"… The storytellers weave the hereafter into the here and now in a deftly formed tapestry of intrigue and subterfuge that has at its pinnacle "The Mob." The scene painting and character development are expert and made me see and love or hate the characters and their surroundings.

The voluminous detail, the labyrinthine plot, the pace, the surprises leading up to the surprise "conclusion," and the acceleration of the action at midpoint are thrilling and kept me immersed in the reading of the novel. The storytelling technique is masterful and done in such a way that I can envision the book being transformed into the soon-to-be-released Web series directed by Deborah."

--- **Dave Crookston**, Writer for Massillon, Ohio's The Independent for 40 years

---

I just finished reading "The Evil That Men Do" by Deborah Fezelle and Sherry Yanow and all I can say is "Wow!" This is a beautifully plotted classic whodunit wrapped in a ghost story set amidst the bright lights of Broadway. The authors have captured the glamorous/sleazy world of show business perfectly, which isn't surprising since Ms Fezelle spent many years performing as a classically trained actress. The characters are rich and three dimensional. The good guys are a little bad and the bad guys are a little good, just like real life. Even the most despicable of them is so vividly imagined that you wish they could find a way out of their predicament and go straight. Nick McDeare takes his place among the great gumshoes of modern detective fiction. Complex, tortured, irresistible to women- he thought love was for suckers until… Let's have another adventure – now please!

--- **Tom Alan Robbins**, Broadway star/playwright.

The Evil That Men Do

The Evil That Men Do

Deborah Fezelle & Sherry Yanow

ISBN 0-615-78788-6
EAN-13 978-061578788-6

Cover by Wendy Prince

"The evil that men do lives after them,
The good is oft interred with their bones."

William Shakespeare
JULIUS CAESAR
Act III, Scene ii

This book is dedicated to the serendipity that brought so many special people together, inspiring our collaboration.

PROLOGUE

New York City's West Side Cruise Ship Terminal was swarming with activity as passengers disembarked from the Italian liner Milano. Eduardo Santangelo slouched against a picture window. Squinting in the early morning sunlight, he watched Andrew Brady wander up and down the terminal, searching for someone. With satisfaction, Eduardo had observed Brady disembark early. The famous actor bought a newspaper and sat in the last chair along the wall. He opened the paper, shielding his face from any glances of recognition. A few minutes later, he tilted his head back and closed his eyes.

Gliding across the tile floor, Eduardo glanced down at his deerskin gloves and the leather jacket slung over his arm. Beneath the ratty jacket he clutched a twenty-two caliber revolver with a silencer. When Santangelo was a foot away from Brady, he snatched one last look around. Pumping up his arm, Eduardo placed the gun's muzzle inches from Brady's temple and fired two rounds.

Eduardo dropped his gloves, jacket, and gun to the floor as he walked to the bank of pay phones, making brief eye contact with a small Hispanic woman and a security guard. He punched in a number, calling his mother like he did every week when he was in port. Act normal, do what you normally do. Those were his instructions.

A woman's scream shattered the busy hum of the cavernous terminal. Eduardo glanced sideways, and smiled.

Andrew Brady lay on the cold tiles, surrounded by a pool of blood.

*

On a dreary April evening two days later, Roosevelt Hospital's Intensive Care Unit was filled to capacity. ICU nurses Penelope Garcia and Rhonda Xavier were finishing their rounds.

"I'm going for a smoke," Rhonda said, digging in her purse for cigarettes. A shrill alarm went off. She glanced at the board. "It's Andrew Brady."

Penelope put out the call. "Doctor Red. Surgical ICU. Doctor Red. Surgical ICU."

The nurses watched as medical personnel flooded Brady's cubicle. Two interns dragged Brady's wife from his bedside, sidestepping the crash cart. A doctor began the struggle to resuscitate the patient's heart.

"C'mon, Andrew," Rhonda whispered. "C'mon."

The doctor shocked Brady six times, his body jerking upwards with each effort. He finally removed the paddles and shook his head, meeting Jessica

Kendle Brady's eyes. A fragment of silence. And then a primitive wail spiraled into the air.

Penelope flinched as the pretty blond woman broke into sobs. "I can't watch this. I'll go with you for a smoke."

The nurses took the stairs to the first floor. They passed the newsstand, their eyes drawn to the headlines. Andrew Brady's face stared back at them. They pushed through the double doors into the chilly night and lit up in silence.

"You know, I saw Brady and Kendle when they debuted on Broadway." Rhonda sucked on her cigarette. "That was only what, seven or eight years ago? It's hard to believe how young they are. I mean, it seems like they've been famous forever."

"According to Brady's chart, he's thirty-three."

"I just saw them in HEART TAKES. My daughter has a crush on Brady."

"Andrew Brady's one hunk of man. Uh, was one hunk of man. God."

"I caught a TV interview with them. They talked about their son a lot. And Andrew Brady was really funny. I can't believe he's dead."

The double doors flew open, jostling the nurses. Reporters jogged for their vans.

"There they go," Rhonda said. "The vultures."

"I'd sure like to know who shot Andrew Brady. Why would anyone want him dead?"

"I'm betting it's that serial killer they keep talking about in all the papers."

*

Nick McDeare slumped against the old-fashioned street lamp across from the Brady brownstone on East Seventy-Fifth. He'd been standing in the same spot for hours, waiting for news on Andrew Brady's condition.

What was he doing here? Nick ran a hand through his thick hair, ebony strands spiking back onto his forehead. He should be at the hospital, not stuck in the middle of a pack of reporters. He wasn't some journalist salivating for a story. Unfortunately, he was a player in this drama. Cursing, he glanced at the Brady residence, ringed by police. Jessica Kendle Brady didn't even know he existed. Nick was supposed to be a surprise. Andrew couldn't wait to spring Nick on his unsuspecting wife.

A cigarette. He fumbled in his jacket pocket and fished out an empty pack. Damn. Nick dropped his head and rubbed his eyes. He couldn't catch a break. A ripple swept through the crowd, the hum of voices rising to a crescendo. Straightening to his full six-foot height, Nick tried to see over the news equipment and locate the source of the commotion.

An NBC News reporter to his right produced a mirror and coiffed his lacquered hair under a portable lamp. The journalist's cameraman snapped on bright lights, scattering the dull darkness.

"What is it?" Nick asked. "Did something happen?"

"Yeah," the reporter said, his eyes fixed on the mirror. "Brady just died. This city's going to go nuts until they find his killer."

Nick reeled backwards, banging his head on the lamppost. His heart was pounding. He couldn't focus. Andrew Brady died. This could not be happening.

"You okay, buddy?" the newsman asked, grabbing Nick by the arm. "Oh my God, you're Nick McDeare."

Nick shook off the man's hand. "Just leave me alone, okay?" Ducking his head, Nick avoided the stares at the sound of his name. He pushed his way through the crowd, stepping over snaking cables and keeping his head down as cameras whirred all around him. He heard every reporter making similar versions of the same statement:

"After surviving for a day and a half following a seven-hour surgical procedure to remove two bullets from his brain, famed actor Andrew Brady died a few moments ago. He is survived by his wife, actress Jessica Kendle Brady, and the couple's five year old son Anthony."

Nick began to run.

Andrew Brady died a few moments ago ...

Andrew Brady died ...

I'm sorry, Mr. McDeare, but your son Jeffrey died early this morning. It was a peaceful death. He slipped away in his sleep ...

Andrew Brady died ...

Your son Jeffrey died ...

Andrew Brady ...

Your son Jeffrey ...

*

Jessica Kendle Brady walked across the glassed-in ICU cubicle, fighting gravity for every step. She sank down on the edge of the bed and stared at her husband. The maze of tubes had been removed from Andrew's body. With the exception of the bandage around his head, he might've been sleeping. An eerie emptiness enshrouded Jessie. It was as if every light in the world had been extinguished when her husband took his last breath.

A sob broke from her throat, but she squashed it, swallowing hard. How could she live without Andrew? He was a part of her. She'd known Andrew forever. At least that's how it felt. From the time they were both thirteen, they'd been inseparable. Twenty years.

This couldn't be happening. Any minute Andrew would sit up. "Gotcha, Kendle!" he'd shout, doubling over in laughter. Andrew's laughter ... the music of their marriage. Jessie knew she'd never laugh again.

And their son. How was Jessie going to tell Anthony that his father was never coming home again? How do you explain death to a five-year-old when you don't understand it yourself?

*

Lieutenant Lyle Barton dragged into his office in the Midtown North Precinct House. He picked up the ringing phone. "Barton."

"It's me. Bushman. Brady just died."

"Shit." Barton exhaled and dropped into his chair. He'd been awake for thirty-six hours straight. He thanked his partner and hung up. The press would

- 11 -

be all over this. Panic was about to sweep the city again, fear the Pervert Killer was back. He'd been hitting along the West Side Highway and Hell's Kitchen for two years now. What better way to grab new headlines than go for something more colorful than transvestites and shoot Andrew Brady dead? The M.O. was the same. A pair of leather gloves, a jacket, and a gun with a silencer left at the scene.

But Barton's gut told him it wasn't the Perv. He could swear Andrew Brady was murdered by someone he knew. He sighed and kicked back in his chair, staring into space. Tomorrow the headlines would scream a killer walked the streets of New York. But in a quiet brownstone on East Seventy-Fifth Street, a young widow would try to find a reason to get out of bed. A little boy would cry himself sick. Barton had seen it too many times. And the Brady family and the entire city would be looking to him for answers.

*

As the world learned Andrew Brady's fate, Eduardo Santangelo was on a plane to Genoa, Italy. His mother welcomed him home with open arms, pleased his days of working as a shipboard bartender were finally over. She had higher expectations for her only son.

So did Eduardo. Eduardo was now a connected man. His benefactor was Roberto Martinelli, head of one of the most powerful crime families in New York City.

CHAPTER 1

Two Years Later

After one final thrust and a slow release of his breath, Nick McDeare rolled off the luscious flight attendant and collapsed onto his back. His heartbeat quickly returned to normal. Turning onto his side, he was asleep in moments.

Just after dawn, Nick bolted straight up in bed, his heart thumping.

"Nick? Honey, what is it?" Kristin Wallingford touched his arm gently. "A bad dream?"

Nick nodded and dropped his head in his hands.

"Want to talk about it?"

Like hell he did.

"You were so quiet all evening. You come home after two years away, and then you sit at dinner staring out the window. What's bothering you?"

"Nothing." Throwing the blanket back, Nick reached for his clothes on the floor. He needed some fresh air.

Kristin grabbed his arm. "Look at me."

"Stop it."

"Please. Talk to me. You never tell me what's on your mind. If something's bothering you I want to know about it."

Nick looked longingly at the bathroom door.

"Typical." Kristin said, folding her arms across her ample chest. "What in God's name is wrong with you? What do you have against women?"

"What the hell are you talking about?"

"I'm talking about the way you treat women, like we're something to be selected from a dinner menu." She leaned towards him. "Only you don't believe in sharing dinner, do you? No, that might require some effort on your part. You might have to give pleasure, instead of grabbing it."

"Okay, stop making it sound like it's a one-way street with me. Let's just get off this subject, okay?" He couldn't believe the conversation was back where it left off two years ago.

"You need to hear this. I thought maybe time in Vancouver with nothing but work would--"

"What? Change me? You thought I'd come back to D.C. and want to settle down?"

"Why not? We've been seeing each other off and on for almost five years. We love each other. What's wrong with—"

"What did you say?" Nick stared at her.

"I said we, love each other?" Kristin squeaked. She shrank back beneath the covers.

"Love each other?" He laughed. "Are you crazy? If I wanted marriage and the whole nine yards, I'd be back in Georgetown with Lindsey."

"You are one cruel bastard."

"Cut it out, okay?" Nick rose and shrugged on his briefs. "Dammit, why do you always do this? Why can't we have a good time together and leave it at that?"

"A good time? You call five minutes getting your itch scratched—your words--a good time?"

"Hey, it was good for me."

"Well, it wasn't for me. Go find someone else to scratch you."

"I have."

Kristin's jaw dropped.

"You thought you were my one and only? We never had a commitment. I told you that from the beginning. Or have you been living in a dream world?"

"I told you I wasn't seeing anyone else. Just you."

"And I told you that was your choice. Not mine."

"Please don't play games with me. I don't deserve this. Tell me the truth."

"Okay, here's the truth." Nick continued to dress as he ticked off a list. "Let's see … Greta scratches me when I'm in Berlin. And then there's Jani in Hong Kong." He grabbed his jacket and yanked it on, straightening his collar. "Darlene, the coffee-shop waitress in Vancouver. And Mandy, the audiologist. And Jennifer, the actress. And—"

"Damn you. Get out of here and don't come back!" Kristin grabbed her cell phone from the nightstand and pitched it at his head. "I mean it! Get the hell out of here!"

Nick ducked. "Gladly. I don't need this, sweetheart." Nick angled her a grin and ambled out the door.

On the street, Nick dug his hands into his pockets and began the long walk to his apartment on New Hampshire Avenue. Walking always cleared his mind. He moved briskly, head down, ignoring pedestrians' curious stares as they recognized him. After ten minutes, he felt a teaspoon of guilt. Some of what Kristin had said--true. Still, she had no right to smother him. Or talk about love. What they had was sex. He'd never given her reason to think their relationship was anything more. Good riddance. He wouldn't miss her nagging or her drama-queen snits. In fact, he wouldn't miss her at all.

Well, wait a minute. Nick's lip twitched. Maybe there was one thing he'd miss. Kristin possessed the one asset Nick coveted in a woman. A gorgeous pair of breasts. Some men liked asses. Others liked legs. Nick was a breast man.

Lengthening his strides, Nick ate up more blocks before he acknowledged what was really bothering him, jerking him awake nights like he was under fire in a foxhole. And it sure as hell wasn't Kristin Wallingford. It was Andrew Brady. The man had haunted him his entire life, and not only in his dreams. But that dream tonight. Andrew again. It was the fourth time Nick had

had the same dream. It was so damned real. He remembered every moment in living Technicolor.

In only a few weeks it would be two years since Nick had stood outside the Brady brownstone, waiting for word on Andrew's condition. He'd left New York the next morning. Two days later he'd been on a flight to Vancouver, B.C.

Nick glanced at the Kennedy Center as he jogged across a busy intersection. Andrew Brady. It was time, he finally admitted. It was time to do something about this. Nick had let things slide for too long. Wasn't that what the dream was trying to tell him? His cell buzzed, and he reached into his jacket pocket. "McDeare."

It was Scott Miller from the NIH Peds Unit, following up on his donation in Jeffrey's name. Nick paused mid-stride, his face softening as Scott spoke. "We've scheduled bone-marrow transplants next week for three children from across the country. They'll be receiving the latest cutting-edge protocols. You've given them a chance, Mr. McDeare."

"I'm glad." A smile lit Nick's amber eyes for the first time since he'd set foot back in D.C. "Today would've been Jeffrey's thirteenth birthday. I'm going to do this yearly. You couldn't have given him a better present."

*

Two Weeks Later

Jessica Kendle Brady sat in front of a blazing fire in the master bedroom study, listening to the rain's steady thump against the windows. The wind whistled around the corners of the old brownstone. The early spring night was as dreary as Jessie's mood. Nestling into the leather couch, she sipped her brandy and stroked Hamlet. The Siamese cat rubbed his head against Jessie's hand. His turquoise eyes had barely closed before he leapt to the floor, jostling the snifter and spilling it on her robe.

Springing up, she eyed Hamlet. The cat was staring at a spot near the mantle, his back arched. "What? Please don't tell me we have a mouse." Ignoring her, Hamlet bolted from the room. Moments later Jessie heard him hurtling down the front staircase.

Heading for the dressing room, Jessie changed into a caftan. Wearily, she sat at the dressing table, staring at her reflection in the mirror. It was the first time she'd examined herself in months. She sighed. She was too thin, her face pale and gaunt. Blue eyes as dull as dust. Her hair drooped to her shoulders, the pale gold dimmed. She'd been sitting in the house for two years. Not eating, not sleeping, and not taking care of herself. She was grieving for a man who was never coming home again.

Jessie shivered. A new furnace had been installed last winter, but the house seemed colder than ever. Her eyes darted to the mirror, a chill dancing down her spine. Was someone watching her? She swung around, scanning the room. Nothing.

Padding into the bedroom, Jessie opened the bedside drawer, dropped two pills in her palm, and chased them with some water. She flipped on the television and burrowed beneath the patchwork quilt. Between the brandy and the pills, she'd finally be able to get some sleep. Hurray.

*

Anthony Brady was in the grip of a nightmare. A stranger was chasing him down a busy street. He had to get away! Rounding a corner, he collided with someone big. The stranger! Twisting and squirming, Anthony searched desperately for an escape. That's when he heard the voice of the one person he could always count on for help. Anthony broke free and ran for Daddy.

His eyes opened wide, awake. Alone. His dad wasn't there, and he would never be there again. But big boys didn't cry. Anthony reached for a tissue. Sitting up, he blew his nose and glanced uneasily around the darkened room. The street lamp outside his window cast moving shadows on the walls, the wind howling down East Seventy-Fifth Street.

Suddenly Anthony knew he wasn't alone, a feeling that had happened a lot lately. It was a good feeling. Anthony lay back down, tugging the blankets up to his neck.

The house was so cold. Yawning, Anthony turned onto his side and stared at his father's picture on the nightstand. "Okay, Daddy, I'm going back to sleep now." Moments later a smile crossed his face, his nightmare replaced by a dream. A dream in which Andrew Brady sat on the bed and once again had a conversation with his son.

*

The rain had stopped when Anthony shook Jessie awake early the next morning. The aroma of coffee and freshly baked cake wafted through the bedroom. Jessie smiled at her son's excitement. "Okay, birthday boy, what's on the agenda at this ungodly hour?"

"Mary's making strawberry waffles. But first I want to go upstairs and open Daddy's present."

"Anthony, what—" But he was already gone. Jessie followed her son up the back staircase to the third floor, where he disappeared into Andrew's old boyhood bedroom at the end of the corridor. She found Anthony on his hands and knees, digging at the floorboards.

"Daddy said it would be right …" Anthony's eyes lit up, and he dug his hands under a board. Jessie watched in amazement as an entire section of flooring lifted up, revealing a small cranny.

Anthony's glee faded. "Oh. They're just books. I thought maybe Daddy hid some toys up here when he was a kid." Springing up, Anthony disappeared in a flash, calling out that he was going to open Mary's present.

Jessie stared at the secret cache, her heart thumping. She sank to her knees and reached for one of the books. My God. These weren't just any books. They were Andrew's journals, journals he'd faithfully kept from the time he'd first moved into the brownstone with Jessie and her father Tony. They were the records of a teenaged boy, an ambitious actor, a husband and a father. There were dozens of them, some leather-bound, some spiral notebooks. They were Andrew's private domain, something he'd shared with no one. Jessie had always wondered what Andrew had done with his journals. Now she knew.

- 16 -

So strange. Anthony had gone straight to this room, to the exact spot where they were hidden. And it was so chilly up here. Jessie could see her breath patch the air. She looked down at the leather-bound book clasped in her hands. If Anthony hadn't led her to this exact spot, Andrew's lasting testaments would have been hidden forever.

*

By the time Jessie got to the kitchen, the sun was streaming through the picture window. Anthony sat on a bench in the breakfast nook. "Look what Mary gave me for my birthday, Mommy!" He held up a digital camera. "Now I can take pictures of Hamlet."

Jessie exchanged smiles with Mary. Mary Bodine was a boxy, middle-aged black woman, raised in Spanish Harlem. It was Mary who ran the brownstone, calling a third-floor suite home ever since she'd come to work for Tony Kendle when Jessie was thirteen. It was the year Jessie's mother had died of cancer, the same year Tony brought Andrew into his home as a foster child. Mary became a second mother to Jessie and Andrew, and now she was helping to raise their son. Jessie thanked God for her on a daily basis.

Mary stood at the island counter, icing a strawberry cake. "You know, Anthony," she said, "you'll turn into one big hive if you continue this strawberry kick."

Jessie looked up at the sound of the front door opening and closing, followed by the whoosh of the express elevator. That would be Jeremy Hoffman, heading for his offices on the fourth floor, separate from the brownstone's living area. An old childhood friend, Jeremy was the Bradys' agent and business manager. He handled an exclusive clientele, with access to his office from a private side entrance. Twenty minutes later, Jeremy hustled into the kitchen.

Dumping a pile of mail on the table, Jeremy exchanged greetings with everyone, affectionately tousling Anthony's hair. Making himself at home, he poured a cup of coffee, chatting about his vacation. "That's all your snail mail, Jessie. And here's the log of office calls. Piled up while I was gone." The brownstone's private line was unlisted. Jessie received few personal calls these days.

Jessie flipped through the envelopes, the usual assortment. Bills. Requests for scholarship money from the Andrew Brady Foundation. Dozens of pleas for personal appearances. Jessie opened one from the American Theater Wing and scanned the letter. "They want me to present the Lifetime Achievement Award to Bill at the Tony Awards. He personally asked for me." Jessie tossed it aside.

"You're going to do it, aren't you?" Mary asked.

"I'm not ready to go back to work."

"This isn't work. This is honoring a man who gave you and Andrew your start, a way to say thank you. If it weren't for him, nobody would know your name."

"Mary, please. I don't want to talk about it anymore."

Jeremy exchanged a look with Mary. "How much longer is this going to go on, Jessie? Bill Rudolph's the most influential producer on Broadway. You can't just say no to him. For the last two years he's been--"

"I said I don't want to talk about it anymore." Jessie knew what Bill was trying to do. He was determined to get her back onstage. But without Andrew at her side, Jessie had no desire to return to the theater. All her creative energy had been buried with her husband.

Jessie picked up the voicemail printout, skimming it quickly. "McDeare. Why does that name sound so familiar?" The man had called the office twice, insisting it was important he speak with her.

"I don't know," Jeremy said, heading for the elevator. "Let me check the database upstairs. Sounds familiar to me, too."

Mary picked up the decorated cake and disappeared through the swinging door to the dining room. "I'll be upstairs. In case anybody cares."

Anthony swirled his finger through the strawberry goo crusting his plate. They were finally alone. "Tell me something, honey," Jessie said. "How did you know about your daddy's journals?"

Anthony whispered, "Daddy told me. In a dream."

"What? You had a dream about Daddy?"

"Last night. He sat on my bed and we talked. He told me he had a birthday present for me, and he told me where to look."

Jessie stopped breathing. "Honey, it was just a dream and--"

"No! He was there, Mommy! We talked for a long time and he told me lots of things."

"What ... kinds of things?"

Anthony propped his chin on his fists. "Well, he said he misses us. And he's worried about you. He doesn't like you staying home all the time. He wants you to go outside more. And he said someone was coming to help us really soon."

"What does that mean?"

"I don't know. Daddy said we'd recognize him right away." Anthony picked up his milk and drained the glass. "Oh, yeah. He said to remind you to put the awards in the bathroom, like you promised."

"The awards?" Jessie's heart bumped up a beat.

"Yeah. The awards you both won for the play. You know. The ones with a guy's name, like mine."

"The Tonys?" Jessie's hands began to shake.

"Yeah." Anthony climbed down from the breakfast bar and trotted towards the stairs. "I'm going to get dressed. Mary said Eric's coming over for some cake." He halted halfway up the steps. "Daddy said he was sorry."

"Sorry? For what?"

"For scaring Hamlet last night and making you spill your brandy." Anthony ran up the rest of the stairs. Good Lord. Jessie pressed her hand to her heart, willing it to slow down. She sucked in a deep breath, transported back to a night in the Brady villa on the island of St. John. The Blue Pelican. Andrew and

Jessie's haven. No critics. No agents or producers or directors picking at them. No fans interrupting their solitude. Nothing but sea and sand and tranquility.

Andrew had dared Jessie to go swimming in the surf naked, and she'd finally given in. They were floating on their backs under a perfect moon and a blanket of stars. The tree frogs were singing, the Tiki torches casting dancing shadows in the hot breeze. Jessie remembered her conversation with Andrew word for word.

"If there really is a heaven, this must be it right here," Andrew whispered.

"You don't believe in heaven anymore?"

"Oh, yeah, most of the time. But do I believe that we're alive one minute and gone forever the next? No. I think those who've passed before us are still around, watching over us and protecting us."

"Andrew, I didn't know you believed in ghosts." Andrew flipped onto his feet and reached for his wife. Jessie slid her arms around his neck.

"My mother claimed she was visited by her dead father," Andrew said, his breath tickling her ear. "She said he came to her in her dreams, only they felt real." Andrew looked up at the stars. "Remember that quote from Hamlet, Jess? The one Mr. Hart kept drilling into us in speech class? 'There are more things in heaven and earth, Horatio, than are dreamt of in your philosophy.' There's so much more to this universe than we'll ever comprehend."

"You're scaring me."

"I'm sorry, honey. I don't mean to." Andrew kissed her softly. "Let's make a pact, okay? I swear to you that I will never leave you. I will always be beside you, watching over you, whether I'm part of this world or the next. I swear to you, Jess." Holding up his left hand, he added, "I swear to you on my wedding band."

Jessie's eyes drifted to her wedding rings. Dear God, did Andrew keep his promise? Was he right here, trying to communicate with them? Jessie clenched her ring hand into a fist. That kind of thinking only opened old wounds. Andrew was gone for good. She had to accept it.

Anthony had probably peeked through the door to her sitting room last night and saw her spill her brandy. He had such an active imagination at this age. He loved to get a rise out of her, just like Andrew. But how did Anthony know about the pledge to put their awards in the downstairs bathroom? No one knew about that but Jessie and Andrew, a silly childhood promise going back to Jeremy. Jeremy's father was Benjamin Hoffman, famed director of film and stage. He had an Oscar and more than one Tony in his penthouse suite's master bathroom. Jessie and Andrew used to lock themselves in that bathroom, each holding up a statuette, and practice their future acceptance speeches. How could she explain her son's knowledge of something so private?

She jumped at the intercom's buzz and hit the connecting button. Jeremy had found a McDeare in the database. Nick McDeare had left several messages shortly before the Bradys departed on that fateful cruise almost two years ago. And Andrew had had a conversation with the man the day before they set sail.

Jessie thanked Jeremy, more curious than ever. Why hadn't her husband mentioned it to her? Why was the name McDeare so familiar? She knew that name! But from where? The police had gone through the phone logs a long time ago, finding nothing suspicious.

Jessie forgot about the mystery for the next several hours as she focused on Anthony and his birthday. But when she finished going through the mail later that afternoon, she found a note from McDeare.

Dear Mrs. Brady,

I'd like to discuss something of great importance with you. Your husband and I spoke on the phone before you left on your cruise. We planned to meet the night you returned. I would very much like to continue that conversation. I'm scheduled to leave for London in the near future, but I'll be home here in Washington for a while. You can reach me on my cell phone at the above number any time of the day. Again, I stress this is of the utmost urgency.

Sincerely,

Nick McDeare

*

Jessie's curiosity finally won out. She called the mysterious gentleman in Washington D.C. that evening. There was a brief pause after Jessie identified herself.

"Mrs. Brady. I'm glad you called me back." A guarded voice.

"You've got me curious." Jessie got straight to the point. "What did you and my husband talk about? He never mentioned that conversation to me."

"Yes, well, he … said he wanted to surprise you."

"I don't understand. Why?"

"Do you think it would be possible to meet in person? I'd rather not do this on the phone."

Jessie raised a brow. "Look, you're the one who initiated this conversation. You never said anything about meeting personally."

"Please. Let me explain in person. I'll tell you everything then."

"Let me see if I have this right," Jessie said. "You could discuss this with Andrew over the phone, but you can't with me?"

"I know how this must sound, believe me, but you'll understand when we meet."

"You really think we're going to meet? About a subject you can't discuss? Are you purposely trying to be mysterious, Mr. McDeare?"

A soft laugh on the other end. "No, I'm sorry. I don't mean to give that impression. It's just that … Look, this is coming out all wrong. I have to come up to New York Tuesday on business. I was planning to stick around for a few days. Maybe we could meet? Anywhere you want."

"I don't think so, Mr. McDeare. Are you a reporter?"

"No. God, no. This is nothing like that."

"Because if you are, I warn you—"

"Please. I want to explain how your husband wanted to surprise you. And why. You'll understand then. I promise. Please do this for Andrew. It was very personal for him, Mrs. Brady. Whatever you're thinking, well, Andrew would want you to do this, trust me."

For Andrew.

It would be perfectly safe, after all. Hadn't he agreed to meet anywhere? Mary would be right here with her. She'd ask Lyle Barton to send a squad car on a drive by. With a sense of disbelief, Jessie found herself agreeing to meet with Nick McDeare early Wednesday evening at the brownstone.

Hanging up, Jessie was surprised to find Mary in the doorway, smiling. "What?"

"I take it we're having company?"

"Just someone Andrew talked to before ... The man will only be here a few minutes before dinner, so don't make a fuss."

*

Late that night Nick sat at his kitchen table, sipping a bourbon and staring down at New Hampshire Avenue. It was finally going to happen. He'd been avoiding this for too long. He had to rock Jessica Kendle's world. He couldn't avoid it any longer.

A cool breeze ruffled the curtains. Off in the distance he heard the wail of sirens. The first buds were sprouting on the ancient cherry tree outside his window. Spring was almost here.

Spring. The season of hope and renewal.

CHAPTER 2

Damn, but he was on edge about this meeting with Jessica Brady. Nick shrugged on his suede jacket and paused in front of the hotel-room mirror. He was used to steady nerves, a man always in control. Nick combed his hair with his fingers, spiky tendrils snapping back onto his forehead. Checking his watch, he quickly slung his leather briefcase over his shoulder, and left the Regency Arms Hotel on the Upper West Side.

It was a beautiful evening, the sun beginning its skid over the Hudson River. The trees were starting to bud, the streets bustling with people. Nick drank in the sights: Ladies walking their dogs. Chinese delivery boys on bicycles. Men in business suits hurrying home, the Wall Street Journal tucked under their arms. Old gentlemen playing backgammon in the small park at West Seventy-Second. Hordes of humanity pouring out of the subway after work, half of them on their cell phones or texting.

Nick found himself smiling as he traversed Central Park and turned north at Fifth Avenue. He jogged across the street, weaving around cars and taxis stapled in place in the congested traffic. Walking swiftly along the stretch of elegant apartment buildings that bordered Central Park's east side, he tried not to get in the way of doormen as they hailed taxis, opened doors, and carried packages for their tenants. New York. There was nothing like it. No other city in the world could compare, and Nick had seen most of them.

The sun dipped further in the west, and the night air grew colder. Zipping his jacket, Nick stuffed his hands in his pockets. Head down, he clipped north, ignoring the glances of passersby who recognized him. Reaching East Seventy-Fifth Street, he halted. What a difference from the last time he'd seen this block. News trucks and reporters had been swarming. Now, with the exception of a few dog walkers, the area was deserted,

Taking a deep breath, he crossed the narrow street, stopping to admire the elegant Brady brownstone nestled between Fifth and Madison. The walls were slate gray granite, the front door sporting a fresh coat of shiny black paint. Brass sconces framed the entrance with a matching brass knocker. A low black iron fence surrounded the building's perimeter.

Nick pushed the gate open and stepped onto the pristine stone path leading to the door. A Siamese cat perched in a first-floor window, watching him. A movement on the second floor caught Nick's eye. Glancing up, he spotted a little boy with dark curls staring down at him. Nick smiled. The child smiled back.

Taking a deep breath, Nick approached the door, stifling an overwhelming urge to turn and hail a taxi back to the hotel. As he raised his hand to the knocker, the front door swung open. "Mr. McDeare?"

Nick cleared his throat. This comfortable-looking black woman must be the housekeeper. "Yes."

"Hello. I'm Mary." The woman shook his hand heartily. Her smile faded as she looked closely at him. "Uh ... come in, come in. Mrs. Brady's been expecting you. Let me take your jacket. She got a long distance call a minute ago. She'll be right with you."

Sensing that he was being watched, Nick glanced up the stairs and saw the little boy, his face poking through the banister's spokes.

"Hello," Nick said.

Mary's eyes followed Nick's. "Anthony Brady, you get back in bed. Do you hear me? I'm going to close my eyes and count to three and I better not see you when I open them. One ..."

"Bye," Anthony whispered, before dashing down the hallway.

"I'm sorry about that, Mr. McDeare. We don't have many strangers come to the house, and he's curious. "

"It's all right. I understand. I know about little boys."

"If you'll just follow me, I'll take you to the study. Be careful," Mary added. "I just waxed the floors this morning and they're mighty slippery for the first few days."

As Mary led the way down the first floor's main artery, Nick took in each room off the hallway. A formal living room was on the right, decorated in shades of white and mahogany. Oriental rugs overlay thick carpeting, a baby grand nestled in the corner. The room was filled with elegantly framed posters of Broadway shows, a ballerina sculpture on the mantel, yellow roses in a Ming vase on the coffee table, dozens of photographs. A formal dining room was on the left, a long oak table running the length of the room with crystal chandeliers overhead.

A bathroom was tucked behind the hallway staircase leading to the second floor. A winterized sun porch lay straight ahead. Nick followed Mary past a roomy kitchen with a picture window and an old-fashioned breakfast nook. The gleaming oak floor was festooned with colorful scatter rugs. A pantry peeked behind a second set of stairs leading to the second floor.

"So, you have a son, Mr. McDeare?" Mary asked. "... Mr. McDeare?"

"Hmm? Oh, I'm sorry. It's just that ... It's been a long time since I've seen a New York brownstone that wasn't broken up into apartments."

"Well, we certainly have a lot of space. More bedrooms upstairs than the Hilton. So, you have a boy then?"

Nick paused. "I have no children."

"Well, boys are a handful." Mary finally stopped at their destination. Opening the double doors to a study, she stepped back and motioned Nick inside. "The bar's right over there. I put ice cubes in the ice bucket. Help yourself to whatever you want. I'll be right across the hall if you need anything."

Dropping his bag on the leather couch, Nick went to the bar and poured some bourbon over ice. Swirling the liquid, he perused the room. Cozy. Lived in. A fire in the grate had been burning. Framed photographs were everywhere, toys scattered. A pair of reading glasses rested on an opened TV GUIDE. And books. Books and mementos filled both sets of floor-to-ceiling bookshelves on opposing walls.

Curious, Nick crossed to one of the shelves. He scanned the titles and chuckled. Backing towards the door, he turned his gaze on an enormous oil portrait of the Brady family over the mantel. Andrew stood behind his wife and son, smiling down at the world.

Hearing footsteps approach, Nick stilled, gripping his glass hard. He heard a scuffle, and a woman mumbled, "Damn!"

Mary's voice echoed across the hallway. "I told you I just waxed those floors." Nick crossed to the doorway just in time to see Jessica Brady right her balance. Mary materialized behind her. "She does this, Mr. McDeare. Onstage, Jessie's as graceful as a cat. It's real life she has trouble with." At Jessie's withering look, Mary backed into the kitchen and disappeared.

*

"Are you all right?" Nick McDeare asked.

"Yes," Jessie said, laughing at herself. She swept her hair off her face and approached Nick. "Well! What an auspicious introduction." Extending her hand, she said, "I'm Jessica—" Jessie's jaw dropped. She stared in shock at the man standing before her.

Nick held both her gaze and her hand. He felt the moment, too. He had to.

"I … see you've gotten yourself a drink," Jessie finally said, shaking off the stranger's penetrating stare. "I think I'll join you." She brushed past him and went to the bar, pouring herself a super-size portion of white wine. God. Taking a swig, Jessie faced the man. She was surprised to find him standing only a few feet away, still watching her closely.

His eyes. His amazing eyes. Jessie wished he would stop looking at her like that. She made her way to the mantel, setting her glass down and gripping the ledge for support. "You said you wanted to discuss something with me? Well, here I am. I'm listening."

Nick walked slowly to her side. Jessie looked up at him. That thick head of dark hair, a strand falling over his eye. Those eyes. She tried not to look at his eyes. "What is it, Mr. McDeare?"

"You see it, don't you, Mrs. Brady?"

"See what?"

"C'mon. Be honest with me and with yourself. What are you thinking right now?"

"I'm thinking …" Jessie swallowed. "You look a great deal like my husband. It's your eyes." A soft brown with amber flecks. Heavy lids, drooping at the corners. Bedroom eyes they used to call it.

Nick's gaze never wavered from her face. "I'm Andrew's older brother," he said gently.

Oh, God. Jessie half sat, half fell down on the ottoman behind her. Nick kneeled beside her. The room was so silent she could hear each individual tick of the grandfather clock in the hallway.

"I'd … forgotten," Jessie finally said. "Over the years I'd completely forgotten." But she remembered now. When Andrew's mother had died suddenly, Tony Kendle opened his home to his daughter's best friend. With the exception of an aging aunt, the boy didn't seem to have any living relatives. But Andrew kept insisting that he had an older brother put up for adoption at birth. Jessie's father had made an effort to find him, but there were no records anywhere. As time passed, Tony had come to believe Andrew conjured up a phantom sibling out of loneliness.

Jessie finally turned her gaze on the man who claimed to be her brother-in-law, crouched at her side like a big cat. With the exception of his dark hair, there was so much of Andrew in him. The same cheekbones and small mouth. The same strong nose. And his eyes. Those Mona Lisa eyes. How could there be any doubt Nick was who he said he was?

"You believe me, don't you? I can tell you believe me." Nick finally rose and retrieved his glass, draining it in one swallow.

"Seeing is believing. You look exactly like him. But it's not just your face or your eyes. It's everything about you. Your build. The way your hair falls across your forehead." They both gazed up at the portrait. "And I just realized … even your voices are the same. My God." Jessie rose and reached for Nick's empty glass. "Let me refill that for you. What are you drinking?"

"Bourbon."

She froze, a small smile flickering across her face. "That's what Andrew drank."

Now it was Nick's turn to smile. Jessie tried to read his face, but he turned away. "So," he said, "Andrew grew up in this house."

"He came to live with us when we were both thirteen." Jessie handed Nick his bourbon and retrieved her glass on the mantel. "Tell me something, Mr. McDeare. How did you find Andrew? I mean, how did you put it together that he was your brother?"

"Actually, I have Andrew to thank. He registered with an agency called The Anderson Cummings Bureau for Lost Relatives years ago."

"You mean his mother registered, right?"

"Andrew registered. Eight years ago."

Jessie sank back down on the ottoman. Eight years ago? Why hadn't Andrew told her? That would have been the year they were working as entertainers on the Milano, the Italian cruise ship. And then Jessie understood. Of course. It made perfect sense. Still, Andrew could have eventually told her about it. Why didn't he?

The answer was suddenly obvious. Andrew knew neither she nor her father believed he really had a brother. Whenever Andrew raised the subject, Tony Kendle's eyes filled with pity. Eventually, Andrew had stopped talking about him altogether. Jessie had always thought the subject was dropped because Andrew finally felt secure in his new family. Now it appears he'd kept quiet to avoid the skepticism in their eyes.

Nick sipped his bourbon, studying her over the rim of his glass. "Okay," Jessie said, struggling for composure under that steady gaze, "so

Andrew registered with some agency. That still doesn't explain how you found him."

Shrugging, he said, "Curiosity. Eventually I wanted to locate my birth parents like a lot of adopted kids. I found Anderson Cummings. Since Andrew and I were both looking for each other, they released the records."

"And all this happened right before ... he died?"

"We spoke the day before you sailed on that cruise."

Unreal. Jessie had thought she'd known everything there was to know about Andrew. That they'd had no secrets. "If you don't mind my asking, what was your conversation like?"

"You can hear it if you like. I taped it." Nick must've seen the surprise on her face. "When I'm home I tape most of my conversations," he explained. "It's a safety net in my business." Nick walked over to his briefcase and withdrew a small digital recorder. "Would you like to hear it?"

Jessie nodded, feeling unsteady. Nick pressed a button and leaned against the bookshelves as Andrew Brady's rich baritone filled the study. It was the first time Jessie heard her husband's voice in two years. She stared down at her wine glass.

"Mr. McDeare? This is Andrew Brady. My office told me you've been trying to reach me."

"Yes, yes, I have."

"Are you the author? The McDeare who writes the mysteries?"

"Yeah. That's me."

That's where she knew his name! Of course. Nick McDeare was a best-selling suspense author. One of Andrew's favorites. This was positively eerie. If she hadn't been locked away in her own world for two years she would've recognized it instantly.

"I'm a huge fan," Andrew continued. "I've read all of your books. So. What can I do for you?"

"Ah ..." A sheepish laugh. "I don't know where to begin. It's not easy over the phone. Could I come up to New York and meet with you?"

"What's this about, Mr. McDeare?" Jessie could hear the hint of impatience in Andrew's voice. Also paranoia. The Bradys had to be careful. Reporters were always trying to intrude into their lives.

"I'm sorry. I don't mean to ..."

"Mr. McDeare?"

"Okay. I ... this is of a personal nature. It's about a long time ago. Your childhood."

"My ..." Now it was Andrew's turn to pause. "What's this about?" he repeated, but this time Jessie heard curiosity in the question.

"Christ, this is hard. I didn't think it would be this hard. I really wish we could talk about this in person -"

"You're my brother, aren't you?" Andrew blurted out.

Jessie sat up straight, listening intently.

"Yeah," Nick whispered, obvious relief flooding his voice. "Yeah, I am. How did you know?"

"I don't know." Andrew's voice was hushed. "I just ... did, that's all. I don't know. How did you find me, after all this time? Anderson Cummings?"

"That's right."

"I've been looking for you my entire life," Andrew finally said. A pause. "I just pulled one of your books off the shelf. No wonder I never noticed the similarity between us. Why do authors always go for those arty black and white photos?" Both men laughed. Jessie stifled a gasp. The same laugh. The same pitch.

"Maybe because writers don't have the high-brow taste you actors have."

"Wait," Andrew said. "I've got a computer right here. I'm doing a search on you as we speak." There was a long pause. Then the sound of Andrew sucking in his breath. "My God. We have the same eyes. Amazing. I never noticed. All this time."

"Face it. Now that you know, we look exactly alike. My apologies"

"Yeah, well, at least I got the hair right. Too bad yours is so dark."

The teasing joy was heartbreaking to hear. Poor Andrew. Little had he known ... Jessie blinked. She glanced at Nick, his head down.

Andrew chuckled. "I can't wait to spring you on my wife. She's not going to believe this. She never believed me when I told her I had a brother. And wait until she finds out my brother's Nick McDeare." Andrew chuckled.

"I don't understand."

"I've been going on about you for years, pressuring her to read you. She always says, 'You and this McDeare. What is it with you and this author anyway?'"

Both Andrew and Nick laughed again. Then silence.

"I think it's time we met, don't you?" Nick finally said.

"You think?"

Jessie felt her gut tighten. The humor. So Andrew. "Hey, it's bad timing," Andrew went on. "My family and I are leaving tomorrow on a cruise. We'll be gone ten days, a working vacation." They made plans to meet when Andrew got back, six o'clock at the brownstone. "Oh, and one more thing," Andrew added. "I'm not going to say a word about this to my wife. I want to sit back and enjoy the look on her face when you show up at the door, all right?"

"Sure. Whatever you want."

"Well," Andrew said. "I guess I'll see you then. And, Nick? I, uh, can't begin to tell you how glad I am we finally found each other." There was raw emotion in his voice.

"Yeah. Me, too." Nick rasped. "I'll see you when you get back."

Jessie swiped the tears from her cheeks and glanced at Nick. Were his eyes misty, too? He had to be feeling what she was feeling, the tragedy of promise unfulfilled. Andrew Brady had never come back from that cruise. The two brothers had never met in person. All they had was one phone conversation before someone put a gun to Andrew's head and pulled the trigger.

Straightening, Nick dropped the recorder into his briefcase. He withdrew a manila envelope. "These are the legal papers I got from Anderson Cummings." With one stride he was at her side, his arm outstretched. "All the forms signed when I was adopted. The direction of my life was decided by the signature of a woman named Chelsea Brady."

His birthmother. Jessie ignored the envelope. "Your life seems to have turned out all right."

"Oh, sure." Nick shrugged, crossing his arms. "I'm an international celebrity. My books are translated into fifteen languages. I have every reason in the world to be happy."

"Let me ask you something, Mr. McDeare. Why did you wait two years before contacting me? What do you want from me?" She had to know.

He chuckled. "I don't want your money or your celebrity, if that's what you're worried about. I have more of both than I know what to do with."

"Then what?"

"I guess I'd like to know my brother's family." Nick's face was inscrutable. "I didn't get to know him, so maybe ..."

Nick McDeare was not a man to wear his heart on his sleeve. But Jessie had heard enough to make up her mind. "Then know us, you will. I don't need to see these papers." Jessie dimpled. "My husband believed you sight unseen, and I trust his instincts, even if I've been told I can't always trust my own. Besides, you look enough like Andrew to be his twin. You're family."

"Did anyone ever tell you you're too trusting Mrs. Brady?"

"More times than I can remember. And I think it's time you started calling me Jessie."

*

Nick began to relax as they settled on the porch. Jessica Kendle Brady was a resilient woman. Stunned but regrouping fast. She would prove important to his agenda. So far, so good.

The sun had disappeared over the Hudson long ago, and the bird feeder was silenced for the night. The sweet hint of spring drifted through the open windows from the rose garden. A gnarled dogwood was close to sprouting a bushel of pink blossoms. The far-off wail of sirens was the only hint to remind Nick that he was in the heart of Manhattan. The white wicker furniture sported over-stuffed green cushions. Stained-glass hurricane lamps cast pools of light on the Oriental rug. Hanging plants would catch the sun's rays through the skylight.

Jessie refilled their glasses again, and Nick sipped cautiously. The last thing he needed was to get drunk. He had so many questions about Andrew, leftovers from the time his brother was alive and he'd looked forward to Andrew answering them all. "Would you mind telling me about Andrew? What was he like?"

Jessie smiled. "I know this is going to sound corny," she said slowly, "but Andrew was probably the finest man I've ever known." She tucked her legs beneath her and took a sip of wine. "He'd never hurt anyone. And he had a great sense of humor. He loved to make people laugh. Whenever Andrew was around, you knew there'd be laughter."

Not exactly a Nick McDeare profile. "And his childhood? What was that like?"

With enthusiasm, Jessie took Nick on a walk through her life with Andrew: The High School of Performing Arts, where they met the first day of school, Andrew's devastation over his mother's death and life at the brownstone, the Juilliard drama division, their struggle in the industry and how it all came together when they teamed up after Bill Rudolph discovered their club act aboard a luxury liner.

Nick was riveted by Jessie's story, but he couldn't help peeking through the window into the kitchen where Mary was fussing with a huge pot on the stove. Nick hadn't eaten since breakfast. Whatever that woman was fixing smelled like ambrosia.

Nick returned his focus to Jessie. "When did you get married?"

"Married?" Jessie laughed. "Um, that was around the time we opened our club act for Bill."

"And?"

"And we got married. I'm not sure what you're asking." She fiddled with the buttons on her silk tunic.

"Were you and Andrew always a couple?"

"I wouldn't say that, not exactly. But in the end we had a closeness that some marriages never see. Something smells good," Jessie added, quickly uncurling from her seat. "Mary's been in a cooking and freezing mood all week. I'll check out the kitchen. I hope you're hungry," she smiled over her shoulder, "since our meeting's turned into dinner."

Nick didn't argue the invite. He washed his hands in the marble bathroom. Two shiny statuettes sat on opposing corners of the sink, Tony Awards. Nick shook his head.

Wandering back into the hallway, Nick couldn't resist stepping into the living room. In front of the hearth, he spotted a cat bed. A coloring book and crayons were scattered on the floor, along with a few magazines. Nick scooped one up and rolled his eyes. PEOPLE'S issue of The Fifty Most Eligible Bachelors.

"I'm sorry. I should have cleaned up in here." Jessie had padded up behind him. "Picking up after a seven-year-old's a full-time job."

"I didn't mean to snoop."

"You're family. Feel free."

Nick arched a brow. His folks Charles and Kate were family, his only family since he'd lost Jeffrey. Now family was suddenly a sister-in-law and a nephew, too. This would take some getting used to. As touched as he'd been by Jessie's sisterly trust, getting to know Andrew's family wasn't the reason Nick was here. Getting to know all about his brother wasn't the real reason he was here either. Not anymore.

Jessie plucked the magazine from Nick's hands, her blue eyes widening. "Oh my God, this is you, isn't it?" She pointed to one of several photos on the cover.

"Ah, yeah." He reached for the magazine, but Jessie pivoted in the other direction. She opened to the two-page spread on Nick. "The Elusive Nick McDeare." Jessie read, glancing up at Nick. "Nice title. 'Thirty-nine years old and holding, Nick McDeare is PEOPLE'S choice for confirmed bachelor.'" Jessie chuckled. "'Thirty-nine and holding?'"

"I'm forty in a couple of months. Are we done yet?"

"Not quite." Jessie continued to read aloud. "'After five suspense thrillers on the NEW YORK TIMES Best-Seller list and another one due out this summer, Nick McDeare's celebrity continues to rise. Tall, dark and handsome, with an exotic sexuality that women of all ages find irresistible, this award-winning former investigative reporter for the WASHINGTON POST leaves behind a trail of broken hearts.'"

Women. "Give me that please."

"In a minute. There's still another paragraph. What qualified you for the eligible bachelor title, Nick? It looks pretty prosaic so far. Married. Divorced for eight years. I'm really out of the loop these days. But a trail of broken hearts? Maybe it--"

Nick snatched the magazine out of her hands. "My private life's private and no one else's business." And he sure as hell didn't need another woman grading his love life.

"Then why did you give the interview?"

"I didn't. They printed whatever the hell they wanted."

"Calm down. I'm not prying into your life."

"Yeah, right. That's what they all say."

"Wait a minute." Jessie faced him squarely. "I don't know who 'they' are, but I'm not one of them. I don't lie. In fact, I'm known for saying the first thing that pops into my head, which tends to get me into trouble. You can do whatever you want in your private life, and I don't care."

"Well, thank you so much for your permission." He flung the magazine onto the couch.

"I don't know anything about your love life." Jessie flicked her hair back, her eyes darkening. "And I don't want to know, trust me." Jessie folded her arms and met Nick's glare. "My life's been dissected and twisted out of proportion every which way for the last two years, and I resent the hell out of it. I don't know what's going on with the celebrity circuit because I avoid it. I know exactly how you feel. So please stop jumping all over me for having a little fun with a silly magazine article."

Nick crossed his own arms. "If you hate gossip so much, why do you read PEOPLE?"

"I don't. Mary does."

Christ. "Um, sorry. Maybe I ...overreacted."

"Well, maybe I was wrong, too. I mean, I--"

"Jessie?" Mary called from the kitchen. "Dinner."

Saved by the bell. As Nick trailed Jessie into the hallway, he spotted Anthony spying through the second-floor balustrade. Anthony put his finger to his lips. Nick nodded. Then his stomach tightened. What if the child had overheard his quarrel with Jessie?

*

Jessie's mind was going in more circles than a hamster on a wheel. She tried to focus on one thing at a time. "Mary," she said, not sure how to begin, "You met Nick earlier, but, well, there's no other way to say this. Um, Nick is ... Andrew's older brother. Remember when--"

"Lordy, Lordy." Mary's jaw dropped and her hand flew to her heart. "I about fainted when I opened that door tonight. You looked so much like Andrew. I knew it was you." She sandwiched Nick's hand between both of hers and squeezed. "I always had the feeling Andrew never stopped looking for you. Welcome to the family, Nick."

"Yeah. The family." He extricated his hand.

"Well," Mary said. "I have dinner all laid out for you on the table. And I turned on some soft jazz. It's soothing for the digestion." She started for the stairs. "I'm going to bed. My arthritis is acting up. If you want to hear all about that brother of yours, Nick, you ask me anytime. Night."

Jessie was touched by what Mary had created for a spontaneous late-night dinner. Two places were set at one end of the long dining room table. Flickering tapers in a pewter candelabra cast a glow on bright stoneware dishes and piping hot crocks of her homemade split pea soup. Fresh corned beef sandwiches were stacked high, accompanied by Mary's special coleslaw and American fries.

Jessie watched Nick dig in, slathering his corned beef with heaping tablespoons of horseradish and mustard. She put aside their argument. Nick was obviously a private person, and she'd poked a sensitive spot. Jessie was an incurable tease. At least, she used to be. For a few seconds, she'd reverted to form tonight. He'd apologized. She'd apologized. Now Jessie figured it was time to answer the questions she knew Nick had to be dying to ask. "You haven't asked about your birth parents. You must be curious."

Nick finished chewing and swallowed. "No."

"Why not?"

He shrugged. "They didn't care about me, so why should I care about them?"

"You don't know that."

"Sure I do. When I was born, they gave me away. Then they forgot about me and went on with their lives."

"Actually, your father didn't stick around for Andrew either."

"No?" Nick snorted. "What a prince. Andrew's the only one I really wanted to ... well ..." He closed his mouth around a spoonful of pea soup.

Jessie wished Andrew were here to deal with his brother. Maybe he would know what-- "Oh my God!" Jessie leapt to her feet and sprinted to the study. She was back within moments, cradling five hardback books in her arms.

"Was it something I said?"

Was he teasing? Yes. His amber eyes were dancing, just like Andrew's. So he did have a tiny sense of humor at least.

"Sorry. Look." Jessie set the books on the table one by one as she ticked them off. "TOKYO BLUES. SHADES OF BLACK. THE GREEN MONSTER. WHITE NIGHTMARE. GOLDEN OPPORTUNITY. Andrew had all of your books. And look here. They're signed by you. To Andrew."

"How …? Did Andrew and I meet at some point? I think I would've remembered."

"Bill Rudolph, our producer friend, got them signed for me. He knows your publisher or editor or something. I gave them to Andrew that last Christmas."

The doorbell rang. Jessie glanced at the clock. Nine-fifteen. Mary always answered the door, but Mary had gone to bed. "Excuse me."

Jessie went to the vestibule and squinted through the peephole. A bombshell of a blond stood on the other side of the door, looking upset. "Yes? Who is it?"

"I'm sorry to bother you. My name's Lindsey McDeare Cromwell. I'm looking for my ex-husband, Nick. His friend Michael told me he was here. It's about his mother Kate."

His mother? The magazine article had mentioned an ex-wife named Lindsey. Jessie turned the locks and swung the door open. "Nick's in there." She pointed towards the dining room. "Is something wrong?"

"You bet there is." The buxom blond pushed past Jessie and made her way to the dining room. Jessie ran after her and saw Nick spring to his feet.

"Kristin. What are you doing here?"

"Kristin?" Jessie moved to Nick's side. "She said she was your ex-wife."

"This isn't my ex-wife. Try one of my ex-girlfriends." Nick approached the woman. "What's going on?"

"One of …? I'm one of your ex-girlfriends?" Kristin slapped Nick hard across the face. He reeled backwards, grabbing the dining room chair.

"Are you all right?" Jessie flew to Nick's side.

"You son of a bitch." Kristin's face contorted. Tears filled her eyes. "You cheating, cruel son of a bitch!"

"Please." Jessie shushed the woman. "I have a young son upstairs."

"A son?" Kristin turned on Nick. "You're despicable. You're going to screw this woman while her son's in the house?"

Still holding his jaw, Nick looked like water on boil. "What's wrong with you? Have you lost your mind?"

"If I have, it's all your fault." Kristin focused on Jessie for the first time. "Oh my God. You're Jessica Kendle, aren't you?" Her eyes smoked lasers at Nick. "You're going to screw Andrew Brady's widow? What a bastard. Next to Jackie O, this woman makes the list of the most famous widows the country has known! It figures she'd be on your to-do list!"

"Get out." Nick grabbed Kristin by the arm and dragged her towards the door.

Kristin jerked her arm free and confronted Jessie. "You have no idea what you're getting yourself into. This man's an animal. He hates women. You know what he calls making love? Getting his itch scratched."

"Dammit, Kristin, shut up."

"And you want to know the funniest part of it all? He sucks in bed."

"That's it." Nick tried to grab Kristin by the shoulders, but she sidestepped him and circled around.

"Oh, what have we here? Your books." Kristin's voice dripped with sarcasm. "This is how he romanced me, too. Big famous author. Women fall at his feet to worship the great Nick McDeare. Women are lucky to be invited into his bed." She whirled towards Nick and held up a book. "This is what your life amounts to, Nick. Pieces of paper." She whipped open the book and ripped out chunks of pages.

"Don't!" Jessie grabbed the book from the woman's hands, but Kristin snatched another.

"Dammit, Kristin, that's enough!"

"Pieces of paper, Nick!" Again, she wrenched pages from the book, avoiding Jessie's frantic attempts to stop her. Lifting the book over her head, Kristin bashed Nick in the chest with it.

"What the hell are you trying to do? Kill me?" Nick backed away as Kristin hurled another book at him, aiming for his head. He ducked. A crystal pitcher on the hutch shattered. More pages torn. A fourth book thrown.

"You're out of control Kristin!" Nick lunged for the woman. Before he connected, the throw rug beneath his feet shot out from under him, landing on the dining room table. It reminded an astounded Jessie of a magician whipping a tablecloth off a table piled with dishes.

Nick lost his balance and struck his head on the corner of the hutch. Looking dazed, he slid down the wall in slow motion, collapsing into a heap.

CHAPTER 3

Nick's eyes opened a crack. He made out a woman's face, floating in front of him. Blurry. She kept calling his name. He remembered now. He was in New York. In his brother's home. Jessie. It was Jessie who looked so worried. Nick tried to sit up. "I'm okay," he mumbled.

"Mommy?" A little boy stood at the foot of the stairs. Anthony.

"Anthony! What are you doing up?" Nick watched Jessie rise and speak to someone else. "Are you happy now? You woke my son."

Nick focused on the other person. Kristin? What...? It all came back. Struggling to his feet, Nick trained his eyes on Kristin. The woman shrank like an accordion. "Did you follow me to New York?" Nick's voice was barely a whisper. "Did you follow me here tonight?"

Jessie took her son's hand. "Anthony, c'mon. Let's get you back to bed." After one look at Nick, Jessie led Anthony upstairs.

"I'm waiting, Kristin. And don't lie to me."

Kristin dropped her eyes. "I called Michael Whitestone."

"Michael? You spent two minutes with my college roommate on one occasion. Michael's the editor of a major newspaper. He doesn't have time to answer your calls!" Nick wanted to throttle her, but he wasn't feeling strong enough. Yet.

"I didn't like what happened between us the night you got home. I wanted to apologize. I left a dozen messages on your cell. You never returned one. I started to think you'd already left for London."

"I'm surprised you didn't call my ex-wife."

"She didn't return my calls either--"

"You what?"

"So I phoned Michael," Kristin croaked. "He told me you were in New York at the Regency Arms."

"You're nuts!" Nick's eyes narrowed. "Michael would never give out that information." Nick took a step towards the woman. "How did you weasel it out of him, Kristin?"

"I, ah," Kristin's face blanched, "I told him that your mother was sick."

"You used my mother to find me!?"

"I'm sorry, Nick, but I had to see you. When I got to your hotel tonight, you were just leaving. I followed you here. I thought maybe you were interviewing someone, but when the hours passed, I ... figured you were with another woman." The tears started to flow. "I'm sorry. I just ... Are you seeing Jessica Kendle? Please. I have to know. Have the decency to tell me the truth."

"You and decency are an oxymoron. We're through! How many ways don't you get that? Who I see is none of your business." Catching Kristin's glance over his shoulder, Nick turned his head. Jessie stood a few feet away, her face stony.

"Nick was my husband's brother," Jessie said. "We're family. That's all."

Kristin's eyes darted to Nick. "Andrew Brady was your brother?"

"That's none of--"

"I'd like you to leave my home." Jessie's tone was firm. "You destroyed my possessions. You attacked Nick. And you woke my son. Isn't that enough for one night?"

"I, I'm sorry. Really." Kristin glanced at Nick. "I'm sorry, Nick. Call me, please, and we'll--"

"There is no we. Get out. Now."

Kristin hurried out the front door. Jessie closed it behind her.

"Dammit, Jessie, that woman didn't deserve an explanation. You shouldn't have—" Nick's breath caught as a wave of pain shot through his head. His fingers came away bloody when he touched a spot above his hairline. "Do you think maybe you could get me a cloth?"

"You need to go to the emergency room."

"No hospital. I'll be the lead item in tomorrow's gossip columns."

"You're bleeding badly."

"All head wounds bleed badly."

"You're an expert on the subject?"

"I was a reporter in the field, remember?" A flashback to Nicaragua. A bullet had grazed Nick's skull, a head wound. Something he had in common with Andrew. But Nick had survived with the help of an experienced medic. Andrew hadn't.

"C'mon. There's a First Aid Kit in the pantry." Nick watched Jessie push through the swinging door. "But you really should have your head examined," she said, bursting into laughter.

"I'm glad you find this funny," Nick said, trudging after her.

"Sit down," Jessie ordered. She choked back a laugh.

"Nice to know I bring out your sense of humor. Look, just give me a Band-Aid. I'm fine." The room started to spin. Nick grabbed for the island counter.

"Yeah. You're fine. Would you please sit down before you fall down?" Jessie stared at Nick, her arms crossed. He met her eyes, not moving. Jessie sighed. "Okay, I'll ask again, nicely. Please let me look at that before I have to scrub down the entire kitchen."

"Give me a Band-Aid and I'll be on my way."

"What is your problem? Is it emasculating to accept help from a woman? Well, don't think of me as a woman. Think of me as family."

Family. This was all Andrew's fault. Nick wasn't looking for family, but family seemed to be part of the deal.

"You're bleeding all over your shirt," Jessie added.

Grimacing, Nick sat on the bench in the breakfast nook. The gash on his scalp throbbed. His jaw was pulsing from the smack Kristin had given him. And he was starving. This evening was a screaming nightmare.

*

Roberto Martinelli was at the pinnacle of his power, one of a handful of anointed men who ran the decimated crime families of New York City. On this cool April evening, Roberto sat in his study overlooking the Atlantic Ocean. Ensconced in a wing chair, his feet stretched across the coffee table, he puffed on a Cuban cigar and sipped Cognac.

There was a discreet knock on the door.

"Come."

Aldo Zappella slipped into the room. He parked his tall frame in a club chair across from his old friend. "We got a problem."

Martinelli had figured as much. When his right-hand man appeared late at night, something was up.

"It looks like Andrew Brady's murder is about to be resurrected."

"That case has been going nowhere." Roberto smoothed back his mane of salt-and-pepper hair. "The cops have been chasing their tails for two years. What's changed?" He offered his friend a Cuban from the humidor.

"Nick McDeare." Aldo bit the tip of the cigar and lit up. A plume of smoke drifted over their heads.

"The author? What about him?"

"He also used to be an investigative reporter. One of the best. It turns out he's Brady's brother. Adopted at birth. He's at the Bradys' Manhattan residence as we speak."

"How do we know this?"

"We bugged the Brady house after the incident, remember, the first floor and phones? The usual routine. That cop--Barton--spent a lot of time holding the widow's hand and keeping her informed. We learned a lot from his big mouth. The case is still open. We've been monitoring the chatter ever since. A precaution."

"Maybe McDeare's there as family?"

"Yeah." Aldo shot Martinelli a look and went to the bar. "And I'm den mother to the Cub Scouts." He poured a hefty shot of Sambucca. "We better cover our asses."

Martinelli sighed. Two years had passed since the Brady situation. Roberto had assumed the case was as dead as Brady. Now this. He rose and paced to the picture windows. It was a clear night. A thousand stars. A half moon was reflected on the rippled inlet leading to the ocean, exploding into a spray of tiny crystals. How many times had he stared out this window, making life or death decisions? "Okay," Roberto said quietly. "We need to put someone on this twenty-four, seven. I want this new development watched closely."

"Especially since we just brought Santangelo back to New York."

"I want to use the kid."

"I'll make sure Santangelo comes to see you in the next couple of days. He's grateful. He'll do whatever you ask. Now. About McDeare, I got

- 36 -

somebody outside the Brady brownstone tonight. He'll follow him home. We also need to watch McDeare's place in DC. Who do we put on this permanently?"

"Isn't it obvious?" Roberto turned to face his old friend. A smile inched across his jowls. "Let history repeat itself."

"Cobra?"

"Cobra. He came through for us two years ago. Besides, we own him now."

*

Nick flinched. "Ouch. Easy, okay?"

Jessie held up her hand and wiggled her fingers. "How many fingers?

"Fifteen."

"Very funny."

"Okay, five. If you want to count the thumb."

"That's better." Jessie applied pressure against the gash. "The bleeding's stopped. That's about all I can do. Are you sure you don't want me to bandage it?"

"No thanks." Nick got to his feet and made a beeline for the front door. He'd stop at a deli and pick up a pastrami on rye.

"Where are you going?" Jessie trotted after him.

"Back to the hotel." Nick grabbed his jacket and reached for the doorknob. "Haven't you had enough excitement for one night?"

"You're not going anywhere." Jessie blocked the door.

"Who's going to stop me? You?" Nick slipped on his jacket. He looked her up and down and chuckled.

"Don't insult me in my own home. It's rude."

"I thought I was being funny."

"Look, I gave in on the hospital because I understand bad publicity. But you shouldn't be alone tonight. You could still have a concussion. You could keel over on the street. That gash is bad, and you were unconscious for a few seconds."

"No, I wasn't. I was just--"

"I don't want to feel guilty if I let you leave and something happened to you. Nick, please." Jessie stepped forward, her eyes glinting metallic blue. "There's a suite up on the fourth floor. You can use it for the night and have all the privacy you want."

"Look, Jessie, I'm fine."

"You didn't tell me you're a doctor. Show me your medical license, and I'll let you leave."

"My father's a doctor. His expertise rubbed off on me."

"Your father's not a doctor. You're lying."

"He's a doctor in the Air Force. I grew up all over the Far East and Europe." Nick rolled his eyes. "Why are we talking about this?"

"Because you're being pig-headed. Now, the subject's closed. You're staying the night."

"Are you sure you're not my mother in disguise?"

"I can imagine the hell you put her through." Jessie began to peel Nick's jacket off.

"Hey, I was a model kid. Straight A's. Taking classes at the university when I was fifteen."

"That only proves you're intelligent. It says nothing about your character. Which, by the way, was on full display tonight with that woman." Jessie hung up Nick's jacket.

"That's none of your business. My life's--"

"Private. I know. Come on. We'll finish dinner. Your stomach's drowning out our conversation."

Nick shadowed Jessie into the dining room. They both came to an abrupt halt. The cat sat in the middle of the table, washing his face with his paw. Nick's dinner plate was licked clean except for the bread crusts. Nick looked at Jessie.

She shrugged. "Hey, he's a cat." It took Jessie only a few minutes to make new sandwiches from Mary's leftovers. They sat across from each other in the breakfast nook and Nick dug in.

"Is your life always this exciting?" Jessie asked.

"Actually, I try to keep it pretty simple." He shivered. "I've got a better question. Is this house always so cold?"

"Lately, yes. There's a sweater in the front closet. Help yourself."

Nick found the closet and the sweater, a thick turtleneck. He removed his bloodied shirt and slipped it over his head, fingering the Irish wool. It fit him like a glove. This must have been Andrew's. The closet had no scent, yet the sweater smelled of pine. Every human being had a subtle scent all their own. Jessie's fragrance was lilacs. Nick brought the garment to his nose and inhaled. Strange how a smell could conjure up a human being.

He wandered back through the darkened dining room and stumbled over one of his novels, splayed on the floor. He picked up the book, the inscription still intact. "To Andrew. Nick McDeare." Nick sighed. Still holding the book, he returned to the breakfast nook.

"THE GREEN MONSTER," Jessie said. "Andrew's favorite."

"Funny. It's my least favorite." The critics considered THE GREEN MONSTER Nick McDeare's finest work, but for Nick the novel was shrouded in heartache. It had earned him one of the literary world's highest honors, but the award was buried in the back of his closet. When a major studio had bought the rights to MONSTER they'd offered Nick big money to do the screenplay. He'd turned them down flat.

The phone jangled, voicemail clicking on. Moments later, an accented voice filled the room. A man. "Jessica? Are you there? It's Gianni."

Jessie ran for the phone. "Gianni? Hi. I'm here ... "

Nick tried not to eavesdrop. Still ... Gianni? Who was Gianni?

*

It was almost eleven o'clock, and Lieutenant Barton was still at his desk. With his wife out of town, no need to rush home to Queens. Chief of Detectives at Midtown North meant thirty-six hours a day.

Lyle slumped over a file, the desk lamp casting the cramped office in shadow. He loved the precinct at this time of night. A skeleton staff of detectives. Uniformed cops making the rounds in patrol cars.

Barton stared down at the smiling face of Andrew Brady. The man's file was frayed from wear, but Brady's murderer remained at large. It ate away at Lyle, aging him fast. His close-cropped brown hair was sprouting frizzy gray, his face as grooved as tree bark. He looked older than his forty-one years.

Lyle had been thinking about Andrew all week. The second anniversary was only days away, but that wasn't what had Barton thumbing through the file tonight. From the moment he'd gotten out of bed that morning, he'd been smelling his uncle's old cotton candy machine at Coney Island. It was the first job Lyle ever had. He'd spied a thief trying to steal money from the cash register and had chased him for a mile and a half. He'd caught him, of course. Barton always got his man. Until Andrew Brady.

Lyle pulled out five more photos. All suspects. All had reasons to want Brady dead or were associated with organizations that spoke with their guns:

Vito Secchi. Resident of Italy, but associated with Roberto Martinelli, one of New York's crime bosses. Secchi had sailed on the Milano's anniversary trip and was in the terminal at the time of Andrew's shooting. Secchi had a violent reputation but had so far eluded arrest. He always had an alibi.

Aldo Zappella. Martinelli's right-hand-man. Also sailed on the Milano that trip. Also in the terminal that morning. Both Secchi and Zappella had a witness, a security guard who'd attested that both men were on the other side of the terminal when Andrew Brady was shot.

Ian Wexley. Former lover of Jessica Kendle Brady. Sworn enemy of Andrew Brady. He believed that Brady sabotaged his acting career and had vowed revenge. An arrest record for more than one assault and battery and attempted rape, no convictions.

Gianni Fosselli. Former shipping-line owner. Another ex-lover of Jessie's, scion of a powerful Italian family. Fosselli had very personal reasons for wanting Andrew dead.

Finally, Eduardo Santangelo, ship bartender. In the terminal at the time of the shooting. A punk with a record in Italy for petty theft and aggravated assault. Also Gianni Fosselli's nephew, the reason he'd avoided Italian prison.

Barton sighed. Cotton candy. He could smell it. He could taste it. It always meant something was about to break. Whatever it was, Lyle knew the break wasn't going to spring from staring at pictures. Whatever was about to occur would pop out of nowhere, like a ghost.

*

"Nick, do you think you could come for dinner tomorrow night? There's someone I'd like you to meet." Jessie loaded their plates into the dishwasher.

"Your friend on the phone? Gianni?"

Jessie nodded.

"Who's Gianni?"

"An old family friend."

"That's it? Just a family friend?"

"Yeah." She wiped her hands on a towel.

Did Jessie run to the phone that quickly for any old family friend? And why so secretive? But he was too tired to make like Sherlock. Nick yawned and stretched. God, he ached all over. "It's a date. I think I'll turn in. Um, where do I go?"

"Take these stairs to the fourth floor. The suite will be right in front of you." Jessie turned back to the sink. "Good night."

"Night." Nick dragged himself up the stairs. He couldn't wait to lie down.

"Hi."

Nick jumped. Anthony stood in the middle of the second floor hallway. Would this night never end? Nick put his finger to his lips. "I don't think your mom would be happy if she saw you up," he whispered.

"I'm Anthony. You look just like my Daddy. It's weird."

Nick laughed. "C'mon. You should be in bed. Where's your bedroom?"

"I'll show you." Anthony dashed down the hall and disappeared through a doorway. He was already under the covers by the time Nick joined him. Hamlet purred on the pillow. "What's your name?"

"Nick."

"Your eyes. They're just like Daddy's. Your face, too. And you talk like him."

"Well, there's a reason for that." Nick sat on the edge of the bed. Might as well say it. He didn't think Jessie would mind once he explained the circumstances. "Your daddy was actually my younger brother, Anthony."

"Huh? Daddy didn't have any brothers or sisters."

"Yes, he did. You see, when I was born our parents put me up for adoption."

"Why?"

"I don't know, Anthony." Kids always got right to the point. Jeffery used to ... "Anyway, when Andrew was born, our mother decided to keep him and--"

"Wow, it wasn't a fairy tale!"

"What wasn't?"

"Daddy's bedtime story. Wait, let me finish it for you, okay?" Excited, Anthony sat up. "The mother didn't give away the second boy. His name was Andy. And the mean father went away for good. Andy and his mom were happy, but they wanted to find Andy's older brother. They looked and looked but they couldn't find him. Andy grew up and whenever he was sad or happy he'd pretend like his brother was there. He even dreamed about him. The two brothers looked like twins, but one had light hair and one had dark hair. And then one day they found each other and lived happily ever after."

Nick could barely breathe. He tried to find his voice, but it was broken.

"That was Daddy's favorite story. He even acted it out sometimes. He'd change it and add things. The last time ..." Anthony paused, "was on the cruise. It was different then. Daddy started to cry. He said the brothers found each other just in time. He said Andy needed his brother now, because he didn't ever want to be alone again."

"Alone?" Andrew wasn't alone. He had a family.

"Daddy's story was about you and him, right?"

"It looks like it, kiddo."

Anthony and Nick stared at each other silently. Anthony got up on his knees and hugged his uncle, Nick fingering Anthony's soft curls. Memories washed over him in waves. He pushed them away. This was Andrew's son, not Jeffrey. Still, it felt good to hold a little boy in his arms again.

*

Jessie poured brandy into a snifter and scrunched into a corner of the couch in the study. The fire had died, but the liquor would keep her warm. She gazed up at the family portrait. Andrew stared back at her.

Amazing. Andrew's long-lost brother had appeared out of nowhere. The one she'd never believed existed. In a way, it was like having a part of Andrew back. Of course, the two brothers were nothing alike, except for an uncanny resemblance.

But the differences were glaring. Andrew was effervescent, an open book who never shut up. Nick was full of mystery, guarded, a man who weighed his words carefully. Jessie twisted a lock of hair around her finger. Andrew used to warn her about misreading people. He always said she saw the good in them and missed the bad. But from what Jessie had seen of Nick McDeare, the man was about as different from Andrew Brady as a man could get and still be the same species.

*

Nick had no trouble finding the suite, but he wasn't prepared for the opulence. The walls were a deep red, the woodwork high-gloss white. The bed was a four-poster with a down quilt a foot thick. A cedar chest rested against the footboard. The carpeting matched the walls. There was a dresser, a wardrobe, a working fireplace, and an oak rocker by the picture window. The bathroom had every personal amenity, including a toothbrush, a razor, and a hairdryer.

Opening a connecting door, Nick found a spacious sitting room in the same colors. A white leather sofa faced another fireplace. A workspace included a phone, a fax and a computer, a small refrigerator built into the unit. Bookshelves topped off at the ceiling. A round table and chairs nestled in the corner. Nick opened the sliding door that led to a terrace and stepped outside into the chilly air.

He looked out at the stars, a twinkly geometric design graphed by some invisible hand. What a night. And his sister-in-law had turned out to be surprisingly down-to-earth. Jessie was a famous actress, a woman the public adored. But inside this home, she was just a mother and a widow--with more sharp corners than a cube.

Nick's lip twisted. Who would have thought that Kristin would show up for a floor show tonight? And that as an encore she'd bash the hell out of him? Dear God.

Touching his head gingerly, Nick returned to the bedroom, stripped off his clothes and slid beneath the cool sheets. He left on a small lamp, an old habit whenever he slept in an unfamiliar place. Within minutes, he was asleep.

*

The dream crept up on Nick slowly. He and Andrew were sitting on the cedar chest at the foot of the bed, deep in conversation.

"You certainly have an effect on the ladies," Andrew cracked. "Look at you. Do all women take pleasure in beating the crap out of you?"

"Hey, what can I tell you? I bring out the beast in women."

Andrew studied him for a moment. "I'm glad you're here, Nick. They'll be safe now."

"Jessie and Anthony? Safe from --?"

"If you'd waited any longer, it might've been too late."

"Too late for what? Get to specifics."

"I can't. It doesn't work that way. You have to find out for yourself."

"Where do I begin?"

"Begin by moving in here for the duration."

"Here? In the brownstone? Are you nuts? I can't do that."

"Don't make me pull another rug out from under your feet."

"What ...?"

Andrew smirked. "You think that rug flew out from under your feet on its own? It was the only way to stop you."

"Stop me from what?"

"You looked like you were going to hurt that woman."

"I may be a jerk, but I don't hit women. You had no right!"

"Yeah, I did. And you hurt women in other ways. You enjoy breaking their hearts. Do you hate women that much?"

"Hey, I love women."

"I know you love their bodies. If I ever see you treating Jessie the way you treat your other ladies, I'll do more than play with a little throw rug."

Are you threatening me?" Nick laughed.

"Just a friendly warning. The real reason I played with that rug was to make sure you stayed here tonight. Now that you're here, Jessie will encourage you to stay. She's hungry for family, even a brother-in-law like you. Give her a chance. She's ready to open up, and you're the person to trigger it. I want you to help her, no one else. Jessie isn't a good judge of character. She's made some big mistakes in the past. She can't afford to make anymore."

"What kind of mistakes?"

"There's a lot you don't know yet."

"Then tell me. We're wasting time. We both know why I'm here. You've been after me, nagging away night after night in my dreams. Okay, you got your wish. I'm going to find out who pulled that trigger. I'll solve your murder. The hell with being here for family."

"We'll see about that. But I can only guide you. I can't intervene."

"Okay, guide me."

- 42 -

"Question everyone carefully. People are hiding things. Look behind their masks. You have a sixth sense when it comes to people. There's a cop you'll meet soon. Lyle Barton. It's important you trust each other."

"I work alone."

"Swallow your pride. And watch your back. There are powerful people who won't be happy you're getting involved. Protect Jessie and Anthony. They'll try to get to you through them. I'm putting my wife and my son in your hands."

Nick's mind raced.

"I have to go." Andrew rose. "Abbie will return to New York next week. If there's anything you want to know about my past or about our mother, talk to Abbie. She knows me as well as Jessie. In some ways she knows me better."

"Who's Abbie?"

"My oldest and closest friend. We've known each other since we were seven."

"Who's Gianni?"

Andrew paused. "A man who'd like to take my place. In this house and in Jessie's bed. More importantly, in my son's heart. Take care of Anthony for me. Call him Bongo. It was my pet name for him. He'll love you forever. "

"He's a good kid."

"Have Jessie take you to The Blue Pelican. You'll understand me better after being there. It's heaven on earth. Promise me you'll move in here. I want you near my family."

"I--"

"Promise me! It's important."

"Okay, okay, I promise. But how? I can't just announce I'm moving in."

"You'll find a way. Just follow Jessie's lead. One more thing. Trust no one. Do you understand me? No one."

Nick awoke slowly, the room easing into focus.

Andrew again. Another dream. Or was it? Nick was sitting naked on the cedar chest at the foot of the bed. The air was chilled, but he felt surprisingly warm.

His brother had been alive here in this room, in a dream. Or a non-dream. He'd come to ask for Nick's help.

Nick couldn't bring his brother back. He couldn't re-do the past. But he could do what mattered most to Andrew.

Find his killer and protect his family.

CHAPTER 4

Nick paced the suite, his eyes darting to the cedar chest. He needed a cigarette, in his jacket downstairs. He didn't want to creep around a strange house in the dark. He glanced at the clock. Five in the morning. He had to calm down and think this through.

Crawling beneath the quilt, Nick tucked his hands behind his head. Okay. He'd been nagged by his brother's ghost in another strange ... dream. For months Andrew had been needling him in his dreams to come to New York and find his killer. And now he wanted Nick to move into the brownstone. Andrew was a demanding sonuvabitch. Nick closed his eyes and willed himself to sleep. A dreamless sleep this time.

When Nick came downstairs the next morning, he found Mary tidying up in the living room, dust rag in hand.

"Apparently I missed quite a show last night," she said, her dark eyes watchful. "It took me two hours to clean up that mess in the dining room."

Ouch. "Sorry. We had, ah, an unruly visitor. She won't be visiting again. Where's Jessie?"

"I heard her shower running a few minutes ago."

Nick ambled around the room, giving the photos Mary was dusting closer inspection. Andrew and Jessie in the musical HEART TAKES. That would've been Andrew and Jessie's last play, according to the news reports. While Andrew was being murdered, some lucky understudy was getting his big break. Hmm ... Nick moved on to a happier subject: Andrew and Jessie in their college caps and gowns, the future at their fingertips. A baby photo of Anthony in Jessie's arms. Several pictures of Andrew and Anthony. Jessie with an older man. Her father? Andrew as Hamlet, holding up his Drama Desk Award.

Nick scrubbed a hand over his jaw, eyeing the pictures of a family unknown to him, his family. A brother he'd never met. A sister-in-law he knew even less about, other than the fact she was a celebrity onstage and screen. He never read the tabloids, and he rarely watched TV. Jessie's past, her family, her love life before Andrew—a blank slate. Which would change when he started his investigation. He'd soon learn more about Jessica Kendle Brady than Jessica Kendle Brady knew. Or wanted him to know.

A photo on the mantle caught Nick's eye. He picked it up and studied it.

"That's Andrew and your mother," Mary said quietly. "Andrew was eleven or so."

Nick nodded. His brother was gangly, all amber eyes and thick blond hair. Chelsea Brady was pretty, with dark hair and the same eyes. This woman was his mother. She gave birth to him and then gave him away like an unwanted puppy. "Are there any other childhood pictures of Andrew?" No response, Mary had disappeared.

"Hi, Nick." Jessie stood in the archway. "How did you sleep last night?"

Like he'd seen a ghost. "Fine. You could open a Bed and Breakfast."

"Just what I need." Jessie laughed. "C'mon. Let's get some coffee and sit in the breakfast nook. I want to ask you something."

And Nick wanted to ask Jessie something. How the hell was he going to wrangle an invite to Jessie's Bed and Breakfast?

Sitting across from each other, Jessie began. "How long are you in town?"

"Why?"

"I wondered if you'd like to check out of your hotel and stay here?"

Jesus.

Jessie waved a hand. "Now, hear me out before you say no. It would be great for Anthony. And I know Andrew would've considered it a personal favor. You haven't really met my son yet, but—"

"Actually," Nick said, wondering where Andrew was right now, "Anthony and I met last night. On my way upstairs. We talked a bit. I, um, I ended up telling him who I was, Jess. That I'm his uncle."

"You're kidding."

"I hope you don't mind? I didn't mean to, but he saw the resemblance. He was this close to guessing on his own."

"Really?" Jessie's eyes clouded over.

"He's a bright kid." Nick smiled. He hoped he looked reassuring. "He was fine with it. Honest."

"Anthony's resilient, yeah. I mean, he's dealt with a lot in his life. But he didn't seem upset? Or confused?"

"Nope. If anything, he was excited."

"Well, maybe it's good it came out so naturally then," Jessie said hesitantly. "I'll have a long talk with him later. He misses his dad so much. And Gianni's always busy. You're going be important in his life, Nick." She trained those brilliant blue eyes on him. "That is, if you want to be."

Gianni again. "I'd like that," Nick said easily. "Ah, Gianni, that's your family friend who called last night, right?"

Jessie nodded. "Anyway, if you stay here you could see Anthony all the time. Consider the suite yours whenever you're in town. It's private and I bet it has all the equipment you need for your work and … well, what do you think? If I'm not being too pushy."

"I guess I could make the sacrifice," Nick drawled. "Sure. Consider me a tenant. For Anthony's sake." His cell phone jangled. "Excuse me." He reached into his pocket. "McDeare."

"Nick, it's Grady again. I'll get to the point and not waste your time, or I'll have to bill you. This call's on the house. Bethany won't back off."

Nick rolled his eyes. The last person he wanted to talk to right now was his attorney. The last person he wanted to talk about was Bethany. "I told you. No child support. Not a dime."

"She swears it's yours."

"Like hell it is. Look, you know women, Grady. They want what they want. And if it's not bedroom gymnastics or a commitment for eternity, it's your mon—" In disbelief, Nick realized Jessie was calmly pouring the contents of her coffee mug into his lap. He leapt up. "What the hell!"

"What?" Grady asked. "What? Should I tell her to get a DNA test A-SAP?"

"Do you know what you could've done to me?!" Nick yelled at Jessie.

"Huh?" Grady said. "How's a prenatal DNA test going to hurt you?"

"Oh, yeah, I know all right," Jessie snapped. "If that was scalding, which it's not, I could've ended your problems with paying child support for any more children forever!"

"It's not my kid!"

"I know it's not your kid, Nick," Grady said patiently. "We've already gone through this. The timeframe's wrong, you used protection, and she's done this before. I told you, my PI found the court records. Sealed. For which you will be billed. Plenty."

"Not you, Grady. I'm talking to Jessie." Nick swiped helplessly at his wet crotch.

"Another woman? Man, you've got to stay away from the ladies."

"She's not that kind of lady."

"Sure she's not."

"I'm sure not your kind of lady," Jessie hissed.

"I'll call you back later." Nick snapped his cell shut.

"Do I really want you in my house?" Jessie asked, handing Nick a towel.

Nick blotted his lap. If it wasn't for Andrew he'd be out of here so fast … Nick forced himself to count to ten. Slowly. In Chinese.

"Yes, Jessie," he said smoothly. "You want me here. For Anthony, remember? My love life has nothing to do with you, remember?" Nick waved his arms. "And I swear that's not my kid! This woman's a scam artist. My attorney has the court records to prove it. She stalks celebrities, gets pregnant, and collects child support. If the DNA doesn't match, she fixes it so it does. She must have five children stashed with her mother for crissake. I slept with her exactly once. Call Grady if you don't believe me."

Jessie cocked her head. "Okay, I believe you. Just keep in mind I'm a woman, too. And treat me with more respect than you treat the other women in your life. Because, believe it or not, we're not interchangeable pieces on the chessboard of life."

"Hey, I treat my mother with lots of respect."

"Remember, there's more coffee where that came from." Jessie made an exit stage left, her head high.

Nick swore. What he'd said about Jessie to Grady was true. Jessica Kendle Brady wasn't like the other ladies in his life. She was worse. He could kill Andrew. Except he was already dead.

Nick dried off his pants with the suite's bathroom hairdryer. "Andrew," he said to the empty room. "I hope you're happy."

*

"We're not having dinner until late," Mary informed Nick when he returned from collecting his things at the hotel. "Gianni Fosselli will be joining us. Also, Jeremy Hoffman, Jessie's agent. His wife has some sort of charity function tonight. I hope you like beef Wellington."

He could grow to like Mary. "Are you kidding? I love it."

"Jessie's on the phone. Long distance to a friend in California."

Nick wandered into the living room. His run through Central Park had helped clear his head. He was back on the case. He'd deal with Jessie in his own way.

Nick was dying to check out the baby grand. What a beauty. Dropping onto the bench, Nick stroked the keyboard. Fabulous tone. He began to play a Mozart concerto. This piano made his little upright in Washington look like a toy. As he brought the piece to a crescendo, he spotted Anthony a few feet away.

Nick stopped playing abruptly. "Hi, Anthony,"

"Don't stop. I forgot how pretty the piano sounded. No one plays it anymore. Not since Daddy …" He sat down beside his uncle. "He was going to teach me."

"Well, I'm sure I don't play as well as your dad, but I could teach you."

"Yeah? I'll ask Daddy if he minds."

Nick's scalp prickled. "What do you mean, ask Daddy?"

"In a dream. I'll ask him when I see him in a dream."

"You dream about your dad, Anthony?"

"Uh-huh. Well, they're dreams, but not really."

"I don't understand." Andrew got around.

"Daddy visits me and tells me things. He told me you were coming to help Lyle catch the bad guys. He said I'd recognize you right away. Now I know what he meant. It's because you look so much like him."

Nick tried to stay calm. "Does your mom know this, that your dad told you about me, that he talks to you a lot?"

"I told her about one dream. That's all," he whispered. "Daddy doesn't want her to know how much he visits me. He said it'll make her sad he doesn't visit her, too."

Good point. Andrew visited his son and his brother, but not his wife? Nick reminded himself there was a lot about Jessie he didn't know. Hadn't Andrew told him to trust no one? Did he mean Jessie, too? It wouldn't shock Nick. Nothing about human nature would shock him. Especially when it came to women.

"Anthony." Mary stood in the doorway. "I just made some peanut butter cookies, your favorite."

Anthony looked up at his uncle. "Want some?"

"My favorite, too." Nick followed his nephew to the kitchen, trying to keep his expression all about cookies.

They sat at the island in the kitchen, a plate of cookies between them. Mary puttered with her dinner, glancing occasionally at the latest member of the family. Nick spotted a colander of salad fixings. "I could cut those for you."

Mary's eyebrows shot up. "Are you sure you're Andrew's brother? That boy was a disaster in the kitchen."

"Hey, the kitchen's one of my favorite rooms in any house."

"So," Mary said. "You write books. You play the piano. And you cook. What's your fatal flaw?"

"I'm a slob. My ex-wife listed it as grounds for divorce." Mary didn't need to hear the rest of his flaws. No reason to get on her bad side yet.

*

Jessie hurried into the kitchen. "Abbie's coming back to New York, everyone! She's sick of L.A. and she misses us." She smiled at Nick, too happy to hold a grudge against her twisted brother-in-law. Anyway, she owed it to Andrew to be nice to him. Nick's personal life was his personal life.

Jessie nibbled on a cookie. "I didn't tell her about you, Nick. I want to surprise her. Maybe I'll throw a party for the two of you next week. You should meet some of Andrew's friends."

"A party?" Nick looked like she'd asked him to hang naked from a billboard in Times Square.

Jessie's high spirits deflated. Nick was right. What in the world was she thinking? What did a party have to do with her life these days? Jessie drifted to the window overlooking the back yard. Daffodils and tulips bloomed in Mary's garden, birds orbiting the feeder. The early evening sun cast the yard in a buttery glow. A new season was descending on New York. For everyone but her.

Spring. Her second spring without Andrew. How could life go on as if nothing had changed?

"I'll get out my recipes and start to plan the menu." Mary flipped on a little television mounted into the wall. "Time for DR. PHIL." Before she had time to change the channel, they saw a reporter standing in front of the West Side Cruise Ship Terminal. In an ominous voice, he reminded his audience that it had been two years since actor Andrew Brady had been murdered and that his killer was still at large.

*

Rosita Hernandez put the plate of empanadas on the kitchen table just as the news about Andrew Brady came on the television. "That poor man."

"Rosita," Miguel warned, reaching for a meat pie. "Forget about it. You want them to send us back to Cuba? You go to the police, that's what they'll do. We got no papers. I'm telling you for the last time. Stay out of it."

If only she could. Rosita turned away, pouring the table wine. She couldn't forget what she'd seen. And heard. The terrible truth was Rosita had been in the West Side Cruise Ship terminal that evil morning to meet a cousin arriving on the Spanish-American Hacienda. But she hadn't been able to find the ship.

While Miguel devoured dinner and watched a Mets' game, Rosita remembered that morning as if it were a movie playing in her head, the same movie she saw in her nightmares every night. As she'd wandered up and down the sidewalk outside the pier, she'd spotted a man who seemed as confused as she was. He'd kept looking down the ramp to the street and glancing at his watch.

"Excuse?" she'd asked, showing him a piece of paper with the word Hacienda printed on it. "You know?"

The man she'd later learned was Andrew Brady had shaken his head and smiled down at her. "I'm sorry." He'd pointed to a security guard inside the terminal. "Ask him. He'll know."

She'd returned his smile. So handsome. Such unusual amber eyes. Like a cat. The guard had told Rosita that the ship would be at least two hours late. She'd decided to sit down and wait. Passengers had streamed off the Italian ship Milano. So many rich passengers with deep tans. She saw Mr. Cat Eyes buy a newspaper and then sit down at the far end of the terminal.

Rosita had decided to call Miguel. Her husband worried when she was late. It was as Rosita approached the bank of phones that she saw a man drop his leather jacket. She wouldn't have noticed except it made a noise as it hit the tile floor. He almost seemed to do it on purpose. She was about to pick it up for him when he made eye contact with her. The look in his eyes made her back up as if she'd seen a rattlesnake. He continued walking away quickly into the crowd. A few minutes later a high-pitched scream pierced the terminal. Terrified, Rosita ran for the doors, for Eighth Avenue and the subway to the Bronx.

Later, the news had been all over the television. Mr. Cat Eyes. Someone had shot him. Then she'd remembered the man with the snake eyes and the leather jacket and shivered. The image still haunted her, but Miguel had warned her to keep her mouth shut. She had no choice. She couldn't tell anyone what she knew. Not ever.

*

Gianni Fosselli never showed up at the brownstone empty-handed. Tonight was no exception. He had a shopping bag in each hand as he arrived for dinner. He handed Mary one of the bags. "I brought the spinach ravioli you like so much." He winked. "You cook them to perfection, Mary, better than my own chef. And Amaretto cookies for Anthony. Where is my handsome boy?"

"Taking pictures of Hamlet," Mary laughed. "He's got that poor cat wearing a scarf and a baseball cap."

Glancing down the hallway, Gianni spied Jessica approaching. Taking her hands, he kissed her lightly on both cheeks, drinking in her delicate scent. Every time he saw her, Gianni resisted the urge to clutch Jessica in his arms and kiss her the way he used to, with passion. It was just a matter of time. He was a patient man when he needed to be. The prize would be worth the wait.

Gianni cocked his head, studying Jessica, so elegant in an ocean-blue silk dress. The pure color mirrored her eyes, the fabric's loose waves flattering her body, too thin now, like a bird. But he would fix that in time. He'd tempt her with his most delicious dishes night after night until she was the Jessica he wanted her to be again. "What's different about you?" Gianni asked softly. Dare he hope that glow in her eyes was for him?

And then Gianni spotted the dinner guest Jessica had mentioned. "L'oh il mio dio!" He was looking at a ghost. With the exception of the dark hair, this man was the picture of Andrew Brady.

Jessie smothered a smile and led the way to the back porch as she explained that Nick was Andrew's brother.

*

Trust no one, Andrew's words. Nick remembered them well.

Nick watched as Gianni Fosselli sat beside Jessie on the wicker divan and lit a cigarette. Nick's instincts as a reporter had served him well over the years. Those instincts were crawling all over him now. Andrew had said Fosselli was the man who wanted to replace him in Jessie and Anthony's hearts. Just how far was he willing to go? Nick pointed to Gianni's silver cigarette case on the table. "May I?"

"Of course," Gianni dug into his pocket and pulled out a book of matches. "You can keep it," he said expansively, as if he were giving a shoeshine boy a big tip.

"Gee, thanks," Nick said, examining the matches. It was a fancy cover, a cruise ship in a tropical setting. Oceano was written across the bottom.

"My restaurant." Gianni crossed his legs.

Nick sniffed the cigarette, imagining taking a deep drag, ignoring Gianni's brief look of curiosity. Ah, the old days. Before he'd quit. A lot had changed since his brother died. Now when he needed a cigarette, it was to sniff. To fondle. To exercise self-control.

Sitting back, he watched Fosselli make small talk with Jessie on his other side. Gianni Fosselli smelled of money. Limousines and caviar. Five-thousand dollar suits and diamond rings. He was wearing a three-piece charcoal gray silk suit, magenta shirt, and matching silk tie. Expensive Italian cut shoes. A gold link bracelet. Nick's lip twisted. Probably a fourteen-carat gold chain around his neck with a religious medal. His dark mahogany hair was combed straight back. He was handsome with a dimpled chin and chocolate brown eyes. Nick felt like a slob in a soft dark blazer over a matching turtleneck sweater.

Fosselli lazily turned his attention to Nick. "So. Your name is different from Andrew's. But you say you are brothers?"

"I didn't say anything. Jessie did."

"Nick was adopted at birth," Jessie explained, pouring Gianni a glass of wine. "When Andrew came along, his mother refused to give up another child."

Yeah, Nick thought. Keep one son. It doesn't matter which.

"Ah," Gianni said, "the stuff of a fairy tale. The favored son and the ... other son." He waved his hand, as if giving a benediction. "There's Andrew, beloved by all. And then there's the child Nicholas. But you seem to have done very well for yourself, Nicholas, considering."

"Gianni," Jessie said. "That was rude. I'm sure—"

"Don't worry, Jess," Nick drawled. "Gianni is essentially correct. Of course, there are always many players in any folk tale. Fables' origins run deep in our shared psyches. In fact, I think Gianni has a place in the tale, too."

Gianni locked eyes with Nick. "How do you see me in your little fairy tale, Nicholas? Please, tell me."

"Well," Nick said, "now that you ask, I see you as the spoiler. The black prince who usurps the rightful heir's throne and wins his princess, the golden-haired bride. Of course, you have to excuse my poor storytelling skills. I'm into more contemporary books these days. But some things are so basic, aren't they? Just fiction, of course."

"Nick," Jessie said, coloring a pretty shade of pink, "let's stop this, okay?"

"No, no," Gianni said, sipping his wine, "let Nicholas run on. This is intriguing. Tell me, my friend, does the black prince succeed?"

"Not in my story, he doesn't. In fact, you know those dungeons in—"

Jeremy Hoffman burst onto the porch. "Jessie, I've had three calls in the last two days from The American Theater Wing. Ooh, shrimp!" He headed for the chilled bowl, dredging several shrimp in the cocktail sauce. "You've got to give them an answer," he said, swallowing. "I can't keep stalling them."

After introducing Nick to Jeremy, Jessie touched Gianni's arm and steered him away from Nick's gaze, chatting about his restaurant. She cast Nick a sharp look, which he ignored.

Anthony materialized in the doorway, skidding to a stop. "Gianni! Did you bring it?"

"You're terrible, Anthony!" Gianni laughed. "Come here." He reached beside the divan and handed the boy a shopping bag. "I'm sorry it wasn't ready for your birthday."

Anthony jerked out a gaily wrapped package and tore the paper away. Inside was a carved wooden sailing ship. He proudly showed it to Nick. Nick whistled. The design's intricacy was stunning, a museum piece.

"Gianni always gives me a ship for my birthday and Christmas. You have to see my collection, Uncle Nick. They're so cool!"

"You like ships?" Nick asked the boy.

"I've only been on one. The one with Mommy and Daddy. But Gianni used to own a whole bunch of them."

"Where's my thank you?" Gianni prodded.

The boy threw his arms around Gianni and kissed him on the cheek. "Thank you so much." Nick eyed them sharply. This old family friend wanted to get into the golden-haired princess's silk panties in the worst way. And he was using her son to get there.

"Anthony," Gianni said. "What did I teach you?"

"Sorry." The boy laughed and kissed the man on both cheeks. He turned to Nick. "That's how they do it in Italy," he said, his chin dimpling.

Nick watched them, his brows knitting. The boy and the man might have been father and son. The hair. The shape of the face. The shape of the eyes, if not the color. That dimple in the chin ... Gianni's a man who would like to take my place. In this house and in Jessie's bed. More importantly, in my son's heart ... Nick shifted his gaze to Jessie. She was staring back at him.

Over dinner, Nick was honored when Anthony insisted on sitting beside him.

"Anthony," Gianni said gently, "you always sit next to me."

"Nick is my new uncle," Anthony explained. "He needs me to show him the ropes. That's what my dad told me when I met my best friend Eric. He said when you get a new friend you show him the ropes. You already know the ropes around here, Gianni!"

Everyone laughed, even Gianni.

Nick said little during the meal, an extravaganza of beef Wellington, creamed spinach and grilled portabella mushrooms. It was second nature for him to blend into the background and watch. Gianni regaled the table with tales about his restaurant and the new addition under construction. The architect from Italy. The imported marble. The new secret recipes the Italian chef had stolen from the finest restaurant in Roma. The movie stars who wouldn't eat anywhere else when they were in New York and got special delivery by private jet to the West Coast.

No one seemed to notice Nick's silence except Jessie. Every time Nick glanced at her, those blue eyes were riveted on him. Nick poured himself another glass of wine and met her gaze innocently. Maybe it was none of his business. What had gone on between Andrew and his wife and Gianni might have nothing to do with solving his murder.

Or it might have everything to do with it.

*

Nick had been lying awake for almost two hours. His body was tired but his mind was obsessively circling Jessie, Andrew, Anthony, and Gianni. He dragged himself up and shucked on jeans and a T-shirt. Grabbing a few items from his duffel bag, Nick headed for the stairs.

A small light over the stove cast the kitchen in shadow. Nick reached for the tea kettle, surprised to find it hot. Glancing over his shoulder, he saw Jessie sitting in the breakfast nook with a steaming mug, Hamlet curled beside her.

"You couldn't sleep either?" she asked quietly. He shook his head. "The tea bags are on the counter."

Nick held up a small tin. "I carry my own." He dropped a tea bag in a mug, poured in some steaming water, and backed towards the stairs. "Sorry to disturb you."

"You're not. Don't go. Please. Join me."

Here it comes. He didn't want to get into this. He'd rather get at the truth independently, in his own way. Nick sat across from Jessie in the breakfast nook. Digging into his pocket, he pulled out a silver flask and poured some liquid into his mug. "Brandy. Helps me sleep."

"May I?"

He looked up in surprise. "Sure."

"I love brandy." Jessie poured a large shot into her mug. "It's been my medicine for the past two years. My preferred medicine at least." She took a sip.

"So, you travel with tea and brandy. What else have you got stashed in that suitcase upstairs?"

"Just a few creature comforts. Nothing special."

"You are a man of few words. Do these creature comforts have some secret meaning?"

Nick shrugged. "Nothing you need to know."

"The more you tell me about yourself, the less I know."

Nick chuckled. "Mystery serves me well in my--" Hamlet leapt to his feet and hurtled up the back stairs. "What's that about?"

"He's been weird lately. I'm sure it's nothing a good mouse couldn't cure." His sister-in-law was not a good liar. Her face was the color of milk. Clearing her throat, Jessie seemed to shake off her dark thoughts. "I did some research on you tonight. On the internet."

"Why?"

"I just wanted to know more about you. You certainly don't fill in the blanks for me."

"There's nothing to know. I was a reporter and now I'm an author. End of story."

"Your summation omits about ninety percent of the story. For example, your ex-wife's some big attorney in Washington. A counselor for the Senate. I also read you have a son. Nick, why haven't you mentioned him?"

Nick swallowed hard. "I did have a son," he said hoarsely. "He died. You didn't research me thoroughly enough it seems."

"He ....? Oh, God, I'm sorry. I'm so sorry." Jessie looked like she wanted to sink through a trap door in the floor. Nick stared at his hands, wishing he could escape, too. It wasn't her fault. The silence ate up the room. He was relieved when Jessie finally changed the subject.

"Uh, I read your book reviews. THE GREEN MONSTER won The Arthur Conan Doyle Award. That's quite an honor." She reached for his flask and added more brandy to their mugs. "I also read your track record as an investigative reporter's one hundred percent. You solved cases that stymied the cops. You were even nominated for a Pulitzer Prize, considered the best in your field." Jessie set her mug down carefully. "You came here to find out who murdered Andrew, didn't you? That's the real reason you're here."

Nick's mouth fell open. He'd thought she was going to bring up ... No matter. She knew why he was here. "Yeah, that's the real reason I'm here, Jess," he said gently.

"Do you intend to turn your pursuit into a book?"

"No! God, no. This isn't about a book." Nick leaned forward. "I want to do this for Andrew. It may be the only thing I can ever give him. Please believe me."

Jessie sighed and dropped her head. "Thank God. That's one fear out of the way."

"Are you okay with this? Will you help me?"

"Yes, I'll help you, any way possible. I want answers. And I want justice." She peeked up at him, her blue eyes wide. "Now for my other fear. You were watching Gianni with Anthony tonight. I saw the look on your face. You know, don't you?"

"I'm not sure what you're talking—"

"You figured it out in one evening, didn't you, Mr. Investigative Reporter? Your reputation's still intact. One hundred percent."

Nick pushed both hands through his hair and wished he could dematerialize like Andrew.

"Nick, tell me. You figured it out, didn't you?"

Why was she putting him in this position? Sticky emotions were not his territory. Neither were emotional women. He was out of here. Jessie grabbed Nick's arm before he made it off the bench. Her hand knocked over his open flask, a pool of brandy washing over Nick's T-shirt.

"Damn!" Jessie rose, reaching for the towel rack. In her hurry, she swept her mug off the table. It crashed to the floor, splashing its contents up to her waist.

Nick raised a brow. "Congratulations. My T-shirt's full of brandy, and your robe's soaked with tea. All in a night's work. And that's not counting this morning's coffee."

Jessie burst out laughing. "Consider yourself warned. My friends take out insurance if they're going be around me for very long."

Nick grabbed a sponge and helped her mop up the spillage. Jessie looked like bone china that would crack at any moment. But in reality she was a brandy-guzzling klutz. At least her clumsiness made her forget about the topic no longer at hand.

"I'm going to change," Jessie said, heading for the stairs. "Are you tired?"

"Hmm?" Nick tossed the sponge in the sink. "No. I mean--"

"Good. Why don't you change your clothes and meet me in my sitting room? I'll light a fire. There's a bottle of brandy in the bar up there."

"Uh, wait, I ..." He was speaking to the air. Great. More talk. He wouldn't underestimate Jessie again.

*

Anthony's moans shattered his bedroom's silence. The stranger was chasing him down the busy street again, and Anthony was running as fast as he could. Anthony sensed his father on the other side of the street, watching. He could feel him. Daddy!

"I'm here, Anthony. You're safe. Open your eyes."

His eyelids fluttered open and he smiled. "Daddy."

Andrew Brady sat in the rocker beside the bed. "Hey, Bongo."

"I keep having that dream, Daddy. But I'm fine once I know you're there."

"Me? I'm in it?"

Anthony nodded. "You're on the other side of the street trying to save me. I know it's you."

Andrew dropped his eyes. "What do you think of your Uncle Nick?"

"I like him. A lot. But he's not like you. He's real quiet. I think he's sad."

"Maybe you can help him." Andrew paused. "Nick's lost a lot in his life. You and your mom have to find a way to get him to talk about it so he's not so quiet anymore. He really likes you, Bongo."

Anthony weighed his father's words. "Okay. I'll talk to him. But what do I say?"

"Let me tell you a story about a little boy named Jeffrey."

*

Nick's cell phone rang as he left the suite and headed for Jessie's sitting room. Who the hell would call him at this hour? "McDeare."

"Hi, baby. I'm lying here all alone. I'm naked, I'm wet, and I'm missing you."

Greta. A hot little German fraulein. "Do you know what time it is here?" Nick whispered in clipped German. He disconnected, enjoying the mental image of a sputtering Greta. He never should have gotten out of bed tonight. The next time he couldn't sleep, he'd guzzle straight from his flask and skip the tea. He strode into Jessie's room.

The two-room master bedroom suite ran from the brownstone's front to its back. The sitting room was a treasure, from the heavy marble fireplace to the overstuffed leather furniture scattered in front of the blazing grate. Hurricane lamps bathed the room in a soft amber glow. There was a bar and a state-of-the-art entertainment center. Windows overlooked the back yard. Nick's eyes were drawn to an oil portrait of Brady and Kendle over the mantel, theatrical yet haunting.

"Welcome to my museum," Jessie said, nesting into the corner of the sofa, a snifter in her hand. "I poured you a brandy, too. On the bar."

"Very impressive." Nick took the glass and examined the other mementos dotting the walls. Framed posters of plays starring Jessie and Andrew. Photographs of Brady and Kendle with celebrities and political figures, one with the president. Dozens of framed hand-written notes from the likes of Dustin Hoffman, Meryl Streep, Al Pacino, Glenn Close, Bob Fosse, and Nathan Lane. Mounted covers of NEW YORK MAGAZINE sporting their famous faces.

"Wow." Nick wandered to one of the leather chairs and sat down. "Why don't you have this parade in the living room?"

"It's part of the past. It has nothing to do with my life anymore."

He took a swig of brandy and winced as it burned its way to his stomach.

"Nick, what we were talking about downstairs, before I played the clown ..."

"I don't want-- "

"Dammit, this is important!"

The volume of her voice surprised him. Such a mighty sound coming from such a small woman. A woman used to commanding the stage, he reminded himself. Nick rose and set his glass on the end table. "Look, this may be none of my--"

"Why are you so intent on running away from this subject?"

"I don't run," Nick said softly. Who was she to presume to know anything about him? Especially when Jessie was the one with the secrets. How much had she kept hidden from Andrew? What lies had she told his brother?

"Then you're doing an awfully fine imitation of it. Tell me. What were you thinking when you were watching Gianni tonight? I have to know. Please."

"You really want to know?" Nick glared down at her. "Okay, I'll tell you. Anthony's not Andrew's biological son. He's Gianni's. You had an affair with him." Silence hung in the room. "I'm right, aren't I?"

He stared Jessie down, waiting for his answer.

CHAPTER 5

Nick watched Jessie in silence. She finally found her voice. "Yes," she said, looking Nick in the eye. "Gianni is Anthony's father. But there's more to it than you can possibly imagine."

"Look, I don't know what went on between you and Fosselli, and maybe I don't want to know."

"I told you. It's more complicated than you can imagine. How did you figure it out so quickly, about Anthony?"

Nick shrugged. "Gianni and Anthony look alike. It's obvious he loves the boy. Hey, let's just drop it, okay? Your secret's safe with me." He'd expose her secrets on his own.

"I can't drop it." Jessie swept a hand through her hair. "It's too big to drop."

Nick pulled a cigarette from his pocket, took a deep sniff, and stuffed his hand back in his pocket. He paced the room. "All right. Let's talk about this then." If she wanted to pursue the topic, fine. He'd get the answers faster that way. But it wasn't going to be pretty. "Did Andrew know?"

"Yes."

"You're sure you're telling me the truth? You don't want to rethink this?"

"What do you mean?"

"I mean, you didn't cheat on Andrew with Gianni? You didn't let Andrew assume Anthony was his son? Two secrets he never knew to his dying day?"

"No!" Jessie flushed scarlet. "Just what do you think I am?"

"A woman, honey."

Nick didn't see it coming. Jessie shot up from the couch and slapped him across the face so hard he reeled backwards.

"Get this through your thick head! I don't lie and I don't cheat. And not all women are tramps and thieves. You can pack your bags and get out of here right now. Gianni and I were a public item before Andrew and I were married. You can ask anyone, including the detective on Andrew's case. Andrew knew everything."

Taking a step backwards, Nick fingered his jaw. Maybe Jessie was telling the truth. Maybe she wasn't. He'd play along and find out. His jaw hurt like hell. What was it with the women in his life?

"Look," Nick said contritely. "You have to understand, Jessie. As a reporter, I saw this kind of thing all the time. You heard my own phone conversation this morning. Lots of daddies out there who have no idea the kid isn't theirs. It happens."

Jessie paced the room. "Well, that kind of woman is not me. You owe me an apology, Nick."

"Okay," Nick said softly. He switched to his sincere voice. "I'm sorry I insulted you, Jessie. I didn't mean to. I guess I'm too cynical for my own good." Jessie's color slowly returned to normal. "Jessie," Nick said calmly, "who knows about Anthony besides Gianni?"

"Mary, of course, and Abbie. And Lyle, the detective in charge of the case."

"Abbie. Your friend in California."

"Andrew knew from the beginning. It was no secret Gianni and I had been seeing each other. Everyone knew."

"Anthony obviously doesn't know who his biological father is."

"No, and I don't want him to ever learn the truth."

"Why not?"

"It's complicated. A long story."

"Wait a minute. You're the one who wanted to talk about this complicated, long story. Start talking."

Jessie stared out the window into the night. "So, what did you think of Gianni anyway?"

"I think he's a smug man who wears his money like a medal of honor."

"You're wrong. Gianni comes from a great deal of money, it's true. But he's been wonderful to Anthony and me ever since Andrew died."

Wonderful? Fosselli wanted his son and he wanted to screw his son's mother. Again. What a naïve woman Jessie was. Assuming she was telling the truth. Nick kept silent, confident it would keep her talking.

"You'll see when you get to know Gianni better. Of course, he's different now."

"What do you mean, different?"

"I didn't see Gianni for five or six years. He came back to the States a few months before Andrew was murdered to open a restaurant. He studied at the Cordon Bleu years ago, but he had to quit when his parents suddenly died."

"A chef?" Nick chuckled. "Gianni Fosselli wanted to be a chef?"

"Trust me. He's excellent. Why do you think he owns his own restaurant?"

"So he can get his name in the papers?"

"Very funny. At one time, Gianni ran the Italian Marine Line. His family founded the shipping company generations ago. That's how I knew him. My father was one of the cruise directors. Gianni watched me grow up. Anyway, Gianni sold the company when his grandfather died."

"His grandfather died. His parents died suddenly. A lot to deal with, hmm?"

"His mother and father died when Gianni was nineteen. His grandfather just a few years ago."

"How did his parents die?"

"I ... don't know. I never asked."

"What about his grandfather?" Nick took a gulp of brandy.

"Who knows? He died of a million old-age afflictions. He was a mean, selfish old man."

"I take it you didn't like the grandfather."

"He jerked Gianni around his entire life, whining he was dying and needed his grandson to run the company. He was dying for twenty years. Gianni was a puppet and the old man pulled his strings."

Nick warmed his hands over the fire. "Gianni doesn't look like the kind of man who would be anybody's puppet."

"Not now. Back then he did everything his grandfather asked. No matter who he hurt."

Nick softened his voice, an old reporter's trick. "And you were one of the people he hurt?"

"Yes," Jessie said in a small voice. "But I was a fool. It was my fault, too." She took a sip of brandy. "There was a time when I thought I was in love with Gianni."

Finally—the real story. "When was this?"

"About eight years ago, the summer that Andrew and I worked aboard the ship doing our club act. That's how Bill Rudolph discovered us. Gianni and I started seeing each other that May. It lasted until September. I guess I was in love with love. Gianni was Old World. European. I was crazy about him." She glanced at Nick, blushing.

Jessie almost looked innocent when she blushed. The last innocent female Nick had spoken to was Mimi Schwartz, in first grade. A redhead. "Go on," he coaxed.

"Andrew didn't like Gianni from the start. Later, he admitted he was jealous."

"You, ah, you were dating Andrew and Gianni at the same time?"

"No. Andrew and I were lovers when we were young. At Julliard. We were also best friends most of our lives. I can't date two people at the same time. It's not my style."

Sure it wasn't. "So what happened, Jess? How did Fosselli hurt you?"

Jessie stared into the fire. "Halfway through the summer I found out he was engaged to a woman back in Italy. Not a real engagement. An arranged marriage."

Nick laughed. "An arranged marriage? C'mon."

"Yeah, that's what I thought, too. But Bianca's father offered to bail the Italian Marine Line out of financial trouble in return for the marriage. When I came along, I threw a wrench into the agreement."

"Did the Fosselli family find out about you?"

"Not until my summer contract ended and Gianni moved into my apartment. Before that we'd been living in his owner's suite on the ship. We were going to get married and tell his family after the fact. And then someone secretly took photographs of us and sent them to Gianni's family. The old man collapsed and Bianca tried to kill herself." Jessie reached for the poker, stoking the flames. "Gianni flew home to smooth things over and tell his family the truth. He said he'd call once it was done."

"But he disappeared from your life instead."

"I'm a cliché, aren't I? A silly woman. Go ahead, take your shot." She watched Nick through lowered lashes.

"I don't think you're silly." Leaning against the mantel, Nick came to a surprising conclusion about his sister-in-law. Jessie was one of the honest ones. Not only was she honest, but she probably assumed other people were as honest as she was. No wonder Andrew said Jessie trusted the wrong people.

Jessie replaced the poker, the fire casting a glow over her ivory skin. "It was three weeks before I heard from Gianni. He wrote me a letter about his grandfather being on the brink of death. I should be patient. That's when I realized Gianni would never get out from under his grandfather's thumb. It was over between us. However—"

"Anthony was on the way."

"To make matters worse, my father died of a heart attack the week before. I was alone. And terrified."

"And Andrew came through for you?"

Jessie smiled tenderly. "Andrew offered to marry me and raise the baby as his own. With Dad gone, it was just the two of us. We were married within a week and moved back into the brownstone. It was the perfect solution. The brownstone's been in my mother's family for generations. Anyway, we began our career on Broadway, thanks to Bill and a lot of press. America's sweethearts. And eight months later Anthony was born."

Nick refilled his glass at the bar. "When did Gianni come back into the picture?"

Jessie plopped back down. "On that last cruise, two years ago."

"Did he ever marry his Italian fiancée?"

"He said he couldn't marry someone he didn't love."

"How did he take the news that you'd married Andrew?"

"He knew about that. Andrew insisted I write him immediately after we were married. I did, but I didn't mention the baby. I never heard a word from Gianni until I bumped into him on the ship. Andrew and I were shocked to see him."

After six years, Fosselli rematerializes and Andrew ends up dead. Andrew, the man who'd taken possession of Gianni's woman and son. It didn't take a rocket scientist to figure this out.

"I know what you're thinking, Nick. Gianni had nothing to do with Andrew's murder. He was standing right beside me when Andrew was shot."

Nick's mind raced. Gianni could've hired a gun. Crossing to the couch, he sat beside her. "Jess, why weren't you with Andrew when it happened?"

"Andrew was lured away by a phony message from Bill Rudolph. Something about a photo shoot and an interview for the Tonys. I stayed behind with Anthony, Mary, and the luggage. Um, Nick, I really don't want to talk about that—the cruise."

"We're going to have to talk about it eventually. If you want to help me solve this case. If," Nick said softly, "it's as important to you as it is to me." Nick shivered again and rubbed his hands together.

"Don't insult me. Eventually is fine, just not now. Look, you're freezing, too. I've got the thermostat set at seventy. I don't understand ... Or maybe I do, which makes it worse." Jessie rose and wandered to the fire, wrapping her arms around herself.

"What is it?" Nick paced to her side, letting her change the subject. A short break wouldn't hurt before they got to the hard part.

She flicked her eyes up to his. "You'll think I'm crazy."

"I think everyone's crazy. Especially women. But you already know that." Nick had a feeling he knew exactly what Jessie was going to say. If she was crazy, so was he.

She took a deep breath. "The cold. It's the same as the other night. It's Andrew. I think he's here, Nick. I know it sounds nuts but Anthony had a strange dream about Andrew. The next morning he showed me something Andrew had hidden under the floorboards he had no way of knowing."

"Jessie—"

"Hear me out. I think Andrew told him in a dream. See, Andrew and I made a pledge on our honeymoon never to leave each other. I think Andrew kept his word." She looked up at him. "Am I crazy?"

Nick's heart was pumping too fast and too hard. "Tell me something," he croaked, "did Andrew call Anthony Bongo?"

She turned as pale as pearls. "I haven't heard that word since Andrew died. How did you know?"

"What's The Blue Pelican?"

"The ...? Did Anthony tell you--"

"Andrew. Andrew told me in a dream."

"A dream?" Jessie's eyes widened. "When?"

"Last night." Nick walked away, rubbing the back of his neck.

Jessie followed him. "What else did he say?"

"Basically, that he wants me to nail his killer."

"That's why it's so important to you to solve this case! You made a promise to-to Andrew. My God."

"Yeah. It's personal. Very personal. Besides crazy." Nick reached for his snifter and took a gulp. "In my dream, Andrew and I were sitting on the cedar chest up in the suite. That's where I woke up."

"You're kidding!"

"Yeah. I always joke about waking up naked on a cedar chest in the frigid zone."

"Has this ever happened before?"

Nick picked up his snifter and went to the bar, pouring a hefty shot of brandy. With a twist of his wrist, the liquid disappeared down his throat. He sighed with satisfaction.

"This has happened before, hasn't it?" Jessie was beside him again. "You're not leaving this room without telling me everything you know about Andrew." Jessie folded her arms.

"Or what? You'll hold me against my will? Jess, you look like a wind chime would blow you over."

Jessie opened her mouth to reply before looking down at herself. "God, you're right. Look at me. I used to be ..." She walked over to a chair and collapsed.

Nick felt a sudden wave of pity. "A little food and exercise can get you back in shape. I was thinking of jogging tomorrow after a good night's sleep. Want to join me?"

"You run?"

"Yeah, I run. Do I look like some nerd who sits behind a desk all day?"

"You just don't seem the athletic type."

"Hey, I've run marathons. I play football. I'm a diehard baseball fan. I used to have season tickets to the Orioles. Jeffrey and I--" Nick raked a hand through his hair and turned away. "So? Will you join me?"

"I can't. I don't leave the house. Not unless I have to."

"May I ask why you're under self-imposed house arrest?"

She stared at the carpet. "People point and stare. Or they ask for my autograph and tell me how tragic it was to lose my husband. The paparazzi follow me. Reporters shove their mikes in my face and ask stupid questions."

"Look, come jogging with me. You know what's great about jogging? By the time people recognize you, you're long gone. It's always worked for me."

"People recognize you that easily?"

"Once you've been on OPRAH, every woman in America knows you."

"You were on OPRAH?"

"Twice. Are you coming with me?"

"I had no idea. What about LETTERMAN?"

"Yeah. Are you coming?"

"I ... no, I can't. I can't, but thanks."

Nick eyed her. There was a whiff of clinical depression about Jessie. Nick recognized the signs firsthand. "You're a chicken, you know that?"

"Nice try. You changed the subject and never answered my question."

"What question?"

Jessie rolled her eyes. "I asked if you had other dreams or visions or whatever about Andrew. And I want an answer."

"Let it go."

"No."

She continued to stare. "Okay. Yes, it's happened before. And that's all I'm going to say. It's private."

"Private? I tell you about a disastrous love affair that produced a child, and your dreams are too private?"

Nick looked skyward, "How did I get myself into this?"

"We're family. That's how. Family talks to each other."

"Okay, I'll make a deal with you. I tell you about my Andrew dreams if you tell me about the day Andrew was shot."

Jessie's face fell like a mudslide. She dropped into the chair again.

"Sure, you want me to confide in you, but you won't do the same."

"I just did. I told you about Gianni."

"And I told you I was prattling into thin air while sitting on a cedar chest naked." He sat across from her. "C'mon. How do I find out who killed my brother if I can't start with you? I need to know what happened that day. Eventually is now."

Jessie clasped and unclasped her hands. "I can't even think about that day. I've never talked about it. Ever. To anyone except the police. Eventually has to be ... eventually."

"I'm not anyone. As you love to point out, I'm family." He leaned forward. "Look, while you were at Andrew's bedside I was walking the streets waiting to hear news of his condition. I couldn't get anywhere near you. I looked like some nosy reporter angling for a story. I was standing across the street from this brownstone when word came down he died. Please. I need to know. It's how I work. And I'm Andrew's brother for crissake. I deserve to know."

Nick sighed. Jessie looked as if she were in a trance, her eyes staring into space. "Okay," Nick said quietly, "you win."

"What do I win, Nick?"

"I'll talk first. If you feel like reciprocating, it's your choice." He took a deep breath. The last thing he wanted to do was talk about himself. "Jessie, I've been dreaming about Andrew since I was a child. I didn't know who he was, but he turned up on a regular basis. As I got older, he got older. Sometimes his face would appear out of nowhere. I'd be writing, and there he was, calling to me. To say I was curious is an understatement."

Jessie stared at him, her face rapt.

Nick rose, idling near the fire. "Right after Andrew died, I took off for Vancouver to write RED ROVER. By that time I knew that the man who'd haunted me all my life was my brother. With Andrew gone, I figured the dreams were gone." He snorted. "Wrong. Andrew appeared as vivid as my own face in the mirror, Jess, his voice pronounced and strong."

"Jess. You keep saying ..." She shook her head. "Go on." Her eyes were alive again.

"He was a physical presence. Real. He kept saying the same thing. He wanted me to come to New York to find his killer. Then something happened that scared the hell out of me. After one of my dreams, I woke up at the kitchen table, exactly where I'd had my conversation with Andrew. I used to sleepwalk when I was a kid. I thought it was starting up again, provoked by Andrew and Jeff-- But when I woke up on that cedar chest this morning, I knew I wasn't sleepwalking. I knew something out of time and place had just happened. At least, our time and place."

"So you think I'm right? You think Andrew's here? It sounds so crazy."

"I know. But think about it. Dreams are something we still can't clearly define, one of the mysteries of life. Maybe Andrew realized a dream was the only way to communicate with us. I lived in the Far East for years. Spirits are a way of life in that culture." Nick shrugged. "I guess you could call me a believer. And myth says cold spots shadow the spirit world."

Jessie walked to the hearth, jabbing at the dying fire with a poker. "If it's true," she murmured, "why has he come to you and Anthony, but not me?"

Nick joined Jessie, tossing fresh logs on the smoldering embers. "I don't know." But despite his earlier doubts, Nick was pretty sure it wasn't because Andrew didn't love his wife. Or trust her. "There must be a logical reason. With me, I think being denied a life together connected Andrew and me in an unusual way." He leaned against the mantel, staring at the flames.

"And Anthony?"

"Maybe Andrew's afraid he'll be replaced in his son's heart," Nick said gently. "Gianni's the boy's biological father. I'm sure the man would love to marry you and claim his son." Nick met her eyes. "Is that possible?"

"I'll never marry again." Jessie twirled her wedding rings. They caught the fire's glow, flicking tiny diamond strobe lights across the ceiling. "I'm never taking these rings off. And Anthony will never know that Gianni's his father. Andrew deserves to have his son's love forever."

Nick knew from experience that there was more to being a parent than blood. Charles and Kate McDeare were perfect examples. But it was time to ask an important question. "Can you think of anyone who would want Andrew dead?" Other than Gianni, he added silently.

"One person. Ian Wexley."

*

Ian Wexley tossed some bills on the sticky bar top. "Night, Max." He brushed a strand of silver hair from his forehead and rubbed his temples.

"See ya, Wex,"

Ian caught sight of himself in the mirror behind the bar and stared. His once beautiful mane of silver hair was limp and oily. His eyes were bloodshot. Veins popped out on his forehead. He looked fifty-five, not forty-one, and like he'd been rode hard and put away wet. He shook his head, trying to get rid of the double image reflected in the mirror. One was bad enough.

Grunting, Ian slipped an arm through the sleeve of his leather jacket, but he couldn't find the other sleeve. "Ah, the hell with it." He handed Max his jacket over the bar and watched as one sleeve mopped up spillage. His wife would buy him a new one. "Keep this for me till tomorrow, 'kay?"

Ian stumbled towards the door, bumping into the frame before pushing out onto the deserted street. Lurching towards his apartment on McDougal Street, he hoped Paula was asleep. He didn't feel like small talk. He didn't feel like any talk. Passing a newsstand at West Fourth Street, he paused to look at THE DAILY NEWS front page. It wasn't easy to focus.

Sonuvabitch. Andrew Brady. He tossed some change at the Peruvian snoring behind the glass and grabbed a paper. What the hell was Andrew doing on the front page again? Publicity hog. Oh, shit. The anniversary. It had been two years since that cockroach had disappeared from the face of the earth. That meant the cops would come calling again. Why couldn't they just call it an unsolved murder and leave him alone for good?

*

"Ian's one of life's greatest mistakes," Jessie hissed. "He's a slimy excuse for a human being. In fact, I won't even call him human. He's sub-human."

Whoa. Such venom coming from his well-bred sister-in-law's mouth. "What was Wexley's relationship to Andrew?"

"They hated each other. Before my relationship with Gianni, Ian and I lived together for two years. Ian was cheating on me, and Andrew knew it. Being the intelligent woman that I was, I chose to believe Ian. When I finally caught him with a woman in our bed, I threw him out."

Nick kept his face a mask. Except for Andrew, Jessie had a disastrous track record in her choice of men.

Jessie took a sip of brandy. "Remember I told you that someone sent photographs to Gianni's family? It was Ian. He vowed revenge when Gianni broke Ian's nose for harassing me after we split. And Ian had done the same thing before. When his brother's wife was screwing around, Ian took photos of her and anonymously sent them to his brother."

Nick whistled. "So how does this make Wexley a suspect in Andrew's murder?"

"I'm getting to that. When I realized Ian sent the pictures, I took my own revenge. Ian was up for a leading role in a play that Bill Rudolph was producing. When Bill asked me about Ian, I crucified him. On my word, Bill blackballed him. He was devastated, went downhill fast. His character Rock Stone on SEARCH FOR LOVE was killed off with an ice pick through the heart. Ian Wexley was reduced to doing dinner theater in Podunk, Iowa." Jessie smiled mirthlessly.

"So where does Andrew come in?"

"Andrew and I had run into him at a wedding when I was pregnant. Ian had too much to drink and insinuated the baby was Gianni's. He threatened to go to the tabloids. Andrew warned Ian to drop the subject. He said he could crush Ian's career with one word to Bill."

Jessie looked down at her wedding rings, moving them from side to side. "You see, that's where I got the idea. From Andrew." She sighed. "So for years Ian has believed it was Andrew who sabotaged his career when it was really me. Andrew never set him straight. Nick, maybe I was responsible for Ian killing Andrew. If I'd just left it alone—"

"That's ridiculous. You didn't put a gun in Wexley's hand and pull the trigger. Besides, are you that sure he murdered Andrew?"

"He's despicable. A sociopath."

"And this is someone you lived with? Someone you shared a bed with?"

Jessie looked like a wounded animal.

Nick paced to the windows. It was time. "Tell me about that last cruise. Please." He purposely kept his back to her. "Do the right thing, Jess. No matter how hard it is. Just begin at the beginning." He waited, holding his breath.

Just when Nick was about to give up, Jessie murmured, "The beginning. It began on an off-note," she said slowly, "just the way it ended. A disaster from beginning to end. In a way, we were forced to do the cruise. We didn't want to, but Bill said it would be good publicity for the Tony nominations. You know, back to our humble beginnings. We could never say no to Bill. Andrew was tense the entire cruise, not himself. He said it was the crush of fans. We stuck to our cabin most of the time."

Nick let her talk, the dam broken at last.

Jessie warmed her hands over the fire. "We ran into Gianni hours after we sailed. Like I said before, we were shocked. I think he knew already. He knew Anthony was his son even before he found him looking at the carved wooden ships inside the gift shop. The way Gianni looked at me. The way he asked Anthony his birthday. Right in front of us."

"How long do you think he'd suspected he was the boy's father before that moment?"

"Gianni has contacts everywhere. At some point I think he knew I had a child, and he knew it could be his."

"You said he sold the line. What was he doing aboard the ship?"

"He told me he wanted to sail one last time as owner. And ... he wanted to see me. He knew Andrew and I would be performing. When we got to the last port at San Juan, I had a headache. Andrew and Mary took Anthony ashore. Gianni cornered me in our suite and demanded to know if Anthony was his. He kept at me until I told him the truth. I made him promise not to tell Anthony. I begged him. I said he could see him whenever he wanted."

"And Gianni was okay with this?"

"He didn't want to upset me more. He saw how close I was to the edge. When Andrew came back, I told him about my confrontation with Gianni. I was hysterical. Andrew assured me it wasn't my fault, that I had no choice but to tell him the truth. But Andrew was so agitated. Worse than I'd imagined."

Nick rubbed a hand over his forehead. "You thought you could keep it from Gianni forever?"

"I don't know. Maybe it sounds stupid now, but Gianni had been out of my life for so long. After a while, I guess I forgot about him because I wanted to." She wiped her eyes. "Do we really need to do this now?"

*

Jessie felt wrung out, her whole being focused on a sliver of tragic memory.

"Jessie," Nick said patiently, "I immerse myself in a case until I live it, until I'm there with the victim. You know my record. You said you wanted me to find out who murdered Andrew."

"You know I do." Somehow she trusted Nick to do that. She sensed that if anyone could find out who killed Andrew, this hard man could.

"You're doing great. Just a little more. Why was Gianni with you that morning Andrew was shot?"

She shrugged. "I don't know. I guess to say good-bye. Right after he knocked on the door, we heard that woman's scream in the terminal."

"How long was this after your confrontation with him in your cabin?"

"Two or three days."

"Did Andrew agree to let Gianni see Anthony?"

Jessie collected herself, the memory an ache in her heart. "I never asked him. Andrew was upset enough . I thought we'd talk when we got home. The ship was no place to discuss it. We put the subject on hold, the elephant in the room."

"And then Andrew was shot," Nick prompted.

"And then Andrew was shot," Jessie echoed. "Gianni stayed with me at the hospital after Mary took Anthony home. He was my rock." Jessie bunched up in the corner of the couch. Nick sat across from her, his legs stretched in front of him, a snifter of brandy balanced on his chest.

Her voice hushed, Jessie told Nick about the two days Andrew Brady lingered between life and death. "Everyone was there," she said quietly. "Everyone who loved Andrew."

"Everyone except his brother."

"I'm sorry for that. You should've been there." Jessie took a sip of brandy. "The surgery took hours. You know the worst part? Telling Anthony. All my life people had taken care of me. My father. Gianni. And Andrew, always Andrew. But at that moment I was the adult and Anthony was the child, and it was up to me alone. I don't even remember the days afterwards or the funeral. There were hundreds of people around me twenty-four hours a day, but I never felt more alone in my life."

"I'm sorry, Jess."

She rose and walked to the fire, keeping her back to him. "And then it was over. Everyone went back to their normal lives. But for Anthony and me there was no normal. There was a great big hole where Andrew used to be. The house was so quiet. I couldn't sleep. I couldn't eat. Finally, Bill put Mary and Anthony and me on his private jet and flew us down to the villa in St. John." Jessie wiped away the tear trickling down her cheek. "But that was even worse. The Blue Pelican was Andrew's and my private little paradise. There I was … without him."

The words dried up. Jessie felt the sobs coming and her shoulders began to shake. The last thing her womanizing brother-in-law was equipped to handle was an emotional female. Suddenly, she felt Nick's arms around her. He cradled her head against his T-shirt and her sobs poured out, unstoppable. He let her cry. Finally she backed away, mortified. "I'm sorry, Nick. You must think I'm a blubbering idiot."

Nick looked down at her, his hands on her shoulders, his heavy-lidded eyes looking as if they held the weight of the world. Her troubled waters soothed under that steady gaze. "On the contrary," he rasped. "I think you faced pure evil and lived to tell the tale. I'll let you rest now. I think we both need it. Good night, Jess."

"Good night, Nick," she said softly.

*

Gianni stood at the picture window in his luxury apartment. From the sixty-seventh floor of his Park Avenue penthouse, the rest of the world seemed tiny and unimportant. The sound of the New York Philharmonic wafted through the spacious rooms. WNYC was the best classical station on the planet.

So, Andrew Brady had a famous brother. Gianni had done a little research on Nicholas McDeare when he got home. McDeare was a world-renowned author. He had quite a reputation as a reporter. He also had a reputation with the ladies. Gianni could understand why. The man had an exotic beauty, mixed with a heavy dose of testosterone.

Was McDeare a threat?

After mulling the dilemma, he dismissed the subject.

He wasn't worried. McDeare was no threat to his relationship with Jessica.

CHAPTER 6

Martinelli closed the file on Nick McDeare and stared out the study window. The bright morning sun glanced off the bay. Gulls skimmed the surface. Sailboats dotted the horizon.

Why did he have to receive alarming news on such a beautiful spring day?

McDeare posed a problem. If what Roberto had read about him was true, the former reporter wouldn't stop until he ferreted out Andrew Brady's killer. What made the situation lethal was that it was personal for McDeare. He'd work all the harder.

There was a discreet knock on the door. Aldo sauntered into the room, trailed by Santangelo. The kid stepped forward, a smile on his face, a shiny new scar streaking his right cheek. "It's an honor to finally meet you, sir."

Roberto sized up the newest member of his family. Eduardo was small and young, but he had already demonstrated his loyalty and cunning. "So, Eduardo, how was Genoa?"

"Boring. Two years is a long time. I'm glad to be back."

"Any questions asked? Any authorities sniff around?"

"No. Not one."

Roberto leaned back in his swivel chair and folded his hands across his ample belly. "Do you know what today is?"

"Yes, sir." He watched Eduardo stand a little taller. "Exactly two years ago I wiped the arrogant smile off Andrew Brady's face forever."

"Any regrets?"

"Nope."

"Sleeping okay?"

"Like a baby."

Martinelli stared long and hard into the coal-black eyes of the man standing before him.

Eduardo met his gaze firmly.

Roberto was impressed. This kid was one cool bastard. "You made your bones with Brady. Welcome to the family, Santangelo."

*

Wearing beat-up sweats, Nick paused in the front hallway and stretched his legs, making sure his muscles were loose before he started a run. He glanced at his watch, already late afternoon. After catching up on his sleep, he'd been working Andrew's case since noon on his laptop.

"Hi."

Nick jumped. Jessie stood a few feet away, clad in a lilac jogging suit.

"Still want a jogging partner?"

"This is a surprise."

"No one calls me chicken and gets away with it." She looked nervous.

"Sure," Nick said easily. "Better warm up first."

Jessie nodded and began to stretch, her honey hair shading her face as she dipped her head. "Wait a minute." Nick scoured the front closet and tugged a black stocking cap over Jessie's head. She produced a pair of sunglasses from her purse. "Do you want to take your cell?"

"I don't have one anymore. I don't go out of the house, remember?"

"Right." Nick jammed on his own hat and glasses. "Let's go. Nick started them out at a slow trot, heading across East Seventy-Fifth Street towards Fifth Avenue. "Has it really been two years since you jogged or even took a walk?"

"It's really been two years."

"We'll take it nice and easy today. Relax. No one's giving you a second glance." They reached Fifth Avenue, jogging in place, waiting for the light to change. "Hey, look at me." Jessie turned in his direction. "You look like a punk. I'd cross the street if I saw you coming." The light changed and he took off running. He heard her laughter, and seconds later she was beside him again. "C'mon," Nick said. "Let's hit the park."

A few minutes later they entered Central Park at Seventy-Second Street. Jessie stopped abruptly and bent over, her hands on her knees. "I can't believe how out of shape I am." She held her hand over her heart. "God!"

*

Lyle Barton maneuvered his car across the Fifty-Ninth Street Bridge. Thank God it was Saturday. The early afternoon traffic was light. He missed his wife. It was time Barb came home and let her mother fend for herself. The house was lonely without her chatter and his daughter's laughter. Besides, eating take-out every night was getting old. He wanted some of his wife's sausage and peppers.

To add to his gloom, today was the second anniversary of Andrew Brady's death. Barton knew this would be a difficult day for Jessie. Mary had called him that morning and invited him to the brownstone for dinner. He never passed up an opportunity to eat Mary's cooking. She'd also mentioned a surprise dinner guest. Normally, the only visitors to the brownstone besides Jeremy were Fosselli, Bill Rudolph, and himself. This could be interesting.

*

"Today's the anniversary," Jessie said, as they jogged down the park's path. "I promised myself I'd put flowers on Andrew's grave, but, well, I haven't been there since ..."

Nick sidled a glance at her. "You want to stop? You look winded."

Jessie nodded. "Sorry."

"Let's walk. Otherwise we'll tighten up." Nick enjoyed the sun on his face. Jessie looked good, some color in her cheeks. The timing was perfect. "Hey, you okay with some more questions on the case?"

- 70 -

"Fire away. After last night, I'm good with this. I want you to find out who killed Andrew. And after you ask your questions, I have something to tell you, too."

Jessie's baby blues were crystal clear in the daylight, like colored water. Nick told himself to stop staring. "It may mean invading your privacy a bit," he warned. "I need to know what makes Gianni tick. You have a complicated relationship with him. If I can understand how you two connect, it'll help me get a better handle on the guy."

"I told you, ask. And then you'll realize he shouldn't be a suspect."

Nick kept his face blank. "All right. I don't want to upset you, but how can a guy like Gianni not be pressing you like hell to tell Anthony who he is?"

"He does press me at times. He's human. He wants his son to know his biological father. But Gianni respects my wishes. He's a very sensitive and honorable man."

Nick smothered a laugh. Did Jessie realize how ridiculous she sounded? He fought to keep his composure.

"When I ask him to back off, he does. Nick, what?"

Nick couldn't control himself another minute. He burst out laughing and put on a spurt of speed. "Hey!" Jessie was next to him in a flash. "What the hell's so funny? Why are you laughing?"

Nick slowed to a walk. "I wasn't laughing."

"Yeah, right. Look, Gianni does respect me. I don't know what else I can say to make you believe me. How can we do this if you never believe me? Do you think I'm an idiot?"

"I don't think you're an idiot."

"Then stop treating me like one."

Nick picked up the pace, Jessie matching him stride for stride. He'd bet his next book's advance Gianni Fosselli was as obsessed with Jessie as he was with Anthony. Was Gianni deviously manipulating Jessie until he got everything he wanted, step by murderous step?

"Okay, Gianni respects you. Let's tease this out a bit further, shall we? Since the murder, has Gianni tried to … be intimate with you?"

"W-what did you say?"

"I said, has Gianni tried to sleep with you since the murder?"

"I told you last night Gianni and I have been over for years. I see no one. This is really going—"

"Oh, c'mon. Get real. I'm not judging you. I don't care who you sleep with. It's no big deal. Now, tell me, what's the situation? Do you have sex with Gianni to stall him from telling Anthony? Don't be embarrassed. I have to learn everything I can about Gi--"

Jessie accelerated like Secretariat. Nick picked up speed and followed on her heels. Jessie reached up and slapped at a low-hanging branch over the jogging path. There was no time to veer. The thick branch ricocheted into his chest like a cuckoo popping out of a clock. Nick skidded backwards, slamming into a jogger behind him. As Nick fought to keep his balance, the man swore, jetting around Nick and bumping his shoulder hard. While the runner shot down the trail past Jessie, Nick did a ballerina twirl on one foot and fell.

Jessie trotted back, running in place. "I tell the truth, remember? I don't sleep with him!"

Two high-school kids jogged past, wearing track-team colors. "Hey, you believe her, man!" shouted the tall kid. "She looks like a nice lady! She don't sleep with the dude!" Their laughter echoing, they kicked up a stone that narrowly missed taking out Nick's eye.

Nick swore, scrambling up and breathing hard. "You should be declared a lethal weapon."

They found their way onto the grass and rested under a tree. Nick took the time to catch his breath. "Are you okay?" Jessie asked sweetly, brushing leaves off Nick's shoulder.

"You can wipe that smile off your face." He tested his ankle. "Yes, I'm okay. Brute force wasn't necessary to get me to back off."

"With your thick head? Of course, it was. Do you believe me about Gianni?"

"For the sake of discussion, let's say I believe you're not sleeping with him. According to you, Gianni respects you. He's an honorable man and had nothing to do with Andrew's murder. He'll wait patiently until you decide the time is right to tell Anthony about him, which you have no intention of doing. Being an honorable man, he'll wait patiently until you're ready to marry him, which you said last night you have no intention of doing." Nick stepped backwards, holding up a hand. "Don't hit me. So, am I correct?"

"Okay, smart mouth. For the sake of solving this case, I told you I'd answer your questions. By the same token, you have to believe me when I say that, as unbelievable as it may seem to your cynical, sexist mind, Gianni will wait until I'm ready to tell Anthony. He'll wait until I'm ready for him. My intentions are immaterial. He'll wait because—get this, Nick--HE respects me."

*

Jessie leapt onto the jogging path and started running. By the time Nick caught up, the anger had begun to pump out and reason set in. Nick was going to try to solve Andrew's murder. He was Andrew's brother. He was living in her house. And besides, when she'd talked to Anthony earlier about Nick being his uncle and moving into the brownstone, you'd have thought Santa Claus was taking up residence. For Anthony's sake alone, she had to make peace with Nick McDeare.

Slowing to a walk, Jessie brushed a hand across her sweaty forehead. "Nick," she begged, catching her breath, "ask me something easy for a change so I won't want to hurt you."

"Like what?" He grinned at her with that white ribbon of teeth, a pirate in the middle of Central Park. "And for the record, I respect you, too, just like Gianni."

"Sure you do. Like ask me if there was anyone else who hated Andrew? Besides Wexley. You might as well be comprehensive, right?"

"Okay. Was there anyone else who hated Andrew?"

Jessie laughed. "I thought you'd never ask. Last night, right before I fell asleep, I remembered something. I've been waiting to tell you about it. I told you that the summer I was seeing Gianni, Andrew and I were performing on the Milano. Well, one night after our act Andrew caught one of the ship's bar stewards stealing money from the tip jar in the late-night club. Eduardo Santangelo. Andrew turned him in."

"I'm glad you're telling me this, but I don't know if that's exactly a motive for murder."

"Eduardo's Gianni's nephew, which makes him an extended part of the Italian family that owned the ship. Which made the theft something out of the ordinary. Gianni was called out of bed to deal with it. We were-- Never mind. Anyway, I wasn't on the scene but Andrew told me Gianni was furious when he found the tip money in Eduardo's pocket. Right there in public, he slapped him so hard Eduardo crashed into the wall and fell to the floor. Andrew said the kid was cursing at the top of his lungs. He vowed that Andrew would pay."

"Did Andrew take him seriously?"

"Not really. Andrew thought he was a punk and treated him with contempt, baiting him. We'd perform on these one-week cruises to Bermuda, a different audience each week. The enmity lasted the summer."

"And what about you?"

"I took Eduardo more seriously than Andrew." Jessie shivered in the sunlight. "The look in Eduardo's eyes was frightening. Eyes as black as night. He was not someone I'd choose to cross. And he was on that last cruise, too. I caught him watching Andrew, more than once."

"Maybe I should've waited before bringing all this up again and upsetting you."

"No, actually I'm glad you did. I was so dazed after the murder— I told Lyle about the hostility between Eduardo and Andrew, but I never really went into why. It came back to me last night, the details about the tip-jar incident. You forced me to start remembering. I'd forgotten all about it."

"Anyone else on the hate list?"

"Yeah, maybe." Jessie stopped, amazed at another memory floating to the surface. "Michelle Davis." They continued their brisk walk. "My father was the Milano's cruise director, and Michelle was his assistant. She hated me. She'd look me up and down--you know, the way two women size each other up when they recognize competition?"

"Competition?" Nick's lip twitched. "Don't tell me. For Gianni."

"Gianni was seeing Michelle right before he hooked up with me. She went from hating me to really hating me. Andrew used to make fun of her. I mean, the woman was outrageous. Long bright red hair, color that can only come from a bottle. A gallon of makeup on her face. Gaudy jewelry. Skimpy clothes. Although I guess she was efficient enough."

"And Gianni was attracted to both of you?" Jessie shot him a withering look. "Sorry. Go on."

"Michelle knew what Andrew said about her behind her back. She hated him for it. I told Lyle about her, too, but I was so out of it after the murder.

I know she was interrogated. Michelle thought Andrew was a snob, especially after Bill offered us a contract on Broadway. That killed her. She was insanely jealous. Working on a cruise ship is like living with family. We'd see her all the time, crew meals, lounges, living quarters. Andrew liked to rub her nose in it. Which was so unlike him. Generally, Andrew was a kind man who went out of his way not to hurt anyone."

"Except for Eduardo, Michelle, and Ian."

"Well. Three people on a hurt list in one entire lifetime isn't so bad, is it?"

"So he was nothing like me when it came to ticking people off?" Those amber eyes glittered.

"Definitely nothing like you." Jessie dashed down the path, forcing Nick to run to catch up to her. Turning Nick McDeare into family wasn't going to be easy.

*

They circled around and left the park the same way they came in, continuing at a brisk clip across East Seventy-Second Street. So far, Jessie seemed to be doing okay. "Jessie," Nick said, "I have to go back to Washington tomorrow, an interview for the new book. The guy's leaving the county for six months, so it's now or never."

"Works for me."

"You're glad to get rid of me? And here I thought we were getting along so well."

"That's not what I meant. I just want you to feel free to come and go."

They turned south on Park Avenue. Nick picked up speed, Jessie intent on keeping up with him. He finally eased up, slowing to a fast walk. He could hear her gasping for air. This jaunt had taken guts. The setting sun cast a glow over the city. Lights began to twinkle on in apartments. Straight ahead, the elegant stone Grand Central Station was a stark silhouette against a fuchsia backdrop.

"Nick," Jessie said, "I asked someone to dinner tonight I'd like you to meet. But there's something else I wanted to talk to you about, get your feedback. Let's stop here a minute, okay?" Jessie leaned against a lamppost, catching her breath. Nick waited, arms folded. Jessie straightened up. "Okay, here's the thing. Jeremy's pressuring me to appear at the Tony Awards in June for a special tribute to Bill Rudolph. He keeps saying I owe it to Bill, that Andrew would want me to do it, too. I'm not sure yet what to do about it."

Why was she telling him this? Because he was Andrew's brother? "I guess you should do whatever feels right, Jess."

"Jess ... You keep calling me Jess. No one but Andrew ever called me that. And you say it with the same inflection."

"Do you mind? Should I watch for swinging tree branches?" He smiled.

"Actually, it's ... nice. So let me ask you something. If I decide to do the Tony's, which I don't think I will, but if I do, I need an escort. Do you think you, well, would you mind filling in if I decided to go?"

"Me?" Nick was shocked. "Wouldn't you rather have the honorable Gianni as your escort?"

"He's a lot nicer than you, true, but it's complicated. He'd turn the evening into something it's not. And the press would speculate I have a new man in my life. But if I go with you," Jessie smiled brightly, "no one will think anything of it at all."

Now Nick got it. Jessie was a star after all, a diva. That's why she'd pretended to use him as a sounding board, to lead up to this. "You need an invisible prop that night, right? Someone who can make it all about you."

"Where did you get that? I just don't want any complications. Being my brother-in-law, you're perfect for the part. Family. See, it wouldn't mean anything to anyone like it would with Gianni."

Nick wasn't used to not meaning anything when he was next to a beautiful woman. He should say no to teach that star ego a lesson. He bet no man ever said no to Jessie Kendle Brady.

Jessie fixed her eyes on him. The lowering sun turned them into pure turquoise. Nick lost himself in their dizzying depths.

"Nick? So?"

"So what?"

"So, would you go with me, conditionally speaking?"

No. "Yes." He coughed. "Um, especially since it doesn't mean anything. Conditionally speaking."

*

As Eduardo entered Gianni's office, his uncle snapped his cell phone shut. "Uncle Gianni." Eduardo strode across the plush carpeting. Oceano's office was as opulent as the restaurant. Very nice.

Gianni looked into the face of his sister's only child. "What are you doing here? Aren't you supposed to be in Genoa wooing Franscesca Mirabella?"

"That was Mama's idea. Not mine."

"And you're here because? "

"Business."

"What are you up to, Eduardo?"

"Me? Just trying to achieve the American dream." Santangelo admired the framed photos on Gianni's office walls. Donald Trump. Bill and Hillary Clinton. Leonardo DeCaprio. Halle Berry. Hugh Jackman. All these famous people wanted to be seen at the city's newest hot spot. "Why isn't Jessica Kendle up on this wall?" He couldn't help baiting his uncle.

"Right here." Gianni picked up a framed photograph on his desk. "To me, she's not a celebrity. She's merely Jessica."

"And when is the happy event?" Gianni's brow furrowed. "Your wedding," Eduardo clarified. "When do you and your lady love finally seal your age-old obsession?"

Gianni stared at his nephew. "Soon."

"I'm glad to hear it. Really. You've been waiting for this day for a long time." Eduardo reached into his pocket for a stick of chewing gum and folded it into his mouth. "Well, I just came by to tell you I was in town."

"For how long?"

"A while."

"Okay, what's going on?" Gianni demanded. "And don't lie to me."

"I'll be in touch." Eduardo spun on his heel and disappeared through the door. Once out on the street, Santangelo breathed deeply, exhilaration sweeping through him like a drug. That was fun. For the first time in his life, he had the upper hand with his uncle. Too bad Gianni didn't know it was Eduardo who had taken care of Andrew Brady. Eduardo Santangelo was the one who had made it possible for Gianni to finally be reunited with his precious Jessica and the kid.

*

Ian Wexley glanced at his watch. Where was Jeremy? He was an hour late. His old friend had been keeping him waiting like this for years. Might as well have another Johnny Walker Red. "Hit me again, Max." That was his limit. He had to keep his wits about him tonight. This conversation with his good friend was important.

The bar was almost empty. Just Ian and a leggy brunette four stools away. "Hey, Max?" He leaned over and whispered, "Get the lady a drink on me, okay?" He watched as Max mixed a strawberry daiquiri and presented it to the woman. Legs Larue smiled sweetly at Ian and nodded her thanks.

Jeremy trotted through the door and plopped down beside his old friend. "It's starting to rain. Every time I come down here it's raining."

"So Lady Sarah deigned to let you see me?" He hated Jeremy's wife, and she hated him, a feud going back to the ancient days of Ian and Jessie. When was that? How many years ago? Ten? Something like that. Ah, who gave a shit?

"Sarah doesn't know I'm here. She thinks I'm meeting our accountant."

"Uh-oh. The Ice Queen will want a complete accounting of every penny."

"Nah. She only spends the money. She never thinks to count it. Three checks bounced last month."

"She thinks you're loaded like your old man."

"Shut up, Ian." Jeremy asked for a beer. "What's so important?"

"Okay." Wexley took a gulp of scotch. "You're around Her Royal Heinie all day. And you see the King of Cops on a regular basis. I want to make sure they're not stirring the pot again on this, the," he threw in his Shakespearean voice with a flourish, "anniversary."

"Why do you insist on behaving like an asshole?"

"It's my best event. Don't knock it."

Jeremy's beer was delivered. He slurped the foam from the top of the stein. "If you're referring to Jessie and Barton, there's been no pot-stirring lately. In fact, there's been little mention of Andrew. Of course, that could change now that his brother's arrived."

Ian set his glass down so hard the contents splashed onto the bar. "What brother? What are you talking about? Andrew didn't have any family."

"Au contraire, mon ami. You're not up on the latest. Not only did Andrew Brady have a brother, but he's now living at the brownstone."

"What the hell are you talking about?"

"Nick McDeare. Nick McDeare's Andrew's long lost brother. A brother who was put up for adoption."

"Nick McDeare? The famous author? The reporter? He's Andrew's brother?"

"Yep."

Ian dropped his head in his hands. "Shit."

*

When Nick came downstairs that evening, he saw Jessie sitting at the island with a tall stranger. The guest she'd mentioned. Jessie had changed into a cream silk blouse and matching slacks. Nick had thrown on a turtleneck over a pair of jeans.

"I was beginning to think you'd fallen asleep," Jessie said. "I'd like you to meet—"

"This is the surprise dinner guest?" the man asked. His flinty voice reminded Nick of an old crime flick. Humphrey Bogart in THE MALTESE FALCON. The Bogart stranger held out his hand. "You're Nick McDeare."

"Yeah." Nick shook.

"Nick is also Andrew's older brother." Jessie explained.

"Brother? There was no family."

"Jessie just found out," Nick said blandly. "One of those reunion things. Except Andrew and I never met."

The guest studied Nick. "You look like him. Now the phone call between the two of you before that cruise makes sense. I thought it was one celebrity talking to another. Or you wanted to write about Andrew."

"How the hell do you--"

"Nick," Jessie interrupted, "be nice. This is Lieutenant Lyle Barton. Lyle's in charge of Andrew's case."

Whoa. This was the NYPD cop with the rep for never giving up. Barton was a bulldog. Nick sized up the rugged detective more closely. He was wearing jeans, a khaki T-shirt, and a worn corduroy jacket. The eyes were intelligent. It was about time they connected. "I see," Nick said. "The phone logs. Of course. You checked them out." Nick surveyed the hors d'ouevres on the island and reached for a stuffed mushroom. He was developing a healthy respect for Mary's cooking. "I was going to ask Jessie about you tonight. I know your reputation."

"Yeah, I know a little bit about you, too. That case you solved in Arlington. That serial killer who—" He stopped abruptly, glancing at Jessie. "Your books are required reading at the station house, McDeare."

"Thanks." Nick respected some cops. Lyle Barton might be one of them. Or not. Whatever, he intended to milk the detective dry for information. But not in front of the family. His questions would wait.

Dinner was Mary's pot roast with red potatoes, glazed baby carrots, and homemade buttermilk biscuits with sweet butter. It wasn't until Nick walked Lyle to his car while Jessie tucked Anthony in bed that he got a chance to talk in earnest.

To Nick's surprise, Barton beat him to it. "Are you here in town as Andrew's brother," he asked gruffly, social manners gone, "or are you interested in finding his killer?"

"The latter. You mind my poking around?"

"Civilians can be a pain in the ass."

"You know I'm not any civilian."

Barton nodded. "Maybe I could tolerate your poking around. Maybe not. Ask me some questions. We'll see."

"You're giving me permission to talk to you?" Nick chuckled.

"Ask now, or make an appointment."

Okay, he'd play the game. "Any suspects?" They reached the car.

"Yep. Nothing concrete on any of them."

"Can I see the reports?"

"Against the rules." Barton's face was stone.

"Let's get to the bottom line. Do you want to play by the rules, or do you want some help in nailing the killer?"

"You're an arrogant S-O-B, you know that?"

"I solve crimes. I want to solve this one. We don't need a pissing contest, do we, detective? We're on the same side."

Barton studied him. "Come by the precinct tomorrow. Midtown North," he finally said. "We can talk privately in my office."

An order, not a question. But Nick would take what he could get. "I can be there early, but not for long. I'm due back in D.C. by dinner."

*

The man known as Cobra blended into the shadows as Nick McDeare crossed his path. He trailed his mark, keeping a safe distance behind.

So Supercop and Supersleuth were doing a dance. Interesting. With a quick phone call, Cobra learned the dinner conversation was superficial. Having the brownstone bugged for the first floor and phones made his life so much easier.

With McDeare stuck in the brownstone and going nowhere, there wasn't much more to do tonight. The chatter was being monitored. Martinelli was giving him a long leash. The rest of the evening was his. He intended to take full advantage of it. He'd swing home briefly and then head out again. The night was young. Somewhere in Manhattan a woman was sipping a Margarita and waiting for the perfect man to walk through the door. Cobra intended to be that man.

*

As Nick pushed through the iron gate in front of the brownstone, he paused and looked around. He had the feeling he was being watched. Sure, it was New York. Hundreds of windows. But this was different. Someone was watching him. He was sure of it.

Glancing up and down the block, Nick noticed nothing untoward. An old man walking his bulldog. A young couple sitting on some steps across the street. A taxi disgorging three ladies. A Chinese delivery boy pedaling his bicycle, bags of food in the front basket. Everything looked normal. Shrugging, he continued into the house. His cell's jangle echoed down the hallway.

"McDeare."

"So where have you been? Why haven't you called me?" Nick recognized the husky voice of Pepper Purdue. "You were supposed to call me days ago."

Shit. He'd told her he'd call the first night he was in New York. Pepper was a leggy blond with a perfect rack. As a rule, she made Nick drool. How could he have forgotten? "I've been busy."

"Busy with what? Another woman?"

Why did he seem to have the same conversation with every lady he dated? "Yeah, as a matter of fact, I've spent the last forty-eight hours with a blond actress. Not only does she have the perfect body and the most gorgeous eyes I've ever seen, but she is also a huge star. Not the jiggle queen of dinner theater."

"You enjoy being a prick, don't you, Nick?"

"No, I don't, Pepper. I also don't like dealing with possessive women. Our relationship is about sex. Why can't you leave it at that?" He got a dial tone for a response. "Fine. Go to hell." He clicked off and started towards the kitchen.

Jessie stood in the archway. She looked ... appalled? Her face was an interesting shade of red. It was obvious she'd overheard at least part of his conversation.

"Um," she said, not meeting Nick's eyes, "Anthony asked if you'd say goodnight." Without another word, she turned and disappeared into the kitchen.

Nick ran his hands through his hair. All that talk about a blond actress. Did Jess think ...? He hustled into the kitchen. Jessie stood at the sink, drying wine goblets. "Jessie, I hope you don't think there's ... that I think of you that way. I was just trying--"

"Of course not. Forget it." Jessie kept her back to him.

"I don't usually talk to a woman like that. I ..." What was he saying? Of course he talked to women like that. Almost all of them. And Jessie had had more than one front-row seat. He had to get out of here, the tension as thick as humidity in August. "I'll say good night to Anthony and hit the sack. I have to leave early tomorrow."

"When will you be back?" She finally looked at him. "Abbie gets in Tuesday night."

"I don't know. The interview could take a couple of days. Plus, I have to get the outline done for the new book. I'm way behind. Don't count on me, okay?"

"Fine."

Nick found Anthony curled in his bed, a dim bedside lamp casting the room in shadow. Hamlet was stretched like a slinky toy against his back. "Hey, kiddo." Nick sat on the bed's edge.

"Hi. I was wondering, Uncle Nick. When can you start teaching me the piano?"

"Whenever you want."

"Tomorrow?"

"I have to go back to Washington tomorrow. We'll start when I get back, okay?" A camera lay on the bedside table, its guts splayed. "What happened here?"

"Hamlet knocked it off the bed and it broke. I just got it from Mary for my birthday. Can you can fix it?"

"I don't think so. Too many pieces snapped."

Anthony sighed. "I never have anything that doesn't get broken. Except my ships. My ships stay nice 'cause I keep them on those shelves."

Nick glanced up at the five carved wooden ships lovingly displayed. Gianni's presents. "You're close to Gianni, aren't you?"

"Yeah. He was a good friend of Mommy and Daddy's," the boy said with importance, obviously mimicking his mother's words.

Nick fingered the camera. "I'm sorry, Anthony. I'm afraid this is history."

Anthony seemed to take it in stride. After losing his father, a camera didn't seem that important, Nick surmised. He fixed the blanket around the boy's shoulders. Suddenly, he saw himself tucking Jeffrey in just like this, the image as vivid as if it had happened five minutes ago. Nick stuffed the vision back into his mental hard drive. It wasn't easy. "I've got a bunch of cameras at home," he said softly. "I use them for my work. I'm sure I have an extra one. It'll be more complicated than this camera though. Think you can handle it?"

"Will you show me how?" Anthony looked excited.

"Sure."

The room suddenly grew cold, and Nick shivered. He looked down at the goose bumps on his arms.

"You feel it, too, don't you?" Anthony whispered. "The cold. It's Daddy. Daddy told me he visits you, too."

Taking a deep breath, Nick scrambled for a response. He didn't believe in lying to children. It only prolonged the inevitable. Worse, respect was lost in the process. "Yeah, Bongo, he has."

Anthony's eyes opened into half-dollars. "Bongo! Daddy told you to call me Bongo, didn't he!"

Nick grinned. "He did. Is that okay?"

"It's cool, Uncle Nick. Daddy told me something about you, too. He told me why you're sad. He told me about Jeffrey."

Nick reeled. He tried to speak, but he couldn't find his voice.

"Sometimes I think if I went with Daddy that morning he wouldn't have died. He wanted me to come with him and say hi to Mr. Rudolph. But I wanted to watch the guys unload the luggage from our balcony. Every day I wish I'd gone with him." His eyes filled with tears. "I know how you feel, Uncle Nick."

How did Anthony know? Nick had never said a word to anyone. How did this boy recognize the guilt he carried with him every day? What the hell was this house doing to him, and where would it end?

CHAPTER 7

"Man, I gotta get to a barber." Steve Bushman stared at his reflection in the grimy wall mirror.

"Yeah," Barton told his partner. "All six hairs are getting long." Bushman was squat and balding at an early age. An ex-Marine.

"You're just jealous 'cause I get all the babes." Bush's eyes flicked out the glassed-in office to the noisy squad room. "Here comes McDeare now." Harry Steinmetz, the Desk Officer, led the famed author and reporter towards them. Dozens of eyes followed his every step. "You sure you want to do this, Lyle?"

"You and I both know that Brady's murder's headed for the Cold Case bin. It's been two years and nothing's changed. Maybe he'll see something we don't."

Lyle rose as Nick came through the door. The two men shook hands. "This is my partner, Steve Bushman. There's a chair over there somewhere." Barton pointed to a mound of papers in the corner.

"You must have the same decorator I have," Nick muttered. "I'll stand. I don't have much time."

The trio eyed each other warily. Barton finally nodded towards a thick manila envelope on the desk. "This goes against the rules. If anyone finds out, somehow you made a copy of the Brady file without my knowledge."

"Got it." Nick dropped the file into his shoulder bag. "Anything else I should know before I catch the shuttle?"

"Everything's in that file."

"How about what your gut's telling you?"

Lyle snorted. "You won't find that on a piece of paper."

"I know that."

Lyle didn't blink. Nick McDeare got the file. That was enough.

Nick finally nodded. "Fine." He hefted his bag onto his shoulder. "I'll be in touch when I get back."

The two detectives watched the reporter weave his way through the squad room. "What a warm and cuddly guy," Bushman said.

"A real charmer."

*

"What's the matter, honey?" Mary asked.

Jessie sat on the back porch, an unopened book clasped in her hands. "I'm just tired, I guess. All the late night activity finally caught up with me."

"Uh-huh."

Jessie recognized Mary's tone. "Okay, what does that mean? If you've got something to say, just say it."

"What's that you're reading?"

"Something I found in the study. It's just a book."

"Let me see it."

Jessie hated it when Mary made her feel like she was ten years old. Jessie handed the book to her.

"TOKYO BLUES," Mary recited slowly. "A mystery by Nick McDeare. Just a book."

"I was curious, all right?"

"Uh-huh."

"May I have the book back please?" Jessie tossed it on the coffee table.

"Dinner will be ready soon." Mary said matter-of-factly, heading for the kitchen.

So what was the big deal? Her brother-in-law was a famous author, okay? Although, Jessie admitted, that didn't mean she didn't hope Nick's book wouldn't tell her more about him. Getting Nick to talk about himself was like getting Anthony to eat his carrots. It required focusing on one carrot at a time. Still, there were a few chinks in Nick's wall. Like his son. Jessie couldn't imagine what it would be like to lose a child. If she lost Anthony, she'd lose her reason for living. She could understand why Nick didn't talk about Jeffrey. And yet, Jessie sensed there was something more gnawing away at the man. Jessie wished Andrew were here right now. Andrew would be able to break through Nick's armor. He could always ...

The cold hit Jessie with a blast. She shivered and reached for the throw on the back of the divan. It was freezing in here. Where did ...? And then Jessie knew. "Andrew?" she whispered. She remained still, her mind running a race with her heartbeat. What was he trying to tell her? What did he want?

"Jessie?" Jeremy suddenly appeared and sat across from her, a newspaper in his hands.

"Do you feel it, Jeremy?"

"Feel what?"

"The cold. It's so cold here."

"The ...? No. In fact, I think Mary's got the heat up a little high today. But the fourth floor offices are always a different temperature."

"Oh." Jessie pulled the throw up around her shoulders. "I must be getting sick."

"Jessie, I think you better take a look at this." Jeremy opened THE NEW YORK POST to page six.

"Hmm?"

"Are you all right?"

"Yeah. Well, no. I don't know. What's up?"

"You need to see this. You're not going to like it." Jeremy handed her the paper. Jessie's eyes widened as she read the headline splashed across the top of the gossip section. NICK MCDEARE - JESSICA KENDLE'S NEW LOVER? Her eyes drifted to five photos. Pictures of Nick and Jessie jogging. Leaning against a tree in Central Park. The photographer had twisted a simple jog into a tryst between two lovers. He'd managed to transform an innocent look and an accidental brush of their shoulders into an intimate exchange.

Hands shaking, Jessie grabbed the paper from Jeremy. Below the pictures was a blurb:

Exactly two years after her husband, actor Andrew Brady, was fatally shot in the West Side Cruise Ship Terminal, Broadway actress Jessica Kendle was seen in the company of ladies' man and best-selling author Nick McDeare. Is a new romance on the horizon for the grieving widow? It looks like Mrs. Brady didn't waste a precious moment in finding a new amour. According to etiquette guru Emily Post, two years is the suggested time to mourn before moving on. Is Jessica Brady moving on with Nick McDeare? Not for long, if the author's reputation holds true. No one yet has been able to snag the confirmed bachelor.

*

Nick met William Brozovic for dinner at an Indian restaurant in Georgetown. The former double agent for England and Russia was forthcoming with insider information. Nick recorded the interview, took copious notes and was home by nine-thirty. Way too early for bed. Maybe he'd call that waitress from the restaurant tonight. Gina. She'd tucked her phone number into Nick's palm as he was leaving. Whistling, Nick turned his cell back on. My God, he had thirty-two messages. What the hell?

The first message was from Mary. "Nick, I don't know if you've seen it, but THE NEW YORK POST has pictures of you and Jessie in the gossip section. They insinuate … well, you have to see it for yourself. Anyway, Jessie's upset. She didn't want any dinner, and I'm worried. Could you give me a call please? I know Jessie gave you the unlisted home number."

Nick pulled up THE POST on his computer. His gut tightened. Damn this trash. Now he understood why he had thirty-two messages. Three were from Mary. One was from his old roommate Michael Whitestone, the POST'S crime editor. He'd called to apologize for his trashy paper. There were a dozen or so calls from reporters who were friends, asking if they could run with the story. Fuck it. There was no story.

His cell rang as he sat still, his mind moving at the speed of light. It was Mary. She asked if he'd seen the article.

"Yeah. Online."

"Do you think … Could you come back to New York tomorrow? I don't mean to intrude into your schedule, but I think Jessie could really use you right now."

Nick was meeting Brozovic for breakfast and then he had a meeting with his business manager. Plus he needed to get that outline to his editor sometime this year. "I can't. I'm sorry, Mary, but I already have a tight schedule." Jessie would have to handle this on her own.

"Can you maybe reschedule? I wouldn't ask if it weren't important."

"Look, Jessie's been dealing with the paparazzi for years."

"Not alone. Not without Andrew."

"Please don't bring Andrew into this."

"I'm not. I just ... You're family now. I can see that Jessie's starting to trust you. You don't know her well, but she's a closed book since Andrew's death. She doesn't need this kind of publicity."

"What can I do that you can't?"

"I don't know. All I know is you're the other person in the pictures." She paused. "Never mind. I'm sorry I bothered you." She clicked off.

Nick tossed his cell on the desk. Jessie had to handle this herself, just like he did. This was a perfect example of why keeping your distance from the rest of mankind made life so much simpler. Forgetting about the waitress, Nick poured himself a hefty bourbon and sat in the dark, brooding. Four bourbons later, he crawled into bed.

A noise woke Nick at dawn. The kitchen. Nick shrugged on a pair of jeans and quietly pulled a pistol from the bureau, cocking it. Nick inched his way towards the kitchen. Someone was sitting at the table in front of the window. The moonlight cast the intruder's face in shadow. Considering his line of work, past and present, it could be anyone. Nick raised the gun and said quietly, "I suggest you don't move a muscle. I won't hesitate to shoot."

The figure turned his head slightly so Nick could see his face.

"Sorry, Nick, but that gun won't work on me," Andrew Brady said, looking amused. "Getting fatally shot's a one-time thing."

Another dream. Another damned dream. Setting the gun on the counter, Nick sank into the chair across from his brother. A bottle of bourbon and two glasses sat in the middle of the table.

Andrew splashed the glasses with bourbon and pushed one in front of Nick. "Go ahead. Drink. You look like you could use it."

Nick took a healthy swig.

Andrew leaned forward. "Mary needed you tonight. It took a lot for her to call you. You should've listened to her."

"I don't listen to most people. What makes a housekeeper special?"

"Mary was a surrogate mother to Jessie and me. She had a hand in raising me. Mary gave me my first journal."

"You kept journals?"

"Forget I said that."

"What journals, Andrew?"

"I kept journals for years. Sorry. That's all I can say. It's up to Jessie to tell you about them. When she finally decides to show them to you, you'll know she trusts you completely."

Nick's mind leapt ahead, trying to figure out a way to nudge Jessie into giving him Andrew's journals.

"Stop it. You can't control everything."

Now his brother could read his mind?

Andrew laughed. "You think I'm some kind of mind reader? It doesn't work that way. But I can read your face pretty well. From now on, I want you to show Mary the respect she deserves. I want you back in New York tomorrow,"

Andrew continued, taking a sip of bourbon. "Jessie needs you. She's not a lone wolf by nature like her brother-in-law."

"What do you expect me to do? I hardly know Jessie."

"You've already managed to do the impossible. You got her out of the house. It's a miracle. That POST article today set her back. I want you to make sure she doesn't retreat from life all over again. Remind her the paparazzi are a part of the business. She has to learn to deal with them if she's ever going to act again. Encourage her to go to the Tony Awards."

"Andrew, you over-exaggerate my influence on your wife. Jessie went jogging to prove she could do it, not because she valued my company."

"You challenged her. Your attitude gets under her skin. If anyone can get her to the Tonys, you can. Jessie needs to walk out on a stage again. To feel the heat from the lights, hear the applause. The Tonys will help bring back the old Jess. Someone you haven't even met yet. Will you do it?"

Nick patted his pockets.

"In the drawer."

"What?"

"Cigarettes. In the drawer. You stashed a pack in there."

"I ...?" Nick opened his junk drawer. There they were. He'd forgotten. He sniffed one deeply, exhaling slowly.

"You haven't answered my question."

"Yeah. Okay."

"You'll do it?"

"I said I would."

"Tomorrow?"

"Andrew, I barely know Jessie. We just--"

"You're family. I know, a foreign concept to you. Look, I'll make a deal with you. If you help Jessie, I'll help you with the family thing."

"I don't need help--"

"The hell you don't. You refuse to open up to your past. To Mom and--"

"My past is something you could never understand. You lived a completely different life than I did."

"Get over it. Here's my part of the deal. When you get back to the brownstone, go up to the attic. In the far corner at the front of the house is a trunk. It's old and tarnished and the lock's broken. You can't miss it. Inside, you'll find a flowered tin, the kind that fancy candy comes in. That tin will fill in some blanks for you. Abbie will fill in the rest."

"What's in the tin?"

"I think I've given you more than enough." He rose. "Do we have a deal? Will you help Jessie?"

"Andrew ..." What the hell. This was just a dream. "Sure."

"Will you go tomorrow?"

"If I can make the time."

"Don't play games with me."

"Yes. Okay. What more do you want, a contract?" Nick returned to the table and drained his glass in one gulp.

"There's one more thing."

"There's always one more thing."

"This is important. This is why I brought you to New York in the first place. This is about me now, not you. I want you to swallow your pride and work with Lyle Barton. Get down to business."

Nick held his brother's stare. "Let's see if I have my orders straight. I'm to go to New York tomorrow. I'm supposed to get Jessie back on the stage. And I'm to play nice with the cops. Anything else, boss? You want me to solve the problems in the Middle East, too?"

"As a matter of fact, there is something else. Keep doing what you're doing with Anthony. You're good with him. I owe you. Thanks, Nick."

"Tell me something. You've shown yourself to your son and your brother. Why not your wife?"

Nick watched as his brother's expression shifted. "It's ... too early. If Jessie saw me now, she'd never leave that house. She'd just sit there waiting for me. She'll see me when the time's right." He stared down at Nick. "I've met Jeffrey."

WHAT?

"He's a remarkable boy. Jeffrey worships the ground you walk on, you know."

Nick couldn't move, trapped in a bubble of space and time.

"You see, Nick? You're taking care of my son, and I'm taking care of yours."

Nick felt his eyes misting. He dropped his head. When he looked back up, his brother was gone. And then he woke up. In the kitchen. At the table. A bottle of bourbon and two glasses sat before him. Nick's hands started to shake. There wasn't a shadow of doubt in his mind that Andrew Brady had been in this room tonight.

*

The next morning, Mary was waiting for him when he got out of the taxi at the brownstone. "How's Jessie?"

"I don't know. She's still sleeping."

"It's almost twelve."

"She does this a lot. She thinks I don't know, but she stays up half the night sometimes."

"Uncle Nick?" Anthony pounded down the stairs. "I can't wake up Mommy."

"What do you mean?"

"I called her name. I even shook her a little but she won't wake up."

Nick lunged for the stairs, Anthony and Mary on his heels. He found Jessie sprawled on her stomach, her honey hair draping her face. Mary pulled a bottle of prescription pills from the nightstand drawer. "Damn."

Nick snatched the vial from the woman's hands. Sleeping pills. In fact, they were ... He leaned over the bed. "Jessie! Wake up. Jessie!" Nick turned Jessie over and shook her. "Dammit, Jessie, wake up!"

Jessie moaned as her eyelids began to flutter. "What?"

"How many of these did you take?"

"Hmmm? How many what?" She focused on the bottle in Nick's hand. "Um, jus' one."

Nick looked closely at the prescription. Fourteen pills were issued. He dumped the bottle in his palm and counted. Three were missing. He asked Mary to get some coffee. "Jessie, did you take three pills?"

"Stop yelling at me." Jessie sat up, sweeping her hair off her face.

"Answer me. Did you take three?"

"I took one last night. And one this morning."

"When did you open the bottle?"

"Last night," she snapped. "I don't need an inquisition. And what are you doing here? Get out of my bedroom."

"You must've taken two."

"Mommy, you promised." Anthony approached the bed.

Mary was back, a mug in her hand. "She promised us. No more pills. Here." She handed the mug to Nick.

"Look, would everyone please get out of my bedroom? What is this, opening night?"

"Drink this." Nick handed her the coffee.

"Who are you to come into my house and give me orders?" Jessie glanced at Anthony's white face. "I'm not yelling at you, honey. I'm so sorry. I'll talk to you later. Everything will be fine. I promise." Mary gave Jessie a dirty look and left the room with Anthony.

Nick concentrated on keeping his temper. He grabbed Jessie's robe at the foot of the bed and tossed it at her. It landed on her head. "Put that on."

"I told you to get out." Jessie flung the robe onto the floor.

Nick came around the bed and hurled it onto the pillow. "Jessie," Nick rasped, "Put on the goddamned robe, or I'll put it on you myself."

"Why are you doing this?" she asked plaintively.

"Look, put the robe on, okay?" Picking up the mug, he waited.

Jessie finally slipped her arms through the silk robe.

"Here." Nick handed her the coffee. "Drink it."

She took a sip. "There. Are you happy?"

"Keep drinking." He watched her take another sip. "Do you know what you just did to your son?" Nick asked quietly. Jessie focused on her mug. "He thought you were dead, Jess. He thought he lost his only remaining parent. When did you start taking sleeping pills?"

She shrugged.

"Did you promise Anthony that you wouldn't take any more pills?"

She nodded, averting her eyes.

"Where did you get the pills?"

"From the doctor."

"Did you get them after you made the promise?"

She nodded.

"You hid them?"

Again, she nodded.

"Do you have more hidden?"

"No."

"You're lying."

"You're a real bastard, aren't you?"

"Oh, yeah. Worse than you thought, honey."

"You like playing the tough guy."

"I'm not playing. Where are the other pills?"

"There aren't--"

"Where are they?!" Nick thundered.

"Dammit, why won't you believe me?" Jessie studied Nick's face. "Oh, I see. You, too, huh?"

It was Nick's turn to look away. "Just tell me where they are."

"I'll tell you where they are if you answer my question about you."

Nick sighed. "Talk, talk, talk. That's all you do." Sliding his hands into his pockets he walked to the front window.

"I'll tell you my story if you tell me yours."

"It's always give and take with us, isn't it?"

"That's your fault, not mine. Normal people just talk. With you it's like trading state secrets."

Nick crossed his arms. "Okay, talk."

"Do you mind if we go into the sitting room?" Jessie swung her legs to the floor. "You have an unfair advantage over me."

Nick's lip twitched. "The bed, huh? Uncomfortable? What difference does it make? We're not a man and a woman. We're family, remember?"

Jessie sprang up and wrapped her robe around her, flinging her hair back. "Don't flatter yourself. I'd feel the same way if I were arguing with Mary. Do you have any female friends, Nick? Are there any women you appreciate for their intellect or their sense of humor?"

"Hey, women are sex objects to me. You know that." He bit back a smirk as Jessie's face turned red.

Jessie picked up her mug and shuffled into the sitting room, dropping into a chair. "Okay," Nick said, "start talking." He perched on the couch arm. "I want to hear all about those little pink pills."

Jessie met Nick's eyes. "Only if you promise to reciprocate."

Nick held up two fingers. "Boy Scout's honor."

"There are no Boy Scouts in the Far East."

"The pills, Jess?"

Jessie sighed. "I told you I couldn't sleep ... after Andrew. Dr. Vasquez prescribed the pills. They worked. End of story. Do I have to spell out the rest for you?"

"Tell me about your promise to Anthony."

"A couple of months ago I accidentally took too many pills. They had to pump my stomach. Bill Rudolph arranged for a private clinic. That's when I promised Anthony and Mary I wouldn't take anymore. But I couldn't sleep. I was dragging around, yelling at everyone. I decided I liked me better on the pills."

"Did you take too many pills again this morning?"

She stared hard at him before nodding. "I must have. I didn't mean to, but I must have. It was a new bottle. Three are missing, You do the math."

Nick rose and circled the couch. "Where are the other pills hidden?"

"Huh-uh. You tell me about your little experience first." She sat back and crossed her arms.

"You're annoying."

"And you're a bastard. At least we're not dull."

He paced the room. "A couple of years ago, not long after ... I got hooked myself." He snorted. "On the same pills as yours. A maid at the hotel in Vancouver found me passed out and called an ambulance." His eyes met hers. "I'm all too familiar with stomach pumps. They checked me into a hospital and I spent weeks with a shrink. That's when I started a rigid exercise routine. Particularly jogging. Physical exercise helped me fall asleep." Nick came around the coffee table and squatted in front of Jessie. "You don't want to do this to your son. He's already been through one trauma. He doesn't need to live with this kind of fear, or worse." Nick's voice was gentle. "Now, where are the rest of the pills?"

"I can't." Jessie's eyes darted nervously. "Please. You don't understand."

"I'll help you. You can't do this to your son. Look at me." When she finally met his eyes, he said, "I promise I'll help you. For Anthony's sake."

Jessie held Nick's gaze. Finally, she rose and went to the fireplace. Nick watched as she played with the wooden frame. A small door swung open, revealing a safe. Jessie turned the combination and reached inside, withdrawing four vials of pills. She walked over to Nick and placed them in his hands.

"Is this all of them?"

"Yeah."

"Do you swear to me on ... your wedding rings? Swear on your rings."

Jessie bit her lip. She stared at her gold wedding band and a solitaire diamond and twirled them around. "I swear," she muttered.

Nick left the room quickly, closing the door behind him. Exhaling slowly, he leaned against the wall in the outer hallway. God, that was hard. Talking about his addiction wasn't what was difficult. He'd come to terms with that long ago. What was hard was seeing Jessie's exquisite body beneath that silk nightgown and robe. What was even harder was remembering that the slender body belonged to his sister-in-law, his brother's wife. Family. Harder? Nick chuckled. Appropriate word. What a gorgeous pair of knockers.

CHAPTER 8

"Your mom's okay, Anthony." Nick sat at the island in the kitchen, trying to soothe the boy's worries. "She promises it won't happen again."

"She promised before."

"You got that right," Mary chimed in.

Nick sent a warning glance in Mary's direction before focusing on Anthony. "This time she'll keep her promise. I'll help her, okay? I'll tell you what. I have to go out for a little while. How about I pick up some supplies on my way home, and we make dinner for your mom, with Mary's help?" He looked up at Mary. "Does everyone like Japanese?"

Mary lit up. "When Andrew was alive we ate Japanese at least once a week. But Jessie never asked me to put it on the menu after ... well." Mary busied herself making Anthony's lunch.

"I think she might enjoy it again now. What about you, Anthony? You like it, too?"

"I think so. Does it have carrots? I hate carrots."

"We'll skip the carrots."

*

The man known as Cobra shifted the disposable cellphone to his other ear and glanced around. "Okay, so tell me. What's McDeare up to? ...That's it? He interviewed some fossilized spy and went home? No roll in the sack with a hot babe? ... What? When? Shit. Okay. Thanks for covering D.C. I can't be in two places at once. I'll be in touch."

He hung up. McDeare was already back in New York? This day was turning into crap pronto. Cobra had thought he'd get at least a week's reprieve from trailing the prick. In fact, he'd made serious plans for the evening. He hoped the lady would take a rain-check.

Cobra glanced at his watch. He hadn't even eaten lunch yet. Well, screw that. If he was going to shadow McDeare for the rest of the day, he'd do it on a full stomach.

*

Nick pushed through the double doors of Gianni Fosselli's upscale restaurant. Pimpish with a veneer of class. Two levels of maritime décor in shades of green and blue. An oval bar designed like a ship's wheelhouse. Tropical fish tanks. Ornate chandeliers. Crystal goblets, bone china, and sterling silver. An illuminated fishbowl on each table. The staff appeared to be Italian. Nick heard thick accents coming from the dining area.

"Hello, I'm Monica." A voluptuous young woman approached Nick with a menu. "One-- Oh, Lord, you're Nick McDeare."

Nick tried not to salivate. "I'm looking for Mr. Fosselli."

"Uh, do you have an appointment?" Monica fumbled with the menu.

"No." Nick softened his voice. "Is he here?"

"I'm not sure. Let me check." Monica backed towards a podium and picked up a phone, her eyes Velcroed on Nick. He'd changed into black slacks, a cashmere V-neck and a black leather jacket. Nick McDeare, successful author and celebrity. Sometimes fitting the image worked to his advantage. Especially when it came to interrogating a snake like Fosselli.

Seconds later Gianni descended the grand staircase, polished in a navy silk suit and powder-blue shirt. He held out his hand. "Nicholas. This is a surprise. I was just having a bite to eat. Care to join me?"

"I just ate, but thank you. Could we speak privately?"

Gianni paused, staring at Nick with those unblinking eyes. "Of course. Come."

"What can I do for you?" Gianni asked as they entered his plush office, gesturing towards some wing chairs.

Nick sat down, feeling a rush of adrenaline, the thrill of the hunt. "As you probably suspect, I'm looking into my brother's murder."

Gianni lifted a gold box on the coffee table. "Cigarette?" He lit up.

"No thanks. To get to the point, I'm trying to find out more about Andrew's mood on that last cruise. Jessie said he seemed preoccupied, depressed. Being such a close friend of theirs," Nick smiled faintly, "I'm sure you must've noticed. Any idea what was bothering him?"

"What if I don't want to talk to you about it? It's not a very pleasant memory. You're not the police."

"True. But Jessie might wonder why."

"Jessica trusts you? She knows you're going to investigate?"

"She trusts me. I'm family."

"Jessica can be too trusting."

Nick chuckled. "That's what I keep telling her. I guess I'll also have to tell her you wouldn't give me the time of day when I tried to ask you a few questions."

The man's eyes were shiny black marbles. "You asked about Andrew's mood on the ship? To be honest, I didn't see much of him on that cruise. Or Jessica, for that matter."

Nick pressed his advantage. "Why not?"

"I'd been in Italy for almost six years, out of touch. And things weren't exactly pleasant between us."

"What do you mean?"

Gianni paused. "Well, it's not really a secret. Jessica and I were engaged at one time."

"Oh yeah. She mentioned it in passing." Nick kept a straight face as Gianni's eyebrows shot up.

"That doesn't sound like Jessica. She is not a frivolous woman. We're still extremely close."

And Gianni wished they were closer yet. Nick leaned forward. "About your engagement. What went wrong?"

"This is very private, Nicholas."

"Jessie didn't seem to think so. I'm just verifying what she's already told me."

"I find that hard to believe."

"Fine." Nick rose. "I'll tell Jessie you refused to cooperate." He started towards the door.

"Wait." Gianni paused. "It's just a very private matter." Nick returned to his chair. "Our engagement ended when I was called home to Italy due to some nasty business."

"Nasty business?"

"Someone exposed my relationship with Jessica to my family."

"Why was your relationship a secret?"

"It wasn't exactly a secret. It's a long story, nothing to do with Andrew's murder."

Nick waited.

"I was engaged to another woman, an arranged marriage between two families. It's a common practice in Italy."

"But you intended to marry Jessie?"

"Yes. When my grandfather found out about Jessica he collapsed, and my Italian fiancée tried to kill herself."

"Your Italian fiancée. As opposed to your American fiancée."

"I don't appreciate your snide remarks. I'm cooperating. I demand some respect in return, or I'll tell Jessica you behaved like a pompous ass."

Nick laughed. "Okay, back to your family. Did you tell them the truth about you and Jessie when you returned home?"

"I intended to. But with my grandfather and Bianca so ill, I didn't want to rub salt in their wounds. I wanted to wait until my grandfather was back on his feet."

Nick nodded. "Jessie said you had trouble standing up to the old man."

"Jessica would never say that. She knows me better than that. I simply have respect for family. Something you obviously know nothing about, having none of your own."

"On the contrary." Nick smiled pleasantly. "My family just got larger. I now have a sister-in-law. And a nephew. My brother's son." Gianni flushed. "So, you decided to stay home with Grandpa and tell him the truth when he got better. Then what?"

"Jessica was furious with my decision and chose to marry Andrew."

"So there was jealousy between you and Andrew?"

"On Andrew's part, yes. Jessica thought of him as her closest friend, almost a brother. You can imagine my shock at their marriage. Anyway, now you see why Andrew would not be inclined to confide in me. In fact, when I showed up on that final cruise, I think he looked on me as a threat to his marriage."

"Weren't you?"

Gianni smiled. "You mean, was I was still in love with Jessica?" He rose and straightened his suit jacket, stubbing out his cigarette. "Of course I was.

But I'm not a home wrecker, Nicholas. Jessica and Andrew had been married for almost six years."

"So things were cordial between all of you?"

"Cordial? Yes, cordial is a good word. We were no longer close, but we were far from enemies."

Nick nodded and got to his feet. Sliding his hands in his pockets, he strolled around the room, examining the framed photographs on the walls. "Jessie said you were with her when Andrew was shot. And that you stayed with her throughout his surgery and afterward."

"That's right. She needed someone. I'll always be there for her. She knows that." He shot a pointed look at Nick.

Nick ignored it. "Did you know that your nephew Eduardo was in the terminal at the time of the shooting?"

"The police told me, yes."

"Was that unusual? I mean, did he always disembark early?"

"I don't know what Eduardo's habits were. I had just come back to New York a few weeks before that cruise--"

"What brought you back to New York?"

"Many things, all of which are none of your business."

Nick shook his head in amusement. "You see, it's answers like that that arouse my suspicion." Nick shrugged. "What's the problem?"

Gianni leaned over the back of the chair. "Because it's my personal life. Because it has nothing to do with Andrew."

"Why don't you let me be the judge of that? It's a simple question. Why did you come back to New York?"

Gianni seemed to be having an inner debate. He came around the chair. "I came back to open my restaurant. I had acquired a prime piece of real estate and wanted to get started."

"How did you acquire this land?"

"How do you think? I had been searching for months."

"And you found this on your own?"

"Of course not. I have people who do that sort of thing for me." Gianni flicked his hand in the air as if waving away a fly.

"So you came back to open your restaurant. Any other reason?"

Gianni looked at Nick with distaste. "Yes. I was closing the sale of the cruise line."

"Oh, that's right. Who did you sell to, by the way?"

"It's a matter of public record. Look it up."

"Why not just tell me? Jessie would be pleased to know you were so cooperative."

Gianni exhaled slowly. "I sold to an American corporation. Pagano Industries."

Nick chuckled. "Now, that wasn't so hard, was it?" He wandered over to the desk and picked up a framed photograph of Jessie and Anthony. "So after six years away, the first time you set foot in New York was a few weeks before that cruise?"

"Yes."

"There's something I don't understand," Nick said, replacing the photograph and picking up another. "If you sold the line, why were you on the ship for that last cruise?"

"The transfer of the line became legal at the termination of the anniversary cruise. I wanted to sail one last time as the owner."

Nick studied the picture in his hand. "Who's this?"

"My mother."

"Pretty woman. Are you close?"

"She died many years ago."

"An illness?"

"No."

Nick waited.

"She ... Both she and my father surprised a burglar. They were murdered."

"Really. When?"

"About twenty years ago."

Nick stared at the photo before setting it down. He moved leisurely to the bookshelves. "Just a couple more questions. Was there anything odd that took place aboard the ship you think may have contributed to Andrew's murder?"

"Odd?"

"Any confrontations? Arguments?" Nick turned around to face the man.

Fosselli remained still, watching him. "What is it that you're afraid to ask me, Nicholas? Ask it. I'll answer your questions."

Nick slowly approached him. "What is it that you're afraid to tell me, Gianni? I get the feeling that you're hiding something."

"What would I possibly have to hide?"

"You tell me."

"We're doing a little dance here, yes?"

"Are we?"

"I think so." Gianni took a step closer to Nick until they were nose to nose, hands planted in their pockets. "Ask me. Just ask me."

"Okay," Nick said softly. "Who is Anthony's biological father?"

They continued to stare at each other, neither man moving.

"I am." Gianni's voice was almost a whisper.

Nick swallowed his satisfaction. "And you and Andrew never had words about his raising your son as his own?"

"Andrew and me? No. Jessica and me? Yes." Gianni moved behind a chair, his head down. "We had a confrontation in her cabin at one point. I forced her to tell me the truth."

"And then what? I would think you'd want to claim your son. Obviously you didn't. Why?" Nick's voice was conversational. Friendly.

"Anthony was so young. I thought it would confuse him. I didn't want to do anything to upset his equilibrium. He was a happy and contented little boy.

As a rule, I'm a selfish man. The decision not to tell Anthony is one of the few times I thought of someone else first. That's how much I love my son. I just wanted to be a part of his life for the time being."

"And what about now? Aren't you anxious to tell Anthony the truth?"

"Jessica and I have been discussing it. And that, my friend, is strictly between her and me."

Nick nodded. "Okay. Thanks." Playing nice, he shook Gianni's hand. As Nick reached the office door, he glanced over his shoulder. "Are you and your nephew Eduardo close?"

"Not really. We're ..."

"Cordial?"

Gianni smiled. "We're a little more than that, but I really haven't seen much of him the last couple of years. After I sold the cruise line he went back to Italy, while I've been here in New York."

Nick nodded and descended the staircase. Before leaving the restaurant, he angled Monica a lazy smile.

Nick hailed a cab, giving the driver an address in Chinatown. Pulling out a small notebook, he jotted down the key points of his conversation with Gianni, then stared out the window. The gray sky threatened a cloudburst, the air damp and chilly. He longed to be in front of a blazing fire with the voluptuous Monica. He'd peel away that skin-tight blouse and lose himself between those two luscious melons. He wondered what Fosselli would think if Nick screwed his hostess?

Nick had to handle the man carefully. Fosselli was a supremely confident man, in complete control at all times. If Nick was to get anything out of him, he had to convince Gianni he wasn't under investigation. Maybe if Fosselli relaxed, he'd slip up. Nick had to admit so far Gianni had been above board with him. The man had confirmed everything Jessie said the other night. There was just one problem.

Nick didn't trust Gianni Fosselli. And that spoke volumes when it came to Nick's kind of work.

*

In his sweats, Nick waited impatiently by the front door. Jessie had told him she was going upstairs to change twenty minutes ago. He could've jogged to Rockefeller Center and back by now.

He could hear Mary and Anthony chattering in the kitchen as they finished cleaning shrimp and slicing vegetables. Nick had gotten Anthony started on dinner before Mary took over, the little boy intent on making his mother a special meal. He'd given his nephew his first piano lesson, too. He'd told Nick he wanted to make his dad proud. A nice kid. A very nice kid. Jessie had done a good job with him.

Nick looked at his watch again. He took the stairs two at a time and knocked on Jessie's sitting room door. "C'mon. Time's wasting."

No answer.

"Jess?"

Silence. Jesus, what if she had more pills stashed? Nick turned the knob, unlocked. He opened the door and looked in. Jessie sat at her desk. She met Nick's eyes. "I'm sorry, Nick. I can't. I really tried. I just can't go back out there. People will see us together and assume the worst."

"The worst?" Nick chuckled. "Being seen with me is the worst?"

"You know what I mean. That article."

"You and I both know the press is part of our careers. They go with the territory. You can't let every trashy article get to you."

Jessie seemed to fold in on herself. "This is different. What that slime printed in the paper made it look like I couldn't wait for two years to be up so I could move on. Everything I do now reflects on Andrew. He's not here to defend himself or our marriage."

"Let me ask you something. When Andrew was alive, how did the two of you deal with the press?"

She shrugged. "We were careful, but we didn't let them prevent us from doing things."

"Exactly. Besides the obvious, nothing's different now. If you stay holed up in this house, they've won. Is that what Andrew would want?" Maybe it was time to spring an idea he'd been working through. "Look," Nick said, "I thought a lot about this on the flight up from D.C." He flopped down in the easy chair beside the desk. "My old college roommate's an editor at THE POST. We're still good friends. How about we fight fire with fire and go to the press ourselves? We give Michael an interview."

Jessie lifted a delicately arched brow. "And what are we going to tell him?"

"The truth. I'm Andrew's brother. Michael can print the whole story. That takes the focus off you and transfers it to me."

"You'd do that for me?"

"Not exactly." Nick pushed himself out of the chair. "My agent's riding me to get my name out more. RED ROVER comes out this summer. I figure the world eventually has to find out about Andrew and me. Why not now? I'm sure other media will pick up the piece. Great PR for the book. And in the process, yeah, no one will question our relationship again."

She thought about that, those indigo eyes brightening. "They'll know we're just family."

"Right. Just family."

Jessie smiled. "Perfect! It'll stop this ridiculous nonsense about anything more going on between us."

Was he Quasimodo? "So, you agree to the interview?"

"Do I have to be there? Can't you just do this?"

"I come up with a solution to your problem, and you want to weasel out of it? We both do it, or we forget about it." Nick moved to the window, looking out on the garden. Here he was offering himself as press fodder, and she wanted more. This was the prima donna he'd expected to meet that first night.

Jessie joined him at the window. "I'm sorry, Nick. I must sound like a prima donna." Nick coughed. "Sure, I'll do the interview with you. Thanks for thinking of it." She studied him. "Serves all our purposes, doesn't it? Very pragmatic."

"Pragmatic pays the bills. So, are you ready to jog?"

"Um, do you mind if I wait until the article's out?"

"For crissake, you--"

"Don't yell at me. It hasn't been the best of days. You took my pills away and now you're trying to push me out the door."

"Jess, how do you expect to sleep tonight if you don't get any exercise?"

"By going ten rounds with you, okay?"

*

"I forgot how much I love tempura," Jessie purred, snaring another piece of crispy shrimp with her chopsticks. "This is the best I've ever had, Nick." The man had a way with food. He and Anthony had worked for an hour putting the Japanese feast together after Nick got back from his jog. It was good to see Anthony act like a normal little boy again.

"And where did you learn to make negamaki?" Jessie asked, attacking the rolled beef and scallions. "Andrew would mow down little old ladies to get his chopsticks around one of these babies."

"I'm impressed, too," Mary said. "You cook other things besides Oriental?"

Nick shrugged. "I can cook almost anything. Asian's my specialty."

"A man who cooks," Jessie teased, reaching for another negamaki. "My God, next you'll be telling me you make your own clothes. So where'd you learn to cook like this?"

"My mom. Living in the Far East made Asian a natural."

"Did your ex-wife cook?" Jessie snatched another piece of tempura from the serving platter. Nick was a font of information tonight.

"Lindsey thought the kitchen was a place to chill champagne. If I didn't cook, Jeffrey, um, would've lived on pizza and McDonald's." Nick concentrated on his food.

There it was again, that reluctance to mention his son's name. Jessie groaned. "I'm stuffed." She pushed herself away from the table. "I can't believe how much I ate. I won't survive if you do this too often, Nick. I'll gain thirty pounds."

"Not if you exercise." Nick cast Jessie a meaningful look as he patiently showed Anthony how to hold his chopsticks.

"I wish you'd get off the exercise kick."

"It'll help you sleep."

"You know," Mary said, stacking the plates, "Andrew talked about converting the attic into a gym. It's huge."

"It's also crammed with generations of stuff." Jessie snuck one more piece of tempura.

"It's time we cleaned out that mess." Mary handed Anthony a fork. "Here, honey. Use this."

"That's the answer, Jess." Nick smiled triumphantly.

"A fork?"

"Our own hands. We'll clean out the attic over the next few weeks, and you can convert it into a gym. Great idea. The exercise will tire you out but good. You'll be exhausted every night and sleep like a baby." He pushed his chair back eagerly. "C'mon. Show me."

Nick McDeare thought he was so smart. He was undoubtedly hoping she'd crash early every night after clean-up detail. After which, he could slip out and find a woman for that itch of his. All those ladies calling on his cell must be vibrating a hole in his pocket tonight. But she was feeling too good to argue. Besides, Jessie had to admit more exercise would be good for her. "Okay, you're on. Follow me up to the fifth-floor stratosphere."

The attic was the mess she'd promised Nick. Windows at both ends cast the room in a musty glow. The space was enormous. It really would make a state-of-the-art gym, just like Andrew had wanted. Nick waded through the clutter, lifting sheets to admire the antiques and moving on to examine the holiday decorations. Jessie lit on box after box, fingering long-forgotten treasures, family relics she'd forgotten had existed.

Suddenly, she froze. Nick glanced over at her. "What's up? Did you find something good?" He worked his way over to her. "What is it?"

She pointed. "Ah, that's ... our luggage. Andrew's and mine. From that last cruise." Jessie swallowed. "I guess Mary brought the bags up here unopened. I never wanted to see them again." Jessie forced herself to resume breathing. In and out.

Nick examined the suitcases. The matching luggage still bore the gay tags of the Italian Marine Line. From the rapt expression on his face, Jessie could tell he was dying to go through them. She supposed their luggage might hold clues only Nick McDeare could decipher.

Jessie moved on, quickly leaving forbidden territory. She stopped in her tracks, transfixed with another set of mementos. "Oh my God, look. I'd completely forgotten. This stuff is yours now, Nick."

*

"What are you talking about?" And then he spotted it. A large trunk with a broken lock. Exactly how Andrew described it during their last chat.

"When your mother died ... When Andrew moved in with us, Dad emptied their apartment and brought a lot of their things over here. This is all yours. Take it to Washington if you like."

Nick stared silently at the odd assortment of items, all that was left of Chelsea Brady. His focus kept returning to the trunk, his curiosity eating away at him. He was afraid of ... what? His birth mother meant nothing to him. She'd squeezed Nick from her womb and given him away.

"What's wrong?"

"Nothing." To prove it, Nick approached the trunk and lifted the lid. It was full of folded clothes and old photographs. Silver candlesticks. A makeup kit. Nick carefully dug throughout the items, looking for ... there it was. A fancy tin for chocolates. Chills did a parade down his spine.

"What's that?"

"I don't know." Nick snapped the lid open.

Letters. It was stuffed with old letters. Nick opened one at random and began to read.

Dearest Patrick,

Today you are ten years old. Ten! I've lost ten whole years of your childhood. How can I ever get those years back? Happy birthday, my precious son. I bought you a gift today. I know it's silly, but I truly believe I'll find you this year, and I don't want you to think I forgot your birthday. It's nothing really. It's hard to know what a ten-year-old boy wants. Andrew's only five, so I've never done ten before.

I hope wherever you are that you're happy and healthy. I hope you're having a wonderful day. I'm making a cake and Andrew will blow out your candles for you. Next year we'll be together. I'm sure of it.

I love you - Mom

Patrick. Nick's name would've been Patrick. How ironic. Kate and Charles McDeare had never met Nick's birth mother, but Nick was christened Nicholas Patrick McDeare.

Nick's hands were shaking. He slipped the letter back in the tin and snapped the lid shut, the lump in his throat threatening to choke him. Chelsea Brady hadn't written this kind of letter to an unwanted, forgotten kid. What the hell was going on here?

CHAPTER 9

"Hey, Lyle." Bushman banged a knuckle against Barton's door before entering. "Better take a look at this." He tossed THE POST on his partner's desk, open to the Metro headline: JESSICA BRADY'S MYSTERY MAN REVEALED.

Barton began to scan the article written by crime editor Michael Whitestone. "So what? McDeare decided to announce to the world he's Andrew Brady's brother. Big deal."

"Read the last paragraphs."

Barton jumped down to the end of the article:

I freely admit I've known Nick McDeare for almost twenty years. We were college roommates and fellow journalism majors. McDeare is relentless, thorough, and deceptively smooth. His track record is one hundred percent. When he is on the scent of a hunt, nothing gets in his way.

Now McDeare is concentrating on finding Andrew Brady's killer. The stakes are even higher this time. It's personal. Someone murdered his brother in cold blood. I predict McDeare will be successful.

There's a killer who walks among us. You may even have passed him on the street. But he won't be around for long.

Nick McDeare has painted a bull's-eye on his forehead.

Barton slammed the paper on the desk. McDeare was offering himself as bait. He was the one wearing the bull's-eye. Lyle grabbed his coat and headed for the parking lot, leaving a gaping Bushman in his wake.

*

As Jeremy walked into the study with the day's newspapers, Jessie put aside the paperwork for Anthony's summer camp. "Thank you. Finally!" Jessie grabbed THE POST from Jeremy, her hands were trembling.

"Hey, give me a break. I have a few other things on my agenda, like stalling the Tony committee."

"Tell them no." Jessie ripped through the paper. She and Nick had given the interview four days ago. It had to be here.

"You're making a mistake. Bill deserves better from you."

She found what she was looking for. "Hmm? What did you say?" She looked up, but Jeremy was gone.

Jessie read Michael Whitestone's feature story carefully, hoping it did the trick. Would the press never leave her alone? Vultures. Her mouth dropped open at the last few paragraphs. Nick didn't say any of this in their interview with Michael. When did he ...? Damn him. The irresponsible jerk.

Jessie hurtled up the back stairs and pounded on the suite door.

"Yeah?"

Throwing the door open, Jessie charged into the sitting room. Nick was at the desk, reading glasses on his nose, dressed in jeans and a faded Baltimore Orioles T-shirt. Chaos surrounded him. Piles of papers. Empty cans of cola. An overflowing ashtray filled with crushed, whole cigarettes. Wadded-up paper sprouting in the wastebasket.

"What's this?" Jessie demanded, waving the newspaper in the air.

"A newspaper?"

"Very funny."

"Is that Michael's article? How does it look?" Nick extended his arm. "Let me read it."

Jessie pitched THE POST to the floor. It landed on a mountain of papers, flattening them.

"Hey, watch it. I've got this stuff organized."

"Organized? This is organized?" Jessie shrieked. "This room is a nightmare. You better hope Mary doesn't see this."

"She did. That's why it looks this way. She refuses to set foot in here."

"Don't change the subject. Why did you do it, Nick?"

"Do what?" He began to read the article.

"Are you trying to get yourself killed? You waltz into our lives and then you set yourself up to be killed?"

"You're repeating yourself. Hey, this is good. I forgot Michael could write like this."

"Are you hearing me? Please don't do this, Nick."

Nick put down the paper and removed his glasses. "I'm not doing anything. Michael's just stating the obvious. He knows me well. Besides, it explains my presence here in town."

"Listen to me. If something happens to you it'll destroy Anthony. He's downstairs working with that ridiculous camera you brought back from Washington for him. A nuclear scientist couldn't figure that contraption out, but Anthony wants to make you proud. Please don't do this to him."

"We don't dare let anything happen to me for Anthony's sake?"

"Don't play mind games with me. You're my brother-in-law. My son's uncle. My family just got a little larger. I'd hate to see it shrink again."

"Family. Right. Okay, I'll do my best to prevent my untimely death. For Anthony's sake."

*

Lyle impatiently waited for Mary to answer the door. He could hear her hustle down the hallway. "Abigail Forrester, is that you?" she called out. "You're early."

The minute she opened the door, Lyle burst into the house. "Where's McDeare?"

"And hello to you, too, Lyle."

"Sorry, Mary, but I've got to talk to McDeare." He paused. "Where's all the shouting coming from?"

She pointed skyward. "The suite. Looks like you'll have to get in line."

Lyle rushed for the stairs.

*

"Shit!" Ian Wexley hurled THE POST across the living room.

"What's wrong, honey?" Paula Wexley appeared in the kitchen doorway.

"Why can't the sonuvabitch just go away, once and for all?"

"What's got you so worked up?" Paula picked up the paper and began to scan the article. "Nick McDeare's Andrew's brother? The famous writer?"

"Just my luck." Ian went to the bar. "It's been two years. Let it alone already."

"You've been cleared. What's the big deal?" She gave him that sly smile he hated.

"You're never cleared, Paula." He poured scotch into a glass and swallowed it in one gulp. "Not until someone's arrested." Another splash of scotch. Another gulp.

"Shouldn't you get ready for your job?"

That whiny voice made Ian's teeth hurt. "You call bartending a job?" He used to be a soap star. Women used to stalk him at fan events, begging for his hotel room number. His key. Him! Now he was headlining as a bartender for a catering service. Paula's family had more money than God. Why did they insist he help support his wife? What bullshit. "Get out of my sight, okay?"

Paula backed into the kitchen.

Ian pulled out his cell phone, hitting a speed-dial number. "It's me. Can we meet?"

*

"Do I have to do everything? Just take care of it." Gianni slammed down the phone. He didn't need this harassment right now. Not when things were beginning to look up. Gianni eyed THE POST. McDeare had stones. At least the man had explained he wasn't Jessica's secret lover. What a ridiculous notion.

Gianni wandered to the living room window and looked down at Manhattan and the East River. His current concern was how to get Jessica to the Tony Awards. Mary had mentioned the ceremony that morning when he'd stopped by the brownstone for coffee. Jessica had changed the subject. But if Gianni could convince Jessica to go with him, the next step would be easy. Who else would she want to escort her on that special night but Gianni? It would be their new beginning. The first time they were seen together in public. And the fact that Gianni had been Andrew's friend would only make it easier. It was always nice to have the first husband's blessing. Give the papers something real to shout about next time.

*

Lyle Barton shot into the suite, waving THE POST in the air. "Are you purposely trying to get yourself killed?" Barton realized he was shouting. He didn't care. "I don't have the time or the manpower to cover your sorry ass while you run around town playing detective."

"Don't bother, Lyle," Jessie said. "I've already tried."

- 103 -

"I've been taking care of myself for almost forty years," Nick said mildly. "I don't need protection."

"You're on my beat now. You get yourself killed, it's one more case on my desk. I don't need any more headaches." He tossed the paper into the mess on the floor. "Good God, what happened to this room?"

Nick stepped over the stacks of paperwork and paced to the terrace door. "Let me ask you something," he said, his back to them. "Have you checked out a conglomerate called Pagano Industries?"

"McDeare, have you heard a word I've said?"

"Have you checked them out?"

Lyle exchanged an exasperated look with Jessie. "No. Why?"

Nick turned around and faced him "That's the corporation that bought the Italian Marine Line, Fosselli's family business. It's one of those organizations with a lot of figureheads, but when you dig into the layers you find all sorts of interesting things. If you know where to look. It took me years on the job as a reporter, but I learned where to look."

"Okay." Barton rolled his eyes. "What did you find?"

Nick crossed his arms. "Georgio Pagano's the owner and CEO. He's got a ton of legit board members and vice presidents in charge of changing the toilet paper. But there's one wing of the business called the M Foundation. It turns out the M Foundation's the real owner of the cruise line under the Pagano umbrella." Nick grinned. "Guess what the M stands for?"

Christ. "Martinelli?"

"Give the man a cigar. Your report says two of Roberto Martinelli's men were in the terminal that morning when Andrew was shot."

"Vito Secchi and Aldo Zappella. But I have an eyewitness who says they were on the other side of the terminal at the time. We checked them out first thing."

"I read that in the report. The witness was a security guard. A man by the name of Joseph Salerno. Italian. A coincidence?"

"Salerno's been a security guard at the piers for forty years. Spotless record."

"Who are Secchi and Zappella exactly?" Nick returned to the desk, stepping carefully over the pile of papers.

"Vito Secchi runs Martinelli's business in Italy. Aldo Zappella is Martinelli's stooge. Zappella delegates the dirty work so Martinelli can keep his hands clean."

"What were they doing in the terminal that morning?" Nick shuffled through some papers, rooting for something.

"Actually, they were passengers. Traveling with their wives. It's my experience that wise guys play it straight around the wives."

Jessie stood with arms folded, quietly following the conversation.

"Okay, let's rethink this," Nick said. "The M Foundation. A personal vacation for two wise guys, nothing to do with Martinelli, who just happens to be their employer. Who just happens to have bought the cruise line."

Lyle began to see Mcdeare's reasoning. Gianni Fosselli had indirectly sold the line to Martinelli. And Martinelli had his key men aboard. Barton wandered to the terrace door. "Had we put two and two together like you did," he admitted, "it would've told us that Fosselli conducted business with the underworld and heightened our suspicions about him. Secchi and Zappella correctly assumed we'd never make the link to Martinelli. Pagano bought the company on paper. The faceless M Foundation meant nothing to us. They had layers preventing us from making the connection."

"Until now. And it explains how Fosselli's standing beside Jessie at the time of the shooting and appears completely innocent."

"So you think either Secchi or Zappella did the job? While traveling with their wives? I don't think so."

"I agree. I think they were there as witnesses to make sure the job got done. We both know La Cosa Nostra has layers of insulation to make sure things go accordingly. More backup than the space shuttle. I think there was someone else in the terminal that morning working for Martinelli. He was the shooter. Identify him and work backwards. I'll bet all roads lead to Fosselli. I've been going over the witnesses statements--"

"Wait a minute." Jessie stared at Nick. "Are you saying Gianni hired someone to kill Andrew? To murder him in cold blood?"

Nick and Lyle exchanged a glance. "It's a possibility," Nick said. "You knew he was a suspect."

"You're crazy!" Jessie threw her hands up in the air. "Gianni's not capable of murder. He didn't even have the backbone to stand up to his grandfather. I knew you were suspicious, Nick, but I thought you'd get over it!"

Nick stared at Jessie. "I'll get over it," he said softly, "when I nail whoever killed my brother. Whether it was one man or ten men."

"You have to see it the way Gianni saw it," Lyle said gently. "Andrew had everything he wanted, including Anthony. Wexley still tops my list, but Gianni's a suspect, too."

Jessie backed away from Barton. "I'm telling you both Gianni did not murder Andrew! And I don't want to hear another word about it." Jessie turned on her heel and hurried from the room.

*

"Mary, what smells so good?" Barton stood over the stove, breathing deeply.

"You want the whole list?" Mary winked at him. "Let's see. Crown roast of pork with sautéed cinnamon apples. Potatoes au gratin. Fresh asparagus."

Jessie sat at the island, making a salad, too angry to speak. She chopped a red pepper in two with a vicious stroke, half the pepper flying off the carving board and onto the floor.

"And a salad," Mary added. "If the vegetables survive."

Jessie scooped the pepper up with a laugh. Mary could always deflate her temper. "Sorry, Mary." The hell with Nick McDeare. She was too ecstatic about Abbie's impending arrival to let Nick ruin it. Abbie was finally coming home. Abbie, Andrew's best friend for over twenty-five years. Abbie, who knew Andrew better than anyone, except his wife. Abbie, who was Jessie's support with Gianni after her world fell apart.

"What's the occasion?" Lyle asked, lifting a lid on a pot.

"Abbie's due home any minute," Jessie said.

"Are you angling for a dinner invitation?" Mary teased.

"Yeah. Barb's still out of town."

"Where's Nick?" Mary asked.

Jessie sliced a black radish. "Probably in his lair. Hopefully changing clothes."

The doorbell chimed. "There's Abbie!" Jessie skittered down the hallway and turned the locks.

Abigail Forrester stood in the doorway, four suitcases at her feet. A large floppy hat covered her mop of sable hair, her pale brown eyes peeking out from under the brim. She wore a wide smile that accented her full red lips, lips that graced the pages of the world's top fashion magazines. Abbie was the darling of every ad exec with a lipstick account. Even though she was a classically trained stage actress and part of Bill Rudolph's family of actors, Abigail Forrester made her living doing commercials and print work.

Abbie was dressed in a pair of black designer jeans and a black baggy sweater. A loopy string of cultured pearls hung from her neck and a Gucci leather satchel purse hung from her shoulder. She was the perfect combination of New York chic and California cool. The two girls threw their arms around each other and started to cry.

Jessie had missed her friend desperately. After Andrew's death, Abbie had spent months trying to hold Jessie together. She'd finally returned to her native California, far from the memories of her best friend. Jessie knew the pain of Andrew's death had sliced through her like a laser.

"God, I've missed you," Abbie whispered. Stepping back, she gave her friend the once over. "You look much better, Jessie. I love that handkerchief blouse. And it matches your slacks perfectly. You should wear turquoise all the time."

"What are you? The fashion police? But what's with the chunky sweater? It's not your style."

"I didn't want to be hassled on the plane, so I decided to go baggy." Abbie tossed her hat on the cathedral bench by the door.

Jessie spotted the matching designer luggage on the stoop. "Hey, guys," she yelled towards the kitchen, "we could use some help here." Jessie picked up one of the bags and dragged it into the hallway. "I see you traveled light, as usual."

Anthony came bounding down the stairs, and hurled himself into his Aunt Abbie's arms.

"What's happened?" Abbie asked, trying to lift the boy. "I can't pick you up anymore. You're getting too big." She began to tickle him. "But I can still do this." Anthony squealed with delight.

Mary materialized and joined in the hugs, while Lyle picked up two of the suitcases. "Hey, Lyle," Abbie said, grabbing the last bag. "This is a nice surprise. It's good to see you." She turned to Jessie. "Okay, where's this mystery guest of yours?"

"I'll show you!" Anthony said, skipping down the hallway. Following Anthony's lead, the entourage made its way to the kitchen. Nick was staring out the window, stuffing a mangled cigarette into his pocket. Jessie noticed he'd changed into black slacks and a sleek black shirt. He looked like a brooding panther.

Abbie stared silently at the tall stranger for a moment. "Oh, my God. You're him, aren't you? You're Andrew's brother. My God! And-and I know you somehow."

Nick fixed her with a look. "I'm him, I guess."

"Abbie," Jessie said, linking her arm through her friend's. "This is Nick McDeare."

Abbie's face lifted in surprise. "Nick McDeare?" She started to chuckle. "Nick McDeare, the author? Of course." When Nick nodded, Abbie began to laugh. "This is too funny. I don't believe it. Nick McDeare is Andrew's brother?"

"If you don't mind my asking," Nick said, "what's so funny?"

"It's just that Andrew was probably your biggest fan. He drove Jessie and me crazy, raving on and on about you. I think I need a drink."

Jessie needed one, too. She maneuvered Abbie into the study, away from everyone else. Going behind the bar, she reached for the bottle of sherry. "Okay, tell me. What brought you back to New York on the spur of the moment?"

"I missed you. Isn't that enough?"

"Abigail Forrester, I've known you since we were thirteen years old. I know you missed me, but I also know you don't suddenly relocate back to New York in a matter of weeks."

"Why do I try to fool you after all these years?"

Jessie plucked a glass from the cabinet and poured her friend a hefty shot. "Okay. What was his name?"

Abbie took a sip of sherry. "Robert Piazza, a photographer I worked with on a shoot."

"Italian?"

"Of course. After dating so many Italians I have marinara sauce in my veins instead of blood."

"What happened? Married?"

"Married. The lying sack of shit."

Jessie hugged her friend. "When are you going to give up on your Italian Romeos?"

"I like hot Italians. What can I say?" She set her glass on the bar. "Now if you'll excuse me I'll exchange this baggy outfit for something a little slinkier. And we'll discuss your new brother-in-law later, too."

"Take the first bedroom on the third floor. Mary aired it out and changed the linens for you." Watching Abbie trot off, Jessie dropped down onto the couch. It was good to have Abbie and her mouth back. And her timing was perfect. Maybe Abbie could help with the sleepless nights and the yearning for the magic pills. It was even harder now than before. She was turning into a wreck.

Jessie jogged every day with Nick, just like he wanted. Each evening he insisted they work on the damned attic, making sure she did her share. The man was worse than the pushiest director. And every night was a struggle to fall asleep. Jessie would drop into bed exhausted. But instead of counting sheep, she'd recite that slimy newspaper article in her head. How Jessica Brady couldn't wait to move on after two years.

Worse, she'd started having flashbacks to the nightmare days after Andrew was shot. The press and their microphones, the celebrity entertainment shows, the media dissecting her life. That horrific evening in the hospital when her world had shattered.

Opening up to Nick had brought the trauma to the surface all over again. Damn him. For two years, she'd managed to bury the memories with her husband. Then along came obnoxious Nick McDeare with his questions and his prodding. Nothing was the same anymore. And to top it off, now he'd painted a target on himself for Andrew's killer. And to top that off, the man thought Gianni was capable of ordering a hit on Andrew. Jessie felt like screaming. If it weren't for Anthony--

"Jessie, I need help!"

Jessie was happy to leave her black thoughts behind and answer Mary's plea. Carrying the pork roast to the dining room table, she found Anthony the sole dinner guest. "Where is everyone?"

"Lyle got a call," Anthony said. "He's outside. I'm starving, Mommy!"

Mary pushed through the swinging door, the side dishes on a large tray.

"And Nick and Abbie?" Jessie asked.

"Aunt Abbie went up to change. Uncle Nick followed her. I think he wanted to show her something."

"I'm sure he did, honey." Leave it to the man to make a move on Abbie the moment she hit town. Nick McDeare should come with a bell around his neck.

"Well, dinner's ready," Mary said, exchanging a look with Jessie. "Anthony, why don't you get them, okay?"

"Never mind. I'll go," Jessie said, mounting the stairs in irritation. The door to Nick's suite open, she moved swiftly through the bedroom into the sitting room. Empty. Where were they? Then she spotted them.

Abbie and Nick were on the terrace with their heads together. Leaning on the railing, shoulder to shoulder, they were speaking in muted tones. Abbie had changed into a pair of skin-tight fuchsia slacks and a sweater. Nick's hip brushed against hers at regular intervals. What a wolf. Yet another reason to dislike him.

Nick and Abbie were so engrossed in their conversation they didn't hear Jessie approach. "Dinner's ready," she said, obviously startling them both.

*

Nick was silent throughout the meal. He noticed Barton wasn't talking much either. The cop ate like a kid set loose in a candy shop. Abbie and Jessie prattled non-stop, catching up on old friends. They spent ten minutes gushing over an actor named Josh Elliott, Andrew's understudy in HEART TAKES. He won a Tony last year for another musical. He was supposedly gorgeous and a sweetheart. Nick found it revolting for any man to be called a sweetheart.

After supper, Nick walked Barton to his car. He'd been impatient all night to get back to the case. "I assume you checked out Andrew's understudy? The man profited in a big way from Andrew's death."

"The guy's baseball and apple pie. His life was dissected. He and Andrew were close. Besides, Elliott owed Brady his career."

"How so?"

"Andrew dragged Bill Rudolph up to Darien, Connecticut to see Josh Elliott's work. Rudolph was blown away, and Josh joined the producer's stable of actors."

Nick nodded. He'd look into Josh Elliott further on his own. "Okay. Tell me why you like Wexley for Andrew's murder."

"You read the police report. It's all in there." They headed towards Madison Avenue.

"I want to know what your gut's telling you. Why Wexley?" They stopped at the light.

"What my gut tells me is my business."

"Look, do you want to play games or do you want to nail this guy? You've been working this case for two years. I've been working it for days, and I've already uncovered something critical you overlooked."

"You want a medal? You're looking at one case. I've got twenty on my desk."

The light changed and they crossed Madison Avenue in silence, reaching Barton's car. Lyle plucked the NYPD sign off the windshield. "I want to get this guy as bad as you do. Let's not go at each other. It's a waste of time."

They stared at each other across the top of the car.

"What if you went at it fresh?" Andrew had admonished Nick to work with Barton. He'd give it a shot. "What if you did another round of interviews? Talked to all the witnesses again?"

"What's different this time?"

"Me. I'll go with you, look at it with new eyes."

Barton chuckled. "You and me? I don't think so."

"Fine." Nick backed away from the car. "Go back to the station house and work on your twenty cases. I'll concentrate on my one." He walked away. Barton had no idea what a concession it was for Nick to make that offer. Nick McDeare worked alone.

"McDeare," Barton called. "Wait."

Nick turned around.

"Look, I have a partner."

"And look where he's gotten you."

"You really think you can work with someone?

"I said I could."

"Okay. Let me think about it."

"Don't think too long. I work fast. I may have solved the case by then."

CHAPTER 10

"Andrew talked about you constantly, Nick," Abbie said, refilling her snifter with brandy. "From the moment we met, two seven-year-old kids at a cereal commercial audition, he told me about the brother he and his mom were going to find one day." She was feeling good. Stuffed but good.

The kitchen was warm and cozy in the candlelight. Abbie, Jessie and Nick were perched on stools around the island, one of Abbie's favorite spots. She'd sat there with Andrew too many times to count. Now she sat across from his brother. Damn. Her buddy should be there, too. Abbie fought her tears. It was times like this that she cursed being an actress at heart. Her emotions always lurked just beneath the surface.

"Andrew even talked about you on his wedding day," Abbie offered.

"I didn't know that." Jessie reached for the bottle of brandy.

"When I went up to the third floor to get him for the ceremony, he was staring out the window. He wished you were there to stand beside him, Nick, when he took his vows."

"You got married here in the brownstone?" Nick asked, looking at Jessie.

Jessie nodded. "We had to put the ceremony together really fast."

Abbie looked at her friend in surprise. "Um, Jessie--"

"It's okay. Nick knows. It took him a whole day to figure out the truth about Anthony." Jessie seemed weary, her eyes smudged.

Abbie looked from Jessie to Nick. "Jessie let you in on a pretty big secret."

"What? You think I'll scoop it on Twitter?"

What a prick. Andrew's brother had a chip on his shoulder the size of a Mercedes. Still ... Nick caught Abbie's eye and looked away.

Nick cleared his throat. "Ah, Abbie, did you ever meet Chelsea Brady?"

"So formal. Sure. I met your mom. Lots of times."

"What was she like?" Nick reached for the brandy.

"She was a sweet lady. But damaged, you know? She worked hard to take care of Andrew. She could never hold down a job, always taking Andrew to auditions. And I think she was lonely. Andrew was all she had."

"Did she ever mention me?"

"Nick," Jessie said, her voice strained, "I could've answered these questions for you. I mean, they're about Andrew's life. Which is the kind of personal thing I should be an expert on, right?"

"I wanted Abbie to answer them."

"You don't trust me?"

"I decided to ask Abbie, okay?"

"So the great investigator's giving me some R'nR at last. How kind of you." Jessie's brittle laugh made Abbie flinch. She poured herself another brandy.

"It's nothing personal. You knew Chelsea for one year. Abbie knew her for seven. She's the best one to tell me about my-- about Chelsea. Where's this coming from?" His eyes hardened. "Or does this have nothing to do with Chelsea Brady and everything to do with my investigation of the honorable Gianni Fosselli?"

Abbie followed the spat as if she were watching a tennis match. Jessie, who could be the most contrary woman in the universe, had met her match in her brother-in-law.

"Spare me," Jessie said, springing up to get another bottle of brandy. "Go on. Knock yourself out."

"So, Abbie," Nick said, "did she ever mention me?"

Abbie glanced in Jessie's direction. "All the time. I don't think she ever got over losing you. That's what I meant when I said she was damaged. Andrew said she blamed herself for not standing up to your father. He didn't want kids. You know they weren't married, right?"

"I don't know anything. I never wanted to know until now I guess. What was his name?"

"Jason. I don't know his last name. Brady was your mom's name. He was long gone by the time I came on the scene. In fact, he left the day Andrew was born. "

"Did he ever turn up again?"

"Nope. And Chelsea never looked for him. It was as if he never existed. All she cared about were her sons." She took a sip of brandy. "Chelsea had a shrine built to you in her bedroom. She used to buy you gifts and wrap them. Then she'd put them on this little table, along with a votive candle that was lit twenty-four hours a day. She called you Patrick."

*

Nick watched Jessie replace the nubs in the candlesticks. The three of them had been sitting around the island for hours, talking about anything related to Jessie and Andrew. Jessie had barely spoken to him, Abbie their buffer. Women kept these lists in their heads like report cards, checking off your faults. Nick surmised he was failing in Gianni, as well as several other subjects.

Nick noticed Abbie was careful not to say anything that would upset Jessie, treating her like delicate crystal. That's how all her friends treated her. Like a figurine in a glass menagerie. Nick had a feeling Jessie was a lot stronger than anyone gave her credit for. Including herself. But maybe she didn't want to be strong. Maybe she wanted to hide forever. Which was exactly what Andrew had told him he was afraid of.

"I heard Bill wants you to present the Lifetime Achievement Award to him at the Tonys," Abbie said.

"I've decided not to do it. I'm not ready yet."

Nick raised a brow. "Wait a minute. Didn't you ask me to escort you?"

"With a qualification. IF I went. I told you I probably wouldn't go. I'm not."

Abbie set her snifter down with a thud. "Jessie, you have to do it. It's Bill. You can't say no to Bill."

"I'm not ready, Abbie."

Nick watched the exchange closely. He was already on Jessie's list tonight. What was one more check? "What are you afraid of, Jess?"

Jessie shot him a look. "Nothing. I just don't want to do it."

"You sound like a spoiled brat."

"Hey, don't talk to Jessie like that." A flash of anger crossed Abbie's face.

"It's okay, Abbie," Jessie said. "It's Nick's style. He does his best to offend everyone he meets, don't you, Nick?"

Nick shrugged. "I just tell it like it is."

Abbie glared at Nick. "Jessie's not some--"

"Why don't you let the lady speak for herself?"

"Who the hell do you think you are?" Abbie's voice rose.

"I said," Nick raised his own voice, "let the lady do her own talking." He looked over at Jessie. "You can speak for yourself, can't you?"

"Of course I can." Jessie's eyes narrowed into turquoise slits.

"Then answer my question. What are you afraid of?"

"Nothing. I just don't want to go to the Tonys."

"Like I said, a spoiled brat."

"Okay, you listen to me, you bastard." Abbie slammed her hand down on the counter. "I don't ever want to hear you talk to Jessie like that again. Do you understand me? She's been through enough without some long-lost brother-in-law showing up and treating her like crap."

"I'm the only one around here who has the guts to tell her the truth. You all tiptoe around her like she's a piece of porcelain."

"Jessie has been to hell and back and doesn't need any shit from the likes of you. Keep your opinions to yourself. I saw Jessie go to the brink once and I won't watch it happen again."

"Abbie, that's enough." Jessie put a hand on her friend's arm.

"What are you talking about? Something besides sleeping pills?"

"You don't know? I thought you knew everything."

"Stop it, both of you." Jessie pleaded.

"Four months after Andrew died," Abbie forged on, "Bill yanked me from HEART TAKES and packed me off to the villa in St. John. Jessie was down there slowly drinking herself to death. She wasn't eating. She wasn't sleeping. And she emptied case after case of brandy."

"Abbie, shut up!"

Abbie jumped to her feet. "Tonight Jessie's been attacking that brandy bottle with gusto again. I'm putting two and two together and I figure it's because you and your lousy attitude are hanging around. So just pack it in and shove it up your royal ass, Mr. Celebrated Author." Abbie headed for the stairs. "You know, if you didn't look so much like Andrew I'd never believe you're his

- 113 -

brother. You're nothing like him. Andrew wore his heart on his sleeve. I'm not sure you even have a heart. If Andrew were here he'd disown you." She charged up the stairs.

Jessie whipped a hand through her hair. "Damn you, Nick. Abigail Forrester was Andrew's best friend. I won't have you treating the people he loved like that."

"I'm only telling the truth" Nick's lip twisted. "Everyone handles you with kid gloves and you allow it. Hell, you crave it."

"I do not."

"Bill Rudolph asked a favor of you. This is supposedly a man you owe everything to. You say no because you just don't feel like it. Sounds spoiled to me. Jessie only does what Jessie feels like doing, right?"

"You are the most arrogant man!"

"Yeah, but you like arrogant don't you? As in the honorable Gianni Fosselli?"

"You ... You are ... You want me to go to the Tonys?" Jessie bolted up, her face as red as a pepper. "Fine. I'll go! But you're going with me."

"I already said I would."

"Are you sure you're man enough to handle it?"

"Big deal. I put on my monkey suit and drink expensive champagne all night."

Jessie looked like fireworks were about to go off inside her head. Instead she dashed up the stairs without looking back.

Nick chuckled. Andrew wanted Jessie back on the stage, and Nick had obliged. Nick was determined to continue to push Jessie back into the land of the living. Let her hate him. Plenty of women did.

Nick chuckled again. Meanwhile, Abigail Forrester was an interesting woman. Fiery. Beautiful. And devoted to her friends.

*

Nick tossed his reading glasses onto the desk and rubbed the bridge of his nose. Eight in the morning. He'd been up all night poring over the police reports. Christ, he was turning into a bat.

He looked at the document in front of him. Wexley's statement. Wexley claimed to have passed out on a friend's couch the night before Andrew was murdered. He went home with a terrible hangover around ten in the morning. Two hours after the shooting. The friend corroborated Wexley's statement.

But that wasn't what had kept Nick up all night. What kept him up was Paula Wexley, Ian's wife. The Wexleys lived on McDougal Street in Greenwich Village. They owned a two-bedroom apartment in one of the more affluent areas of the city. Where did the money come from? Not from Ian, with barely two nickels to scrape together in washed-up actors' purgatory. No, the money had to come from Paula.

He'd called an old buddy in D.C at three in the morning, a cop turned private investigator. Jack was doing an all-night surveillance and bored out of his mind. He said he'd look into Paula Wexley and get back to Nick early in the morning.

Nick scrubbed the stubble on his jaw and drifted to the terrace door. This was where his brother grew up. Andrew had walked these floors and played down in that yard. He'd probably climbed that tree and raked leaves in the fall. If he and Andrew had grown up together, they'd have shared secrets and jokes. They'd have protected each other and argued like hell, the way brothers did. Maybe if they'd grown up together, Andrew wouldn't be lying in a cold grave at the age of thirty-five.

Nick turned out the desk lamp and wandered into the bedroom. Spotting the flowered tin on the bureau, he picked it up. Chelsea's letters to her long-lost son. For the first time in his life, he was actually curious about his biological parents. Nick snapped the tin open and pulled out a letter at random.

Dearest Patrick,

It's been a month since the nurse at the hospital ripped you from my arms. I cried and begged her not to take you but I'd signed the forms. Jason convinced me not to change my mind. I haven't stopped crying since. Jason keeps telling me it was a decision we both made. I thought you'd be better off with parents who were married and could give you a good home. I was worried I wouldn't be able to give you nice things.

But then I couldn't do it. I kept hoping that when Jason saw you he would want you, too. Now I don't know where you are. I miss you so much. Somehow, someday, I'm going to find you. I promise you, Patrick.

I feel better having written this letter. It's as if you can hear me. Thank you, my beautiful little boy.

I love you.

Mom.

Nick dropped into the rocker. After almost forty years of bitterness, he was having trouble embracing the reality that Chelsea Brady had loved him. That she'd regretted giving him away.

Nick's cell phone rang. "McDeare."

"It's Jack. I got your info. I put Paula Wexley's name into the system. The computer lit up like the Fourth of July."

"And?"

"She's connected. To the Martinelli family."

Nick's heart began to pound. "How?"

"Her maiden name's Zappella. Roberto Martinelli's closest confidante is Aldo Zappella. Paula's his sister."

*

Jessie's party in Nick's honor was three days later. As the gala wound down, Nick slumped against the refrigerator, a glass of bourbon in his hand. He couldn't wait for the guests to go. Jessie and Mary had been preparing for the festivities since the night Abbie had come home. Nick had retreated to his suite, using the precious time to take the police report apart, word for word. And stay out of Jessie's way.

Nick glanced around the kitchen at the stragglers. Actors. Self-centered, pushy actors, dressed in anything they thought would grab attention. Nick looked down at his own attire. A pale gray suit with a charcoal gray shirt and a silk tie that shimmied both shades to perfection. As a rule, Nick lived in jeans and T-shirts, but residing in Hong Kong had enabled him to fill his closet with the finest materials in the world. He was used to beautiful women flocking to his side when he chose to dress for success. But the females at this soiree seemed more interested in what a famous author might do for their careers than in Nick McDeare. Jessie stood out from the self-involved glitter like a diamond in a mess of glass and glue.

Nick scanned the crowd. Besides himself, Barton and his partner were the only non-thespians. Bushman had been following Abbie around for hours. And Abbie was sticking to Gianni Fosselli like a tick to a dog. She was wearing a dress that would stop traffic on the George Washington Bridge. A skin-tight yellow strapless thing with a slit from knee to hip. Nick licked his lips and admired her breasts, two juicy grapefruits that appeared to be standing on their own. Abbie was chatting away in Italian with Gianni. Fluent in Italian himself, Nick had been eavesdropping on their conversation all evening. It was the party's most entertaining event.

Jessie swung through the door from the dining room, arms full of dirty dishes, her apron hiding her violet sheath. Nick thought she looked stunning. Jessie's dress was long-sleeved with a high neckline. It clung to her sleek body, making a man fantasize about what was underneath.

Seeing Jessie yawn, Nick smothered a smile. She had a right to be tired. Jogging each day. Spending every spare hour in preparation for the party. Working all night cleaning out the attic. But she'd survived eight nights without a pill, and Nick was proud of her contrary self.

Barton sidled over to Nick, a bottle of beer in his hand. Barton's idea of dressing up was changing his shirt. Tonight he wore khaki slacks, a crumbled white shirt, and a jacket that looked like a bag of burlap. "What happened?" Lyle cracked. "You were the life of the party."

"Funny man." Nick sipped his bourbon. "I'm used to running through my bag of social tricks to sell books. My brother wasn't the only actor in the family."

A middle-aged man with long hair, wire-rimmed glasses, and a bandanna tied around his forehead strolled past Nick with his arm around a girl who looked sixteen. "I hate actors," Nick muttered.

"They were Andrew's peers. You haven't met the worst of them yet. Wexley." Barton took a swig of beer. "You've read the police report by now. What do you think of Ian Wexley?"

"So you want my opinion?"

"You're the one who said we should work together."

"Let's take a walk."

Drinks in hand, the two men wandered out of the brownstone, halting inside the iron fence. "Okay," Barton said. "Who do you like for your brother's killer?"

"It sure as hell wasn't your report's serial killer. The M.O. was the same, but the victim wasn't. And your Pervert Killer doesn't strike in the middle of a crowd. Cute name, by the way."

"The press came up with that handle." Lyle took a chug of beer. "I don't think it was the Perv either, but the department's been on my back for two years to hand Brady's case over to the Perv's Special Task Force. The hell with that."

"One of two men killed Andrew. Wexley or Fosselli."

"Which one?"

"My gut says Fosselli." Nick slid a hand in his pocket. "In Gianni's mind, Andrew stole Jessie and Anthony from him. If Gianni had known that Jessie was carrying his child, he would've returned to New York immediately. I've spent some time in Italy. Nothing matters more to an Italian man than his son."

"What about his mistress?"

"She comes after the son. We know Fosselli sold the cruise line to Martinelli," Nick continued. "Which means Gianni had the contacts to have Andrew killed. Jessie says Fosselli's not a violent man, that he couldn't even stand up to his grandfather. I think she's wrong. Beneath that suave demeanor lives a man who would think nothing of snuffing out a life."

"Wexley's just as ruthless. Maybe more so."

Nick rattled the ice cubes in his glass. Now was the time to drop another nugget in the cop's lap. "Did you know Paula Wexley's maiden name is Zappella?"

Lyle stared at Nick, his mouth ajar. "As in Aldo Zappella?"

"Paula's Aldo's sister."

"Are you purposely trying to humiliate me, McDeare?"

"Nah. If I was doing it on purpose you'd be flattened by now."

Barton took a gulp of his beer and collapsed against the fence. "So Fosselli's not the only one with connections. All this time I've been thinking Wexley pulled the trigger personally. You saw his record. Assault and battery. Attempted rape. Got off each time. Hell, he still could've done it up close and personal. He could've gone to his brother-in-law for the weapon and the cover."

"Maybe."

Lyle grimaced. "What really sucks is Andrew's shooting was set up to look like the Perv's handiwork. The department's kept the Perv's MO under wraps. Which means the NYPD has an informant on its payroll."

"C'mon, Lieutenant. You and I both know that the mob has their hand everywhere. They can get any information they want with the snap of a finger."

"Now it's a tossup as to the killer."

"My money's on Fosselli."

"I was leaning towards Wexley from the get-go. Now that his wife's connected, I like Wexley more than ever." Barton glanced at Nick. "Should make for an interesting partnership. Tomorrow let's start by interviewing—"

"Hold it. I fly to D.C. tomorrow. An interview for my new book." No way could Nick cancel. It had taken months to set up this meeting.

"When are you back in New York?"

"When I get here. I've got a book tour coming up in June so we better take advantage of May."

"I thought finding your brother's killer was your number-one priority."

"I have a job, just like you. Are you dropping those twenty other cases to concentrate on Andrew's?"

"You've got an answer for everything, don't you?" Lyle jingled his keys in his pocket. "This is already May fourth. That doesn't leave us much time."

"I don't need much time. I have a short list of people I want to interview."

"Forget the I business, McDeare. We have a lot of people to interview."

*

Jessie gathered the dirty plates on the secluded back porch, relieved to have a few moments to herself. After two years in hibernation, her social skills were creaky. Thank God, surprisingly enough, for Nick. The loner was adept at mingling with people. When she'd questioned him about it, he'd winked and reminded her book tours meant charming strangers you never had to see again.

Gianni materialized at Jessie's side. "I've been trying to find a moment alone with you all evening." He took the plates from her hands and set them on a table. "Abigail is an interesting woman, but I think she enjoys the sound of her own voice more than I do. Nicholas finally took her off my hands for a while."

"Nick?" Why would Nick want to talk to Abbie? The two had hardly spoken since that first evening. "Where are they?"

"I don't know. Maybe the study. Could we sit down for a moment? ... Jessica?"

"Hmm?"

"Could we sit down?" Gianni repeated.

"Sure." Jessie dropped onto the wicker divan. "Is something wrong?"

"Not at all." Gianni eased down beside her, opening the button of his black silk jacket. "Jessica, I heard you talking with your friends tonight about going to the Tony Awards. That will be a big night for you. A return of sorts, yes?"

Jessie nodded. Every time she envisioned walking out on that stage without Andrew, a lump lodged in her throat. She didn't know how she was going to get through it.

"I know how difficult it will be for you. Andrew and all. I'm sure it will be emotional." Gianni took a deep breath and covered her hand with his palm. "I would very much like to escort you that night, Jessica. I'm sure you could use a steady arm to support you. I've been your support before. I can be again."

Jessie blinked, speechless. Thankfully, Gianni didn't seem to notice. Jessie could feel his palm sweating. She freed her hand, using it to brush a strand of hair behind her ear.

"I want to make that evening as easy as possible for you," Gianni continued. "You can't do this alone. And I'm sure the press won't make a fuss about me being with you. After all, I've been a friend of the family for years."

Jessie wavered. Should she tell Gianni she'd already asked Nick? She didn't want to hurt him. But why should he be hurt? Nick was her brother-in-law, family, not some hot date.

"Gianni, that's very thoughtful of you. And I'm sure you'd be able to keep me together for the evening. It's just ... I asked Nick to take me." Seeing his crestfallen face, Jessie added quickly, "Let me explain. My appearance at the Tonys will be my first time back onstage since Andrew died. Everyone will want to see if I fall on my face without my husband at my side. I don't need any whispers about the man I'm with on top of it. If I go with my brother-in-law, everyone will accept it." She looked up at him. "Do you understand? He's family. Real family."

Gianni stared at the Oriental rug and said nothing for a moment. "Do you really think the press will question your being with me, a friend of the family who knew your husband well?"

"Look at the fuss they made over an innocent jog with Nick! They'll jump on anything for a headline. But they can't say a word about Nick this time. It's all been said and dealt with. Do you see what I mean?"

"Honestly? No. No, I don't, Jessica." His back as stiff as a church spire, Gianni rose and stalked to the window, looking into the night. "How much longer is this going to go on? It's been two years since Andrew died."

Jessie sighed and pushed herself off the divan. "I'm too tired to get into this with you tonight. I'm not ready to date again. In fact, I may never be ready. I was Andrew's wife. Now I'm his widow. That's who I'll always be." Jessie felt so tired, like she was a hundred years old.

Gianni spun around to face her. "Don't be a fool. You're young. You have your whole life ahead of you. You and I--"

"The subject is closed." Jessie turned on her heel and escaped to the hot kitchen. It was time Gianni realized that there was no great love affair waiting to be rekindled. That had died years ago. And now she was dead inside, too. There was no fire inside her, just cold ashes.

Jessie looked around the deserted kitchen. Where was everybody? She wandered across the hall and into the study. Nick and Abbie sat side by side on the leather sofa, their backs to her, talking. Jessie inched closer. "What's going on, guys? Oh, wait. Let me guess. I'm interrupting one of Nick McDeare's infamous come-ons, right?"

Nick glanced over his shoulder at Jessie. "Great timing. I was just getting started. A few more minutes and ..." Nick eyed Abbie, his gaze lingering on her lips.

Abbie laughed. "Asking me about Andrew's childhood's a come-on? That's getting started?"

"Hey, give me a little more time, sweetie. I'd have you purring in a matter of minutes. Forget Gianni. Besides, that steamroller approach you took with him tonight's a turnoff. I'm surprised you haven't learned that by your age."

"I'm some geriatric with baggy hose?" Abbie stood up. "Look, you egomaniac. The only reason I'm nice to you is because you're Andrew's brother. Jessie filled me in about your gentle touch with the ladies."

Jessie gulped. "Abbie, I --"

"So get this through your egotistical head. You and I will not be taking a tumble beneath the sheets,"

Jessie realized Nick and Abbie had forgotten she was there, an unwilling spectator.

"Oh, get real. You came on to me the moment you walked through the front door. You're attracted to me and you know it."

"You're unbelievable."

"I don't hear you denying it. Admit it. You like me."

"I like Italians. You don't qualify."

"You like men, baby. Any male with a healthy libido who'll give you the time of day."

"Go to hell!" Abbie headed for the door. "Good night, Jessie. I'm going to bed."

Nick laughed as he stood up. "Sure you don't want some company?"

Jessie glowered at her brother-in-law in Abbie's wake. Would this night never end? "Nice job. You just ticked off your brother's best friend."

"No, I didn't." Nick picked up his glass and swirled the ice cubes. "To Abbie, fighting's foreplay."

"Don't use Abbie as one of your sex objects."

"I haven't heard that phrase in years. She's a woman. I'm a man."

Jessie could feel her face burn. She turned and headed for the hallway. Nick was obnoxious. It was his second nature.

"Hey, Jess?"

Jessie pivoted. "What?"

"What if I'm the sex object and Abbie's the user?"

Jessie left the room without another word, Nick's laughter ringing in her ears. Sometimes she almost came close to liking Nick McDeare. Sometimes she plain loathed him. But she had to admit she never felt dead with him.

*

Nick was too wired to sleep. He sat at his desk going over his notes on Andrew's case. He had the nagging feeling he was missing something, something that had been a red flag when he'd first seen it. He carefully reread page after page, finally placing a finger on an entry. Ah, there it was.

Gianni Fosselli's parents were killed in their Genoa villa when they surprised a burglar. Nick reread the police report, then flipped through the official file and pulled Fosselli's statement. Gianni had told the police the same thing. And Barton had confirmed his statement with the Italian authorities. The

Fosselli Genoa villa was ransacked, the parents found dead in an outer building Paolo Fosselli had used as his office.

Nick had lived in Siena for a year while researching a book. While there, he'd worked with a private investigator, Ozzie Mancuso, one of the best. Nick had kept in touch with Mancuso over the years. Siena was further down the coast and inland from Genoa, but Ozzie had contacts everywhere.

Right now it would be morning in Siena. Nick put a call through and moments later he was speaking with his old friend in Italian. After exchanging pleasantries, Nick got to the point. Would Ozzie look into the deaths of Paolo and Teresa Fosselli? "You and I both know that the Italian authorities look the other way if there's a whiff of Le Cosa Nostra being involved in a murder," Nick explained. "Something's not sitting right with me about this. Oh, and one more thing. This couple's son, Gianni. See what you can find out about him, too."

CHAPTER 11

One Week Later

The man known as Cobra slipped behind a flower stand at Tenth and West Streets and punched in a number on a disposable cell. "It's me. I heard from my contact in D.C. McDeare'll be back in New York tomorrow."

"What's he been doing in D.C.?"

"Hanging around with some retired reporter. All the chatter was about his book and spy stuff in London. Not a mention of Andrew Brady.

"Did your friend check McDeare's home computer?"

"Yeah. Nothing. Apparently, everything's in the laptop he's got with him."

"We need to get to McDeare's laptop. Anything else?"

"Yeah." Cobra snickered. "As per my contact, McDeare's screwing some model in D.C. with the biggest bazookas he's ever seen."

*

"Abigail, what a pleasant surprise." Gianni trotted down Oceano's sweeping staircase and kissed Abigail on both cheeks. The woman was as subtle as a gladiator's short sword.

"I've always loved that quaint Italian custom," Abigail said. "Did you know that the Dutch kiss you three times?"

"The Dutch are obsessive." Gianni stepped back to admire her scarlet pantsuit. "You certainly know how to wear color. What brings you here on this beautiful spring day?"

"I was out apartment hunting and thought I'd drop by to see what your place looked like." She glanced around the restaurant. "Very classy, Gianni."

"Thank you. Have you had dinner? Would you like to join me?"

"I'd love to." Abigail smiled, Gianni's eyes fastening on her glossy lips. Gianni led Abigail to a corner table by the window. He snapped his fingers at a waiter and ordered a bottle of Bolla. She was really making this too easy.

After chitchat about the weather and the merits of California versus New York, Abigail raised the subject of Jessie's return to the stage for the Tonys. "Jessie's terrified. I'm worried she's not going to be able to pull this off. Andrew was always her anchor."

"I offered to escort her, but she wants Nicholas to do the honors."

"Oh, God, don't mention that man's name to me."

Gianni hid his surprise. "Why?"

"Nick McDeare's the most obnoxious man I've ever met. He's nothing like Andrew."

"I won't argue with you." Gianni met Abigail's caramel eyes. Idly, he wondered if Jessica would be jealous if he slept with Abigail. "Anthony told me Nicholas has gone back to Washington."

"He'll be back. There's too much here that he wants. Call it my feminine intuition, but I think Nick likes living in the brownstone his brother called home. With Jessie and Anthony." She leaned forward and whispered, "If you ask me, I think Nick wouldn't mind slipping into Andrew's life."

"Are you saying Nicholas McDeare is attracted to Jessica?" Gianni's heart leapt into his throat.

"I wouldn't call it attracted. Nick sees women as utility workers. Just between us, I think he'd like to utilize Jessie so he can make the brownstone his permanent residence."

The waiter uncorked their wine and poured a small amount in Gianni's glass. Gianni waved him off impatiently, almost hitting him in the face. The young man swiftly filled Abigail's glass and backed away.

Abigail leaned across the table. "Look, Gianni, I don't know if you're aware of this, but I'm one of the few people who knows the truth about Anthony."

"Jessica told me."

"I know how much you love your son. If I were you, I'd make sure I spent a lot of time in that brownstone when Nick's in town. Anthony's crazy about his uncle, and it looks like the feeling's mutual. I have to admit that Nick's great with his nephew." She took a sip of wine, swirling it in her mouth. "This is excellent."

"You're alarming me, Abigail."

"I don't mean to. Truly. It's just that ... I get the feeling Nick's used to getting what he wants. And Jessie and Anthony may be what he's set his sights on."

"You really think Nicholas wants Jessica?" Gianni couldn't believe what he was hearing. But why would Abigail lie?

"I think Nick wants his brother's life and he'll do what's necessary to get it, including marry Jessie. Look at the man. Sure, he's written books, but he has no personal life. He antagonizes everyone he meets. He treats women horribly, so he can't keep a relationship."

Abigail was an insightful woman. "I did a little research on Nicholas McDeare and his reputation with women," Gianni said. "I didn't like what I read."

"You know how trusting Jessie is. She's blind where Nick is concerned, Andrew's brother. Sure, she knows Nick's a ... well, never mind. But Nick's family, so Jessie will forgive him anything. If Nick turns on the charm around Jessie, who knows what can happen? I saw him in action. He came on to me, and I have to admit, um, he's very sexy."

Those full lips pouted, distracting Gianni for a minute. He poured more wine into his glass and drained it. "You're right. I'm going to have to watch the situation closely."

"Listen, I have a suggestion." Abigail's eyes sparkled with mischief. "Want to go to the Tonys with me? If Nick's going to romance Jessie, he'll pour it on that night. If you're there, I think he'll back off. He knows your history with Jessie. I'm going because the Tony Committee wants everyone close to Bill Rudolph to be there." Abigail smiled, licking her bottom lip shiny. "Interested?"

Gianni smiled back. "I like the way you think, Abigail."

*

Jessie threw back the quilt on the bed and bolted up. It was no use. She couldn't fall asleep. She'd tried everything. Nothing worked. Damn Nick for taking away her pills. Another black mark against her brother-in-law. Jessie squinted into the dark, thinking. She vaguely remembered hiding some pills in a blazer pocket in the back of her closet. Jessie swung out of bed.

After rummaging through her clothes, she came up empty-handed. Feeling silly, Jessie hustled out of the walk-in closet, hooking her foot on something bulky. She fell and struck her forehead on a shelf. Blood trickled down her face. "Damn!" What the hell did she trip over? Lifting up on her elbow, Jessie spotted Andrew's dance bag. She sat up and skated her fingers across the black leather, as soft as seal.

Tony Kendle had given his daughter and Andrew dance bags when they were accepted into Juilliard. Jessie's bag had worn out years ago, but Andrew had taken loving care of his. When she and Andrew were working, this bag went everywhere with them, filled with music, stage makeup, scripts and little bits and pieces of their lives. The last time the bag was used was on that cruise. It was draped over Jessie's shoulder when she was rushed to the hospital. She'd held onto it for hours, waiting for Andrew to come out of surgery. For months afterward, she'd kept the bag by the bed, touching it like a talisman when she couldn't sleep.

Fighting tears, Jessie flashed back to tucking Andrew's journals in the bag for safekeeping after Anthony discovered them. Jessie wiped her eyes, seeing blood mixed with her tears on her hand. She must be a mess. Secreting the precious bundle back into the closet, she padded into the bathroom and looked in the mirror. Blood welled from the cut. Her nose was running, and her eyes were shot with red. She looked like a wartime refugee on a news clip.

And Nick ... Oh God, Nick would notice the cut immediately. He had a way of staring at her with those eyes ... She took a deep breath. The heck with it. She'd tell him the truth. She'd tripped. He knew what a klutz she was. Jessie blew her nose and covered the gash with a band-aid.

Feeling better, she headed downstairs, settled into the breakfast nook and filled a snifter with brandy. Jessie winced at the first gulp, then took another. The house was so quiet, the only sound the ticking of the grandfather clock. Hamlet perched on the island, his lantern eyes alert. Jessie was suddenly chilled. "Andrew?" she whispered.

Silence.

A wave of loneliness swept through her. Jessie missed her husband tonight. She wanted to hear Andrew's laugh. His laugh ... Jessie gasped. She couldn't remember what Andrew's laugh sounded like! Dear God, what did it sound like? And then she remembered and relaxed. But it wasn't Andrew's laugh, she realized with surprise. It was Nick's. So much like Andrew's.

Nick. He was coming back to New York tomorrow. Nick could be a pain, but the house seemed empty without him. How had that happened?

*

When Nick returned to the brownstone the following morning, he found Mary stirring a huge pot of Marinara sauce. "God, that smells great."

Mary grinned. "It's Gianni's recipe. I'm making lasagna. Anthony loves it."

"He's not the only one. Where's Jessie?"

"Out back."

Nick found Jessie on her hands and knees, surrounded by gardening tools, focused on a small shapely tree with purple leaves. "Hey, Jess. The prodigal has returned."

"Welcome back, prodigal." Jessie rose, removing her gardening gloves.

"What's with the tree?"

"It's not just any tree. It's a plum tree. I'm fertilizing it." Lifting a watering can, she sprinkled around the base of the tree. "Dad bought this for Andrew when he moved in with us. It was up to Andrew to make sure the tree survived. Well," Jessie said with a laugh, "you would've thought this tree was Andrew's child. He fussed over it year round. It's old for a plum, but it's still thriving, even though he's gone."

Nick eyed Jessie closely. "You look rested."

"I feel good."

Nick had been worried Jessie would hit the pills again while he was gone. He hoped he was wrong. "Why the band-aid?"

"I tripped. Jessie the klutz strikes again." She chuckled as she gathered her tools, not looking at him.

"How did it happen?"

"The usual way. I tripped over something." She started for the small tool shed.

"Where?"

"What is this? Twenty questions? I tripped. It's no big deal." She deposited her tools in the shed.

Nick's heart sank. "C'mon. What really happened?"

Jessie spun around. "I'm getting tired of your calling me a liar."

"This is about the pills, isn't it?"

Nick watched as surprise flashed across her face. Jessie started for the house. "I'm putting an end to this inquisition."

Nick grabbed her arm and whipped her around. "I'm not into playing games. Tell me the truth. Did you take any pills while I was away?"

Jessie jerked her arm away. "Who the hell do you think you are? I'll answer your questions about Andrew's murder. Otherwise, stay out of my personal life. Isn't that what you always say to me?" She ran for the porch. Nick caught up in two long strides. "Leave me alone!"

"Not yet. Look, this isn't about your personal life." Jessie looked as reasonable as a hornet. Nick clasped her hands. "This is about Anthony. This is about a promise I made to you. I said I would help you every step of the way with the pills, and I intend to keep my promise. You may not think much of me, but there's one thing you can always count on. I never break a promise." He softened his tone. "I won't be angry if you slipped up. I know better than anyone how hard it is to give up those pills. We can start over. No big deal." He looked into those blue eyes. "Tell me the truth. Did you take any pills?"

"No." Jessie's voice was a whisper. "But I tried. I thought ... maybe I had some hidden in the closet. When I was searching, I tripped over Andrew's dance bag." She bit her lip, her eyes filling with tears.

"Good girl. I'm proud of you." Nick wrapped his arms around her. "You got through a week on your own without pills. You're stronger than you or your friends realize. God, it's uncanny."

"What is?" She peeked up at him.

"Andrew's dance bag. Andrew was looking out for you in my absence. Obviously, he doesn't want you taking pills either." Chuckling, he tapped Jessie's nose. "I'll see you later. I have to meet Barton."

Whistling, Nick slung his jacket over his shoulder and left the brownstone. It would be a relief not to have to worry about Jessie taking pills when he was out of town. Andrew would watch over her for him.

*

Nick and Barton drove out to Oakdale, Long Island to interview the security guard on duty the morning Andrew Brady was shot. Joseph Salerno was the witness who'd verified Vito Secchi and Aldo Zappella were nowhere near Andrew at the time. "So we take it from the top," Lyle said as they climbed out of the car. "Do it all over again."

Nick eyed Salerno's home, painted frame chipped, front garden overgrown. "And see if a new memory shakes out. I've seen it happen before. Especially when we surprise him like this, assuming he's home."

He was. "Mr. Salerno," Lyle said, when the white-haired man opened the door, "I'm Lieutenant Barton, NYPD, and this is Nick McDeare, an investigative reporter assisting me on the Andrew Brady murder case. You may remember me."

Nick quickly sized up the man. Salerno looked wary. He was wearing saggy corduroys, a frayed shirt, and a cardigan sweater that could use a run through the wash cycle. Nick knew that the Port Authority of New York and New Jersey paid its security guards well. This man looked like he ate in a soup kitchen every day.

"Yeah, I remember you," Joseph said. "I told you everything two years ago."

"We're retracing our steps," Barton said, "seeing if we overlooked something. Mind if we come in?" Lyle was already halfway through the door.

Salerno stared at Nick, blocking Lyle's entry. "You're that famous author, right?"

Nick nodded. "I'm also Andrew Brady's brother."

"His ...? Oh, right. I read about that."

"Would you mind if we came in and talked for a few minutes? We'd really appreciate your time." Nick kept his voice friendly. "Nothing new, Mr. Salerno. You've done it before."

Salerno continued to stare. Finally, he nodded and led them to a den, collapsing into a weathered recliner. Nick and Lyle sat across from him on the sofa.

"Refresh my memory please," Barton asked. "You've been a security guard at the West Side Shipping Terminal for how long?"

"Forty-two years. I retired a year ago."

"You probably knew all the VIP's down at the piers, right?" Nick asked.

"Sure. Over the years I got to know 'em real well."

"And is it safe to say that you were able to spot someone who didn't belong?" Nick continued.

"Anyone suspicious stood out. That's what I was trained to look for."

Lyle showed the man a picture of Wexley. "It's been a while since you've seen this, so take your time. You ever see this man around the piers?"

Joseph squinted at the photo. "His face seems familiar, like I said last time. But I still can't place it. I seen him but I can't remember where or when."

Barton handed him another photo. "What about this man?"

Salerno chuckled. "Gianni Fosselli. I knew him. His family owned the Italian Marine Line. Can't say that I liked him much. Don't think I said that last time."

"Why didn't you like him?" Barton asked.

"He thought he was better than everybody. Treated us like we worked for him and not the Port Authority. He was around a lot for a while, and then he just up and went back home. He was gone a long time. Then he came back for that last cruise."

Nick saw a glass ashtray on the coffee table with two cigarette butts, both smoked down to the filter. He reached into his pocket and pulled out his own cigarettes. "You mind?"

Joseph shook his head.

Smiling, Nick extended the pack to the old man. Salerno took one and accepted a light. Nick lit up and placed the pack on the coffee table. Trying not to quiver in ecstasy at his first smoke in two years, he asked when Fosselli first showed up before the cruise.

Joseph took a deep drag on the cigarette. "I seen him the day of the anniversary sailing. But before that I don't remember."

Barton showed Salerno another photo. "The kid's name's Eduardo Santangelo. We already know he was in the terminal that morning." Lyle scanned his notes. "Last time we talked, you didn't remember seeing him. Do you remember now?"

Nick watched a lightning flash of terror streak across the old man's face. "No, I ... still don't remember seeing him. Those other two Italian guys were standing a few feet away from me. That's how I knew they didn't do it."

He glanced at the picture again and handed it back to Barton as if he'd stuck his hand in broken glass.

"Did you know him? Think hard," Barton said, holding up the picture of Eduardo again.

"He was a bartender or something. Trouble with a capital 'T,' always scrapping with the other crew members. He used to get off the ship every Saturday and make a bunch of phone calls. All them guys did. Calling their wives or girlfriends or mothers back home."

"Did you know my brother?" Nick kept his voice soft.

"Sure. I knew him and his wife. Tony Kendle was a cruise director and both them kids were around the piers when they were growing up. They were real nice people."

"Did you see my brother that morning, before he was shot?"

"Yeah. Andrew Brady disembarked a couple minutes before everybody else. I figured he was getting off the Milano early because he wanted to avoid the crowds. You know. Being a celebrity and all. He and his family boarded early on sailing day for the same reason."

"Didn't you wonder where the rest of his family was?" Barton asked, pocketing the photo.

"You accusing me of something?"

"No one's accusing you of anything, Mr. Salerno," Nick said. "We're here because of your trained eye. We need all the help we can get. Now, did you see what happened that day? Did you see my brother sitting in that chair along the wall?"

"No. It was getting busy in the terminal by then. There was a ship from South America delayed for three hours, supposed to dock on the other side of the terminal. Everybody waiting was jabbering away in Spanish, milling around. My Spanish is pretty good, living in the city and all, but these people talked so fast."

"But you helped them, gave them directions in Spanish?" Nick asked, intent on keeping Salerno talking. The timeframe was crucial. The more he knew, the more vivid the crime scene, the better.

"Yeah. There was this one Hispanic lady who could hardly speak English, real nervous, and she asked me about the ship. I told her it would be late into port so she sat down along the wall. That's when we heard a scream and this lady, she up and ran out of the terminal like a frightened mouse."

"Wait a minute," Barton said. "A Hispanic lady? You never mentioned her in your original interview."

"I didn't? Well, she didn't shoot Andrew Brady because I was watching her when she, uh, when she got up and ran, you know, from the place."

Barton flipped through his notes. "Not one person mentioned a Hispanic lady."

Nick shot Barton a look. "Mr. Salerno," Nick said, "let me make sure I have this straight. This Hispanic woman was sitting along the wall when the scream was heard. Then she got up and ran from the terminal, right?"

"Yeah."

"You just gave us a new piece of the puzzle. That lady may have seen who shot Andrew. Do you remember what she looked like?" Nick asked.

Joseph shrugged. "It's been a long time."

"I'll get a sketch artist over here pronto," Barton muttered, scribbling in his notebook.

Nick saw irritation cross Salerno's face. "Mr. Salerno," he said quickly, "those two Italian men, uh, Zappella and Secchi. Did you know them? I mean, had they been around the piers much before that morning?"

"No."

Nick exchanged a glance with Barton. "Then what made you notice them? You said the terminal was busy. What made them catch your attention?"

"I don't know. I don't remember."

Nick reached into his briefcase, producing a map of the interior of The West Side Cruise Ship Terminal. Nick had done an expose of waterfront corruption a few years back. He knew the place inside and out. In the upper right quadrant, Nick had marked a red X, signifying where Andrew was shot. A row of public pay phones ran down the center of the cavernous room, wide crossovers at each end. "Now, will you please show me where you were standing at the time of the shooting?"

Joseph pointed to a spot on the opposing side of the terminal, in the lower left quadrant. Nick drew a circle on the spot and wrote the initials JS in it. "And where were Zappella and Secchi?" Salerno signified that the two men were only a few feet away from him. "Okay. Now the Hispanic lady. Where was she sitting along the wall?" Joseph pointed across the terminal, to the far lower right corner. "Okay, I've got it now. The phones running down the middle of the terminal would've blocked your view of the shooting, but you had a clear shot of the Hispanic lady directly across from you at the far end of the terminal."

"That's what I been saying."

Nick folded the map and returned it to his briefcase. "Thank you, sir. You've been extremely helpful with this Hispanic lady. She may have seen the shooting."

"Okay, that's all for today," Barton said rising. "I'm getting a sketch artist over here this afternoon."

Joseph Salerno glared at the lieutenant. "I'm busy this afternoon."

"Look, this is damned more--"

Nick turned to Lyle. "Hey," he said impatiently, "can I have a moment alone with Mr. Salerno, if you don't mind?" Barton's look of surprise morphed into anger. He turned his back on Nick and Salerno and stalked from the room.

"Sorry about the lieutenant," Nick said gently. "He's frustrated, that's all. How long have you been married, Mr. Salerno?"

Joseph looked down. "Almost forty years. Angela died three months ago of cancer."

"I'm sorry," Nick said softly. "I know firsthand that kind of pain. But at least you had those forty years. Jessica Brady only had six years with her husband. She's raising their son by herself. She needs answers, Mr. Salerno. So do I. Whoever did this to my brother robbed Andrew and me of the chance to finally meet." Nick reached into his pocket, handing the man a card. "That's my cell phone number. Call me at any hour of the day or night if you remember something. Anything. And it would be extremely helpful if you'd work with a sketch artist. Will you do that, sir?"

Joseph nodded. "Yeah. Okay."

"When would be a convenient time for you?"

"Uh, tomorrow's fine. Anytime. But make sure the lieutenant stays away, okay?"

*

"You can send your sketch artist over tomorrow morning," Nick said as he climbed into the car.

"That worked like a well-oiled machine."

"Not bad for two rookie partners." Nick absently searched for his cigarettes.

"You left them back there. You also don't usually smoke."

"Oh, right. Guess I forgot. I stopped smoking for the most part when Andrew died."

"But you like to carry them around."

"Yeah." Nick had forgotten on purpose. That shabby house. Cigarettes smoked down to the filter. The man's worn clothes. Salerno had probably spent his life savings on his wife's illness. "Joseph Salerno's lonely. I'm betting he eventually gives me a call on the premise of remembering something."

"He's hiding something," Lyle said, as they pulled out of the driveway. "He's scared. I had that feeling before. It's stronger now."

Nick glanced over his shoulder at the house. Joseph Salerno was watching from behind a grimy curtain as the car pulled away from the curb. "I agree. I think Salerno knows exactly who killed Andrew. We have to take everything he says with a grain of salt. And pick away at it until we get to the truth."

CHAPTER 12

Two Weeks Later

"I've got a sketch of the Hispanic woman posted in all five boroughs," Lyle Barton told Nick. He pulled away from Midtown North.

"Good." Nick reached in his shirt pocket for a cigarette. He inhaled the rich scent, using all his self-control not to light up. It was Tony night and Jessie was a neurotic diva, swooping down on everyone. Nick was going to need every crutch in his arsenal to survive Jessie's nerves.

He eyed the city streets as Lyle threaded in and out of wall-to-wall traffic. It was the first week of June. Pushcarts selling Italian ices were doing a booming business. Air conditioners hummed. Movie theaters lured people into their cool cocoons. Central Park exploded with activity: touch football, neon-colored kites, dogs catching Frisbees, sun-bathers on the rocks and grass, joggers and rowboats, pedestrians on their cell phones.

Nick was finally going to meet the infamous Ian Wexley. He and Barton had spent the past two weeks methodically interviewing every available witness in the terminal that day. They were getting down to the end of the list, only Wexley and a handful of others left. Last week, Nick had spent a morning at the crime scene, soaking up the terminal's atmosphere on the same day and time Andrew had been killed. All to make it come alive so he could work the scene in his head.

"How's Jessie doing about tonight? Barton asked.

"She's driving Mary to drink, and Jeremy's popping tranquilizers like bubble gum. Anthony's been sticking to me, trying to stay out of his mother's way. Tell me," Nick asked, as they approached the West Village, "how does your partner feel when we exclude him from these interviews?"

"Pissed. But he finally agreed it's time for a fresh eye. This case is the only pimple on our record."

"How long have you been riding together?"

"Seven years."

"It's good?"

"The best." Barton double-parked in front of Wexley's apartment building on McDougal Street, propping the NYPD badge in the windshield. The doorman buzzed the apartment, and they rode the elevator to the eighth floor.

Wexley was waiting for them. "Let's make this quick," he snapped. "I have an appointment in half an hour."

Nick had seen pictures of Wexley. The suspect standing before him looked as much like those photographs as a cadaver like the living man. This

Wexley had bloodshot eyes, a puffy face, and stringy pewter hair. And he kept his hands tightly in his pockets to hide the shakes. Ian Wexley was an alcoholic.

Ian looked Nick up and down. "So you're the famous author. Amazing. Jessie loses Brady and a spare turns up. She's a pretty boring screw, don't you think?"

"Boring? Jessie?" Nick laughed. "Actually, I don't have much time either. I'm taking Jessie to the Tonys tonight. You remember what the Tony Awards are, don't you? They're given for excellence in--"

"Shut the fuck up and let's get on with it." Ian plopped down on the couch and took a gulp from a mug.

Nick snatched the drink and sniffed. "A touch early for scotch, don't you think?" He set the mug down hard on the coffee table, splashing the mahogany. Ian didn't seem to mind. His wife would just buy another one.

"A little case of nerves after my call this morning, Ian?" Barton cracked.

Wexley laughed. "And I thought actors had all the ego."

"Let's take it from the top, shall we?" Barton said. "Tell me once again where you were when Andrew Brady was shot."

"You have got to be the dumbest cop who ever wore a badge. Okay. One more time. I was asleep. On my friend's couch. I was hung over. I got home around ten. Ask my wife."

"Where is Paula, by the way?" Lyle perched on the arm of the couch.

"None of your business."

"Do me a favor. Next time have her here."

"There isn't going to be a next time. And why would I do you a favor?"

Barton grinned and pulled a small notebook from his breast pocket. "Is your friend, uh, Luke Fallon, still in town?"

"Yep."

"Tell me about you and Andrew," Nick said, sitting on the opposite couch arm from Barton.

Ian took another swig of liquid. "We hated each other. He was a malicious asshole who destroyed my career. He blackballed me with Bill Rudolph, the most powerful man on Broadway."

"You're sure about that?" Nick was about to muddy the waters, with Jessie's blessing.

"No one else would do something that fucked up."

"What if I told you it was Jessie who blackballed you?"

Ian looked up at Nick, his mouth open. "Brady was the one who screwed me over. Jessie's a dumb bitch, but she'd never do something-- "

"Jessie told me flat out she did it. She's been consumed with guilt that you killed the wrong person."

"Bullshit. This is a load of crap!"

"Jessie told Bill Rudolph you were trouble. She did it because of those incriminating photos you sent to Italy, the ones that showed Jessie and Gianni in compromising positions. Those photos put an old man in the hospital and drove a young woman to attempt suicide."

Ian bolted to his feet. "I'll say this one last time. I did not send those photos to Italy." He looked at Nick. "Okay?" Ian turned to Barton. "Got it? Are we through?"

"For now," Lyle said, pocketing his notebook. He and Nick started for the door. "Oh, by the way," Barton said, turning back to Wexley. "Why didn't you tell us Paula's maiden name was Zappella?"

For a brief moment Ian was Bambi, caught in the headlights. Regaining his composure, he said, "What's the big deal? What difference does it make?"

Nick's lips thinned. "You don't know? Two of Roberto Martinelli's men were in the terminal at the time of the shooting. One of them was Aldo Zappella. Your brother-in-law." Nick turned away. "Nice meeting you, Wexley."

Nick and Barton had barely cleared the front door before it slammed. They rode the elevator downstairs. "So, what do you think?" Barton asked.

"Wexley's tricky. His despicable personality takes center stage. You have to wade through the bullshit. His drinking could be important. He could even have killed Andrew in a blackout and not remember. Sure, it's possible Wexley killed Andrew, one way or another. Or it's possible Eduardo did Uncle Gianni a big favor and did the honors. A lot of things are possible."

*

Ian Wexley paced the living room, breathing hard. He punched in a number on his cell. "Aldo? It's Ian. Listen, I--"

"Well, well, if it isn't my favorite brother-in-law. Are you being a good little boy, Ian?"

"Listen, I just had a visit from--"

"Are you being good to my sister? Are you keeping your pants zipped?"

"Dammit, will you listen to me? That cop and Nick McDeare were just here. Nick McDeare! Now I've got this big-shot reporter all over me. Can't you do something about this?"

"McDeare was there?"

"Yeah. They're not going to let up on me."

There was silence at the other end of the line. "Don't worry," Zappella finally said. "It's being taken care of."

*

Jessie stood before the full-length mirror in her bedroom and dared one last look. Everyone was waiting for her. On the inside she was quivering like the last fall leaf in a strong wind. On the outside she looked … Jessie didn't know. The gown was a Henri original, black with bugle beads that would sparkle under the lights. Full-length and long-sleeved, the bodice was form fitting with a plunging neckline and back. The skirt boasted yards of floaty fabric with more layers of material underneath. The gown had movement. It had grace. But did the rest of her work?

A simple diamond choker, stud earrings, and a slender emerald bracelet were her only accessories. Gifts from Andrew. Jessie touched her throat. She'd feel her husband with her tonight. Damiano, Jessie's personal hairdresser, had

- 133 -

come to the house earlier to create her signature style. A simple French twist with fair wisps framing her face.

Jessie went to the window and took deep breaths, trying to calm her nerves. Two limos were parked outside the brownstone. A crowd had gathered across the street, including the paparazzi.

"I wish you were here tonight, Andrew." she whispered. "I can't remember the last time I walked onto a stage without you."

*

Abbie had spent a fortune on a white silk Valentino creation. She swept down the brownstone's back stairs, hoping Gianni appreciated her taste. "You're stunning," he said. "A vision." Abbie smiled. Sleeveless and high-necked, with tiny seed pearls sparkling in the light, the gown dropped straight to the floor with a deep slit up the back. "You look angelic in white."

She laughed. "No one's called me an angel me since I was five." Abbie straightened Gianni's tie. "You look spectacular yourself." Gianni was wearing an Armani tux. Very nouveau.

Gianni slipped an arm around Abbie and kissed her lightly on the lips.

"Well, thank you, sir."

"What did Jessica say when you told her I would be escorting you?"

"Not much. She knows I love Italian men," Abbie teased. Seeing his smile fade, she added, "Jessie hasn't been saying much of anything this week. She's a wreck."

"Maybe I should talk to her."

"I wouldn't. Her bedroom's a war zone. I just stopped by on my way down and she threw me out. As much I loathe the man, I don't envy Nick this evening. Tonight karma may get him for all his sins." She laughed lightly.

*

Nick straightened his cuffs and smoothed his jacket as he glanced into the mirror. He was wearing a classic black tuxedo. It fit his toned physique like a glove. Dark strands of hair spiked his forehead, accenting his eyes. Nick chuckled. Who knew what lucky lady would catch his eye over the course of the evening?

Coming down the back stairs, he met Mary on the second-floor landing. The unflappable Mary was a mess. "Nick, could you please talk to Jessie? She's holed up in her bedroom, a nervous wreck. She keeps telling me to give her more time. Time just ran out!"

Nick took a deep breath. "I'll see what I can do." He approached Jessie's bedroom hesitantly. Who knew what lurked on the other side of the door? A grizzly bear? A weeping willow longing for her pills? Nick had encountered too many creatures in the form of Jessie over the past week. He knocked lightly. "Jess? Are you ready?" No answer. "Jess?"

"Come in. If you dare."

He pushed the door open and stepped into the room. Jessie stood by the window, toying with her wedding rings. Nick froze, his eyes drifting from her chiseled face to her black satin heels. She was breathtakingly gorgeous, a slender column of femininity and grace, a marble statue come to life. The

- 134 -

elegant black gown set off her porcelain skin and upswept flaxen hair to perfection. My God.

"What's wrong?" Jessie asked quickly.

"Uh, nothing." Nick told himself to breathe again. He approached her. "Nothing's wrong. It's just that you, ah, you—"

"You hate the dress. On paper it looked fine, but now … I should've worn a brighter color."

"No. No, the dress is perfect. You're—"

"Tell me the truth. My hair's old-fashioned, and I'm wearing too much makeup. The stage lights wash you out, but less is more and—"

"Will you please shut up?" He stood before her. "You're beautiful. The dress, the hair, the makeup, beautiful."

A tiny smile tweaked her lips. "Really?"

Nick nodded. Jessie dropped her head. "I don't know if I can do this, Nick. Not without Andrew."

Nick took a step closer. Cupping her chin in his hand, he lifted her face and looked into those sky-blue eyes. "Yes you can, Jess. You can do it, for Andrew. He'll be standing right beside you." He watched her eyes glisten. "No tears. You'll crack your makeup." He finally made her laugh. "I'll make a deal with you, okay?"

"You and your deals."

"Hear me out. I think you'll like this one. If we leave now and you walk out on that stage and present Bill Rudolph with his award, I promise to be on my best behavior all night. You won't hear one sarcastic word. I'll be so nice you'll swear I'm Andrew instead of his dastardly brother. Deal?"

"This I have to see." She nodded, smiling tremulously. "Okay, deal."

Spotting a black beaded evening bag on the bed, Nick picked it up. "Ready?"

"No." They both laughed. Jessie took the bag and tucked her hand under his arm. "Are you sure you're ready?"

"For what?

"The lion's den. The vicious world of the theater."

*

Eduardo felt on top of the world. Roberto Martinelli, the Big Man, had given him more than he could ever hope for. Eduardo had a beautiful apartment on the Upper West Side, and Martinelli was using him in the organization in a major way.

Tonight he had a few errands on his to-do list. Then he had a rendezvous with a luscious blond babe. He intended to screw her until she couldn't walk. America! What a great country. Anything and everything was possible.

*

Nick and Jessie glided down the staircase. Anthony waited for them, camera in hand. As they moved into the hallway, Nick saw a small group of Jessie's friends gathered behind him. He knew Gianni, Abbie ,and Jeremy. Beside them were an older man with a mane of silver hair and an aristocratic-looking woman. The man stepped forward, taking Jessie's face between his hands. "Thanks for doing this, dear girl. How are you doing?"

"Um, nervous." She turned to Nick. "Bill and Marcy Rudolph, this is Nick--"

"McDeare," Bill finished, shaking Nick's hand. "Of course. You look so much like Andrew. I'm a huge fan of yours."

Nick smiled at Rudolph and his wife. "It's a pleasure to meet you, sir, Mrs. Rudolph." He meant it. William Rudolph had owned the Great White Way for half a century. Even he knew that.

"Call me Bill. And this is Marcy."

Jeremy shepherded everyone to their limos, leaving Jessie and Nick for last. Anthony used the pocket of time to photograph them.

"Okay, let's go, you two." Jeremy kept looking at his watch.

Jessie appeared rooted to the floor. Nick placed his hand in the small of her back. "Ready?" She met his eyes briefly before nodding. Nick could see terror in her every movement, but she walked towards the front door like a robot.

Cameras flashed and onlookers began a patter of applause at the first sight of Jessie. Nick glanced at her. She smiled briefly at the crowd before ducking into the limo. Abbie and Gianni sat facing them. Nick met Gianni Fosselli's cold eyes and tried not to burst out laughing. Jealousy oozed from every Italian bone in the man's body.

As the entourage pulled away from the curb and headed for Radio City Music Hall, Nick kept a close eye on Jessie. She sat like an ice queen, staring out the window, twirling her wedding rings around her finger. Nick reached over and covered her small hands with his own. She looked up at him, a fragment of a smile flitting across her face before curling her fingers through his.

Nick caught Abbie's eye. The woman's stare was inscrutable. Somewhere down this long road Nick intended to get to know Abigail Forrester better. The woman was one surprise after another. But she was nothing he couldn't handle.

*

The entourage came to a halt in front of Radio City. A white-gloved attendant opened the limo's door, and Jessie got her first glimpse of the crowd gathered on the sidewalk. Enormous. Mounted policemen had corralled the fans behind ropes, but the press swarmed everywhere. Jessie longed to be home in her kitchen with a mug of tea laced with brandy. Abbie and Gianni left the car and made their way into the theater. Frozen, Jessie hung back, gripping Nick's hand.

"You do know you're cutting off my circulation," Nick said lightly. "C'mon. Give your fans their due. Without them, no one would know your name."

"Right now that sounds like a good idea."

"You can do this, Jess. For Andrew." Nick stared at her, those amber eyes exuding confidence, his voice calm and steady. She began to feel his strength giving her strength, like one battery charging another. Jessie reached within herself and nodded, the warm current flowing through her nerve endings.

Nick emerged from the car and reached back for her. As they stepped onto the red carpet, the police moved in. Jessie slipped her hand under Nick's arm and they glided through the crowd. Cameras whirred and the crowd called her name. Suddenly it all came back to her. She felt the fans' excitement, buoying her. She smiled, turning her head from side to side, working the crowd. Thank God no one could see her knees shaking beneath the black gown.

Clinging to Nick, Jessie glanced up at him. He met her eyes, a curious look on his face. What was that new look in his eyes? Admiration? Yes, that was it. Nick McDeare admired her right now. The realization made her stand a little taller. Jessie flashed him her winning smile, suddenly proud to have Andrew's brother at her side.

*

Paula sat in front of the television, watching the annual Tony Awards. She loved everything theatrical. She sighed, wishing her own fledgling career had taken off. Even with the family's money backing her, she hadn't gotten to first base. Talent sometimes did win out, and Paula knew her talent was minimal. The only thing her doomed career had brought her was Ian Wexley. When she'd met the hunky soap star at a friend's party, she'd thought she'd hit the jackpot. They were married two months later.

Then her husband's career had gone into free fall, all because of Andrew Brady, or so Ian claimed. The money disappeared, and they'd been forced to live off her family. Finally her brother Aldo had put his foot down and forced Ian to get employment. Ian hated being a bartender. It was beneath him.

Paula sighed and reached for her sherry. She had drunk very little before she met Ian. Now she drank every night. She glanced at the clock. Where was her husband tonight? He'd claimed to have a big Tony bash to work, but she knew Ian would slit his wrists before being anywhere near actors on Tony night. Paula suspected Ian was lying to her, again. Several years ago, Aldo had shown up at the apartment unannounced one afternoon, catching Ian in their bed with a trashy divorcee from the second floor. Paula had been having lunch with their mother. After that, Ian had vowed to toe the line. But Paula feared her husband would never be able to keep his promise of fidelity. Ian was not a man to trust, in or out of bed.

One of these nights, she was going to follow Ian and see where he went. Paula bit her lip. She hadn't followed her husband on his nighttime escapades since ... since the night before Andrew Brady was murdered.

*

Jessie paced nervously in her dressing room, mouthing the words to her speech. Thank God Jeremy had insisted she be secluded. Most presenters gathered in a large communal room, but Jeremy had known how difficult this would be for her.

Nick sat on a divan, watching a television monitor. The network went to commercial, and Jessie heard a voice-over. "Coming up next: Josh Elliott and Jessica Kendle."

- 137 -

There was a knock on the door, and Jeremy poked his head in. "It's time, Jessie. You should be on in about five minutes."

"I want Nick in the wings, okay?"

"Sure. Whatever you want. Let's go, honey." Jeremy led Jessie and Nick through a labyrinth of corridors, emerging onto the stage right wing. The cavernous backstage area was crowded with singers, dancers, and actors, all staring at Jessie. A lively production number from one of the season's nominated musicals was on the stage.

"Hey, stranger," a voice said over Jessie's shoulder. Josh stood behind her, handsome in his tux, his yellow hair a swirl across his forehead. Jessie hugged her old friend, holding him close for a long moment. "It's so good to see you again," Jessie whispered. "Abbie and I have been talking about you all week."

"Abbie's here too?" Jessie nodded. "Are you going to the party?" Josh asked.

"Yeah. Josh, I want you to meet Nick McDeare, Andrew's brother."

As the two men shook hands, the stage manager came out of his booth to shush them. Onstage, they heard Josh being introduced as last year's winner for Best Actor in a Musical. Josh kissed Jessie on the forehead and walked confidently out onto the stage to thunderous applause.

That was Jessie's cue to get in place. Butterflies fluttered in her stomach. She looked up at Nick. He smiled. "Go. Go be brilliant."

Jessie's jaw dropped.

"What? Did I say something wrong?"

"No," she croaked. "Not at all." Jessie took a deep breath, pivoted, and walked quickly to the upper corner of the stage, just out of sight of the audience.

Go. Go be brilliant. It was what Andrew had always said to her before they walked onstage. Was Andrew here tonight, guiding their actions?

Trying to relax, Jessie shook her hands, rolled her head back and forth, and lifted her shoulders up and down. Everyone backstage seemed mesmerized by her, but she blocked them out, the way she was trained to do. Concentrate on the job at hand. Tunnel vision. Jessie dropped her head, closed her eyes and remained perfectly still. If only her knees would stop shaking.

Josh presented the Best Actor statuette to this year's winner. Jessie heard him clear his throat before saying, "Ladies and Gentlemen. Miss Jessica Kendle." The orchestra launched into the theme song from HEART TAKES.

Jessie lifted her head, squared her shoulders and strode onto the stage, moving at a steady pace. Multiple spotlights zeroed in on her. The warmth of the lights made time stand still. It was three years ago and Andrew was by her side as they swept hand-in-hand down the stage to present at the Tonys. Her instincts kicked in. She was in control again. She owned the stage. Her nerves were replaced by adrenaline. She felt like she could touch the moon.

The applause that began as her name was announced became a roar. As Jessie reached the glass podium, she instinctively looked to her right, expecting to see her husband standing beside her. Instead, she saw Nick smiling at her from the wings, applauding, never taking his eyes off her. She took a deep breath and fought to keep her composure.

Catching movement out of the corner of her eye, Jessie looked back at the audience, surprised to see them rising to their feet. Some were clapping over their heads. Some were crying. She blinked, fighting back her own tears. Smiling and scanning the audience, she recognized friends down front and nodded to them. She shook her head, swallowed hard, and looked back up, all the way to the balcony, the way she'd been taught. The television cameras kept swinging for different angles. Jessie ignored them. She had hit her mark on the stage floor. The rest was up to the cameramen.

Finally, the applause began to fade, and the audience sat back down.

"Eight years ago," Jessie began, in a steady voice. "William Rudolph took a chance on two unknowns, a young couple whose club act he happened to catch while vacationing on a cruise ship. Six months later, my husband Andrew and I opened at his new club, Dickasons, right here in the theater district. A year later, we starred on Broadway."

Jessie willed herself not to cry. "My story's not unusual, not when it comes to Bill Rudolph. Over five decades, he's launched the careers of hundreds of people. He's kept Broadway alive with new musicals, new playwrights, new composers and fresh faces. Here's just a sampling of Mr. Rudolph's long and celebrated career." She looked back at the large screen that dropped down over her head as the lights dimmed.

Jessie clenched her jaw and tried to think of something else as she fixed her eyes on the short film highlighting Rudolph's successes.

*

While the film ran, Nick stared at Jessie onstage, this stunning creature. This was a new Jessie, a woman he'd never seen before. This was not the brandy-guzzling klutz addicted to pills. The contrary woman afraid to venture from the house. This woman was Jessica Kendle, a renowned actress, a Tony winner, a tragic figure emerged intact from the crucible. This was the woman his brother had fallen in love with, but stronger. She had a presence, an otherworldly aura that demanded attention. And she was radiant, more beautiful than any woman he'd ever known.

Nick turned his attention to the clips on the screen. Jessie and Andrew singing, their voices perfectly tuned. Dancing, as light and graceful as twin sunbeams. Jessie and Andrew connecting in a tearful emotional scene. Andrew and Jessie had had it all before evil had ripped their lives apart. The tribute concluded with Jessie and Andrew singing the theme from HEART TAKES, the camera freezing on their faces before fading out.

Nick rubbed his eyes. If he felt like this, what must Jessie be feeling? He could see she was fighting tears. At that exact moment, her eyes darted to him, and he nodded.

When the stage lights came up, he watched Jessie turn to the audience again and welcome Bill Rudolph to the stage. The audience was on their feet again, this time for Bill who bounded to the stage like a kid, not a seventy-one-year-old man. He accepted the statuette from Jessie and hugged her tightly.

As Bill moved to the podium, Jessie stepped back, applauding with everyone else. Nick could see her clenching her teeth, trying not to cry. When Bill's speech was finished, the famed producer put his arm around Jessie and the two of them left the stage.

Jessie flew into Nick's arms. He pulled her into the shadows and away from curious stares. He could feel Jessie shaking, on the verge of losing it. "You were brilliant, Jess," he whispered.

Jessie looked up at him, shock on her face, her eyes wet and spilling over.

"What? What's wrong?"

"Brilliant. That's the word Andrew always used." Jessie nestled against his chest, the tears flowing. Nick kissed the top of her head. She was so small. Her body melted into his, soft where he was ….

Whoa. He was responding to her. This was wrong. This was his sister-in-law he was holding in his arms. His dead brother's wife. Who happened to be a beautiful, talented woman filling him with an aching desire so sweet it shocked the hell out of him.

CHAPTER 13

Nick fought a sudden impulse to tip Jessie's head up and cover those raspberry lips with his. Jeremy interrupted Nick's exquisite torment, cracking the mood like a hammer on crystal. "What's wrong with Jessie?"

Ignoring Jeremy, Nick whispered, "Come on, Jess. Let's get out of here." Shielding her from the stares of her fellow actors, Nick led Jessie from the backstage area. "Get the car," Nick ordered the agent.

"Hey, you may be Andrew's--"

"Damn it, get the car. Jessie walked out on that stage with her head held high. Do you want everyone to see her fall apart now?"

Jeremy didn't look happy, but he got the car.

*

Nick told himself the explosive sexual chemistry he'd just experienced with Jessie was an aberration. She was a woman and he was a man with a libido, that's all. It ended there. He used their moments in the limo to help Jessie get her emotions under control. She dabbed away at her running mascara with his handkerchief and reapplied her makeup. By the time they were joined by the others, he was relieved to have her laughing. "You do know this handkerchief's ruined, don't you?" he teased, stuffing it back in his pocket.

After a stop at the New York Hilton for the official Tony party, the group headed uptown. Bill Rudolph's private party was more Nick's style, a smaller gathering of two hundred guests in a nightclub overlooking Central Park. There was a sunken stage for dancing, flowing champagne, and a full bar. Servers moved through the room, offering baby portabella mushrooms stuffed with crabmeat, miniature Quiche Lorraine, bacon-wrapped sea scallops, chilled prawns with cocktail sauce, caviar and sour cream on toast points, spinach and feta baked in phyllo dough, and pate de fois gras.

While Abbie greeted old friends, Gianni honed in on Jessie, smoothly guiding her away for what he called his private congratulations. Nick watched Gianni slip a jewelry box from his pocket. He heard Jessie's gasp as she fingered a strand of, Nick squinted, diamonds. Lots of them. Nick let Gianni have his moment and gave an interview to a local New York TV station. He got the cute reporter's phone number when she was done. Colette.

Then it was time to mingle. Jessie was calm and collected, but Nick kept a close eye on her. He knew how much Andrew weighed on her mind tonight. Nick downed a goblet of champagne and fingered Colette's number, reminding himself New York was loaded with enough gorgeous women to scratch every itch in this lifetime. Women who weren't his sister-in-law.

More champagne flowed from a fountain that looked like a loaner from Versailles. Nick politely answered the same questions ad nauseam from guests and reporters about being Andrew's brother and whether he was planning to adapt one of his novels to the stage. A reporter from the NEW YORK TIMES introduced himself. "We were in Iraq together, remember?" Nick didn't, but it didn't matter. This was Jessie's night. He excused himself and skated through the crowd at Jessie's side. Every so often she clutched his hand and he squeezed back, letting her know her brother-in-law was there for her. Family. Jessie was surrounded by old friends everywhere she went. She laughed at bad jokes, graciously accepted the condolences of fellow actors, and talked about the merits of the current Broadway season. She was the picture of grace under pressure.

People-watching was one of Nick's favorite sports, and this was a particularly interesting crowd. The worst of the phoniness seemed to have been left behind at the Hilton. Still, actors were actors. Producers were producers. Directors were directors. Writers didn't seem to have that much power in the hierarchy. There was ass-kissing and glad-handing like there was no tomorrow.

While Jessie hugged an actress Nick recognized from a movie musical, a toned man with a beautiful manicure took him aside. "Quentin Maxwell," he said, flashing a business card. "COLD BLOOD AND GUTS. My film. You might've heard of it. Almost nominated for an Oscar three years ago. Golden Globe nominee." Max flipped the card into Nick's pocket. "I read all your books," he said, flashing a perfect white smile. "I'll get to the point. You persuade Jessie Kendle to star in my next movie and you write the screenplay and get a percent of the gross. No one's business but ours. You name her price."

Nick retrieved the card from his pocket. "I'll get to the point, too, Quentin," he said pleasantly, tearing the card into tiny pieces and stuffing them into Maxwell's jacket pocket. "You stay the hell away from my sister-in-law, or it'll be your blood and guts all over the floor." Nick smiled amiably. "Got it?"

Jessie materialized at Nick's side, smiling at Quentin. "Do I know you?" she asked.

"Actually," Nick said, "Quentin here, movie producer, was just telling me how much he admired your stage work. Right, Quentin?"

Maxwell eyed Nick nervously and downed his martini with one gulp. "Right," he said. Quentin snaked away.

Jessie raised a brow. "I won't ask what you said to that man. I don't want to ruin your record of being a good boy tonight. Our deal, remember?" She smiled wickedly. "Excuse me while I powder my nose."

Nick watched Jessie sway seductively across the room, pleased she had no idea of the lascivious thoughts that had consumed him earlier. To prove that he was almost cured of wanting his sister-in-law in the worst way, Nick flirted with a Brazilian beauty headlining a Broadway musical import. He got Evita's number, too. Hell, how many more did he have to collect before he could boot Jessie out of his head—the entire room?

A lavish meal was served at midnight. Nick and Jessie were seated with Bill and Marcy Rudolph at a round table for twelve. Bill's closest friends joined them, including Josh Elliott, Abbie, Gianni, and a stunning six-foot tall Ethiopian model about to open in a new Rudolph dance extravaganza.

Nick studied the dinner selection. Ancient Rome had nothing on these people. Nick had his choice of filet mignon, lobster, or Russian blini with caviar, sour cream and butter. Following crab bisque with sherry or chilled strawberry soup and salads with various lettuces from the world's gardens. He was afraid to check out the groaning dessert table. Anyone who indulged was going to feel like a Moulard duck on its way to becoming foie gras.

Nick's cell phone rang just as his lobster tails were delivered. If it was a woman from another time zone he was going to hurl the phone across the room. "McDeare."

There was a pause before a voice rasped, "Leave it alone, McDeare. Let sleeping dogs lie. Otherwise Jessica Brady will be planning another funeral."

Then, nothing but a dial tone.

*

"Did I tell you I found an apartment today?" Abigail asked, as Gianni guided her around the dance floor between dinner courses.

Gianni's attention was split between the lovely Abigail Forrester in his arms and the arrogant Nicholas McDeare across the room. Had the man made inroads with Jessica? He could swear McDeare had a smirk on his face as he glanced their way.

"A high-rise at Seventy-Second and Riverside Drive," Abigail continued. "It's time for me to get out of the brownstone and into a place of my own."

"Hmm? I'm sorry. What did you say?"

"Where are you?"

"I'm sorry, Abigail. It's Nicholas. He's been giving me strange looks all night. Almost like he's taunting me."

"He probably is, but I don't know why. There's nothing going on between Jessie and Nick. He's just trying to get a rise out of you. Ignore him. I promise I'll tell you if something starts up between them."

"If you move out, how will you know?"

"Mary." Abigail smiled. "She's the eyes, ears, and nose of the brownstone. Nothing gets by her."

*

When Nick's cell phone rang again, he was ready, his adrenaline flowing. He snapped open his phone and listened. Silence hung on the line.

"Hello?" a voice asked in Italian. "Nick? It's Ozzie." Nick let out his breath. His private investigator friend from Siena.

"Hi, Oz. I'm here. Hold on, okay?" Nick spoke in English, hoping Ozzie understood him. He glanced at Gianni who had just returned from the dance floor with Abbie. The Italian kept eying Nick while dredging a piece of filet mignon through Béarnaise sauce. "I'll be right back," Nick whispered to Jessie.

He headed for a remote corner of the lobby. Now was not the time for Fosselli to learn Nick spoke fluent Italian. How many times had Nick overheard a suspect incriminate himself in a foreign tongue? "What have you got, Ozzie?" he asked, switching to Italian.

"Okay. First, Paolo and Teresa Fosselli's murder. You were right. It was a mob hit. I tracked down the family housekeeper. She closed up like a rotten clam, but she gave me a list of the other servants. That's when I hit the jackpot. I coerced a little signorina to spill her guts."

"I can imagine how you, ah, coerced her."

"I'm the king of pillow talk, just like you, eh? Anyway, Paolo Fosselli was dealing in fine leather with the Martinelli family in America. A little side business separate from the shipping line."

"The Martinelli family?"

"Paolo was cooking the books. The Martinellis found out, and Paolo was eliminated. His wife was his bookkeeper, so they took her out, too. Now, here is where it gets interesting."

"Hold on a minute, Oz." Nick strode to the hostess' podium and grabbed a piece of paper and a pen. "Okay, go ahead." He began scribbling.

"The son, Gianni, showed up at the Fosselli villa right after the hit. He was home from school for the weekend, a surprise visit. He found the villa deserted and his parents dead. The little maid I spent time with hid with the rest of the servants, but she ventured out long enough to see the killer threaten Gianni if he talked."

"They left him alive, a potential witness?"

"He was a nineteen-year old kid, studying at the Cordon Bleu. He knew nothing about the father's leather-goods venture, a chef. They knew they could terrify him into silence. I also think Martinelli wanted Gianni alive as the heir to the shipping throne. Potential future business. You know how it works."

Nick's mind raced. Gianni's link to Martinelli just grew stronger. "Did the maid recognize the killer?"

"One of the most feared men in Genoa. Vito Secchi."

Nick felt his breath catch. Vito Secchi. Martinelli's man in Italy. One of two connected men who were in the terminal the day Andrew was shot.

"One more thing. You asked me to look further into Gianni Fosselli. An acquaintance of mine worked for old-man Fosselli for years. Marco said Gianni was anointed to take over the shipping line after his parents were murdered. No more Cordon Bleu. He divided his time between Italy and living aboard the fleet in the States, learning the business. About eight or nine years ago, the old man sent Gianni to America on his own. A test run. Apparently, he got involved with the wrong woman and almost botched a huge financial deal for the family. Gianni was ordered home and Grandpa had Marco look into this American woman ... uh, let's see, Jessica Kendle."

Nick leaned against the wall, his heart doing a jackhammer.

"When this Kendle woman married someone else, Gianni tried to kill himself. He aimed his Ferrari at a tree after drinking a bottle of grappa. A Ferrari! He spent five years rehabilitating. Anyway, Marco discovered the woman had been pregnant when she married, and the old man was convinced the child was Gianni's. He ordered Marco to keep an eye on Kendle and her son. The plan was to snatch the boy at some point."

"Why didn't he go through with it?"

"How did you know he didn't?"

"Jessica Kendle's my sister-in-law. The boy's my nephew."

"Jesus, Mary, and Joseph. So this one's personal, eh?"

"Jessie's husband was my brother Andrew. He was murdered two years ago. And Gianni may be involved." And Ozzie didn't know the half of it. "So, why didn't they take the boy?"

"Alzheimer's. The old guy's memory failed. The file on the woman and boy was forgotten. Until the grandfather died and Gianni discovered it when he cleaned out the old man's office. He sent Marco to the States to take photos of the kid. When Marco delivered the pictures, he said Gianni locked himself in his villa for days. Within a matter of weeks, Gianni Fosselli sold the shipping line and the family villa and relocated to New York."

Nick tried to calm his heart. He was going to need a pacemaker soon. "How long ago was this?"

"Let's see ... two years ago last February."

Andrew was killed the following April. Did Gianni come back to New York for the express purpose of killing Andrew Brady and reclaiming Jessie and Anthony?

*

Nick had to collect himself. He went to the men's room and splashed water on his face. As he was washing his hands, Fosselli emerged. "Well, Nicholas, our Jessica was a big success tonight, yes?"

"She's a strong woman, stronger than she ever was."

"Yes, it looks like Jessica has finally come to terms with Andrew's death."

"Come to terms?" He chuckled. "Maybe, but she'll never get over it. Losing someone you love changes a person forever."

"I know all about loss, Nicholas."

"I bet you do."

The two men locked eyes.

Gianni turned away first. "Anyway, it's good to have the old Jessica back."

"The old Jessica's gone for good. But the new Jessie?" Nick crumbled his towel and shot it into the bin like a basketball. "She's emerging intact. Ready to start over." Nick whistled as he headed for the exit.

"Nicholas?"

Nick looked over his shoulder.

"Jessica loves me. Her future is with me and our son."

Nick smiled and pushed through the swinging door.

*

A waiter appeared the moment Nick returned to the table to tell him they'd be bringing him a new plate of lobster tails. Nick smiled his thanks and dropped into his chair.

He spotted Jessie on the dance floor with Josh Elliott. Photographers circled them as they swayed to the music, their arms around each other. Nick studied Elliott. A head of dandelion hair, athletic body, mid-thirties. Jessie's smile as she gazed up at him was genuine. A dart of jealousy swept through Nick. It was a novel feeling. He didn't like it.

His fresh plate was delivered. Nick dug in. The potatoes were tender and piping hot, his lobster dripping in butter. Tonight he wasn't going to worry about eating healthy.

Bill Rudolph sidled over to Nick, asking for a private word. He wasn't meant to eat tonight. Nick followed the man to the back of the gilded room. "Nick, Mary told me tonight you're the one responsible for getting Jessie to appear at the Tonys. A major coup, son. I've been trying to get her back on a stage for two years."

Nick nodded. Where was this going?

"Mary seems to think you know Jessie better than anyone right now, so I want to ask you a question. A lot of time and money rides on your answer." He glanced around. "Do you think Jessie's strong enough to return to Broadway in a major production? Is she ready for a leading role and all that goes with it?

Nick didn't know what went into taking on a role. Still, he did know Jessie better than most these days. He leaned against the wall and slid his hands in his pockets. "I don't know about the emotional pressure," he said softly. "Physically, she's back in condition again. I think you should ask her."

"I'm afraid she'll turn me down flat, like she has in the past."

"Maybe not, if you go to her with a specific project. Convince her it's a complicated role, and no one can do it but Jessica Kendle. Tell her if she turns you down, you'll scrap the whole production rather than take a chance on someone else." Nick's lip quirked. "Guilt works well on Jess. And she can't resist a challenge."

"I've got a project in mind." Bill clapped him on the shoulder. "Thanks for what you've done for Jessie. Your brother would be proud of you."

Nick drifted back to the table. Would Andrew be proud of him if he knew his graphic and lewd thoughts about Jessie weren't going away like they were supposed to? Nick devoured the lobster, focusing on every succulent bite. He had to win this battle. No crossing the line into sex. Sex made it messy. Sex was trouble. Still, on some level, it would be nice to know he could have Jessie if he wanted Jessie. Call it male pride.

Jessie returned to the table, her own plate untouched. "What were you and Bill whispering about?"

"You noticed?"

"I'm not blind."

"You seemed focused on the hunk."

"That was for the cameras, but Josh is really a--"

"Sweetheart. I know."

"So ... about Bill?"

"Ah, we were talking about Andrew."

"Of course. Everyone's talking about Andrew tonight." Jessie picked at her food.

"You okay?"

"Yeah." Jessie dabbed at her lobster as if it were cat food.

"Uh-oh," Nick whispered in her ear. "Don't look now, but Gianni's coming around the bend. I bet he wants a dance."

"Oh, God, I'm not in the mood. C'mon, Nick. You and I haven't danced all evening."

Nick angled her a look that experience had taught him women found seductive. "You want to dance with me?"

"Not really," Jessie said lightly. "I just want to see if you have any of your brother's talent on the dance floor."

*

Rosita slipped out of bed, careful not to disturb Miguel. Leaving the cramped bedroom, she padded to the window. It was too hot tonight to sleep. The windows of their cracker-box Bronx apartment looked out on a cold-air shaft. Still, it was better than Cuba.

Rosita mopped her brow and sighed. It was more than the heat keeping her up tonight. She'd spotted a police poster in the Red Apple supermarket and the subway, horrified to find her own face staring back at her. She'd prayed that Miguel didn't see it on his way home, but, of course, he had. He had screamed at her all through dinner, making her wish she could disappear off the face of the earth. Then she'd seen Jessica Kendle on television tonight, a mark of tragedy stamped on the actress' face. That look never went away. It scarred you for life. Rosita knew all about tragedy. She'd witnessed the execution of both her brothers and her father. She wanted to help Andrew Brady's widow. Maybe if the woman knew who killed her husband, it would give her some peace.

But if Rosita came forward, she and Miguel would be sent back to Cuba. What should she do?

*

The orchestra was playing a slow jazz piece as Nick and Jessie moved onto the dance floor. He slid his arm around Jessie's waist and pulled her close. She curled against his chest and sighed, closing her eyes. "Right now I'd give anything to be home with a cup of tea and some brandy," she whispered. "I'm hot and I'm tired."

Nick reached into his pocket and produced his handkerchief. "You're perspiring." He dabbed at her brow and nose, making her laugh. "Tonight's been a pressure cooker for you. You're finally letting down." His heart was racing all over again, and his palms were sweating. Maybe it was the fact that she was forbidden. That had to be the reason she was driving him mad.

Jessie looked up at him, her eyes inches from his lips. What would it be like to take this fragile creature to bed? Would she be ladylike and blushing? Probably. Would she expect to talk after sex? Definitely. After appreciating her body, Nick would be expected to appreciate her mind. There was nothing worse than talking after sex. After sex you either left or went to sleep.

"Thanks, Nick," Jessie whispered.

"Hmm?"

"For keeping your promise and being a perfect gentleman tonight. And for holding me together when I fell apart."

Why did she have to be nice to him? Clearing his throat, Nick said, "You look dead on your feet. Want to go?"

"You read my mind. Let's go home and have some brandy."

Nick wanted to go home and mash his face into his pillow and fall into a deep dreamless sleep. He wanted to wake up to find his runaway sex drive back under control. He did not want to have a brandy with Jessie.

She gazed up at him, her eyes clear blue crystals. In the Dark Ages, women had been burned at the stake for that kind of witchery.

"Okay?"

"Sure," Nick croaked, "brandy would be perfect."

*

Nick and Jessie slouched across from each other in the breakfast nook, steaming mugs of tea and brandy in front of them. Jessie's shoes and jewelry had never made it down the long hallway. Neither had Nick's bow tie, cummerbund, and jacket. He watched Jessie's face, tired but glowing with the triumph of the evening. Nick scrubbed a hand over his sandpapered jaw.

"Tonight I kept thinking of A TALE OF TWO CITIES," Jessie mused. 'It was the best of times. It was the worst of times.' That's exactly how it felt tonight."

"What was the best?"

"Being back on that stage again. Feeling the heat of the lights and spots on my face. Seeing that green glow coming from the stage manager's booth. Hearing the stagehands cueing up for the next set change. The live orchestra down in the pit. Just ... Everything. I didn't realize how much I've missed it."

"What about the applause?" Nick had never seen Jessie shine like this. Her eyes were sparkling, her cheeks rosy. She was getting a second wind.

"It's like an addiction. Once I have a taste of it, I want more. It lifts me up on my toes. It makes me feel like I can fly."

"And the worst?"

"You know the worst. Not having Andrew there. Being back, but without him. Everything seemed off balance. There was a big hole where Andrew should've been." She rubbed her forehead. "I was having so much fun tonight without Andrew."

"You think if you have a good time, you're not showing proper respect for Andrew, right?"

She nodded.

"You don't want to laugh because Andrew can no longer laugh. If he can't have a good time, you shouldn't either."

Again she nodded.

"I know exactly how you feel."

"You haven't lost a spouse."

"I lost a son. And a brother."

"Are you telling me I'm turning into you? Dear God!"

"Hey, thanks a lot."

"You know what I mean."

"No. Tell me."

"Well, you're so ... closed off. You don't let anyone in. Is that how I am?"

"Go on." Nick's lips flattened into a thin line. "Tell me more about myself. It's insightful."

"There." She pointed at him. "Right there. That attitude of yours. That's another thing. You can be so condescending. You hurt people. Is it because of your losses, or were you always this way?"

Did Jessie really think so little of him? "I thought you knew," he snapped. "I sprang from the womb like this. From the moment my mother tossed me out, I became a hateful human being. My greatest pleasure in life's hurting my fellow man."

"Nick, I didn't mean-- Look, you know how you are."

"Sure. I know exactly how I am." He pulled himself to his feet. "Thanks for reminding me." He headed for the stairs, pausing. "I'm sorry I'm not Andrew. Apparently he was perfect. I should've been the one who was killed, not him."

"Don't be ridiculous."

"Just taking my cue from you. He was a saint."

"I hate your talking about Andrew like that. Besides, you have no right. You didn't know him."

Nick felt his throat catch. "You're right. I didn't," he said quietly. "My misfortune."

CHAPTER 14

Nick glanced at the bedside table. Five o'clock. He hadn't closed his eyes once. An early morning light was filtering into the room, gauzy and fine. Rolling onto his back, he tucked his hands behind his head and stared at the ceiling. Jessie's critique hurt. She'd basically told him he was a worthless human being. Living in this house wasn't a picnic. Maybe he should go home for good. He turned onto his side and punched the pillow. How could he stay away? He'd promised Andrew he'd find his killer. He was starting to make progress with Barton. Anyway, he already had more than one ball in the air when it came to his investigation. Things were ... complicated now, in ways Jessie didn't suspect. Damn.

Nick peeked at the clock again. Two whole minutes had passed. He spied his handkerchief lying on the bedside table with his spare change and watch. Feeling ridiculous, he brought the fabric to his nose. Jessie's scent. Lilacs. The most exquisite woman at the Tonys. No competition.

There was a light knock on the door.

"C'mon in, Anthony. Door's open." The boy often visited his uncle after a nightmare. Nick would calm him down until he was ready for sleep.

"It's not Anthony," Jessie said, poking her head into the room. "May I come in?"

"Uh, sure." Nick bolted up, tucking the sheet and blanket firmly around himself. He wasn't wearing a stitch. He quickly shoved the handkerchief under his pillow.

Jessie floated into the room in a cloud of powder-blue silk nightgown and matching robe. "Nick, I-I'm sorry. I'm so sorry for the things I said. I don't know why I said them," she whispered.

Nick eyed her. "It's not like I haven't heard those things before," he finally said. "Maybe more than once."

"You've done so much for me. The pills. The attic. Jogging. You even got me outside again. And the Tonys tonight."

"You mean last night. Believe it or not, it's a new day."

"Okay." She gave a small laugh. "Last night. I never would've gone if it hadn't been for you. I never would've had the courage. You have a talent for, I don't know, lighting a fire under me."

"Probably my winning personality." He smiled. "Or I'm a pyromaniac."

"I'm really sorry." Jessie perched on the side of the bed. "Abbie says you're nothing like your brother. I've thought that at times, too. But last night, Nick," Jessie angled him a glance from under her lashes, "last night you were more like him than you'll ever know. Andrew was always the strength of our team, the leader. I was the follower. Last night you had that same strength.

Every time I thought my knees would buckle, I looked at you and felt your strength."

"Jessie, you don't have to—"

"No, I want to say this. At the end of the evening when I was so tired I could drop, you were still right beside me, holding me up. Having you with me was like having Andrew there." She waved a hand. "Don't get me wrong. I know you're not him. But last night I could tell you were his brother. Do you know what I mean? I know I'm rambling. Sorry. And I'm not saying he was perfect. He wasn't."

It had taken guts for her to apologize. "I know what you're trying to say, Jess. I appreciate it."

Jessie shook her head. "I'm sorry I'm so needy. I think I've always been that way. First my dad took care of me. Then Ian and Gianni. And Andrew. Always Andrew. Now you've inherited the job, and—"

"That's not—"

"Let me finish. It's not fair to you. I don't want to be that way anymore. It's time I took care of myself. Sometimes I think Anthony's more of an adult than I am."

"Did it ever occur to you men like to take care of you? That it makes them feel good? Maybe men encourage it."

"Why? Other women aren't like that. Abbie certainly isn't."

"Abbie is-- Well, never mind."

"Why? I really want to know." The top of Jessie's robe fell open. Nick could see the spaghetti-strap negligee. He could also see what was beneath it.

He cleared his throat. "You're small and pale, like a china doll. You make men think you break easily." She also made men fantasize about what it would feel like to have her long legs wrapped around their hips while they plunged inside that slick, velvety sweetness. Nick swallowed.

"But I don't break easily. I survived losing Andrew."

"Exactly," Nick rasped. "You're tougher than you realize."

Jessie got up and padded to the window. The dawn's light outlined her luscious body beneath the fragile silk. Nick licked his lips and shifted his position. He told himself to think of something else, but that was like telling a dog to ignore steak.

"I haven't been able to sleep," she said. "I felt so guilty. I had to apologize to you. I know you're starting your book tour today. I thought I might miss you in the morning."

"That's okay. Actually, I don't leave for the airport until noon."

Turning around, she leaned against the windowsill. "When will you be back?"

Nick stared at her body through the smoky blue veil.

"Nick?"

"Um, it's a quick swing through the Midwest, back in a week. Then a few days in town before heading out to the West Coast for two or three weeks." Nick told himself to keep talking about the book. Books were safe.

"That long?"

"Don't tell me you'll miss me."

"Of course I will. So will Anthony. You're becoming a fixture around here."

Like a lamp. Christ. "By the way," Nick heard himself say, "the day after I get back from Chicago I'm guest of honor here at an event hosted by the National Booksellers. How'd you like to go with me? It's better if I have a woman along," he added quickly.

"To keep you from being mauled?"

"Something like that."

"Wouldn't you rather take one of your bimbos? Someone who'll keep her mouth shut all night?"

"Didn't you just apologize for saying mean things about me?"

"I just did it again, didn't I?" Jessie sat on the bed again, facing him. "I'd love to go. It'll be fun to see the best-selling author in action." Jessie flashed him a dazzling smile and sprang up. Nick breathed a sigh of relief. "Well, I've had my say. I'll leave you alone." She paused at the door. "Come by my sitting room before you go. I have something for you. Good, um, morning, Nick."

"Morning, Jess." The door clicked closed.

Finally alone, Nick stared at his lap. Judging from the fact Jessie hadn't run screaming from the room, it was safe to assume that she hadn't noticed what she was doing to him. Maybe she needed glasses.

*

Later that morning, Nick found Jessie at the desk in her sitting room, reading the Tony coverage in the papers. Nick read over her shoulder. "Wow. You should be happy. 'Miss Kendle's appearance was electrifying. This is a woman who has been to hell and back. She appears to have survived her nightmare and is stronger and more radiant than ever.'"

"Not a bad picture of you and me, huh?" Jessie pointed to a large photo of the two of them on the red carpet. "There's some coffee over there. Help yourself. I'll be right back." She disappeared into the connecting dressing room.

Nick poured himself a cup and sat down on the leather sofa. Jessie was back a moment later, a black leather bag in her arms. She dropped down beside him and took a deep breath. "This was Andrew's dance bag. When we were working it went everywhere with us." She lifted out a small leather-bound notebook. "This, all of these, are Andrew's journals."

Finally. It had been killing him, but Nick had forced himself to keep quiet about the journals. You didn't fool with a ghost, especially a sonuvabitch like Andrew.

"I think Andrew would want you to read these," Jessie continued, running her fingers over the book lovingly. "Maybe they'll tell you a lot more about him."

"Haven't you read them?"

"Not yet. I'm not ready. Someday."

Nick remembered his brother's words. "When she finally decides to show them to you, you'll know she trusts you completely."

So Nick had earned Jessie's trust. He wondered if Jessie would still trust him if she knew everything he'd been up to? He eyed her thoughtfully as she continued to caress the book. "Are you sure about this? There may be things in there that could be, well, embarrassing for you. Intimate things you'd rather I didn't know."

Jessie colored. "If there are, I trust you'll have the decency not to rub my nose in them."

"You trust Nick McDeare to be decent?"

"About this, yes."

A smile streaked across his face before he grew serious. "I'm asking honestly Are you sure about this?"

She hesitated, seeming to weigh his words before handing him the journal. "I'm sure. I lived these years with Andrew. You didn't. I think he'd want you to read them. If he were alive, he'd probably give them to you himself."

In a way, that's exactly what Andrew had done. "I'll take good care of them." Nick reached over and pulled Jessie into a hug. "Thanks for trusting me with them."

Before Nick left for the airport, he sorted through the journals, selecting three to take with him. Andrew was diligent about keeping his records. The diaries stopped the day he left on that fateful cruise.

*

Jessie spent the week helping Abbie settle into her new apartment. They shopped for furnishings, stocked the kitchen, gossiped, ordered in Chinese, and had an old-fashioned picnic on the hardwood floor. Gianni joined them more than once and treated them to dinner at Oceano one night. He reserved his favorite table in a glass-enclosed corner of the restaurant and selected the menu himself. The three of them nibbled on clams casino for a starter and moved on to veal piccata and gnocchi in cream sauce.

Glancing out the walls of window at the bright city streets charged with energy, Jessie decided being out felt good. She'd noticed Abbie spending time with Gianni, but she hadn't brought it up. Abbie always gravitated to Italian men. If Abbie could keep Gianni off Jessie's case that was fine with her. What went on behind closed doors, well, Jessie told herself she'd rather not know.

"Gianni," Abbie said, "that's the best meal I've had in years." The waiter delivered espresso and cordials of Sambucca.

"I agree," Jessie added.

Gianni smiled appreciatively. "So, Jessica. How long is Nicholas gone?"

"Right now, for a week, but I think he'll be in and out of town for a while. I'm not sure how a book tour works."

"Pardon me for being nosy," Gianni continued, "but is Nicholas now living at the brownstone permanently?"

"He stays with us when he's in town. That's all."

"He seems to be in town a lot."

Jessie searched her purse for her lipstick. "He's helping Lyle with the case. Tracking down Andrew's killer."

"I see." Gianni appeared thoughtful. "Doesn't Nicholas have a life in Washington? Some special woman perhaps?"

Jessie laughed. "All women are special to Nick." She was used to Gianni being protective. But this topic was becoming ... uncomfortable.

"Doesn't that bother you, Jessica? From what I hear, Nicholas is used to getting what he wants. Aren't you afraid you'll wake up one night and find him standing over your bed?" Gianni's eyes darkened. "With the man's legendary track record of using women, how do you know he isn't capable of, well, I hate to even say the word. And what about Anthony? What kind of example does Nick set for the boy?"

Jessie's jaw dropped. "Are you accusing Nick of ...? Are you crazy?" When did protective slide into controlling? Had she invited this by letting herself lean on Gianni since Andrew had died?

"I'm sorry, Jessica, but with Nick's reputation you should be careful."

Jessie reminded herself Gianni was her son's biological father. She just needed to set some boundaries. "First of all, Nick's private life is none of my business, and it's certainly none of yours. And, I'm not afraid of him. It's laughable that you would even suggest such a thing. It shows how little you know him. As for Anthony, he and Nick spend hours together, at the piano, working with photography. Nick even bought Anthony some baseball stuff, and he's going to teach him how to play. Anthony loves his uncle. They adore each other."

Jessie watched Gianni and Abbie exchange a guarded look. "What? What's wrong now?

"Nothing," Abbie said quickly.

Jessie looked from one to the other before rising. "If you'll excuse me, I'm going to fix my face. Then I'd appreciate it if you'd get a taxi for me." She hurried to the ladies' room. She didn't like what Gianni had just insinuated regarding Nick. She didn't like it at all.

*

"I told you Jessie was defensive of Nick," Abigail told Gianni after he put Jessica in a cab. They were seated at the bar, sipping Sambucca. "You shouldn't attack Nick like that, Gianni. It'll backfire every time."

"I couldn't help it. I loathe that man." Gianni didn't want to swear in front of a lady. He clenched his fists. Jessica should not put her trust in a man like Nicholas. She needed someone to protect her.

"Play nice." Abigail placed her hand on Gianni's arm. "You'll only antagonize Jessie by criticizing Nick."

Gianni stared at her a moment. "Tell me something, Abigail. Why are you helping me like this? You loved Andrew, and Nicholas is his brother. I would think you'd rather see Jessica with him. And what does Jessica say about our seeing each other? Is it a problem?"

Abigail didn't lower those liquid brown eyes. "Jessie and I are big girls. We don't talk about whom we see or don't see. Besides, Jessie isn't the same since the murder. She doesn't do 'girl talk' anymore. And I told you. Nick's nothing like Andrew. I have a feeling Andrew wouldn't have liked Nick if he'd gotten to know him."

"So you're on my side? You want to help me win Jessica back and be a father to Anthony?" Gianni couldn't believe he was this fortunate. Abigail would be an invaluable ally. And maybe more, until he achieved his goal.

"Look," Abigail said slowly. "I'll be honest with you. Anthony's your son, and I think you have every right to have him in your life. I'll do everything I can to help. As for Jessie, I know what happened when you went off to Italy. When Jessie and Andrew suddenly decided to get married, I was the lone dissenting voice."

"You were? You, Abigail? You were always on Andrew's side."

"Exactly." Abigail smiled at Gianni. "I was worried that Jessie would hurt Andrew, just like she always had. She could be so callous with his feelings."

"Not on purpose. It's not in Jessica's nature to be cruel."

"Maybe not on purpose. But everyone seemed to know Andrew was in love with Jessie except Jessie." Abigail's eyes narrowed. "I also know she was still in love with you when she married Andrew."

"You're a very astute woman." Gianni reached over and squeezed Abigail's hand.

"I thought what they were doing was rushed and not well thought out."

"Do you think Jessica still loves me?" Gianni held his breath.

Abigail was quiet for a moment. "I'm not sure Jessie's capable of loving anyone right now. Something died in her when Andrew died." She looked up at him. "But do I think there's hope? I do. I really do."

Gianni caressed her cheek. "Have I told you lately how much I like you, Abigail?"

*

Jessie had trouble sleeping that night. Gianni's words still rankled. Nick might be a prickly entity, but he'd never do anything to hurt Anthony or her. Of that, she was sure. She'd always thought Gianni respected her, but apparently he didn't respect her judgment. In fact, he tended to treat her as a child. A treasured child. Maybe that was partially her fault. Maybe, as Nick had said, there was something about her that made men want to protect her. And maybe she used to like it that way. But not anymore.

Jessie rolled onto her stomach and hugged a pillow. Sleep still eluded her, but the thought of a pill never entered her mind. Those days were behind her, thanks to Nick. If it weren't for him, she'd still be sitting in this house feeling sorry for herself, shutting out the world. Sharing her grief with Nick had forged an unlikely bond between them no one would ever understand,

Jessie got out of bed and padded to the sitting room. Pouring a brandy she wandered to the window overlooking the back garden. The little plum tree was bathed in a silvery shaft of moonlight. It was Andrew's living legacy, one of many. That's why she intended to take good care of it. Next year she'd turn the responsibility over to Anthony.

*

Anthony wasn't happy with Uncle Nick gone. When his uncle was around, it was almost like having his dad back. And his nightmare came back that week, the dream where a scary stranger chased him down a busy street. When he awoke, his heart pounding, there was no Uncle Nick to promise him everything was okay. To ease his fear, Anthony began creeping up to Nick's bed and sleeping with the light on. If he closed his eyes, he could pretend his uncle was there.

In the gap between the end of school in late June and overnight camp in July, Anthony wandered around the house taking pictures. Then he got an idea. Mary had told him Nick's birthday was in July. Anthony decided to make his uncle a scrapbook of his new family. He spent hours sorting through old photographs, adding lots he'd taken himself.

*

After taping a morning interview with a local television station in Cleveland, Nick flew to Columbus for a book signing at Border's. Then he boarded a flight to Cincinnati for a late afternoon cocktail party. By the time he got to Chicago, it was past nine. Tired and hungry, he picked up a Gino's deep-dish pizza and a bottle of bourbon. No city had thick pizza like Chicago. He intended to settle into his hotel room and continue reading Andrew's journals. Tomorrow would be a nightmare. A book signing, a luncheon and two radio interviews. The week's tour would culminate in a national hour-long live television interview with Carolyn Adams, a shrew with a reputation for taking no prisoners. His agent had warned him not to turn Carolyn down again.

Nick changed into jeans and a T-shirt. He cranked up the air conditioning, poured a bourbon and grabbed a slab of pizza. Settling at the desk, he got back to his brother's scribbles.

Two hours later, he pushed his chair back and stared into space. Nick drifted to the window. Below him, he knew Lake Michigan was a glassy shimmer and the Magnificent Mile was dancing with light. But it might've been the stockyards for all Nick saw. His mind was reeling as he tried to assimilate what he'd just read. "Dear God, Andrew. You carried around a helluva secret. The question is, did it get you murdered?"

*

After his interview with Carolyn Adams the next evening, Nick returned to his hotel and quickly poured himself a bourbon. He gulped it down, feeling as if he'd just battled the mythical Hydra. For every intrusive question about his private life he lopped off, Carolyn had tossed out two more. Exhausted, Nick fell into bed, tossing and turning all night. Finally, he dreamed of Jessie. They were on the beach in something out of FROM HERE TO ETERNITY, and he was plunging deep inside her, pulling out lazily before thrusting again--

Nick awoke with a jolt. The room was silent, the city traffic a muffled hum. He glanced at the clock. Four-thirty. Groaning, Nick turned over and floated back to fantasyland, Jessie's sweet lips closing over his ...

Someone cleared his throat.

Nick flashed back to the call he'd gotten at the party after the Tonys. Had someone followed him to Chicago?

"I know you're awake," a voice said.

Nick bolted upright. "Okay, why are you here, Andrew? What'd I do now? Yell at Hamlet?"

"Relax. I came to ease your mind about Jessie." Andrew leaned against the terrace's glass doors. "She's gotten to you, hasn't she? Jessie cast her spell on Nick McDeare." He laughed.

"You find this funny? This is your wife we're talking about."

"I'm dead. Jessie and I are no longer married." Andrew lifted his left hand, wiggling his ring finger. "No ring. Jessie took it off me in the hospital. Did she tell you our wedding rings originally belonged to her parents? The rings mean everything to her."

"Enough with the walk down memory lane." Nick threw on his jeans.

Andrew opened the door of the terrace and stepped outside. "I always loved Chicago. Jessie and I worked here for six weeks once. Standing ovations every night." He turned around and slid his hands in his pockets. "You and Jessie have my blessing, you know."

Nick stood in the doorway, the bottle of bourbon in his hand. "To sleep together?" He took a swig of liquor, wiping his mouth with his hand.

"It always comes down to sex with you, doesn't it?"

"Damn it, just say what you came to say."

"You don't understand women at all."

"I'm sick of your cryptic pontificating. Hindsight's twenty-twenty." Nick lifted the bottle and drank again.

"That's your answer. Bourbon."

"Bourbon, sex, same difference. Hey, I'm just a poor sinner. I'm not Saint Andrew." Nick set the bottle on the floor and moved to the railing. The hot wind whipped his thick hair. "What do you want from me? You want me to admit I lust for your wife? Okay, I lust for your wife."

"You lust for every woman. I want you to admit you have feelings for Jessie that go beyond sex. Admit it."

Nick dropped his head in his hands. "I am so sick of your telling me what to do. I don't even know who I am anymore. I should've stayed in Washington. I never should've come to New York and gotten involved with your family."

"And where would that leave Anthony?"

Nick paused, staring at his brother.

"You're such a bitter man. Mom didn't throw you away. She loved you. She tried to find you."

"Shut up. Ghosts shouldn't be able to move around. Don't you have to stay anchored to a house or a city or something? You shouldn't break the rules. There might be hell to pay. Literally." Nick turned away.

"I can go anywhere you go."

"My tough luck." Nick headed back inside.

"That's right. Run away."

Nick halted, his back to his brother.

"You run from anything that makes you connect with another human being. Are you going to run from Jessie, too?"

Nick glanced at Andrew over his shoulder. "You're so good at giving advice, aren't you, little brother? Let's turn the tables, shall we? You were far from perfect when you walked the face of this earth."

"Here we go. I wondered when we'd get to this. My secret I kept from Jessie. Not that you don't have your own."

Nick laughed. "Apples and oranges. Yeah. Your secret. Or maybe I should say, your bombshell. Jessie never suspected?"

Andrew shook his head.

"Why didn't you tell her?"

"I tried. More than once. I couldn't do it. It would've been easier to tell her I'd slept with another woman."

"Did you?"

"Keep reading. My life's in those journals." Andrew was still, his eyes fixed on Lake Michigan. "Are you going to tell her for me when you get home tomorrow?"

"I should. It would make us even. You wouldn't be perfect, and I wouldn't be the devil."

"Jessie won't like your secret either. But we'll never be even. Not to Jessie." His voice was melancholy.

"Right. She'll always love you. She'll never take her rings off. That's her mantra. And she'll put up with me because I'm the closest thing she can get to you."

"That's not true. You're not some substitute for me."

"Right."

"Promise me you won't give up on her. That you won't run." Andrew locked eyes with his brother. "Listen to me carefully. Jessie's about to trust you in an enormous way. You have to be there for her. Promise me you won't run."

"What are you talking about?"

"I've already said too much. Just promise me. Please!"

"Okay, okay. Now go, so I can get back to my dirty dream about your former wife. I've got to get up early for my flight." He headed for the bed.

"Nick?"

"Yeah?"

"Are you going to tell Jessie? It'll kill her."

Nick rubbed his eyes. He was so tired he could sleep for a week. "I don't know, Andrew. Honestly. I just don't know."

CHAPTER 15

"Gianni, I don't think it's anything to worry about," Abigail insisted. They were in his luxury apartment, high over Manhattan. "Nick's taking Jessie to a party for his new book. Strictly business. I think he likes being seen with her because she draws a crowd. He got back from his book tour yesterday and he's already using her to his advantage tonight. It's all publicity to him."

Gianni admired Abigail as she moved around the living room, examining his artwork. Her red knit dress molded her body's sleek curves like the paint on a racecar. He liked this woman. She was brash and bold, like the city. Gianni poured two Amarettos, handing one to Abigail. "I still find it hard to believe that you would want to help me and not Andrew's brother."

Abigail stared at him. "How many times do I have to tell you? I can't stand Nick McDeare. I'll love Andrew till my dying day. But Nick? Forget it. If he dropped dead tomorrow I'd throw a party."

Gianni wasn't convinced. He had the feeling Abigail was playing him. Was she a plant for Jessica? Was it her job to keep Gianni occupied while Jessica dallied with McDeare? It was time to put his theory to a test. And he knew exactly how to do it.

*

The National Booksellers party was in the ballroom of the luxurious new Othello Hotel in Midtown. Nick's agent Liz Scott closed in on him as soon as he and Jessie entered the gala. A willowy brunette with a foghorn voice, Liz looked Jessie up and down before turning away and looping her arm through Nick's. "You look gorgeous," she cooed. Nick had dressed carefully in a three-piece black silk suit, mint shirt, and matching tie. "You didn't like Carolyn Adams, did you? Naughty boy. I'm still waiting for an outline and sample chapters. You're overdue. When are you going to London to get to work and earn your keep?"

Disentangling himself, Nick reached for Jessie's hand. "Could you get us some drinks, Liz? Thanks, hon," he said, dismissing her and guiding Jessie in the other direction.

"Did I wear the wrong dress or something?" Jessie asked. Nick recognized her catlike look of mischief. Women.

"Never." Nick took in Jessie's new designer creation: a strapless frothy swirl of turquoise and lavender gauze with a fitted bodice and a full skirt that stopped mid-calf. A simple amethyst choker and stud earrings sparkled at her throat and ears. Jessie clutched a tiny jeweled bag that would hold a safety pin. Her shiny flaxen hair cascaded to her shoulders, mirroring the chandeliers' glitter. She had to know she was the most beautiful woman in the room, the neighborhood, and the city.

Nick's lip quirked. "Liz can be a bitch, but she's the best literary agent in the business. She just happens to be jealous right now, which I think you know. And she's angry with me for running late with the new book. I'm a bunch of dollar signs to Liz."

"Oh, I think you're more than that to her. Is she a girlfriend?"

"I never mix business with pleasure." Plus, he didn't think Liz would be pleasure in the true sense, just sex. Now Jessie on the other hand ... God, but he hated it when Andrew was right.

*

Gianni and Abigail were enmeshed in each other arms on his couch, their Amarettos forgotten. When Gianni slipped his hand up her silky thigh, Abigail put a stop to it.

"What's wrong? I thought you wanted this as much as I do."

"I do. That's not the point. It's-it's Jessie."

Gianni felt his chest constrict. He'd been right. He straightened up. "I think you'd better go. I'm onto the game you and Jessica are playing with me."

"Jessie and me? What are you talking about?"

"Your little act. Keeping me occupied while Jessica gets involved with Nicholas."

"Jessie and Nick?" Abigail started to laugh. "Are you nuts? That's ridiculous."

"I don't believe you."

"You think I'm lying?" Abigail leapt to her feet. "Fine. I don't need this." She looked around for her purse. "I was right to stop things before they went any further. You'll never get over Jessie, and I won't play second fiddle to her again." Spotting her bag on the end table, she grabbed it and sailed to the door.

"Abigail, wait. What did you say?" Gianni was across the room in a flash, grabbing her hand.

"You think I'm going to bed with you and let you pretend I'm Jessie? Forget it! I've been down that road before with Jessie, and I won't do it again. I'm worth more than that. I must've been crazy to let things get this far. Now let go of my hand." She squirmed to get away.

"Stop fidgeting. What do you mean you've been down that road before with Jessie?"

"Can't you figure it out? With Andrew!"

"You slept with Andrew?" He was stunned. "I thought you were just good friends."

"The best. But we were also a man and a woman. You think we didn't end up in the sack at some point? Are you as dense as Jessie?"

Gianni shook his head, trying to make sense of all this. "You just called your best friend dense."

"My best friend? Jessie?" Abigail laughed. "Andrew was my best friend. Not Jessie." Her eyes filled with tears. "I stood by and watched Jessie hurt Andrew for years. That man was in love with her from the moment he set eyes on her. He used to pour his heart out to me about her, and all the time I ... I loved him, Gianni." She wiped the tears from her face. "It was a ridiculous situation. A mismatch for us all."

Gianni would never understand women. Their minds were full of twists and turns, like some monstrous Los Angeles freeway. "Come. Let's sit down."

Abigail followed him to the couch, grabbing her Amaretto. "I was devastated when Andrew offered to marry Jessie when she got pregnant. I'd always hoped Andrew would see Jessie for what she was. And now he's dead, courtesy of Ian Wexley, another ex-lover. Jessie might as well have killed Andrew herself!"

Gianni took her hand. "Jessica's not responsible for what someone else did. You're being irrational." He laughed softly. "It appears you and I have been on the same side for a long while, but just didn't know it." He took her glass and went to the bar for a refill. "This is all starting to make sense. You want to punish Jessica by taking me away from her, but you're afraid I'm so in love with Jessica that I would use you as a substitute for her. Just like Andrew did, right?" He handed her the glass.

"Mmm, sort of, without the male ego part. Yes, I want to punish Jessie, but," Abigail cast him a watery smile, "my plan was to help you get custody of Anthony. Jessie cares about her son more than anything else in the world. I, um, didn't know I was developing feelings for you. Not beyond the usual sexual attraction, you being Italian and all. Not until tonight."

Reaching for her purse, Abigail dug out a mirror and tissue, dabbing at her eyes. She looked at him, tear-streaked and enticing. "I can't do this to myself again; do you understand now? I won't. I'm out of here."

Gianni reached for her hand before she could go. "I'm going to tell you something no one else knows, not even Jessica. You think you were devastated when Jessica and Andrew got married? I was so distraught I tried to kill myself."

"What?"

He laughed bitterly. "And I didn't even know about Anthony at the time. I didn't find out I had a son until years later. Yes, I still love Jessica, but I've had a hard time forgiving her for that."

"So we've both been hurt by Jessie."

He squeezed her hand. "Please, don't go. I care about you. I'm not going to tell you I love you because that would be a lie. But I don't ever want you to feel like you're second to Jessica. You occupy a different place with me, with the possibility of so much more to come." Gianni realized he meant most of it. "How about some dinner?"

Abigail nodded. "I feel better, now that everything's out in the open."

*

The palatial Othello Ballroom was packed with booksellers and fans. Jessie tried to remain in the background, keeping the spotlight on Nick. It was the first time she'd entered his world. The loner morphed into an effusive Nick, laughing easily, charming his fans, focusing on each in turn. Nick was a powerful figure, Jessie realized, a mover and a shaker in his own right. And yet he'd taken time from his busy life to help a sister-in-law he'd never known and befriend her son. Even when she'd given him hell.

Occasionally Nick angled her a look, a private smile passing between them, or they came together to quickly clasp hands before moving on again. More than once, Jessie fought the urge to reach up and glide her fingers through Nick's inky hair, feathering the silky strands off his forehead. It was crazy.

For the evening's highlight Nick gave a reading from his novel, the setting Vancouver's purple velvet mountains as Chinese mercenaries hunt for refugees from Hong Kong. The audience was rapt and the applause thunderous, Jessie clapping enthusiastically.

After a Q and A session, waiters drifted through the room with trays of crab puffs, rumaki, caviar and pate. Nick spent hours sitting at a table signing copies of RED ROVER. Every so often, he dropped his hand to his side and flexed it. Periodically, he rose and stretched his legs, rubbing the back of his neck and upper arm. People continued to shake his hand, and he responded genially, but Jessie could see he was tired and hurting.

As the party wound down and the waiters began to clean up, the ballroom finally emptied. Nick stood up, rubbing his right shoulder. "Come here," Jessie said, patting the desktop. "Sit down. I might be able to relieve your pain."

"Should we rent a room?"

"Shut up and give me your hand."

Nick extended his arm, flinching and grasping his shoulder. "This always happens when I have a signing. I've been to specialists around the world. Nothing's helped. But give it a shot. Let me," Nick said softly, "see more of the real Jessica Kendle Brady, miracle woman and healer."

"I'll do that," Jessie said, wondering at the look in his eye. It wasn't teasing anymore. It was ... something else. Ignoring the prickles dancing from her spine to her scalp, Jessie moved closer, clasping his hand. Nick suddenly curled his fingers through hers. He stroked gently, flesh on flesh. A jolt of heat shot up every one of Jessie's nerve endings, startling her. Jessie could sense Nick's eyes on her, his face only inches away. Jessie swallowed. This was the first time Nick was treating her ... like more than a sister-in-law.

"You feel it too, don't you, Jess?" he rasped. She finally peeked at him as he continued to massage her hand with his fingers. "You do. I can see you do."

Suddenly, all her senses heightened. The color of Nick's eyes, those mesmerizing amber flecks. His scent, all male. His breathing, so near. His touch, the pressure he was applying, it was as erotic as if, my God. Jessie shifted as she recognized a familiar tingle, a sensation she hadn't felt since she last held her husband in her arms. How did he do that? "It-it scares me."

"Me, too, trust me. What do we do about it?"

Jessie cleared her throat, breaking the spell. "Um, right now why don't we focus on getting rid of your pain? And not that kind of pain."

"Okay," he croaked. "Your call."

She flashed Nick a small smile and turned his hand up, grateful he was letting the charged moment go. Later, she'd tackle it. Later. Jessie concentrated on the task in front of her, emptying her mind of everything else. Working with her fingertips, she massaged and pressed specific areas of Nick's palm, finding the knots of tension and intently working her way down to his fingers. She moved on to his wrist and forearm, methodically repeating the procedure.

"Anyone ever tell you you missed your calling?"

"I'm so glad you're enjoying yourself," Jessie said, forcing herself to focus. She was so close to him, so close. Jessie told herself to move up to his shoulder. She kept a firm but gentle touch. At the last moment she held his shoulder with one hand and clasped his upper arm with her other hand, sliding her grip down to his fingertips. "Shake it out," she instructed. "Go on."

Nick did as he was told, gasping. "That's amazing. Where did you learn that?"

She grinned. "Juilliard. It's called the Alexander Technique, releases tension. That's where your pain's coming from."

"All the pain and stiffness are gone." He bent his arm and wrist and flexed his hand. "You really are a miracle worker." Nick pushed himself off the table and necklaced his arms around her, catching Jessie off-guard. "There are a few more miracles you could work," he whispered, "if ... you want to take a chance, Jess."

Had she imagined the catch in his voice? Jessie gulped. Nick was staring at her lips. Was he going to kiss her? Did she want him to? Jessie stepped back. She needed time. And space. "I'm, um, going to make a quick trip to the ladies' room." She was gone before Nick could say a word.

The ladies' lounge was deserted, the banquets and meetings long over. Jessie was freshening her lipstick when the lights went out, plunging her into darkness. Great. The custodians didn't realize someone was still in here.

As she inched her way to the door, someone grabbed Jessie from behind, smothering her scream with his hand before shoving a cloth into her mouth. He dragged her back into the room and slammed her headfirst into a wall, bringing tears to her eyes. Trying to break free, Jessie was shoved again and pinned against the wall. This time she almost lost consciousness as white streamers of light danced in front of her eyes. An arm circled her neck in a death grip, cutting off her air. "Don't move a muscle," a man whispered hoarsely, "or I swear, I'll kill you with my bare hands." The stench of garlic combined with a sickeningly sweet cologne made Jessie gag. "You understand me?" Panicked, she nodded.

"Put your hands behind your back. DO IT! That's a good girl." He roughly bound her hands with something coarse while keeping her pinned with his chest. Jessie was shaking so violently her forehead was banging against the wall. This couldn't be happening! The man yanked the dress zipper down, the bodice falling away. He pawed her roughly, grasping her breasts and squeezing, his foul breath hot on her ear. She tried to scream for Nick, tears coursing down her cheeks, the gag muffling her wail.

His hands groped beneath her skirt, ripping away her panties with violent force. Jessie felt lightheaded. This wasn't real! Nick. Where was Nick? Her assailant twisted her around and tossed her onto the floor. Jessie's head hit the tiles with a thud. The next thing she knew, he was on his knees between her legs, fumbling with his belt and yanking his zipper down. Jessie called on a last reserve of strength she didn't know she had. Jerking her leg up, she blindly aimed a kick at his groin with her pump. He yelped in pain.   ′

"You bitch!" The last thing Jessie felt was a powerful slap across the face and a sense of floating before everything went black.

*

A knot began to pull tight in Nick's gut. Jessie had been gone too long. Something wasn't right. He jogged to the hallway and looked in both directions. Deserted. Hustling towards the ladies' room sign, his fear began to choke him. Nick broke into a sprint and burst into the darkened room, groping for the light switch and flipping it on.

Jessie was lying on the tiled floor, bound and gagged, her dress open to the waist, her skirt up around her thighs. Racing to her side, Nick dropped to his knees and felt for her pulse. She was alive, thank God. "Jessie?" Fighting his panic, he pulled off the gag and worked on untying her hands. "Jessie, can you hear me?" The rope was so tight her wrists were bleeding. Nick dug in his pocket for the tiny knife attached to his nail clippers and worked to cut through the rope. "Jess?"

His eyes flicked to her bare breasts, ugly purple bruises in the shape of handprints. He turned her on her side and tried to zip up her dress. The zipper was broken. Stripping off his jacket, he covered her. Nick scooped Jessie into his arms. "Jess? Can you hear me, honey?"

Jessie's eyelids fluttered, opening a crack. Nick caressed her bruised cheek with his thumb. Suddenly her eyes widened and she became a wild woman, twisting and pounding on his chest. "Jessie, stop! It's me. It's Nick!" He grabbed her wrists and pressed his face against hers. "It's Nick," he whispered.

The tension in her body snapped like a rubber-band. "Nick?"

"Yeah. It's me."

She dissolved into tears, curling against his shirt and gasping for breath, her sobs ripping through him. "We've got to get you to a hospital."

"No! No hospital. It'll be all over the news. Promise me. Promise me! No hospital!"

"Okay, okay. No hospital. I promise." Nick fished his cell out of his pocket and called Barton. Then he phoned Mary and asked her to find a doctor who made discreet house calls. Finally, he paged their limo driver and barked at him to bring the car around to the side street.

*

Nick paced in the sitting room off the master bedroom. Jessie was being examined by Dr. Walter Logan, Bill Rudolph's personal physician.

Nick glanced at Mary as she sat immobile on the leather couch. Nick had been impressed with how she'd taken control, calling Bill and then Abbie. Abbie had shown up with Gianni. The three of them were downstairs with Anthony. The little boy was terrified his mother was going to die, just like his daddy. Lyle leaned against the window frame, his arms folded. Nick was grateful for his presence. Fosselli had been a nuisance, trying to take charge and demanding to hold Jessie's hand while she was examined. Barton had brusquely asserted his authority with a crime victim and ordered him downstairs.

The doctor joined them. "The good news is I found no semen and there's no sign of forced entry."

Nick breathed a sigh of relief. "And the bad?"

"Jessie has severe contusions all over her body, lacerations on her neck and wrists, and a cracked rib. But I'm most concerned about her head injury. She should be watched closely for the next twenty-four hours for a concussion." He handed a bottle of pills to Nick. "For pain as needed. I just gave her one. I'll check in with you in the morning."

"What exactly happened to her, doctor?" Mary asked. "Did she tell you?"

"She's not talking. At all. You might want to call in a professional to speak with her."

*

Cobra met Zappella at a Chinatown coffee shop just before dawn. Aldo took one look at the man and burst out laughing. "Your own mother wouldn't recognize you."

Cobra felt ridiculous in a mahogany rug, fake beard and mustache, green contact lenses, padding, and horn-rimmed glasses. "This fucking cologne's gagging me."

"I told you. Smell's a victim's strongest sense. Trust me. She'll remember that crap and nothing else. God, you stink. So. It went according to plan?"

Cobra tossed Jessica Brady's turquoise panties across the table.

Aldo smiled. "I assume you had a good time."

"You're one sick mother, you know that?" Cobra headed out the door, trying not to limp. Zappella would never know what a royal fuck-up tonight was. Jessica Brady's heel to his groin was still causing excruciating pain. That little bitch was vicious.

*

Bill and Dr. Logan finally left. Even after Mary helped Jessie change into a nightgown, Nick noticed she still wore his suit jacket, clumsily pulling it back on. Nick asked Mary about that as they headed down to the kitchen and Anthony. Gianni was standing watch over Jessie for now.

"You figure it out, Nick," Mary said, fixing her dark eyes on him. He combed a hand through his hair. Mary didn't know the half of it, the part about where Nick and Jessie had been heading before Jessie's fateful trip to the ladies' room. What animal had attacked her?

- 165 -

For the next few hours, Nick drifted in and out of the bedroom like a tumbleweed, unable to sit still. He'd talk to Lyle about the attack later, in private, after Jessie was able to give a statement. For now, Lyle had unmarked units cruising the street. Barton took up residence in the bedroom, sitting in the rocker and scribbling in a notebook. The cop's presence seemed to annoy the hell out of Fosselli. Nick smiled, his eyes cold. Abbie was guarded, saying little, never far from Gianni's side. Anthony clung to Nick, his blue eyes ringed with fear.

Over the course of the night, Gianni decided the assault was Nick's fault. Nick bit back his anger and kept out of the man's way. His insinuations were nothing Anthony should hear. As dawn approached, tempers grew shorter. The group finally gathered in the kitchen, leaving Lyle alone with Jessie.

Gianni glared at Nick. "What were you thinking, letting her wander around alone in a hotel at that hour of the night? I know you have no respect for women but--"

"Nick?" Mary interrupted. "Would you put Anthony to bed? Look at him. He's sound asleep on your lap."

"Let me, Mary," Gianni said, rising.

"I want Nick to do it."

"Sure." Nick said, hefting Anthony into his arms. "I'll relieve Lyle." He shot Gianni a lethal glare and climbed the stairs.

As he cleared the landing, he paused, hearing Mary turn her fury on Fosselli. "Now you listen here. I've put up with your snotty remarks all night, but I've had it. How dare you talk to Nick like that in his own home?"

"His own home? He's a guest."

"He's a member of this family, which makes it his home."

"Are you forgetting that I am also a member of this family?"

"You're a friend as far as Jessie's concerned, and if you don't start treating Nick with more respect, you won't even be that." Nick was stunned. This was motherly Mary?

"I can't believe you're speaking to me like this," Gianni's voice rose. "After all I've done for this family! What has Nicholas done besides set a bad example for Anthony?"

"Are you blind? Nick's become a second father to Anthony."

"Don't make me laugh. Anthony belongs--"

Abbie interceded. "Gianni, keep your voice down."

"Get out! Get out of my home right now!" Mary's voice filled the downstairs.

Anthony stirred, and Nick quickly tiptoed towards the boy's bedroom.

"Your home?" Gianni's voice echoed through the main hallway. "This is Jessica's home."

"Gianni, please." Abbie's voice was placating. "I think we'd better leave."

Nick heard Gianni and Abbie's heels click out the door, shutting with a bang. As Nick carefully tucked Anthony into bed, the boy sleepily reached out for his uncle. Nick hugged him, running his fingers through Anthony's tangled curls.

"Uncle Nick? If something happens to Mommy, will you take care of me?"

He lay the boy back down and fastened the blanket around his shoulders. The room was frigid. Was Andrew hovering? "Your mom will be fine."

"But if something ever happens, would you?"

Nick cleared his throat, his emotional battery on empty. He was exhausted from Jessie clinging to him, Mary depending on him, and now Anthony needing him. Taking care of people was not his best event. "We're, ah, family, Anthony," Nick said, his voice husky. "We stick together. I'll always be here for you."

*

Jessie was floating with Andrew in the tranquil waters of their private cove in St. John. The heavens were ablaze with a million twinkling stars on a bed of blue velvet. She was at peace with the world.

They were drifting, Jessie's arms and legs wrapped around Andrew, the warm water lapping at their naked bodies. His lips found her ear, what they laughingly called Jessie's erotic zone. When his tongue began to dance, Jessie shivered and turned her face to kiss him. But it wasn't Andrew. It was Nick who covered her mouth with his.

Her eyes snapped open. "Nick," she whispered. Oh. It was a dream. Only a dream. But it felt so real.

"Jess?" She followed the sound of the voice. Nick was sitting in the rocker, worry creasing his face. Why was he worried? And what was he doing in her bedroom? She took a deep breath. Streaks of pain shot through her body. Her face ached. Reaching up to touch her cheek, she saw her wrist was bandaged. What … ?

She remembered. The dark bathroom. That man. His rough grasp. His hideous cologne. His garlic breath. The grinding sound of his zipper. Jessie pinched her eyes closed, trying to shut out the images. Tears trickled down her cheeks.

She felt the mattress shift. Nick sat beside her, saying nothing, just taking her hand. The sight of his thick-lashed eyes broke the dam. They were filled with such deep sadness and pain, for her. Jessie sobbed, unable to stem the tide. Nick took her into his arms. He let her cry until she had no more tears, and she fell asleep.

*

Gianni watched the reflection of the late afternoon sun ripple across the ceiling of his bedroom. It reminded him of his days aboard the Milano. Those lazy days when he and Jessica had nestled beneath the sheets in the owner's suite. Now it was Abigail stretched out beside him, her arms tossed comfortably over her head.

Gianni was still reeling from the past twenty-four hours: Abigail's startling revelations. The attack on Jessica. Mary's vitriol towards him. It had

- 167 -

been a welcome diversion to tumble between the sheets with Abigail. Abigail was a revelation in bed, supple and stealthy. A constant surprise. If it weren't for the situation with Jessica, Gianni would feel on top of the world.

He no longer worried about trusting Abigail. Amazing. He had found a true partner, someone who thought of him before anyone else. She even managed to make his memories of Jessica recede a bit. Of course, Gianni would always love Jessica, but Abigail was delicious in her own way. And she would be invaluable in his quest to claim his son.

"Abigail, tell me something. With Andrew dead, why did you come back to New York?"

"Truth?" Abigail rolled onto her side. "A romance gone bad in L.A. I wanted to get away for a while. New York was my home off and on from the time I was fourteen."

"Were you really serious about helping me obtain custody of Anthony?"

"Of course."

Gianni outlined her lips with his finger. "I've decided it may be time to act soon. Will you help me when I'm ready?"

"Just tell me what you want me to do."

*

Nick's eyes opened a crack. Jessie was asleep on his shoulder, her breathing deep and steady. He studied her face, her lovely features ringed by bruises, one cheek swollen. Gently, Nick swept a tendril of hair back from her eye. Inexplicably, he wanted her more than ever. If only he were waking up after a long night of making love. If only he could shake her awake and tease her into a few more hours of passion. Life was definitely not fair. Tomorrow he'd be on his way to the West Coast for three weeks.

Nick knew he needed to get out of there, before he did something stupid. Carefully pulling his arm from under Jessie, he stiffly tiptoed from the room. The aromas from the kitchen were tantalizing, but Nick climbed the stairs to his suite. Peeling away his wrinkled clothes, he luxuriated in a steaming hot shower that got his joints back in working order. He pulled on a pair of jeans and a polo shirt.

A trunk in the corner of the room caught his eye, Chelsea Brady's trunk. Mary had it removed from the attic and deposited here while he was in Chicago. Nick lifted the lid and began pulling out items. Neatly folded clothes. A box of cheap jewelry. A stuffed panda. Nick set that aside. Paperback books. A Bible listing family births, deaths and special events dating back to 1907. Nick ran his finger down the roster and stopped at his name. Patrick Michael Brady. July nineteenth. So, his birth was officially recorded in the Brady family bible. He set it beside the panda and kept digging. Perfume. Dazzle. He opened the bottle and breathed deeply. Was this the scent his mother carried? Light, with a hint of vanilla. The perfume joined the bible and bear.

Nick spotted flashes of jeweled colors towards the bottom. Gifts. Eighteen gaily wrapped packages with dates marked on each, Chelsea Brady's birthday presents to her missing son Patrick. Nick removed the one marking his eighteenth birthday and added it to the other items. Mementos from a childhood he'd never known. He placed the saved treasures carefully back in the trunk, on top of the pile.

Padding to the bureau, Nick opened the top drawer and removed a small ring box. He snapped the lid open and touched the contents lovingly. Jeffrey. A memento from a childhood unfulfilled.

*

Nick slipped into Jessie's darkened bedroom and set the tray of food on the dresser: Prime rib. Yorkshire pudding. Mashed potatoes. Buttered green beans with almonds. Comfort food. Starving, Nick had piled two plates with Mary's scrumptious food, hoping Jessie felt like eating.

But Jessie was nowhere to be seen. Moving into the sitting room, he found her gazing down into the back yard, his black jacket dwarfing her frame. "You okay?"

"The plum tree. It's wilting. I'm worried."

Nick glanced at the tree, its leaves drooping. "It just needs some water."

She shook her head. "I've been watering it. I'm going to call someone to look at it."

Nick watched her closely. She seemed in a fog. "Need another pill?"

Her eyes flickered to his face and back. "No," she said quietly. "No more pills. I don't want to go down that path again." She continued to stare at the tree. "His voice was familiar."

"Who?"

"The man. The man who ... attacked me. I've heard that voice before."

Jessie was starting to remember, a good sign. "Don't push yourself. It'll come back to you." He tilted her chin up to the light to examine her bruises. "He really did a number on you."

She surprised him by slipping her arms around his waist and burying her face against his chest. She seemed so small. But by magic their bodies molded together perfectly. Nick kissed the top of her head and stroked her hair. "You want to talk about it?"

She didn't answer, and Nick let it go. Then, in a faltering voice, her words muffled, Jessie told Nick what happened. Her voice cracked, and she was crying, but she told him everything. She drew back and stared up at him with those soft blue eyes. Melty soft, shifting in the light. He'd never realized how many different shades of blue there were: Azure. Cerulean. Sapphire. Robin's egg. Soldier blue. Sky blue. All in one woman's eyes. Incredible.

"Thank you, Nick. For what you did for me. Bringing me home. I owe you. So much." She looked down at his suit jacket. "I think this is ruined."

"On the contrary," he rasped. "It's never looked better. You're in it." Jessie was clinging to his jacket, as if she needed him near her. Him. Not Andrew. Nick brushed her cheek with his knuckles, carefully avoiding the bruises.

This was what Andrew had meant when he said Jessie was about to trust him in a major way. Nick lowered his head and kissed her as softly as a summer breeze. Their lips barely touched, but an electric current thrummed through his body at the contact. He wanted her so much he ached.

His cell shrilled, the moment shattered. With irritation, Nick fished it out of his pocket. "McDeare," he snapped. Silence. "Hello?"

"This time was just a warning," a gravelly voice hissed. "Leave it alone, McDeare, or next time the Brady woman comes home in a body bag. And so will her son." The connection was severed.

Nick couldn't breathe. So this had been no random attack. It was linked to the threatening call at the Tonys. But it wasn't about him anymore. This was about danger to family. HIS family. He couldn't let Jessie see him crumble. Nick felt vulnerable in a way he hadn't felt since ... losing Jeffrey.

"What's wrong? Who was that?"

"No one. A wrong number."

Jessie stepped back from him. "Don't do that. I told you, I don't want to be coddled anymore. Tell me the truth. That call shook you up."

Nick stared out the window, avoiding her gaze. "It-it was a warning. What happened to you last night ... they were trying to scare me off Andrew's case." He finally met her eyes. "I'm sorry I got you involved in this." If Jessie knew they'd threatened Anthony, too, she'd come apart at the seams. Nick suddenly wished he'd never set foot in the brownstone. All of them would've been better off if they'd never met. He was already keeping too many secrets from her. Andrew's secret, his own secret ...

She put her arms around him. "Why me? Why not go after you?"

He hugged her, nuzzling his chin against her satiny hair. "They probably figured I don't care about danger to myself, but I might care about someone I ... about my family."

"Nick, do I know everything? Is there anything else you've been keeping from me?"

"No. Nothing."

For the first time in his life, Nick felt guilty about lying to a woman.

CHAPTER 16

While Nick was on the West Coast for three weeks, Jessie concentrated on getting well. Her rib was on the mend, and she had several long sessions with a rape counselor. She'd survived losing Andrew. She could survive anything, including this. After getting Anthony off to camp in Maine, she hired a contractor to convert the empty attic into a gym. It would be done within days. And for the first time since she'd lost Andrew, she answered a call from Bill Rudolph without letting it go to voicemail and calling him back.

Nick phoned every night. She knew he blamed himself for what had happened to her. No matter how many times Jessie had pleaded with him before he'd left not to think that way, Jessie knew Nick felt responsible. So they carefully avoided any mention of Andrew's case on the phone, a sticky subject.

Lyle kept Jessie abreast of his investigation, Nick working doggedly with the detective long-distance. Lyle had a black-and-white stationed outside the brownstone around the clock. Jessie was sure there were plain-clothes cops hovering over the family she didn't even know about. Some of the Othello Hotel staff remembered a man with mahogany hair and horn-rimmed glasses lingering outside the ballroom that night. But no one could remember his features, only his noxious cologne. Jessie kept trying to pinpoint the man's voice, but she came up blank.

Gianni showed up every day, fussing over Jessie and trying to feed her Italian delicacies. Jessie didn't have the heart to tell him to back off. And Mary wouldn't do it for her.

*

Nick turned the locks in the brownstone, grabbed his bags and jogged down the hallway. "Hello? The nomad has returned." For a minute he expected Anthony to come bounding down the stairs. But then he remembered the boy was at camp. "Jess? Mary?" The kitchen and study were empty. Nick decided to grab a shower and unpack.

Forty-five minutes later he trotted downstairs, and Jessie hurtled into his arms, laughing. "I was up with Jeremy in the office when you got home. Sorry, Nick. I have the biggest news. C'mon. I have drinks, chilled shrimp and baked brie on the porch." She dragged him outside, curling up on the divan and tugging him down beside her.

Jessie looked radiant, wearing a white gauze skirt and a matching halter top, her hair slicked back in a French braid. This was not the bruised woman of three weeks ago. Nick couldn't take his eyes off her. "Where's Mary?"

"Having dinner with her sister in the Bronx." Jessie took a sip of wine. "So, don't you want to know my news?"

"By the way, you look gorgeous. And, yes, I want to know your news," he teased.

She laughed again. "I-I'm going back to Broadway! Jeremy sealed the deal an hour ago with Bill."

Nick's jaw dropped. "Broadway? Jessie, that's great!"

"Rehearsals begin in late August. We open at Dickasons in October, a revival of TO HAVE AND TO HOLD." She waved a hand. "It follows a couple through thirty years of marriage, a tour de force for Josh and me."

Josh Elliott? The sweetheart?

"I'm terrified," Jessie enthused, "but I'll be comfortable with Josh, and I'll have you for moral support."

Here was trouble. Nick hated to step on her enthusiasm, but Jessie had to learn the truth sometime. He'd been dreading this conversation. "Um, Jess," he said softly, "I'm leaving for London soon. I have no choice."

"Leaving?" Jessie's face crumbled. "I mean, I knew it was coming. The new book, the one your agent asked about?"

He nodded, miserable. "My publisher's threatening breach of contract if the manuscript isn't in their hands by December. I'm way overdue with my first chapters. I have to live the place to write it. It's how it works for me. And the book's set in London. Liz keeps trying to put it off, but—"

Jessie touched his arm. "Nick, I had no idea how I've been holding you back."

"Don't be silly. I've been here and not London because I've wanted to be here and not London. You know I have to leave. You know I'd never leave you if I didn't have to."

"I understand. You'll be gone ... till December? That's half a year."

Nick grazed a finger across her cheek. "You can do this. You're ready." But was he?

"What about the case?" Jessie tossed up her chin.

"Well," Nick said, admiring the hell out of her, "I won't be on the case anymore. That's over."

"Nick!"

He sprang up, a cramp plaguing his calf. "C'mon, let's take a walk in the garden. I sat on that plane for five hours. I'm as stiff as hell."

Nick held out his hand, and they picked their way past vibrant roses to the linden tree's shade. "Actually," Nick said, "the case is the good part to come out of this. Whoever attacked you wants me out of the way. Lyle and I have it all worked out. A computer keeps me on top of things. Lyle will share everything with me. But to whoever's watching, it looks like I've been scared away. Which means they'll let their guard down and get sloppy." Nick smiled, hoping he looked reassuring. "Best of all, you," and Anthony, Nick vowed silently, "are safe again."

"I'll miss you like crazy." Jessie swallowed. "But if anyone understands being on the road, an actor does. I know you have to do this. And it's not like you can't visit."

Nick looked into those huge eyes, reflecting the cloudless blue bowl of sky. "And it's not like we can't make ... memories to keep us warm at night." Cupping Jessie's face, Nick dipped his head and kissed her lightly on the mouth. He drew back and gazed at her lips, still parted, then at her eyes, smoky with desire. Nick held her eyes with his own, wordlessly asking if she wanted more. Her eyes said yes, her hands embracing him, her fingers tangling his hair. Nick was suddenly aware he was breathing hard, as if he were running an invisible race.

Clutching Jessie in his arms, he kissed her with passion this time, exploring her mouth, getting to know every delicious part of her. She returned the exploration, teasing him on. Nick felt the lush curves of her body press into his, fitting in all the right places. Too well. He was hard. He wanted her here, right under the damn Linden tree.

Their lips broke apart as forcefully as they'd met. Jessie sucked in a deep breath. "It feels like a roller coaster," she gasped. "When you kiss me. Or touch me."

"Let's take another ride," Nick whispered, closing his lips over hers.

*

Paula parked herself in front of the television, sipping her third rum and coke. She could hear Ian shuffling around in the bedroom as he dressed for his bartending job. "Don't wait up for me, sweetheart," he said, as he came through the living room. "This party could go pretty late."

Hearing him leave, Paula grabbed her purse and ran to the door. After a few seconds, she flew down the stairwell, catching sight of him as he left the building. Paula followed her husband down the street and into the subway, keeping up with him when he got off at West Ninety-Sixth Street. He entered an apartment building's glass vestibule on West Ninety-Seventh Street, just off Riverside Drive, and was buzzed upstairs. Paula watched the overhead elevator dial take Ian to the fourth floor. Stepping inside the entryway, she waited for an opportunity to present itself.

*

Nick reclined across the wicker divan, Jessie cuddling against his chest like a cat. She felt like purring. "How's the plum tree? I didn't see it when we were in the garden. I had, um, other things on my mind." The sun had set, hurricane lamps casting the porch in a soft amber glow.

Jessie laughed. Those other things had morphed into dashing back to the porch and kissing and caressing until they couldn't keep their hands off each other. They'd finally broken apart, breathing hard, seeming to need a break before going any further. Jessie was tingly and moist all over, her body one big erogenous zone. She cast her eyes to the tree, the smile fading. She told Nick the plum was dying. Jessie had been devastated when the greenhouse expert told her the tree had lived beyond its life expectancy. It stood barren in the back yard, surrounded by dead leaves. "I'll have it cut down."

"You can get another tree." Nick rubbed her back under her top, his fingers gentle on her skin.

"It's not really the tree. It's that Andrew --"

- 173 -

"Please don't be sad. Not in the little time we have left." Nick lowered his head to hers, and he kissed Jessie hard, driving every coherent thought out of her head.

They came up for air, Jessie staring into Nick's amber eyes, mesmerized. She wanted him in every sense of the word. She wanted him inside her. Now. Reading her mind, Nick untied her halter, his hands caressing her breasts. His breath came in gasps, hot against her cheek. She closed her eyes and felt that moist tingle erupt into a tremor. Breathing fast, Jessie unbuttoned Nick's shirt, sliding her hands over his hard chest, enjoying his groans as her fingers played with his flesh, exploring his body's every ridge, feeling his heart thump. He swiftly unbuckled his belt. Jess fumbled for his zipper. She moaned, "Andrew, I love --"

Time stopped. Horrified, Jessie felt Nick's body tense. "Oh God, Nick. Oh, God. I'm sorry, so sorry. I didn't mean to ... "

Nick sat up. A solo cricket chirped into the silence. Jessie swallowed as Nick rose and quickly put himself back together. Without a word, he strode from the room.

*

Paula's moment had arrived. An elderly man with a cane gallantly let her in when she pretended to have lost her keys. When they reached the fourth floor, she said good night and waited for the elevator doors to close. And then she crept along the hallway, listening for Ian's voice. At this hour of the night most of the apartments were quiet, the tenants in bed.

Paula's eyes filled with tears. Behind one of those doors her husband was in bed, too. Ian wasn't bartending for the catering company tonight. There were no parties in progress on this floor.

Ian was stupid to play Paula for a fool. Paula Zappella Wexley could destroy his house of cards with one phone call.

*

Jessie couldn't sleep that night. What had possessed her to call Nick Andrew? She'd known full well it was Nick making love to her. Had her own subconscious prevented her from making a terrible mistake? But would it have been a mistake? She wanted to run upstairs and wrap herself around Nick right now. How could a yearning that intense be wrong? Jessie flipped onto her side, squeezing her pillow. "Andrew, I wish you could hear me," Jessie whispered. "Tell me what to do. Was I being disloyal to you?"

Jessie dozed off just before dawn. When she awoke a few hours later, she felt clearheaded. Nick deserved an apology. What had almost happened between them was no mistake. She'd love Andrew until her dying day, but she didn't want to live like a nun in a brownstone cloister anymore. She still had her life ahead of her.

She climbed the stairs to the suite, surprised to find the door open. Nick was gone, the drawers and closet empty, his laptop missing. He'd left behind Andrew's files and the trunk's contents. The things he'd acquired since coming to New York. Oh, God.

Jessie flew down the back stairs and into the kitchen. "Mary, Nick's --"

- 174 -

"I know," Mary said, not looking up from the newspaper. "He left about six this morning. Went back to Washington."

"Did he tell you why?"

"He wasn't talking. And judging by the look on his face, I didn't want to ask. What happened between the two of you last night?"

*

Wexley awoke to daylight streaming through the bedroom windows. He glanced at the clock. Shit, he'd fallen asleep in Nancy's bed! In a panic, he dressed and raced to the subway. He punched his cell back on, sure there would be a dozen messages from his wife.

Nothing. He was a lucky man. She must still be asleep and not realize he wasn't home yet.

Twenty minutes later, Ian stood in the middle of his deserted McDougal Street apartment, a letter from Paula in his hands. She was giving him twenty-four hours to get his things out of the apartment. If not, he'd deal with her brother Aldo.

*

Jessie spent the day calling Nick's cell, leaving dozens of messages. After another restless night and another day of silence, her spirits plunged. She skipped dinner and retreated to the rocker in her bedroom, the same spot she'd chosen when Gianni disappeared to Italy all those years ago. Where Andrew had found her and proposed to her. Now Andrew was dead. And Nick was gone. Jessie hadn't felt this empty and alone since ... since she'd said goodbye to Andrew for the last time. It was intolerable. She couldn't live like this. She wouldn't.

The next morning, Jessie called Bill and asked to borrow his plane. She needed to get away to the villa, the one place she could heal. And she wanted to go alone. She had to learn to take care of herself. She had a play to prepare for. She didn't need a man to complete herself. She had her memories of Andrew for that, memories she'd replenish at the villa to keep him alive in her heart. Maybe she'd needed to learn her lesson the hard way. By six that night, Jessie was sitting on the beach of The Blue Pelican.

Solo.

Independent.

Nick McDeare not needed.

*

Nick slumped at his desk in his New Hampshire Street apartment, sipping a bourbon. The sun had set hours ago over the steamy capital, about the same time Nick had given up writing. Rubbing his hand over his two-day stubble, Nick crushed a cigarette in half with his other hand, the tobacco spilling onto his desk.

It had been forty-eight hours since he'd returned to Washington, but he was still replaying the scene with Jessie in his mind, a mental CD that wouldn't fucking quit. All this time he'd thought Jess had seen him clearly. But in the end, he'd been a stand-in for her dead husband. He didn't need that crap. Nick McDeare could have any woman he wanted. There was just one problem. He wanted Jessie. Nick shuffled to the bedroom. He collapsed on the bed, wearing his jogging shorts and Washington Redskins T-shirt. An hour later he was snoring lightly.

He awoke at dawn to find Andrew sitting in an easy chair. His eyes slits, Nick sat up, his shaggy hair hanging in his eyes. "Let me guess. You're here about Jessie, right?" He stumbled to his feet. "I'm not supposed to be upset when she mistakes me for you." He lurched to the living room, unscrewing the bottle of bourbon and taking a swig.

"Sit down, Nick."

"No, thanks. I'm going back to bed." Clutching the bottle, he brushed past Andrew.

"Sit down!" Andrew roared, spinning him around.

Nick teetered, brushing off his brother's steadying hand. "Well, well, Saint Andrew has a temper."

"You have no idea how hard it was for me to come here tonight to say the things that have to be said. Now, sit down."

Nick sat.

Andrew sank onto the coffee table. "I begged you not to run away, and that's exactly what you did. You overreacted, you bastard. Jessie doesn't substitute you for me. She made a mistake. That's—"

"Go on," Nick pressed. "Let's have the rest of it and get it over with."

"This is your fork in the road. You either put this behind you, or you forget you ever met my wife and son."

"What did you say?"

"I don't think you realize how serious this is. This is deja vu for Jessie. Gianni left her. I left her. And now you've left her."

"Kind of puts us on equal footing, doesn't it? We're both to blame for sending Jessie into a slump at one time or another."

"Is that supposed to be funny? This isn't the time for sarcasm. It's time for honesty."

"You're giving me lectures on honesty? That's a laugh. A man with a secret like yours? The only reason I haven't told Jessie is because it would kill her."

"Don't forget your own secret, Mr. Honesty." Andrew shook his head. "Look at you. You're not eating. You're torturing cigarettes. Your eyes are bloodshot. You haven't shaved. Your hair's matted. You look like a bum."

"This is your fault. Yours and Jessie's. If you'd stayed out of my life—"

"Stop blaming everyone else for your own mistakes. Look, do you want to take a chance and go forward? Or do you want to remain locked in your shitty past?"

"Now we're playing Scrooge? You're taking me on a trip to my past, my present, and what's next, my future?"

"I'm serious."

"Okay, I'll humor you. My past wasn't so bad. No pressure from anyone. Just me, my books, and a lot of travel." Nick dropped his eyes. Last

Christmas he'd sat alone in a Vancouver deli, eating a cold turkey sandwich. He couldn't remember what he did on his last birthday. Probably screwed one of his bimbos. His fortieth birthday was hovering, and his prospects looked just as bleak. "Okay," he said softly, setting the bourbon on the desk. "You win. I've seen the future without Jessie. I'll go back to New York and apologize."

"She's not there. Jessie's at The Blue Pelican."

"Then we can forget it. Jessie doesn't allow anyone into the villa. That's where she goes to be with you."

"Exactly. Jessie's turned the villa into a shrine to me. It has to stop or she'll never be able to move on. You have to get down there and help her jump her last hurdle. She needs to leave me behind. Be there for her. In every sense of the word."

"Andrew, I'm telling you. Jessie will never let me in."

"Oh, but she will. I predict you'll be sitting on The Blue Pelican's beach late this afternoon. Here's what you have to do ..."

*

Wearing a lavender bikini, her hair tied back in a ponytail, Jessie lounged on a throw on the beach, a cooler at her feet. She watched as gulls skimmed the cove's turquoise waters. The mid-summer heat was oppressive, but she was used to it. Adjusting her sunglasses, she plucked a bottle of water from the cooler and buried her nose in a book.

A shadow fell across the page. Shielding her eyes, Jessie glanced up. Nick stood at her side, barefoot, wearing cut-offs and a white tank top, a pair of opaque sunglasses on his nose. A breeze swirled his hair across his forehead. "Surprised?"

My God. "Uh ... try stunned?"

"Mind if I join you?" Not waiting for an answer, he dropped down beside her.

They eyed each other silently. "How the hell did you manage this? How did you find me?"

"It's a long story, but ... Andrew did it."

"You mean the other night. Look--"

"I'm not talking about the other night. I'm saying Andrew's responsible for my being here. I ... had another dream about him. He told me to get my ass down here."

"Andrew did that. Right." So what was Nick's real agenda? Just when she was finally making sense of her life, the one person she didn't need messing with her head was Nick McDeare.

"Mary actually arranged it, with the help of Bill's private plane and Hannah and Kelvin." Nick leaned back on an elbow. "Did I get the names right? The couple that live here?"

"They're year-round caretakers, dear friends. I'm surprised Mary helped you. She knows how I feel about this place." The sun glinted off Nick's sunglasses, his expression impossible to read, an enigma inside and out. One she wasn't up to deciphering anymore.

"You mean, no outsiders allowed. Is that what I am to you now? An outsider? Should we redefine my status in our dysfunctional little family?"

"I don't know what you are anymore." She eyed him warily. "I do know you don't look so good."

"I haven't been in the best frame of mind the last couple of days." He lifted his sunglasses, revealing bloodshot eyes. "I was hitting the sauce." Nick flipped the glasses back in place. "Look ... what happened between us, I overreacted. I'm sorry."

"I tried to reach you." Jessie closed her book. "To apologize."

"I know." Nick picked up the book. "RED ROVER?" He tossed it back onto the throw. "So you were thinking about me, hmm?" He ran his fingertips down her spine, goose bumps shadowing his touch.

Jessie inched away, his hand stroking air. "Why did you come down here? It's a long way to go for an apology."

"I want your body. I figured down here you'd be a captive audience."

*

Aldo entered Roberto Martinelli's study unannounced. "We're lucky we kept the Brady place wired. I just heard from Cobra. McDeare took off for the Brady woman's villa in St. John. Private plane. I got the flight plan from our air traffic controller friend. What do you want me to do? You think he's really off the case?"

Martinelli sat back in his swivel chair. "We stick to the status quo, but let's send a couple of men down there tonight. Call our contacts in the Virgin Islands." Roberto reached for a cigar in his humidor and sniffed it. "I want a backup plan, just in case. A little extra insurance. And a look at that laptop."

*

"Let's take a walk," Jessie said. Ah, progress. She could've poured her water bottle over his head. They strolled the beach, following the inlet encircling the cove. Nick had never seen anything so beautiful, and he'd seen almost every exotic corner of the world. Crystal waters lapped white sand, lush foliage nestling against sculptured gardens and stone benches. Pelicans strutted the grounds. A sleek yacht was tied up to a dock, the Anthony B. Security was state-of-the-art. A ten-foot high iron fence surrounded the property, wired with an elaborate alarm system. Lasers protected the mouth of the cove from intruders. The Blue Pelican seemed to be a fortress.

"On the other side of all that foliage's the ocean," Jessie said. "But in here it's a private little world. This was Andrew's haven." They meandered back to the picnic basket. Jessie shimmied into a pair of white shorts and sleeveless cotton top. "I'll show you the house ... now that you're here."

Uninvited. But he wasn't about to give up. They climbed flagstone steps, passing two hammocks strung between palm trees. The villa was a series of two-story pale blue stucco buildings connected by breezeways, shaped like a "U." A tiled patio was filled with palm trees, its centerpiece a pool with a small island capped by a towering palm. Nick followed Jessie into a huge tiled kitchen-dining room, filled with flowering tropical plants, native pottery, and hooked rugs. As they padded down the east wing, Nick caught sight of a game

- 178 -

room and a gym. Traversing a breezeway, they entered a greenhouse cluttered with palm trees, flowering plants, and a stream with its own miniature waterfall and drawbridge. Nick whistled. "Magnificent."

"You should see it at night," Jessie said tonelessly, as if she were a bored real-estate agent. "The illumination's beautiful." Retracing their steps, they passed through the kitchen to the Great Room. Glass walls overlooked the terrace. Lazy overhead fans spun the air over tropical plants and native pottery. Photographs were scattered everywhere. A grand staircase spiraled to the upper floor.

"What's all this?" Jessie pointed to two large boxes by the front door.

Nick shrugged. "Mary said they were supplies we'd need. Customs went through them while I was boarding the plane. I didn't see what was inside. Honest."

"What you do is your business, Nick."

Nick rolled his eyes. Andrew had been right. Jessie had retreated so far away that she might as well be on the moon. Wandering down the west wing, they passed a library and several bedrooms. Another breezeway crossed to an adjoining building, but Jessie halted and started up a staircase. "Wait. What's in there?" Nick asked, gesturing to the building.

"The master bedroom suite."

"I'm not allowed into your boudoir?"

"I've been sleeping in another bedroom," she said coolly. "No reason for you to see it."

The hell with that.

"Nick, wait!" But Nick was already through the breezeway. Pushing the door open, he stepped into the sitting room of an amazing two-story palace. A glass wall faced the ocean, a white mesh curtain drawn against the harsh sun. In fluid shades of green and blue, the room drew in the ocean beyond the glass. A white baby grand piano stood in the corner, a kitchenette in an alcove. It was fit for a king. And his queen.

Nick climbed an elegant circular staircase to the bedroom, a majestic wall of floor-to-ceiling glass leading out onto the terrace. There was a fireplace to chase out the damp. A lavish bathroom equaled the size of Nick's first apartment. Nick glanced over his shoulder. Jessie was picking her way up the stairs as if walking on eggs. "You should be using this suite."

"I'm not ready."

Sliding his hands into his pockets, Nick ambled to her side. "You didn't think you were ready to set foot in the world again. Or present at the Tonys. Or return to Broadway. But you did it." He brushed a strand of hair from her eyes. "You're ready for this."

"Don't tell me what I'm ready for, okay?" Her eyes flashed blue sparks. "Who the hell do you think you are? You show up here uninvited and start giving me orders? Well, screw that. Maybe you're right, and we should redefine your status in our dysfunctional little family. So you know exactly where you stand." She spun on her heel.

"Let's start talking then. Wait!" Nick grabbed for her arm, but Jessie was as elusive as mercury. She slipped out of his grasp and dashed out the door.

*

As soon as Mary answered the front door, Gianni brushed past her into the brownstone, dozens of pink sweetheart roses in his hands. He hurried down the hallway.

"Jessie's not here."

He stopped. "I'll wait."

"She's out of town."

"Where did she go?"

Mary stared, her face a mask.

Gianni bit back his temper. "Look, Mary, Let's end our feud, yes? We were both tired and short-tempered and worried about Jessica the night she was attacked. I'm sorry if I offended you."

Mary's face didn't change expression.

Gianni handed her the flowers. "These are for you. Now, where's Jessica? I'd like to call her and see how her injured rib is mending."

"Jessie's fine. And she asked not to be disturbed. She's about to start rehearsals for a new play. She needs time to herself."

"A new play? I'm pleased to hear that. I'm glad Jessica will start living her life again. But she didn't mean me."

"Your name wasn't on the list."

The woman should be fired. Gianni glared at Mary before striding through the open doorway. He heard Mary slam the door behind him.

*

Jessie sat at the kitchen table, a note from Hannah in her hands. The Traphagans were staying with family in St. Thomas for the night, Hannah due back in the morning. Jessie shook her head. This was Mary's doing. Trying to push Jessie into Nick's arms.

She fingered both hands through her hair. If someone gave her a lie detector test right now, the needle would be jumping all over the place. She wished Nick would leave. She wished Nick would stay. She wished Nick would make love to her. She wished a jellyfish would sting Nick where it hurt. Bottom line: The man was lethal to her sanity. She was better off on her own.

Nick jogged down the stairs and hefted his duffel bag and laptop. Without a glance in her direction, he disappeared into the Great Room. Jessie crossed her arms and stared out the window. The sun was dipping down the painted sky.

Movement caught her eye, and she saw Nick cross the far breezeway and enter the master bedroom's first floor. What the hell was he doing? She'd ignore him and pretend he wasn't here. Maybe he'd disappear altogether. Jessie picked up her script of TO HAVE AND TO HOLD. Work would get her mind off her brother-in-law.

Nick was back a few minutes later, whistling. As he headed for the refrigerator, his cell phone rang. "McDeare. Hey there ..." Nick chuckled. "Mmm, so-so."

Jessie snuck a peek at him, the phone pressed to his ear. "Yeah, okay. Sounds good. I'll be in touch." Nick tucked his cell away.

"Another one of your bimbos?"

"What do you think?" Whistling again, Nick opened the refrigerator.

*

Mary sat in the breakfast nook, sipping iced tea and watching the sunset over her rose garden. It felt good to relax, her joints aching today.

The doorbell chimed. Mary pulled herself up and shuffled down the hallway. With a quick glance through the peephole, she turned the locks and swung the door open. Abbie smiled and stepped inside.

*

Nick surveyed the contents of the refrigerator. He'd never seen so much food. He pulled out two fresh tuna filets and tossed them onto the island. Checking the pantry, he discovered fresh plantains and crusty seven-grain bread. He grabbed a mango, kiwi, papaya, pineapple, passion fruit, and honeydew melon.

"What are you doing?" Jessie asked.

"I'm making us dinner. Or would you prefer a juggling act?"

"I'm not hungry. Or in the mood for clowns."

"Suit yourself. I haven't eaten much in days. I'll eat your half, too." Examining the spice rack, he began to liberally sprinkle some of the bottles into a bowl.

"Why did you take your things to the master bedroom?"

"I'm sleeping in there tonight. Andrew told me all about it. Actually, I don't think he'd mind if you joined me."

"You're unbelievable." Jessie's face flushed. "You'll do anything to get a woman into bed. Even use your dead brother."

"Andrew told me a lot of things that might surprise you."

"Like what? Go ahead. I need a laugh."

"Well, let's see." Nick rubbed the spice mixture into the tuna fillets. "Like you and he used to take midnight swims. Naked." That got her attention. "Also, the two of you used to go dancing at a local eatery called ... The Octopus?"

Jessie stared at him. "The Pickled Octopus."

"What else? Oh, yeah. The convertible. He said you have a 1971 Cadillac convertible down here. After dark, you'd drive to a spot that overlooked the ocean. It was very romantic. In fact--"

"Stop. Just stop it." Jessie propped her elbows on the table, and dropped her head into her hands.

Nick padded to her side. "It scares you, doesn't it?" he asked softly. "Andrew manipulating our lives. Bringing out the past. Making you face your feelings."

"It doesn't make any sense." She lifted her head and looked at him, her eyes wet. "Why doesn't Andrew come to me if he really told you anything? Why doesn't he communicate with me himself?"

"I'm not sure, Jess." Nick reached over and brushed away a tear. "I'm sorry I upset you. Look, let me get dinner ready and we'll talk about this some more. Wait till you taste my grilled tuna. You'll swear you're eating fillet mignon. Hey, maybe you'll even like me again."

"I'll eat your dinner. But tuna won't make me like you again."

"We'll see about that."

CHAPTER 17

At Abigail's news, Gianni sat stony faced on the living room sofa. "Mary stated unequivocally that Nicholas was with Jessica at the villa, and they didn't want to be disturbed?"

"I'm sorry, Gianni. Really I am."

"And you think there's something going on between them down there?" He was having trouble grasping the situation. It just wouldn't sink in.

"You haven't seen the villa, have you? It's the most romantic spot in the world."

Gianni grimaced. "I've only seen pictures. Jessica never invited me. And I've dropped a multitude of hints."

"She's very protective of the place because of Andrew." Abigail leaned closer. "You know, now that I think about it, maybe I'm wrong. I can't see Jessie fooling around with Nick on hallowed ground. She's probably focusing on the new play and Nick's, well, just being Nick. Jessie won't be under his thumb anymore, now that she's working again. She'll be going to rehearsals, costume fittings. Bill will have her working the press, giving interviews. She'll be back in the real world."

"You really think so?"

Abigail smiled, her luscious lips parting like the Red Sea. "Yeah, I do."

*

Jessie called a truce. She was hungry, and she needed to regroup. She and Nick packed a picnic basket, spread a blanket on the sand, and cooked their meal on the beachside barbecue. The sun had scooted out of sight, and the sky was aglitter with stars. The Tiki torches flared, and the tree frogs warmed up for their nightly gig. A warm tropical breeze had kicked out the oppressive heat of the day.

The grilled tuna was perfection, the fried plantains and fresh fruit the perfect complement. They washed it all down with a fine bottle of Pinot Grigio. Groaning, they repacked the picnic basket and opened a second bottle of wine. Tucking beach pillows behind their heads, Jessie and Nick sprawled on their backs and stared up at the picture postcard sky.

"So tell me more about your Andrew dream," Jessie said lightly. "What else did he say?" At least she'd get to the bottom of Nick's tall tales.

"He told me you wouldn't believe any of it, so he gave me irrefutable proof." Nick took a sip of wine.

"What kind of proof?"

Nick smiled, that band of white teeth gleaming in the torchlight. "I don't think you're ready for it yet."

"This is all a hoax to get me into bed, isn't it?" Nick hated to lose, especially when it came to those notches on his belt. That's what this was all about. He wanted to finish what they'd started at the brownstone. The jerk.

Nick sat up and stared down at her. "Look, I know you have a pretty low opinion of me, but I'd never use my brother to get you into bed. A sister, maybe, but I don't have one."

"I want to hear your so-called proof." Jessie scrambled to her feet. "It's been a long day. I have a script to study."

Nick sprang up. "Calm down." He mittened her hand. "Let's walk in the surf, okay?"

Jessie jerked her hand away. The man had more moves than a belly dancer. "Fine." She looked at her watch. "You've got fifteen minutes." They set off down the beach in silence, the torches lighting their way.

"Andrew paid me a visit before the sun came up this morning," Nick finally said. "He doesn't want you to feel guilty about us being together. He wants you to live your life and be happy and move on."

Jessie laughed in his face. "Move on to you, you mean. I don't believe you."

"It's the truth."

"Right." Jessie planted her feet in the sand, her patience fraying. "Well, let me answer your question about your place in this family. You are my brother-in-law. You are the man trying to solve Andrew's murder. You are Anthony's uncle. But you are not my lover and you will never replace Andrew and thank God I realized that in time. And that," she poked him in the chest, "defines your place in this family."

"You're the one who has a problem with the truth." His eyes glittered. "You're running from me because I was stupid and I screwed up and I ran from you first. And that took you to a very dark place, and scared the hell out of you. I'm sorry about that." His eyes softened. "I'll try very hard to never let you down again. But I don't want to replace Andrew. No one can. I do want to be your lover. Andrew does want you to move on and stop using his memory like a crutch. And he told me two things that no one but the two of you would know to prove I'm telling the truth."

Convenient psychobabble from a man with no scruples. Jessie checked her watch. "Your fifteen minutes are up. I'm calling your bluff. What are those things?"

"Okay, since you won't give me a break, we'll do this your way. The first thing is your erotic zone. Andrew told me all about it." Nick pressed his lips against her ear. "Have I hit the right spot?"

A bolt of lightning skittered down Jessie's spine. Was it the moist touch of his lips and tongue, or was it his shocking words?

"Am I right? Admit it."

"Yes," she squeaked, scared out of her mind by how right he was.

"And there's more," Nick said savagely, not giving an inch. "You and Andrew were superstitious about opening nights and followed a strict routine. On every opening night you both pinned your St. Genesius medals on the inside of your costumes. Your dad gave you both those medals when you graduated from the High School of Performing Arts. St. Genesius is the patron saint of actors. You carried --"

"Stop!" No one, absolutely no one, knew about that superstition. Not even Mary. "I believe you," she whispered, stunned. "I believe you."

Nick grabbed her upper arms. "Say it. Say exactly what you believe. I want to hear you say it."

She looked up into his eyes, boring into hers. And then she froze. "How do I know you didn't read all this in Andrew's journals? I have no idea what he wrote on those pages, and you know it."

"You can't be serious. I'll show them to you when we get back to New York."

"You can have the writing forged."

"You know I hold one thing sacred in this world, Jess, don't you? What is that one thing?"

"Your son. Jeffrey."

"I'll swear it on Jeffrey's name then. Andrew told me these things. He wants you to take another chance on me and put away the guilt about betraying him. Can you believe me now?"

He was telling the truth. She could see it in his eyes, searching hers. She licked her lips. "Okay. I-I believe you've given me a sign from Andrew. I don't have to feel guilty about-about ..."

"About us. Say it."

"About us," she croaked. She wanted him. Jessie finally admitted it to herself. For all his faults, she wanted Nick McDeare in all kinds of ways. In her bed and in her life and in her family. Andrew had set her free. It was time to move on.

Nick smiled into her eyes as if he could read every thought. The tension broke. Reaching out, he skated a hand over her cheek, as gentle as a falling leaf. Jessie shivered as he gently pressed his lips to her ear. Slowly, she surrendered, curling her arms around his neck. She let her fingers flit through his inky hair. She lifted her face to his, silently asking him to love her. Nick bent his head and covered her lips with his. Her insides melted ... And then, out of the corner of her eye, Jessie saw lights flick on. She stiffened.

"What's wrong?"

"Lights. In the master bedroom. Look." Jessie pointed to the illuminated building.

"What the hell? Maybe Hannah --"

"Hannah's gone for the night."

"I'll check it out."

"Nick, no --"

Nick sprinted towards the flagstone steps leading to the master bedroom, taking them two at a time.

"Stop! Please. I'm afraid."

It was no use. He reached the patio level and quickly scaled the staircase to the second-floor balcony.

"It's locked!" Jessie yelled. "Please don't--"

Too late. An arc of light sliced across the terrace as he disappeared inside.

"Nick, no!"

*

As Nick crouched low and slid into the master bedroom, the lights flickered out, plunging him into darkness.

"Nick?" He heard Jessie hurtling up the steps outside.

"Stay there!" Nick shouted. Searching the wall for a light switch, he flicked it on, relieved to see the room bathed in light. He grabbed a poker from the fireplace and scanned the empty bedroom. Everything seemed undisturbed. He dug his cell out of his pocket and asked the operator for the police.

Nick checked the closet and the bathroom. Empty. Locking the door to the breezeway, he crept down the staircase and made sure the sitting room was vacant. Scaling the stairs, he dropped the poker and opened the terrace door. Jessie fell into his arms, trembling.

"God, when you went through that door --"

"There's no one here." His heart was tap dancing, but he tried to sound calm for Jessie's sake. "I called the police."

Jessie flipped a switch on a wall monitor, a live picture of the gate materializing. "We'll see them pull up."

An hour later, Nick was arguing with an Islands cop treating him like a rich-and-famous idiot complaining about a banana peel on his yacht. "There's no one here, Mr. McDeare," the policeman said overly patiently. "We've checked every inch of the estate."

"Then what the hell caused the lights to flicker?"

"Could've been a short. Or a power surge. Happens all the time in the islands."

"A power surge in only one building?"

"How do you know it was only one building? I stood on that beach tonight. From there, the only building visible was the master bedroom."

The cop had a point. The steep drop down to the beach hid the other buildings. And with the Islands' primitive electrical hookup, a power surge could've flicked on the lights even with the switches off.

As Jessie showed the policemen out, Nick paced the kitchen. He couldn't shake the feeling that someone had gained access to the grounds. And if they'd gotten in once, they could get in again. You saw one cockroach, and its pals were waiting in the trenches. As soon as Jessie returned Nick asked if there was a gun in the villa.

"The police said it was a short or a power surge. Why do you need a gun?"

"Better safe than sorry."

"You're scaring me, Nick."

"I'm sorry about that," Nick said levelly. There was no way around this. He needed a way to protect them. Sometimes it was good to be scared.

"Do you know how to use a gun?"

"My dad taught me to shoot when I was twelve. I'm licensed to carry in D.C." She still didn't move. "Jessie," Nick said, not trying to disguise the edge to his voice, "I need the gun. Now."

Jessie finally nodded. "In the pantry. What dark thoughts are rolling around in that brain of yours? Don't shut me out. This is my home."

"Something doesn't feel right. I want you to come with me after I get the gun. We're going to the master bedroom."

"Now you're giving me orders?"

"Now I'm keeping you safe. Unlike last time. Don't argue with me. You mean too much to me. Do you understand what I'm saying? And I'll need a magnifying glass, a flashlight, and sandwich bags."

"I'm not hungry anymore," she quavered.

"It's not that kind of sandwich."

"A joke."

He stared at her. "I will not let them get to you a second time. Forgive me if I'm not being particularly nice right now, but I'll die before I let anything happen to you. Let's move."

Jessie looked at him a long moment, then led Nick to the pantry and handed him a revolver. It was a 380 semi-automatic, the kind cops used as an ankle backup. She scrounged up the other items while he checked out the downstairs' rooms one more time. Hand-in-hand, they padded back to the bedroom suite. Nick locked all three doors and tucked the gun into the nightstand's drawer. With a magnifying glass and flashlight, he got to work, crouching on his hands and knees. "This could take awhile," he said, examining the floor and carpeting. "Make yourself comfortable."

"What are you doing?"

"You'd be surprised what people leave behind. A hair or a stray fiber. A scuff mark from a shoe."

"But it could've been left by a maid or even one of the exterminators. Besides, if someone got in or out, they would've tripped the alarm system."

"Security systems can be breached."

*

Jorge Menendez worked for Cruz Bay Security. He left work at the end of his shift that night with a thick wad of bills in both pockets. He had no idea Roberto Martinelli's private plane carrying Aldo Zappella and three of his men had touched down in the U.S. Virgin Islands earlier that evening. Aldo and his companions had rendezvoused with Bobby Nori, Martinelli's main man on the Islands, at a dilapidated building nicknamed Sandpiper high in the hills of Charlotte Amalie. All Jorge knew was that Bobby Nori had bribed him with a year's worth of wages to switch off The Pelican's security system at a prearranged time and give him access to client records.

While Jorge had worked his shift, Nori had led Aldo and his men, flashlights in hand, to the villa. With a decoder, they had tripped the gate's lock and crept up the driveway, fanning out to check the caretaker's cabin on the grounds. It was empty. Following a security map, they'd made their way to the master bedroom in the main house. Once their job was done, they had packed their gear and phoned headquarters. Aldo had conducted an equipment test, setting off an accidental power surge and catapulting them out of the villa and through the gate in seconds. A quick page to Menendez had reinstated the security system.

As Jorge began the long walk to the ferry, he moved to the side of the road as a car approached. The car slowed, and Jorge found himself staring down the barrel of a gun. His scream ended with a shot to the head.

*

Stretching, Nick lurched to his feet after hours of searching for evidence. He'd found several hairs, now sealed in the sandwich bags. He glanced at Jessie, sound asleep. Nick grabbed a quilt and covered her. Her face was sunburned and minus makeup. She looked healthy and radiant, and he'd be damned before he'd let evil touch her again. Nick brought her hand to his lips, kissing it tenderly.

Nick filled a glass with bourbon at the bar, silently blessing his brother for sharing his taste for Kentucky rotgut. Taking a swig, he rubbed the back of his neck and checked his progress. Only the floor around the bed left to search. Might as well get it over. A few minutes later, Nick dug in his pocket for a plastic bag and scraped what looked like miniscule paint or plaster chips into the bag. Narrowing his eyes, he examined the textured ceiling carefully.

There it was. A tiny hole blending perfectly into the bubbled texture. Unless you were looking for it, you'd never see it. The roof of the suite was sloped. Which meant there might be a crawl space up there. Nick found what he was looking for in the walk-in closet, a ceiling trap door with a ladder attached. Nick's adrenaline propelled him up the rungs. Swinging the door up, he hoisted himself over the lip.

As realization sunk in, Nick felt his blood pressure rocket. Three little blinking lights stared back at him. Three green lights atop three video cameras. One was trained through the hole in the bedroom ceiling. The other two were focused through small openings onto the patio and the beach. In a rage, Nick let loose with a string of whispered expletives, not wanting to wake Jessie. He yanked all three cameras off their cases, disabling them within minutes.

*

As the Martinelli plane was en route back to Islip, Long Island, Aldo's cell rang. It was Bobby Nori. "We got a problem down here. I'm looking at a bunch of dead screens."

"An electrical failure?"

"Either that or McDeare found the cameras."

"Shit."

"Give me a couple of hours. I got an idea you'll like."

Aldo clicked off. Just what he needed. He pulled out a cigarette and patted his pockets for his lighter. Hell, he must have left it back at Sandpiper.

*

Nick paced the bedroom, a bourbon in hand. Every sip burned a hole in his gut. The discovery of the cameras had sent him into a white-hot anger, the kind of rage lawyers used to explain why an otherwise sane client had committed murder. He forced himself to calm down and think this through, or he wasn't going to be of use to anyone.

The villa's high-tech security system had been compromised. Nick needed to speak with the Traphagans. He also wanted Jessie to get in touch with the security company A-SAP.

Who'd want X-rated footage of Nick and Jessie and why? Nick had ostensibly backed off Andrew's case. What other reason could there be? Blackmail? Possibly. Jessie would be willing to fork over big bucks to prevent nude photos from hitting the rags. Maybe this was some sleaze hoping to cash in with the tabloids. Someone who'd caught Nick's TV interview with Carolyn Adams.

He set his glass down and knuckled his eyes. It was almost five in the morning, but he was too wired to sleep. When the sun came up, he wanted to check out the gate and the driveway.

Nick glanced over at Jessie, sleeping peacefully. He'd hoped to call her his lover by this time. The best laid plans of mice and men. Especially men.

*

Sitting up, Jessie swept her hair off her face and glanced at the clock. A little past eight. "Nick?" Spotting a note taped to the door, Jessie relaxed. A few minutes later, she found him at the kitchen table, his laptop in front of him.

Hannah Traphagan, a munchkin of a woman with copper skin and piercing blue eyes, poured Jessie a cup of coffee. "Nick and I've been getting acquainted," Hannah said in her lilting island voice. "He's some detective. Now, if you'll excuse me, I have to check on the girls. The local maids are in today. Kelvin's fishing with his brother, back in a few days. With luck, swordfish for dinner next week." She turned on her heel and power-walked towards the east wing.

"She's a trip," Nick said, his eyes fixed on the computer screen. "She walks and talks at the speed of light."

Jessie sat down beside him. "What's going on?"

"Hmm?"

"Hannah said you were some detective. Were the police wrong? Was someone in the villa last night?"

Nick sighed. "Yeah. And probably more than one person."

Jessie's mouth opened, but it took her a moment to find her voice. "Burglars?" Please let it be burglars.

"I wish it were that simple. They, God, this is hard." He took her hand and squeezed it. Jessie braced herself. "Jess, they set up cameras in the crawl-space over the master bedroom. They were hoping to make some X-rated films of us."

Jessie went numb. She forced out the word. "Who?"

"At first, I thought maybe a tabloid. But then I found this on the driveway when I was inspecting the grounds." Nick pulled a Zippo lighter from his pocket. Bottoms Up NY, NY was etched below a cartoonish female body with breasts that threatened to topple her. "On a hunch, I called Barton. He just got back to me. It's from a strip club in the Bronx … owned by Roberto Martinelli."

Jessie felt sick. "This is still about Andrew, right? That connection you think the killer has to Martinelli?"

Nick veiled his eyes. "It looks like it," he said evenly. "The question is, what was their purpose? They already threatened me by attacking you, and I backed off. I also found my laptop reversed in its case this morning. I'm meticulous about my laptop. They probably wanted a copy of Andrew's file." He chuckled. "It's password protected, almost impossible to penetrate."

"Why didn't they just steal it?"

"Because it would've tipped me off someone had gotten in. I'm sure they didn't expect me to find the cameras."

Jessie's fear returned like the four horsemen of the Apocalypse. She forced herself to keep it together. She could handle this. Nick was here. "So what happened with the lights? Did they accidentally turn them on?"

"Maybe something went wrong when the cameras were turned on." Nick paced. "I just can't figure out how they got past the security system. Maybe they had someone on the inside. Their tentacles stretch everywhere."

"How do we know they're done?"

"We don't. That's the scary part." Nick washed a hand over his mouth. "Jess," he said softly, "you think this is my fault, don't you? I arrive and the next thing you've got Watergate on your hands. I wouldn't blame you if you wanted me gone."

Jessie sprang to her feet. "Don't be ridiculous! This started way before you arrived. It started with Andrew. You have to know that. I'm terrified but I'm okay as long as I have you watching my back." Jess flew into Nick's arms, her momentum sending him reeling backwards.

Nick finally laughed. "Okay, okay. I get your point."

"Whatever this is all about has to do with Andrew. Maybe me, God knows. But you can't blame yourself. Promise me. I mean it."

"All right," he said slowly. "I promise I'll try." He yawned. "Right now I'm too damned tired to think. I've been up all night. Call your security company. See if they can give you some answers." He touched her cheek. "I'll try to get some shut-eye." He brushed her lips with his. "Come join me later, okay?" Jessie watched Nick head for the west wing, fatigue in every step.

Hannah materialized. "Are you going to open those boxes Mary sent? We need to get cracking."

"Boxes?"

"The boxes Nick brought! Open them. There's a lot to do."

Jessie hadn't a clue what Hannah was talking about, but she dutifully ripped open the cartons. One thing she'd learned over the years was that it was impossible to ignore Hannah. Looking inside, Jessie started to laugh. My God, she'd forgotten! What incredible timing.

*

For the most part, Barton loved his job, everything but the paperwork. Today he couldn't avoid it. As the day shift ended, he growled for everyone to leave him alone and hunkered down in his office.

When the desk officer knocked on his door, Barton shot him a glare. "Sorry, Lieutenant," Harry Steinmetz said, "but there's a woman out here who insists on seeing you." Steinmetz stepped aside, revealing Paula Wexley. She was good-looking, spiraled dark hair brushing her shoulders. She wore a teal print dress too tight in the hips.

"Thanks, Steinmetz. Uh, get Bushman before he heads home." Lyle rose, motioning Paula into the office. Bushman appeared a few seconds later. "Bush, you remember Paula Wexley."

"Sure. How ya doing, ma'am?"

Paula nodded, silent.

Lyle cleared off a chair. "Have a seat, Mrs. Wexley." He sat back down. "What can we do for you?" Barton smelled that Coney Island cotton-candy machine, and it wasn't Paula's perfume. Something was about to break, a signal that made his heart speed up like a jet engine. With an effort, Barton forced himself to not yell at her to blurt it out already.

Paula sighed. "This isn't easy. I lied to you, Lieutenant. I lied about my husband's whereabouts at the time of Andrew Brady's murder." She started to cry.

*

Nick's cell jangled. He jerked awake and looked at the bedside clock. Six PM. Christ. He'd slept the day away. Charles and Kate McDeare were calling from Tokyo, wanting to wish their son a happy birthday. Nick groaned. Today was his fortieth birthday. He'd been trying to forget it.

Nick hung up after the best wishes and stared out the window. A torrential rain pounded the villa's stucco walls, the ocean disappearing behind the downpour. The palm trees swayed on the blurry horizon, bowing to Mother Nature. So much for sunny paradise.

He showered and shaved, shucking on shorts and a T-shirt. Nick's stomach growled as he headed downstairs. He hoped Jessie or Hannah had dinner in the works. He found the kitchen deserted and the stove cold, but a note from Jessie asked him to join her in the VIP suite. Nick grabbed a banana on the counter and wolfed it down

Trotting up the steps, he knocked lightly before entering. Jessie was stretched across the four-poster bed, sound asleep. Clad in a clingy cranberry wrap-around dress, one shoulder bare, it was obvious she was wearing only panties underneath. Her fair hair framed her face, her sunburn mellowed into a golden tan. She looked breathtakingly beautiful and as sexy as hell. And asleep. Nick sighed.

RED ROVER was open beside her. Brass lamps on the bedside tables were lit, ditto two thick candles under glass. His attention was drawn to a small dining table in front of a bay window. Nick wandered across the room, weaving his way around the antique furniture. Despite its size, it was a cozy room, with Wedgwood blue walls.

He paused in front of the table. A small banner scrawled with "Happy Birthday, Uncle Nick" hung from the window. Silvery balloons and blue ribbons cascaded to the floor. Two place settings of blue china and crystal flutes. A bottle of Dom Perignon chilled in a sterling-silver wine cooler. A chocolate cake with a single candle awaited lighting.

Three gifts were on the table. Filled with curiosity, Nick scanned the tags. They were from Mary, Anthony, and Chelsea Brady. Her gift to her son Patrick on his eighteenth birthday. Mary or Jessie must've found Chelsea's present to him in that trunk. He should've known Mary hadn't tricked his birthday out of him for nothing months ago, luring him into relaxing his guard after one of her homemade desserts. Apple pie.

Nick stared out at the tropical downpour. He wasn't used to this kind of fuss. There was a reason he didn't do birthdays anymore. Birthdays ate a hole in his gut. Nick winced as a memory washed over him ... Jeffrey's eighth birthday party. Nick had given him a ring he'd bought in Johannesburg. Jeffrey loved all things African. Tarzan and jungles and elephants and diamond mines. Jeffrey had put the ring on and he hadn't taken it off, not until ... Nick sucked in a breath. Damn. Dammit to hell.

CHAPTER 18

Lyle handed Paula a box of tissues. "Take your time," Lyle said gently. The Andrew Brady case was about to explode like a geyser. He could afford a few minutes of making nice.

Paula blew her nose. "I should have come to you right away but ... he's my husband, you know?"

"Hey, just start at the beginning, Mrs. Wexley."

"I, um, suspected Ian was cheating on me from the beginning. My brother caught him with a woman the first year we were married. Every time he went out after that I was sure he was seeing somebody. He said I was paranoid. I'd get my cousin Arthur, and we'd follow him. I could never catch him in the act." She looked down at the tissue in her lap. "Until the night before Andrew Brady was murdered. Only it wasn't ..."

She plucked another tissue. "I wish I'd picked another night. Ian wasn't with a woman that night. He met a couple of men in an all-night coffee shop on West Street."

"Do you remember what they looked like?"

She shook her head. "We couldn't risk Ian catching us, so we didn't see or hear much. Besides, he wasn't with a woman, so I didn't care what they were talking about."

"Why didn't you just go home when you saw he wasn't with a broad?" Bushman asked.

"I thought maybe they'd connect with some women later. Anyway, we waited until before dawn, when they walked over to a warehouse on Tenth Avenue. Ian came out about fifteen minutes later with a gym bag and took the subway up to Fiftieth Street. He walked to the river and waited under the West Side Highway. Like, an hour passed, and we saw the Milano dock at the piers. I remember thinking how weird my brother Aldo's on that ship having a good time, and I'm hiding under a highway waiting for my husband to do God knows what."

Barton flashed her an understanding smile.

"Anyway, around eight or so, a man approached Ian."

"What did he look like?"

Paula shrugged. "From that distance, it was hard to see. He was shorter than Ian, dark hair. Maybe he looked Hispanic from where I was standing."

"What about his age?"

"Mmm, mid-twenties, early thirties."

Lyle pulled a file from a bottom drawer and handed her a picture of Santangelo. "Could it have been this man?"

Paula studied it. "Maybe. The hair's right, but I couldn't say for positive."

"What happened next?"

"Ian opened the gym bag and handed the guy a jacket and some gloves. And then he pulled out a gun."

"Are you sure it was a gun?"

"I saw the barrel gleam in the sun coming up. The guy grabbed it and took off towards the ramp to the piers."

"Did he put the jacket on?"

"He had it slung over his arm. But he put the gloves on before he touched the gun."

"Was Ian wearing gloves when he handled the gun?"

"Black leather. His Christmas present from me." Paula blew her nose again.

"What did Ian do after the man left?"

"He headed back towards Midtown. I figured he was going home, so Arthur and I got out of there. I had to get home so he wouldn't know I followed him."

"Did he come home?"

"Not for hours. I don't know where he was, maybe with that friend, like he said. I couldn't figure out what it all meant. I worried maybe Ian was involved in some shady business, trying to make some bucks on the side? But a few hours later, when it was all over the news about Andrew Brady, I remembered how much Ian hated him."

"Did you ever tell Ian you were under the highway that morning?"

"Not in so many words. But sometimes when he pisses me off, which is a lot, I'll hint I know more than I'm saying. It makes him crazy."

Lyle Barton sat forward. "Do you honestly believe Ian hated Andrew Brady enough to have him killed?"

Paula dabbed at her nose with the tissue. "Lieutenant, my husband is a vain man. He was a soap star. Women followed him around, drooling over him. He got his picture in soap magazines. If Andrew Brady hadn't nixed the idea to Bill Rudolph, Ian would've starred on Broadway in a Rudolph production. His career meant everything to him. He would've been set for life." Paula sniffled. "So Ian ends up being a bartender for a catering company while Andrew Brady's the toast of the town. Do I think Ian would want revenge for the way his life turned out? Hell, yes. Ian's vengeful. He plots. But did I think my husband was capable of murder?" Her big brown eyes filled with tears. "Not until that morning under the highway."

*

Jessie was back in the ICU. The doctors were frantically trying to jump-start Andrew's heart with the paddles. Someone held Jessie back, preventing her from getting to her husband no matter how hard she struggled. It was the man at the Othello Hotel! She wrenched herself free and ran to Andrew. But it wasn't Andrew on the gurney. It was Nick! She heard an animal howling. But, no, those awful sounds were coming from her, her wails echoing down the halls. She was shrieking--

"Jessie."

She heard Nick calling her. But he was dead. Nick was dead! Her screams multiplied. "Jessie. Wake up!" Her eyes snapped open. She was sitting up in bed, and Nick was beside her. "My God, that must've been some dream. You were screaming."

Jessie sobbed. "It was awful," she whispered. "You were dead. It wasn't Andrew. It was you."

He cradled her in his arms. "It was a dream. I'm right here. And I'm not going anywhere. I promise."

Jessie curled her arms around Nick, listening to his heartbeat. He ran his hand across her bare shoulder, making her skin tingle. "I'm sorry. I wanted everything perfect for your birthday. And then I fall asleep and you find me screaming. Are we cursed, or what?"

"Hey, I know better than anyone that you can't control your dreams." Nick smiled. "Besides, how could this ruin my birthday? We're finally in bed together."

Jessie laughed through her tears. She was so relieved Nick was in her arms and not on that hospital bed. Her fingers glided down the hollow of his cheek. His mouth was open slightly as she outlined his soft lips. "I couldn't stand it if anything happened to you. I mean it. I couldn't live through it again."

Their eyes jammed. Nick was still, not a flicker of a muscle as he stared down at her. Jessie lost herself in his eyes, sparkling like gold dust in the candlelight. Nick slowly lowered his mouth to hers, his lips brushing hers and withdrawing, brushing and withdrawing, until her insides churned. Taking a breath, Nick covered her mouth with his, his tongue probing, making her crazy with wanting him.

Jessie slid her arms around his shoulders, his muscles rippling at her touch. Her fingers crept under his T-shirt, kneading his taut skin. Lifting up, Nick peeled the shirt over his head as Jessie fumbled with the string of her wrap-around. She watched as Nick reached over and opened her dress himself. His hand skated up her stomach, cupping her breast, his touch gentle, his thumb dusting her nipple until it felt so good it hurt. His lips and tongue took over, sending melty ripples cascading into a chain reaction down her body, pooling in her core. Her back arched, and she moaned as his fingers took on a life of their own. Down they crept, slipping beneath the wisp of silk separating his hardness from her moist ache. Nick's lips trailed behind, shadowing the silk as he lowered it.

Nick's gaze drifted up her body, his eyes caressing her. She felt her face grow hot. An amused smile flashed across Nick's face as he moved up to lie beside her. "I love that blush of yours," he crooned, "and I love that I put it there." He cupped her face in his hands and kissed her hard. She returned the kiss, harder.

When their lips finally parted, Jessie slithered across Nick, beginning a journey of her own. She rubbed her face against his muscular shoulders, burrowed her forehead against the downy hair on his chest, pressed her lips to his toned stomach. Unbuttoning his shorts, she lowered the zipper. Slipping her fingers beneath his briefs, Jessie inched them over Nick's hips and tossed them to the floor. Her eyes took in every inch of him before her hands reached tenderly, followed by the gentlest of kisses. Nick moaned, whispering her name.

*

"Mrs. Wexley, why did you keep quiet all this time?" Barton asked, yawning. It was past eight o'clock.

Paula shrugged. "I loved him. I didn't want to lose him. And then I caught him with a woman a couple of nights ago. Why should I protect someone who treats me like dirt?"

"A wife can't always testify easily against her husband. Legally or emotionally."

"I filed for divorce this morning. By the time this goes to trial, I won't be his wife."

Barton tapped a pencil on the desk, his mind whirling. "Why didn't your cousin Arthur come along to verify everything?"

"He's out of town. At a hairdresser's convention in Baltimore."

Barton glanced at Bushman, his partner trying not to laugh. What a cast of characters. Paula plucked a business card from her purse. "His cell. He knows I'm here and wants to help."

Barton nodded, extending his hand. "I appreciate your telling us the truth. We'll be in touch."

Paula shook the lieutenant's hand. "What happens next?"

"We look into it and arrest your husband, if it's warranted. Mrs. Wexley, you do know you could be prosecuted for obstruction of justice?"

"I don't care." Paula sighed. "I don't care about much anymore."

*

Nick had lost control the moment he stretched across Jessie, the first electric moment his naked body touched hers. Her fingers molded his back like clay, working their way down his spine. He couldn't wait any longer or he'd implode. Nick took a deep breath. Holding Jessie's eyes, he entered her with one smooth thrust, watching as she arched her back and sucked in her breath. A shadow of a smile flickered across her face, as she closed her eyes and purred his name. His name. Her fingers dug into his back and her long legs curled around his hips. Lifting up, Nick burrowed further into her slick heat, driving deep. Their bodies were fluid motion, moving to a single passionate beat. It was erotic and fiery and emotional. It was something Nick had never experienced before. He wanted it to go on forever. And then he wanted to do it all over again.

*

It was after nine when Lyle climbed into his car and headed home to Flushing. He was tired, but his mind was racing. He'd called Paula's cousin Arthur Bettino before leaving the precinct house. Arthur verified he was with Paula the night in question and agreed to give a statement as soon as he returned to town.

But something was niggling at Lyle. He couldn't put his finger on it, but he trusted his instincts. Paula seemed genuine and straightforward, and yet … Maybe it was that, in the end, it had all been so easy.

*

Jessie began the dizzying descent back down to earth. Nick's damp forehead brushed her ear. He lifted his head and met her eyes. His hair was rumpled and a smile crept across his face. He rolled onto his back, exhaling slowly. Jessie shivered and crept under the blankets. Nick joined her and pulled her into his arms. She closed her eyes.

"You're so quiet."

"I don't want to break the spell."

"Neither do I." His stomach growled, sending them into fits of laughter. "I'm starving. I had a banana for dinner last night."

"Well, there's a feast in the fridge downstairs just waiting for us." Jessie sat up. "I'll get it."

Nick slid his fingers down her spine. "This is just a fuel stop."

Jessie laughed, leaning over and kissing him before scooting to the closet. Grabbing a silk robe, she wrapped it around herself. "Do you have a robe in that duffle of yours?"

"Nope."

Jessie stared at Nick a moment, hoping Nick was as right with things as she thought he was. "I'll be right back." She scurried to the master bedroom and returned a moment later, holding a man's black cotton robe in her hands. "It ... was Andrew's. I got it for him on his last birthday." She held it out, but Nick didn't move, staring at the fabric as if it were a loaded grenade. "Never mind. Bad idea, I guess. Sorry." Jessie hoped Nick didn't think she was testing him. With an easy smile, she tossed the robe on a chair. "I'll get the food."

*

His eyes on the robe, another birthday floated through Nick's mind, a birthday he could usually push away because he pushed away all birthdays. Until now. Jeffrey had been ten. He only had a few more months to live, although Nick hadn't known it. If only he'd known. If only you had the luxury of knowing the last time you'd take a picnic with your child. The last time you'd take him to an Orioles game. The last time you'd play catch with him or say goodnight or I love you.

Nick's birthday had fallen in the middle of a book tour for THE GREEN MONSTER, and he couldn't get away. Jeffrey had pleaded with him to come home to celebrate. Nick rubbed his eyes, the memory of that phone call a permanent ache etched in his heart. If he could do it over again, he'd be on a plane the minute he hung up the phone. He'd pay any price to see his son and hug him one last time. But people didn't get the luxury of second chances. Nick knew that now.

Months later, when Nick finally went home to bury his son, his ex-wife had hurled Jeffrey's birthday present at Nick. "Here, you son-of-a-bitch. Choke on it!" It was an Orioles jersey, signed personally by Cal Ripken: "I'm Nick McDeare's greatest fan. You're lucky to have a son who loves you so much." Lindsey had hissed that Jeffrey asked Ripken to sign it when the legendary baseball star had visited the children's wing at the hospital. Jeffrey had told his mother exactly how to frame it for his dad ... in case he wasn't there to give it to him. The jersey had lived in Nick's closet ever since, alongside his Arthur

Conan Doyle Award for THE GREEN MONSTER. The mementos were proof Nick had failed as a father. All he had to do was look in that closet. He lived with that knowledge every day of his life.

Nick sighed and stared at the robe. It commemorated another birthday for another man. It had taken guts for Jessie to give him Andrew's robe. Nick gingerly picked up the robe and slipped it on, tying the sash. The robe fit him perfectly, and it was comfortable. Okay, he liked it.

His eyes came to rest on the stack of presents on the table. He picked up Chelsea's gift, the red, white, and blue colors still vibrant.

"Nice robe." Jessie stood a few feet away, a picnic basket in her hand, her eyes shining.

"Yeah, isn't it?" Nick said, replacing Chelsea's gift and taking the heavy basket from Jessie's hands. "My lover gave it to me."

"Your lover has good taste," Jessie said, looking Nick up and down. "Lucky lady."

"We're both lucky." Nick nuzzled Jessie's ear and set the basket on the table. He sidled another glance at Chelsea's gift.

"Why don't you open it?" Jessie asked casually, unpacking the basket. "It's been waiting a long time."

Nick picked up the package. Why not? This present had been on layaway for twenty-two years. He tore the paper away to reveal a jewelry box. Inside lay a solid gold pocket watch and a note.

Patrick -

Today you are eighteen. A man. It's time for me to pass this watch on to my oldest son, a tradition in the Brady family. You see, you are Patrick Michael Brady the IV, so the initials still apply. I hope one day you will pass it on to your oldest son ...

Love, Mom

Nick snapped open the watch cover and saw the initials PMB. He wound it. Still working. The watch was exquisite, with a mother-of-pearl face and intricate hands. He ran his fingers across the timepiece, smooth and heavy in his hand.

"You okay?"

He shrugged, not trusting his voice.

"It's nice Chelsea saved this for you. She could have given it to Andrew, but she didn't."

Nick nodded, dropping the watch into its box. Suddenly, he was full of feelings. So many feelings he didn't know what the hell to do with them.

"Okay, time for food," Jessie said. "Mary planned the menu, and Hannah and I took care of the rest. We have sushi from the best Japanese restaurant in the Virgin Islands, calamari salad and marinated mushrooms from The Pickled Octopus. We also have cold sesame noodles, compliments of Mary's recipe file, Hannah's homemade sourdough rolls and a fresh fruit salad assembled by moi. Eclectic, but perfect for a hot summer day." Jessie pointed to the wine cooler. "How about opening the champagne?"

While Nick devoured everything in sight, Jessie filled him in on the situation with the security company. "Their records show security was down for thirty-three minutes last night, but they can't explain it. The owners of The Pickled Octopus recommended their own company to me. I think I'll switch. In the meantime, I've hired an independent security guard to sit outside the gate every night, highly recommended by the police."

"My, you have been efficient." And as tough as titanium. "The system had to have been shut off," Nick mused, "when the intruders were installing the cameras. They worked in the dark, probably used penlights."

"It all makes sense, doesn't it? Anyway, I'm also thinking about bringing in a decorator to redo the master bedroom. I think I'll have the whole suite done over."

"Jessie's taking charge, hmm? And you're not afraid anymore?"

"I'm glad you know who's in charge, McDeare. And how can I be afraid with my detective on top of things?"

"I've created a monster. C'mere." They kissed in between courses. Finally stuffed, Nick sat back, eyeing the other gifts.

"For God's sake, stop looking and open them."

He opened Mary's first. The large box contained everything he'd need to make sushi, including a bamboo roller, sticky rice, wasabi, pickled ginger, black Japanese plates and onyx chopsticks. There was even a sushi boat for serving. He couldn't believe that Mary had gone to so much trouble.

Anthony gave him a scrapbook. Nick gently parted the paper on the gift, opening the thick pages slowly. It contained a pictorial history of Andrew, Jessie and Anthony, with a special section of Nick at the end. "My Family" was carefully painted in gold on the front, Nick's name printed at the bottom. "This must have taken him forever," Nick said, his voice catching as he ran his hand over the cover. He felt a sudden stillness descend over him, as if a supernatural power were whispering him a blessing. Anthony had given him more than he knew. So much more. Anthony and his mother.

Nick and Jessie took their champagne back to bed, turning out the lights but leaving the candles flickering. The rain pounded the windows, but in the big bed it was cozy and warm.

"Nick," Jessie purred, her fingers gliding down his chest, "I don't want you to think that I didn't get you a gift. I did. It's just not ready yet. In a few weeks."

"What do you mean you didn't give me anything? You did."

"I did?"

"Your gift to me is a second chance. Yours and Anthony's. I'll explain one day. I promise. But first, this ..." He kissed her on the mouth. He kissed the pulse beating in her throat. He kissed her delicate shell of an ear, eliciting a moan. He kissed every delectable part of her. She returned his kisses one by one, and they made sweet love.

*

Early the next morning, Hannah buzzed the Kritter Krunchers truck through the gate. When the doorbell rang, she let in the two men from the exterminating company. "Hey, Max, how you been?" she chirped. "Ya got another new assistant, I see."

"Yeah, good help's hard to find."

"Let me know when you're finished." Hannah returned to her pot on the stove, and the men headed down the west wing.

Once out of sight, Bobby Nori told Max to do his business. "When you get back to the truck, Jo-Jo will give you the rest of the money. Jo-Jo and your assistant are probably sitting in that truck getting drunk while you're in here spraying your shit." He laughed. "Lucky them. Hey, stop looking so worried. I just want some pictures of Jessica Brady for my paper. I'll be done in a couple of hours."

"But how do you get back out past security? It's wired, man."

"I'm a pro, don't worry about it. Now go on. And when you're finished, if the old broad asks where I am you say I got sick and went back to the truck." Bobby slapped Max on the back and disappeared into the foliage off a breezeway. He crept along the shrubbery until he found a secure hiding spot, sitting down and making himself comfortable. Opening his bag, he extracted a bottle of water and a camera with a powerful telephoto lens.

Max sprayed his treatment around the villa and left, saying goodbye to Hannah. He found his assistant Diego on his way to getting drunk with Jo-Jo. Jo-Jo passed the bottle to Max and paid off the two men. They all left together, drinking and traveling down a deserted stretch of road bordering the ocean. Jo-Jo insisted on driving.

The drunken exterminators were bewildered when Jo-Jo stopped the truck and whipped out his gun, silencing them in minutes, one bullet each. A dark sedan cruised to a stop behind the truck. Two men emerged and helped Jo-Jo hurl the bodies into the water, joking about Jo-Jo exterminating the exterminators. Both vehicles sped away.

*

Laptop in hand, Nick padded down the flagstone steps to the beach. He'd thrown on bathing trunks under shorts and a tank top. He eyed Jessie lounging on her stomach across a throw, a bikini sculpting that lithe dancer's body.

Nick inhaled a gulp of air so sweet he could bite it and looked out over the turquoise water. It was a perfect tropical day with a bright sun. He smiled at Jessie. "Hi, gorgeous. How long have you been up?" He dropped down beside her. "I can't believe it's the middle of the afternoon."

Jessie cast him a wicked smile. "When you stay up all night, mornings tend to vanish."

Nick kissed her, images of making love the night through flipping through his mind like a slideshow. Their lips parted, and they smiled into each other's eyes. "So, did you follow through with our plans?"

"Hannah's gone back to her cabin for the day. The exterminators have come and gone, and I sent the gardeners home early. We have the villa to ourselves."

"Perfect." Nick's eyes drifted around the cove. Total privacy. They could walk around naked. They could make love on the beach with only the fish to watch. Nick had never felt this kind of freedom. He felt like ... Adam with his Eve. And no snake in the garden.

"Hungry?" Jessie cast him a seductive look.

"Starving." They both laughed.

"Well, let's fill our stomachs first and then, ah, move on to other delicacies."

Nick eyed a cooler sitting in the sand. Opening it, he found poppy seed bagels smeared with smoked salmon and cream cheese, a salad of mango, strawberries, melons, and a thermos of Mimosas. His cell jangled. It was Barton.

Nick listened in stunned silence as Lyle described Paula Wexley's confession. "Christ, this came out of nowhere." Nick pushed his hand through his hair. "Why can't I get excited?"

"I know the feeling."

"Something smells. I don't like it."

"Me, neither. But the department's salivating to arrest Wexley."

Jessie cocked her head at Nick's words. Nick held up a finger.

"And," Nick asked, "Paula identified Santangelo?"

"Close. Santangelo resembles our hit man. But she mentioned a jacket and gloves. Those details weren't released to the press."

"There's more to this. I know it. So do you."

"Tell that to the brass. They want this case put to bed."

If Wexley put the hit on Andrew, why did it feel so wrong? "Let me do a little more fishing, okay? I'll contact a PI friend in Italy to look into Santangelo."

"What good will that do? It still means Wexley arranged it."

"I just want to cover all our bases. You never know."

"Look, I got a favor to ask. I know how you feel about protecting Jessie, but maybe you and your connections can get through to the hotheads downtown and win us more time. You pull weight with the NYPD. Any chance you can get back here?"

Nick glanced at Jessie. If he helped Barton, he might be putting Jessie and Anthony at risk. How long could he keep being back on the case a secret? "Let me think about it." Nick clicked off.

"Think about what? What about Eduardo?" Jessie asked anxiously.

"Barton wants me back in New York." While Nick accessed Ozzie Mancuso's number on his cell he explained to Jessie. "Paula Wexley paid Barton a visit yesterday. She said she saw Ian—"

"Ian!"

"... on the piers the morning Andrew was murdered. He handed a gun over to someone who looked like Santangelo."

Nick punched in Ozzie's number. Voicemail. "Oz, it's Nick again," he said in rapid Italian. "I need another favor. Eduardo Santangelo. Can you check him out? He's Gianni Fosselli's nephew, probably lived in the Genoa villa with the family. I need this A-SAP. I'm sorry to be such a pain in the ass." Nick clicked off. He didn't like what he was thinking. How could he have been so wrong?

"I knew it had to be Ian," Jessie said tonelessly, "one way or another." Her eyes drifted out over the water. "Has he been arrested?"

"Not yet. Barton thinks … we both think we should move slowly on this."

"Why? You've got a witness, and Ian had motive."

"It's not that easy. There could be--"

"Why won't you accept the fact that Ian had Andrew killed? Jessie waved a hand in the air. "There's not a shadow of doubt in my mind it was Ian. He used that crazy Eduardo who had his own grudge against Andrew to do his dirty work. Ian's good friends with Jeremy from way back. He could've easily found out Andrew's enemies from him. Andrew told Jeremy all about Eduardo after that incident with the tip jar."

"Well there's doubt in my mind. And Barton's."

"I don't believe this. This is about Gianni, isn't it? You still think he's a suspect."

Nick sighed, Andrew's secret weighing heavily on his mind. Nick had been convinced the secret got Andrew killed. But if Paula was telling the truth, the secret had nothing to do with it. "Look, I don't want to fight, okay? Let's just say Barton and I aren't convinced Wexley arranged it, and leave it at that."

Jessie wrapped her arms around her knees, staring at Nick thoughtfully. "Are you jealous of Gianni?"

Nick's lips tightened. "I was a professional investigative reporter. Don't insult me. And the last time I looked, I was the one in your bed, not Gianni."

"I'm not talking about you and me," Jessie said softly. "I'm talking about Anthony. Gianni's Anthony's father. Professional or not, you're human. Are you jealous of their relationship?"

Nick rubbed his eyes. "Point taken. I'm sorry. As far as Anthony's paternity, my brother is Anthony's father. Not Gianni. It's nothing personal." Nick turned away from her, opening his laptop and reaching for a bagel.

*

Rosita paced her cramped living room. Miguel had been missing for over forty-eight hours. She hadn't thought much about it at first. Miguel often stayed out all night playing poker, showing up hung-over the next morning, his pockets empty. But as of today, he'd missed three breakfasts.

Yesterday morning she'd asked around the neighborhood, but no one had seen Miguel. Rosita started to panic. He'd just lost his dishwasher job, and he was desperate for money. What if he'd been caught stealing and put in jail?

And fresh posters with Rosita's face had popped up in the neighborhood a few days ago. One of her friends had teased she resembled the lady in the picture. Rosita had laughed and skipped away.

She couldn't go to the police about Miguel. They might recognize her. And if they discovered she had no papers, they'd send her back to Cuba. Dios Querido, what should she do? Rosita dropped her head in her hands and cried.

*

While Jessie studied her script, Nick was buried in e-mails. There were dozens of scathing messages from Liz Scott, admonishing him to get to London immediately. He tried to placate her in a long e-mail, explaining the situation with his brother. His cell shrilled.

It was Anthony. "Did you like the scrapbook, Uncle Nick?" His voice brought a smile to Nick's face.

"I loved it, kiddo. I can't believe you went to all that trouble."

"It was fun. Now when people ask about your family, you can show them the scrapbook." Nick felt a lump in his throat. Anthony told Nick he was bored. He wanted to come home.

"Your mom said you loved camp last year."

"I didn't have you last year."

Kids always cut to the chase. "I think you should talk to your mom about this." Jessie's arm stretched for the phone. "Uh, here she is. Bye."

"What's going on?" Jessie asked Nick as she took the cell.

"Ask Anthony." Nick suddenly felt the world closing in on him. Liz and London. Barton and Andrew. Jessie. Now Anthony.

"Anthony," Jessie was saying, "you need to spend more time with kids your own age. Let me think about it, okay? I'll call you in a day or so. I love you, honey." She glared at Nick and clicked off. "This is your fault."

"What …?"

"He worships the ground you walk on, and you encourage it."

"That's bull." But Nick knew there was truth to what she said. He loved his relationship with Anthony. And part of that relationship was being looked up to. Like a dad.

"If Anthony misses you when he's at camp for a few weeks, what will he do when you're off to London for six months?"

Nick had been thinking the same thing. Unfortunately, he knew exactly how Anthony would react.

"You can't do this. You can't just disappear from a child's life like that. How did Jeffrey handle your long absences?"

Could she read his mind now? "Look, leave it alone."

"I can't. I'm the one who has to pick up the pieces for Anthony."

"Back off, okay?" God, she sounded like Lindsey.

"This is about Jeffrey, isn't it? Whenever you get that pinched look on your face, you're thinking about your son. Will you ever explain Jeffrey's death to me? Please, Nick. Please tell me what happened--"

"Shut up." Nick grabbed his laptop and leapt to his feet. He sprinted for the stairs, feeling like an elephant was sitting on his chest.

CHAPTER 19

Lyle and Bush lounged in the lieutenant's office, drinking scotch from Styrofoam cups. It was after five, and the day shift was long gone. Barton was tired and in a foul mood. He'd spent most of the afternoon listening to the brass push for Wexley's arrest. Lyle had urged caution, at least until he could interview Paula's cousin. His superiors had given him twenty-four hours to either cast doubt on Paula's story or arrest Wexley. That's when he'd called McDeare.

"I don't know," Lyle said. "I don't think Wexley killed Brady anymore. I can't believe I'm saying that, but I am." Lyle took a chug of scotch. "Something stinks."

"I still think it's the Perv. But how do we refute eyewitness testimony?"

"The Commish wants to close this case. It's been two and a half years. Paula made his day. I think he's buying her dinner." He looked Bush in the eye. "Do you think Wexley had Brady killed?"

"Wexley's a drunken asshole who blames Brady for his sorry life. Brady could get in people's faces, ya know? I mean, he was supposed to be this great guy who loved his wife and son. But he was also an egotistical little fuck who loved to rub his success in other people's faces."

Barton nodded. They'd taken too many statements from actors who said Brady's ego was ugly. Jessie was madly in love with the guy. She never saw it. "So," Lyle clasped his fingers behind his head, "if we arrest Wexley, we have a fifty-fifty chance of being right."

"Let's hope the jury gets it right. Hey, at least the case will be off our desks."

*

Jessie checked her watch. Nick had been gone over an hour. Damn her temper. She'd been miffed Nick still considered Gianni a suspect. And she'd been worried sick about Anthony's reaction to Nick leaving for London. So she'd been an idiot and set Nick off by saying every wrong thing possible. Jessie stared glumly at the blue sky. How could such a gorgeous day have gone wrong?

Nick's cell rang. He'd forgotten it, and it had been jangling every five minutes like an alarm clock. Mary had been after Jessie to buy a cell now that she was working again, but she hated to lose her privacy. Exasperated, Jessie finally answered. "Nick McDeare's phone."

"Give me Nick. This is his agent."

"Nick's busy. Can I give him a message?"

"Look, tell Nick to zip up his pants and get his ass to London. Playtime's over. I can't stall Linden Publishing anymore. Bruce Linden says either he sees a manuscript by Christmas or Nick sees a lawsuit. Think you can remember that, honey?"

"Hmm, let's see ... Nick ... ass ... London. I wrote it down so I wouldn't forget. You know how we are."

"We?"

"Nick's bimbos. Big busts. Little memories."

"Who the hell is this?"

"This is Jessica Kendle," she said in her full stage voice. "Don't worry, Nick will get your message. And, Liz? A little advice. You could use more playtime. It might help your disposition. Honey." Jessie clicked off, smiling. Then guilt hit like a lightning bolt from Zeus. What had she done? This was Nick's career she was toying with. Jessie tore upstairs to deliver Liz's message.

She halted at the VIP suite's open doorway, hesitating. Nick was facing away from her, slouched in a chair. His head was down, a jewelry box clutched in his hand. He obviously didn't hear her, focused on that box.

Jessie glanced down at Nick's duffel. It looked like a bomb had gone off inside, clothes sprouting in all directions. Soon the duffel would be repacked for London. God help her, she didn't want him to go. Why wasn't life ever easy, not even when you finally had all the pieces for happiness in place? Soundlessly, she backed away.

*

Bobby Nori was sweating bullets. Worse, he probably had third degree burns on his face and arms from being out in the fucking sun all day. He'd been waiting patiently to see some action between McDeare and the Brady bimbo. So far, nothing, but things were looking up. Jessica Brady had just set a fancy table on the patio, candles and all that shit. Bobby licked his lips as he ogled the famous actress. Natural blond hair? Big blue eyes. Decent tits. And those legs and hips. He couldn't wait to see her naked. The sunburn would be worth it if he saw some action.

*

Nick stared at the jewelry box, lost in another time, another place. Jeffrey ... The doctor had just told him that Jeffrey ... Nick closed his fist over the little box. Jeffrey's ring. Nick's last link to his son. God, it had been over three years, but losing Jeffrey still hurt like an open wound. It was as if time had called a moratorium on Nick's feelings for his son and decreed each day his grief would be as fresh as the day before.

Anthony crept into his mind. If it were up to him, Anthony could come home tomorrow. He wanted to treasure every minute with the boy like a miser with his gold. Nick dreaded seeing the disappointment in Anthony's eyes when he told him about London. But Liz and Linden were breathing down his neck. What choice did he have? His career was his life. His manuscript was due in December, and he hadn't written one chapter. The lawsuit was no idle threat. Linden was a notorious stickler for churning out books as per contract date.

Cursing, Nick headed to the bathroom. He splashed cold water on his face, staring in the mirror. He was a forty-year-old man who'd always traveled light, no strings attached, even when he'd been married for five years. The bloom had fallen off that rose after the first year. Nick McDeare always had a woman in his bed and another in the wings. It was a life many men envied. Now he suddenly had more strings than a puppet and decisions to make. London and the book. Lyle and Andrew's murder. Jessie. And Anthony, a little boy too wise for his years. A little boy like Jeffrey ...

Nick squeezed his eyes shut, seeing Jeffrey clearly, those amber eyes and dark hair a miniature version of his own. He and Jeffrey were in Nick's apartment. After a short visit home to see his son, Nick was packing for Hong Kong to finish THE GREEN MONSTER ...

"Daddy?"

"Hmm?"

"Am I going to die?"

Nick froze. "We're all going to die, Jeffrey."

"You know what I mean."

Nick didn't believe in lying to children. He looked at his son, a brave nine-year-old boy facing his own mortality, a cosmic case of life being unfair. It was tearing Nick apart, eating him alive from the inside out. "There's something I haven't told you. I began a search for my birth parents. To see if their bone marrow's a match."

Jeffrey's face lit up. "Yeah? Cool."

"Don't get too excited yet. It may take some time to find them."

"How come you never looked for them before?"

"There was never any reason. Now there is."

Jeffrey threw his arms around his father. "This means we'll have a bigger family, right? Maybe we can have family reunions, like my friend Curtis. Maybe I've got cousins and aunts and uncles."

Jeffrey hadn't dwelled on the fact that finding lost relatives might save his life. All he'd cared about was having a big family. Nick rubbed his jaw. Memories came hurtling back, slicing through his heart. A phone call from Jeffrey eight months after that last conversation. His son was back in the hospital, and Nick was frantically packing to fly home from Hong Kong ...

"Daddy, promise me something, okay?" Jeffrey's voice sounded small and weak.

"You name it."

"Promise me if you find your family you'll do a bunch of stuff with them. Picnics and Christmases and birthdays and baseball games. Promise me you won't be sad."

"We'll do all those things with them, Jeffrey." Nick's voice cracked. "You and me together."

"Promise me."

"Yeah. Okay." Nick cleared his throat. "Now you hang in there. I'm on my way. I love you."

Jeffrey had come home again after that hospital stay, the last time Nick had seen his son alive. By the time the Anderson Cummings Agency informed Nick he had a brother named Andrew Brady, Jeffrey had been dead for almost a year. Finding Andrew had no longer been about Nick saving his son.

Nick swallowed hard. In a twist more powerful than any fiction he'd ever written, had his finding Andrew and Andrew's family become more about Jeffrey saving his father than his father saving Jeffrey?

*

Anthony awoke in a sweat, his eyes wide and afraid. His nightmare had come back, but it was worse this time! The man chasing him got closer. The traffic sounds were louder, horns honking, people yelling. And then he heard his dad shout his name. It had to be Daddy! He started to run towards him ... and then he woke up.

Anthony scooted out of his sleeping bag and looked up at the stars. Finding the brightest one, he wished all his energy on it, just like his daddy had taught him. "Please make Mommy and Uncle Nick let me come home. Please."

*

It was almost nine o'clock when Nick jogged downstairs. Jessie was probably furious, not speaking to him. Sure enough, he found her standing at the kitchen island, crying. Jesus, what was wrong with him?

Jessie looked up and laughed. "How embarrassing." She dabbed at her face and lifted her script. "It's a scene in the play. I lose my son in the Vietnam War and have to stand over a flag-draped coffin, singing the toughest song. Whew. I'll never get through it without completely losing it." Jessie tossed the script aside. "I made dinner for us. Why don't you relax outside and open the wine. I'll be out in a minute."

Was their earlier fight a dream? Jessie was giving him a pass on his behavior. Nick had no intention of reminding her he was a jerk. He wandered outside. A table by the pool was set, the underwater lights casting a cool aqua glow on the patio. Overhead a full moon shimmered off the cove. As he uncorked the Australian Cabernet, Nick scanned a crazy quilt of stars overhead. Could Jeffrey see him right now? Did he know how much he missed him tonight?

Jessie appeared a few minutes later with a Japanese salad for two: strips of medium-rare filet mignon, red onions, sautéed Portobello mushrooms, mandarin oranges, fresh bean sprouts, slivered almonds, celery, water chestnuts, all dressed with a sesame vinaigrette. Eying the fixings, Nick realized he was hungry.

"Mary called a little while ago," Jessie said as they sat down, "I told her how much you loved her gift."

Nick nodded. He should have called Mary himself to thank her. "This looks great. Thank you."

"Nick," Jessie said, picking at her salad, "I owe you an apology, for earlier. I never should've ... well, anyway, I'm sorry." She peeked up at him. "I was also sort of rude to your agent earlier. Your cell kept ringing, and finally I picked up. Liz was demanding that you get your ... that you get to London immediately. I didn't like her attitude." She dropped her eyes. "Sorry."

"You answered my cell?" Christ, what if it had been some other woman, like Greta?

"I know I shouldn't have, but I thought it might be important. I'm sorry."

"That's okay. It doesn't matter." Nick realized he wasn't hungry anymore. Eating was suddenly way down on his list of priorities. The real world outside The Blue Pelican wouldn't leave him alone, and he had decisions to make. And he was afraid not one of them would make him a happy man.

*

Eduardo felt important for the first time in his life. Roberto Martinelli had welcomed him back with open arms. He'd made his bones by shooting Andrew Brady, and now he was climbing the ladder to success. He intended to keep his mouth shut and do what he was told. He was finally part of a family, a family that appreciated him.

Aldo had given Eduardo an important job, believed in him from the very first day they had met, almost three years ago. He treated Eduardo like a younger brother, but to Uncle Gianni he was the village idiot. One day Gianni would realize what Eduardo had done for him and show his nephew the proper respect.

Tonight Eduardo was being rewarded for his good service. The blonde call girl Gigi was a class act, and she definitely knew how to recharge his batteries.

*

Jessie was worried about Nick. He was too quiet. She knew it wasn't the food—his eyes had lit up when he'd first seen dinner. Was it his agent? Her? The case? "You okay?"

He nodded, silent.

She poured more wine. "Are you going back to New York to help Lyle?"

Nick shrugged.

"What about London?"

"Nothing's changed."

Jessie was becoming exasperated. "Okay. I'll try another question. What do we do about Anthony?"

"We?" Nick took a swig of wine. "Anthony's not my son. Why don't you ask Gianni?"

"Gianni's not the reason Anthony wants to come home from camp. You are."

"Look, I don't know, okay? I'm going for a swim. This place's too damned hot."

Jessie said nothing, watching him stride across the patio. Nick and his wall of silence. How was she going to reach the man?

*

Nick floated in the cove, the water soothing. But it couldn't wash his troubles away. Slipping beneath the water, he resurfaced, slicking his hair back. His life had changed since he'd signed that contract with Linden. One of those changes was Jessie. Nick had expected rage from her and instead he'd received an apology and a romantic dinner. And what did Nick do in return? He was an ass. She deserved better. Well, that was one decision he could make and feel good about.

Nick quickly swam for shore and headed for the house. He found Jessie in the pool, her head resting against the tiles, eyes closed. Soft jazz oozed from the patio speakers. The aqua water looked cool and inviting, like liquid candy. Nick slipped through the water to Jessie. "I'm sorry." He reached out and she glided into his arms. "I don't know what's wrong with me tonight. Thank God I have you."

"Whatever's bothering you ... I want you to know I'm always willing to listen."

"No more talk, okay?" Nick kissed Jessie gently, his lips and tongue moving languidly to her ear. He felt her shiver. He smiled, pressing her back against the cool tiles. Combing the wet tendrils from her forehead, he kissed her again. Gently clasping the hollows of her knees, Nick curled her legs around his hips and molded his body to hers. Jessie dropped her head back, her blue eyes locking with his. Pitching her bikini top onto the patio tiles, Nick's hands moved tenderly across her breasts, eliciting a quick intake of breath from both of them before he slicked off the rest of her suit.

*

Bobby Nori lifted the camera and focused the powerful lens. The lovers came into clear view. Clicking rapidly, he watched McDeare lift the naked Brady woman up high and then lower her slowly as she snaked both her legs back around him. She was a natural blond all right. Moments later their bodies began to move to an erotic rhythm, their eyes glued together like they were in some kind of trance. Nobody got that look in their eyes when they got laid. That look was reserved for your mama's cannelloni.

Bobby licked his lips. He could hear their moans float across the villa. He began to sweat and lowered the camera to wipe his brow. He shook his head and went back to work, reminding himself he had a job to do. This was better than any skin flick.

*

Wrapped in beach towels, Jessie and Nick headed inside to raid the refrigerator. Life, Jessie told herself, was good again. She spotted a pint of chocolate chip ice cream and squealed with delight. Nick grabbed two spoons and they huddled up at the island, stuffing themselves.

Jessie reached over and rubbed the stubble on Nick's cheek. "I like this pirate look, Captain McDeare."

"Good, because I hate shaving. By the way, I've decided to go back to New York tomorrow to help Barton. Don't worry, I'll be careful. I won't march into the Police Commissioner's office and announce I'm back on the case. I won't put you in harm's way again."

Jessie realized that on some level, she'd known all along that's what Nick would do. If Lyle needed him, Nick would be there. Jessie nodded. "I'll go back with you. What do we do about Anthony and camp?"

"Maybe we should let him come home. Especially," he said heavily, "if I go to London next week."

"Next week?" Jessie felt herself deflate. "So soon?"

"You heard Liz. Bruce Linden won't hesitate to sue if my manuscript isn't in his hands by Christmas."

"I don't suppose there's any chance the deadline could be extended?"

"C'mere." Nick wrapped his arms around Jessie. "I've used up all my reprieves. I'm sorry. December's already an extension. I ran late with RED ROVER when Andrew was killed."

Jessie hugged him tightly, burying her face in his neck, his skin smelling of sea and sand. "Maybe we'd better tell Anthony right away. Give him some time to get used to it."

"I love that kid. The last thing I want to do is hurt him."

"How did you handle it with Jeffrey?"

Nick released her. "Poorly."

"But how?"

"I don't want to talk about my son, okay?"

Here we go again. If Jessie knew anything about human nature and grief, she knew it was time Nick opened up about Jeffrey. Especially if he was about to disappear for six months. She needed to know the truth, and Nick needed to tell it. "Nick," she began carefully, "do you remember that night in my sitting room when you forced me to tell you what happened on that last cruise? It was horrible, resurrecting those memories. But it was also cathartic. The weight I'd been carrying around began to lift." Jessie rubbed his arm. "You have to talk about Jeffrey, honey."

Nick chuckled. "You're a psychologist now?"

"I'm a battle-scarred veteran. You helped me. Now I want to help you."

Nick turned around and opened the refrigerator, studying its contents, his profile as stony as Mount Rushmore.

"What happened between you and Jeffrey?" She waited. Nick continued to stare into the refrigerator. "I don't even know why Jeffrey died. An illness?"

"Just leave it alone, okay?"

"Nick, please tell me. What was the cause of Jeffrey's death?"

Nick slammed the refrigerator door and headed for the stairs. "I'm going to bed."

"Oh, sure, run away," Jessie said, exasperated. "That's what you like to do."

Nick swung around. "A little arrogant, aren't we? We have hot sex and suddenly you think you know everything about me?"

Jessie sucked in a deep breath. "I probably know you better than anyone. And what we had was more than sex, and you know it. Insulting me won't make me shut up. We're past that." Jessie inched closer to him. "I hit a nerve so you want to lash out. Go ahead. Get it out of your system. Then tell me about Jeffrey."

Nick dropped his head. "For the last time, drop it."

"Okay then, answer a question. You close yourself off to almost everyone, but you got close to Anthony right away. Why?"

Nick looked at her as if she were a moron. "Because he's my nephew."

"There's more to it than that. You're patient and funny with Anthony, as if you've known him forever. You treat him like an equal, not a child--"

"Don't." Nick lifted his hands, backing away from her. "Don't make me out to be something I'm not. Look, I don't want to talk about this anymore." He headed for the stairs. "Let's go to bed and just drop it."

As if she could. "You have a special connection with Anthony, and I think it has to do with Jeffrey. Please. Tell me about Jeffrey. At least tell what the hell he died of!"

"Leukemia, okay? Leukemia! Are you happy now?"

He began to climb the stairs but Jessie ran after him and grabbed his arm. "Nick, listen to me. I'm the one person who may understand what you're feeling."

"Because you lost your husband? It's not the same as losing a child."

"Of course not. But Andrew was my entire world, just like Jeffrey was yours."

"Stop presuming things you know nothing about."

"Then tell me so I'll understand. Please!"

Nick wrenched his arm away. "I told you I didn't want to talk about it." Turning on his heel, he scaled the stairs two at a time.

*

Rosita Hernandez couldn't sleep. The steamy temperature outside hovered just below one hundred degrees, but that wasn't what was keeping her awake. Rosa was convinced her husband Miguel had met with disaster. She couldn't sit here day after day, crying. She had to do something about it. Their small stash of money was running out, and the rent was due.

She made a decision. Tomorrow she'd call that policeman who was looking for her. Maybe she could barter information about Mr. Cat Eyes' murderer in exchange for the cop not sending her back to Cuba. She couldn't go on like this. Maybe for the first time since that evil day she could fall asleep and not have nightmares.

CHAPTER 20

Jessie sat morosely at the kitchen table. She'd failed miserably at getting Nick to open up about Jeffrey. Who did she think she was, Dr. Phyllis? It was her own damn fault for pushing too hard, for trying to make up for the lost time when he'd be in London. No one should know better than Jessica Kendle Brady you couldn't push opening up.

Turning out the lights, Jessie made her way to the bedroom. Nick was asleep, facing away from her. After she washed up, Jessie climbed into bed, mirroring Nick's position. Just as she began to nod off, she felt the bed shift. "Jess? Why is it so important to you? Jeffrey?"

The question surprised her. "Because it's important to you. And because, well, I care about you, about us. I think talking about it would help. But I was wrong to press you. I'm sorry."

Nick was lying on his back, one arm tossed over his head, staring at the ceiling. He closed his eyes and Jessie turned away, willing herself back to sleep.

"I was in London," Nick said, his husky voice piercing the shadows, "about to receive the Arthur Conan Doyle Award for THE GREEN MONSTER. Lindsey called, hysterical. She said Jeffrey was dying and I should come home immediately."

Jessie rolled onto her back, watching him in the moonlit darkness.

"Lindsey used to call all the time with inflammatory statements. She resented being the one who always had to deal with Jeffrey's illness. She loved to push my buttons. I thought this was another ploy to get me home. He'd been in the hospital off and on for so long ... I told her I'd catch a flight after the ceremony that night."

Jessie saw Nick's face constrict, and he swallowed. "When I got to the hospital in Bethesda the next morning ... Jeffrey's bed ... was empty, the sheets removed. Bare. A doctor told me--" Nick's voice cracked, "Jeffrey had died an hour earlier."

Finally Jessie understood. Guilt was what drove Nick. Guilt was the wall he'd built around himself. Guilt for not being there when his son needed him the most. Guilt for not being able to say goodbye. No wonder he hated THE GREEN MONSTER. The book was a reminder of his failure as a father.

"I wanted to see his-- to at least say ... but Lindsey had already taken ... He was already at the funeral home. No one could tell me which one. It was a nightmare."

Nick paused. "The house in Georgetown was full of Lindsey's Senate cronies and the people who'd loved Jeffrey, his friends and their parents. Lindsey threw me out. She yelled I was a selfish bastard who couldn't even come home to see my son die."

Nick rubbed his eyes and sat up. "I was hailing a cab, and Jeffrey's best friend Curtis ran after me and handed me a box. There was a note taped to it. It was a ring I'd bought my son in Africa. Jeffrey had given the ring to Curtis so Lindsey wouldn't take it. He wanted me to have it. He was a very smart kid. Much smarter than this father. Anthony's wise beyond his years, just like Jeffrey. That's the connection. Each of them is worth ten of me."

"Nick, don't do this to yourself." She touched his shoulder.

"Jeffrey loved that ring. If he gave it to Curtis, he obviously knew he was dying. And where was I? Picking up some shitty award."

*

Bobby had taken lots of pictures for Mr. Martinelli with his fancy camera. Extremely hot stuff. As soon as he was back at Sandpiper, he'd download the pictures onto the computer and e-mail them to New York.

What he wouldn't give to fuck that babe. She'd lit Bobby's candle the moment McDeare had peeled her clothes off. McDeare sure gave her a ride, but she had kept up with him.

Bobby settled into a patch of soft grass behind some bushes and closed his eyes. Despite the sunburn, not a bad day. Martinelli would get his porn, and Bobby had watched exclusive X-rated erotica for free. Live.

*

Nick was swallowed up by one tragic moment in time. Once he'd opened the vault of memories, the words had flowed on their own. He didn't think he could've stopped them any more than he could've plugged up Niagara Falls.

Jessie propped herself against the pillows. "You know," she began quietly, "I've replayed Andrew walking down that gangway a million times in my mind. I can see him smiling up at Anthony and me as we stood on that balcony. He mouthed, 'See you later.'" Jessie laughed mirthlessly. "Three words we say every day. I kept thinking, if only I'd left the ship with him or sent Anthony with him. If only. But we can't turn back the clock. We make random choices every day, some life altering. We can't see into the future."

Nick leaned back, his shoulder brushing hers.

"There's more, isn't there?" she asked gently.

"I ... came close to killing myself that night. I walked around Washington, going nowhere, ending up on the Fourteenth Street Bridge. I stared down at that murky water. I thought, why not join Jeffrey? If he couldn't laugh or go to a ball game or, Christ, breathe, I didn't want to either. Fair is fair, right?"

He crossed his arms. "You know what stopped me from jumping? A kid walking his golden retriever recognized me. He'd read all my books and said he wanted to grow up to be a successful writer just like me. I thought, hey, that would be just great. A writer who kills himself. What kind of example was that? If that kid hadn't happened by ..."

"I'm so glad you told me," Jessie said quietly. "I'm so glad that kid happened by."

He looked at her long and hard. "Me, too. Believe that." Nick brushed his lips across Jessie's shoulder and slid down under the sheet, yawning. He was drained. Jessie snuggled into his arms. It was comforting to have her beside him and hear her steady breathing. Jessie had her own torture chamber of regrets. She didn't try to make him feel better by mouthing platitudes. He wasn't sure he deserved her.

Right before he fell asleep, it came to Nick that Andrew had brought Jessie and him together for exactly this moment in time, deserve her or not. They would be there for each other. And tonight maybe they would both sleep well.

*

Gianni stood at the picture window in his living room. A steady drizzle had been falling all night, converting the lights of Manhattan into a million tiny stars, their blurry points rippling into the ether.

Anthony was on Gianni's mind tonight. He'd called his son at camp that afternoon. Anthony missed his family and he wanted to come home. Gianni smiled. The sooner the boy came home, the sooner he would learn Gianni was his father.

It had been two and a half years since Andrew had died. Anthony had had his time to mourn the man he believed to be his father. The waiting game was over. If Jessica continued to deny him his rightful place as Anthony's father, Gianni was poised to take matters into his own hands at last. It was just a matter of waiting for fate to deliver the perfect moment. He would take it from there.

*

The next day, Nick and Jessie headed north on Bill Rudolph's private jet. First they'd pick up Anthony, then home to the brownstone. Nick hung up the passenger phone and eyed Jessie's empty seat. When she'd scooted into the conference room to work on her script, Nick had quickly phoned Barton. Lyle had gotten the Police Commissioner on a secure line, and Nick had persuaded him to grant an extension on Wexley's arrest. He got two days. What could he accomplish in two fucking days? At least it was something.

Nick and Commissioner Donahue went way back, to Nick's investigative reporter days when he'd helped the NYPD collar a serial rapist terrorizing the Upper East Side. Nick had sworn to Donahue there was enough reasonable doubt that he didn't want to risk a wrongful arrest. Now he had to find it. Nick had attached one condition. No one but Nick, Lyle, and the Commissioner could know he was involved again. Not the NYPD. Not even Jessie, other than his vague comment earlier. He couldn't afford one leak, not even a trickle.

*

Eduardo guided the sleek black Porsche across the Triboro Bridge into Manhattan. Glancing in the rearview mirror at the back seat, he watched Aldo thumb through dozens of four-by-six color photographs of McDeare and Jessica Brady at The Blue Pelican. Aldo was on the phone to Nori in St. Thomas. "You did a great job, Bobby." He laughed. "I'll make sure Mr. Martinelli knows the lengths you went to." Aldo laughed again. "Yeah, well, you don't get your own live nudie show every night. Maybe you have a future ahead of you in Hollywood, kid."

Aldo clicked off. "Pull off onto East Ninety-Sixth Street," he directed Eduardo. "Stop right here." Aldo got out of the car and pulled a twenty from his wallet. "I'll be about fifteen minutes. Grab us some espresso."

Eduardo nodded and watched Aldo disappear into a luxury high-rise. Hustling out of the car, he jerked open the back door and grabbed the photos. Flipping through the stack, his pulse quickened. Keeping his eye on the high-rise entrance, Eduardo rapidly sorted through the pictures again and pocketed five. Che cosa l'inferno? Who would miss five out of a hundred eighty?

Five little grenades that would explode Uncle Gianni's cushy world. He couldn't wait.

*

Lyle sat in his office, rereading every statement from the Andrew Brady murder case. Every cruddy, blurry word. There had to be something, a clue, a sentence. With only two days to conjure up reasonable doubt, the clock was ticking. Like a bomb. His phone buzzed, and he grabbed it, cursing. "What?"

"Call for you on line two, Lieutenant. Some lady with a thick accent. She wouldn't give her name, but I think it's in reference to the Andrew Brady case."

Barton's heart did a jumping-jack. Salerno's mysterious Hispanic woman? Taking a deep breath, he punched line two. "This is Lieutenant Barton," he said quickly. "How can I help you? ... Hello?"

"You say name?"

"Lyle," he said more slowly, cursing his nerves. "My name is Lieutenant Lyle Barton. Can I help you, Ma'am? Are you there?

"Si. I here."

"What can I do for you?"

Silence. Then, "I the lady you look for."

Barton leapt up and tapped on the window overlooking the squad room, motioning Bushman to trace the call. They could have the location in seconds; the department had been pouring millions into new technology that could trace a man on the moon. "I see," Lyle said. "Um ... Miss? ... Mrs ...?"

"No name."

Barton had been a city cop for over twenty years. His Spanish was more than passable. "Would you rather speak in Spanish?" he asked in her native tongue.

"Si. Gracias."

"Okay, so ... you don't want to give me your name. Did you have something to do with Andrew Brady's death, Senora?"

"No!"

"Did you see who killed Andrew Brady?"

"Uh ... I think so." She sounded frightened.

"Did someone threaten you if you talked?"

"No."

Barton chuckled. "Okay, help me out here, Senora. If you didn't kill Brady and you haven't been threatened, what's the problem?" Then it hit him. "You're here illegally, aren't you?"

There was silence, then a dial tone. "Shit!" Lyle slammed the phone down and ran from his office, dashing down the stairs like it was an Olympic event. Bushman met him at the bottom.

"We got it," Steve panted. "A pay phone at McClellan and Gerard Avenue in the Bronx. I got a car checking it out now."

*

Gianni strode into Oceano and paused at the hostess' podium. Scanning the reservation list, he saw Mayor Bloomberg had a private party scheduled in one of the side rooms. Gianni made a mental note to stop by and schmooze. As the hostess joined him, Gianni told her to see to it that the mayor's party got complimentary wine from the private stock.

"Yes, sir." Monica reached under the counter and handed Gianni a small manila envelope with his name scrawled on the front. "That came for you earlier."

Gianni nodded and climbed the sweeping staircase to his office. Sitting down at his desk, he opened the envelope. Five photographs tumbled out. Photos of ... "L'oh il mio dio!" He dropped the pictures, staring in shock at the images polluting his desk. Nicholas and Jessica ... nude ... having intercourse ... all kinds of--

Gianni ran for the bathroom, hugging the toilet as his stomach heaved. This couldn't be happening. Not again. How could Jessica give her body to a man like McDeare? How could she allow that cretin to use her in such a vulgar way?

A new thought struck Gianni, propelling him back to the desk like a mad man. Maybe the photographs were fakes, the man Andrew with Nicholas' face superimposed. Gianni had enemies—this would be child's play. Gianni hesitantly reached for the pictures and forced himself to study them closely. No. Judging from the head angles, it would be impossible.

Gianni slumped into the swivel chair. Jessica ... What had happened to his sweet Jessica, the delicate young woman he had fallen in love with all those years ago? His fragile pale rose. The woman in these pictures was a tramp. A whore. What decent woman allowed a man to ...? He couldn't think it. It was too revolting.

Lifting his head, Gianni's eyes rested on an ornate seashell awash in pastels, a memento from that summer aboard the Milano. He and Jessica had walked hand-in-hand down the beach of the El San Juan Hotel in Puerto Rico. That had been the night Gianni had realized he was in love with Jessica. Staring at the shell, he clutched it and hurled it against the wall, watching it shatter. That was his heart. Shattered.

A new thought vibrated in Gianni's head. Who had delivered this envelope? Who wanted to torment him like this? He punched Monica's extension, but she had no idea how the envelope had arrived. She'd just found it at her station. Gianni slammed the phone down. The woman was useless. If men could reproduce on their own, the world wouldn't need females. Whores.

He smacked his hand flat on the desk. Maledizione del dio esso! Where did these pictures come from?! Jessica and McDeare were supposedly at the villa alone. There must have been someone else there. Unless ... Had Nicholas set up a tripod without Jessica knowing? Gianni had seen the man working with Anthony. McDeare knew his way around a camera.

On a hunch, Gianni dialed Abigail's cell and asked her to find out if Jessica and Nicholas were back in town. Abigail, bless her, called him back within minutes. Not only were they home, but they'd picked up Anthony on their way back. The boy, Gianni's SON, was home from camp early.

Gianni's eyes filled with tears. Pulling out his handkerchief, he wiped his eyes and blew his nose. He was a sentimental fool, that was his problem. He was too soft with the people he loved. McDeare must have been the one to deliver the disgusting pictures. McDeare was fornicating with Jessica, and he wanted Gianni to squirm with the knowledge. Copulation was the man's specialty. He wanted to show off. Well, Nicholas McDeare had just met his match. No more playing the fool for Gianni Fosselli.

Gianni sat upright in his chair, his face stony. There would be no more tears spilled for Jessica. It was time for level-headed thinking. Everything was about Anthony now. Anthony was Gianni's only reason for living. His son.

*

Nick unpacked his duffel. It felt good to be back. He stuffed his dirty laundry in a pillowcase and set it by the door. Jessie liked things orderly. Since she'd most likely be sleeping up here, Nick intended to accommodate her. Nick couldn't bring himself to sleep in Andrew's bed. He hoped Jessie felt the same way. If not, there were all kinds of delightful ways to convince her.

When Nick trotted into the kitchen, he found Mary unpacking the box of sushi equipment she'd given him. "Thanks again for all this, Mary," Nick said, admiring the bamboo roller. "You went to a lot of trouble finding everything."

She grinned, her dark eyes alight. "There was a method to my madness. If you have all this, I won't have to make dinner so often. I can give my rusty joints a rest."

"I'll make dinner any night you want." With the exception of his six-month exile in London.

Mary answered the phone and handed it to Nick. "Lyle."

"Don't you answer your cell anymore?" Barton was practically shouting. "I left you a half dozen messages."

Nick dug his phone out of his pocket. "I have to recharge it. I've been on a plane most of the day, remember?"

"Listen, I heard from her. The Hispanic lady. She thinks she saw what happened that morning."

"What? A witness? Who's the shooter?"

"Cool your jets. She got scared and hung up. We traced it to a pay phone on McClellan and Gerard in the Bronx, but by the time we got there, no Hispanic lady. I think she's an illegal."

"Makes sense. That's why she hesitated coming forward."

"I talked to a buddy in Immigration. He said maybe we can work a deal. I toyed with putting a plea on television. You know. To get her to call again."

"And tip off the whole world."

"Exactly, which is why I nixed the idea. We have to hope she calls again. In the meantime, I've got surveillance on that phone."

*

Gianni finally disentangled himself from Abigail and collapsed onto his back. Anger had fueled his lovemaking tonight, but he'd been careful to hide it from Abigail. He'd been attentive when they met for a late dinner. And he'd come up with a casual lie about why he wanted to know if Jessica was home. Abigail was a jewel beyond compare. Gianni needed her now more than ever.

He'd sat in his office for hours, coldly formulating a plan. It stunned him how quickly his love for Jessica had evaporated at the sight of those lewd photographs. She'd become damaged goods the moment Nicholas McDeare had put his filthy hands on her. Jessica was nothing to him now, other than the mother of his son. Which made her an obstacle.

The goal was custody of Anthony, and Gianni would begin by finally telling him the truth. The boy would be shocked to learn that Gianni was his father, of course, but with time he would adjust. Their father-son love for each other would be the foundation of their new relationship. Blood would bind them. That was the way of the world.

Gianni fully expected resistance. He was prepared to take Jessica to court. Ironically those pictures were a blessing in disguise, the boy's mother openly having intercourse with her dead husband's brother. Any judge in the country would be appalled. Gianni had been waiting for the perfect opportunity after summer camp to tell Anthony he was his father. Fate had just intervened on his side. Besides, Gianni smiled, judges could be bought. A generous contribution to a re-election campaign would work wonders. He had the contacts to further explore that avenue, should it be necessary.

Actually, Gianni thought he should be able to curry favor with the court from the outset. Jessica had willfully kept Gianni from his son for eight years. She'd lied to Anthony about his biological father's identity. And she wouldn't win any admiration with her home situation. Jessica and McDeare were living in sin in front of an impressionable young boy. America and its conservative sexual standards would be an asset in this fight.

And he had yet another trump card, a delicious one. If he married Abigail, he would be able to provide a loving home for the boy. The marriage would make Gianni an American citizen and a deserving parent to any judge. He glanced at Abigail. She loved Anthony. This wouldn't be hard at all. He drew her into his arms, kissing her with passion, sucking in her heady fragrance. "I love you, Abigail," he whispered.

She pulled back and searched his face. "What ... did you say?"

"I love you." He swept her back into his arms. "I don't want to chase an illusion anymore. I've wasted so much time lusting after a memory. Life's too short." He ran his fingers through her shiny sable hair. "You're real. I love you. I mean it."

Abigail smiled as her eyes filled with tears. "I love you too."

He kissed her tenderly, hoping enough of his genuine feelings for her were seeping through to accomplish his goal. "Marry me."

"You want to marry me?"

"We could have a wonderful life together. I'm going to get my son back, and we'll be a real family, the three of us." He paused and studied her. "You do love Anthony, don't you?"

"Of course I do. What kind of silly question is that? It's just ... this is all ... so sudden."

Gianni laughed. "'We've been seeing each other since last April. We're almost into August. That's enough time to know how I feel about you. We're adults. Maybe you ... aren't as serious as I am about our relationship?"

"Of course I am," she said quickly. "You know that. It's just ..."

"You need some time. I understand. There's no hurry. This is a big decision. For me, marriage is forever, Abigail. Just remember that I love you. I truly love you." It was almost the truth. It was close enough to make them all happy.

*

"Damn it, Jessie, you've got to be kidding me!" Nick and Jessie squared off on the second floor landing. "Are you saying we can never sleep together in this house?" Nick couldn't believe this.

"Shhh. Calm down. I'm not saying never. I'm just saying for now. Let Anthony get used to the idea of us as a couple first. I don't want to confuse him. Can you imagine if he walked in on us while we were making love?"

"Doors have locks."

"And Anthony has nightmares. How many times has he come up to you after a bad dream?"

Damn it, Jessie had a point. "All right. But we've got to figure out a solution, even a temporary one. Fast, before I go to London."

Jessie covered her mouth with her hand.

"Are you laughing at me?"

"No!" she protested before dissolving into gales of laughter. "I'm sorry, but you act like I'm cutting off your air supply or something."

"You are." Nick pulled them out of sight of Anthony's bedroom door. Backing her against the wall, he kissed her, molding his body to hers. "Just so you know what you're missing."

"As if I can forget." Jessie reached up and drew him into another melty kiss. "Just so you won't forget either."

"God," he rasped, smothering her mouth with his. He caught his breath. "I have an idea. How about I call you on the intercom when I get upstairs. We could, uh--"

"Phone sex?" She dimpled. "Give me five minutes to get into bed. Oh, this is so exciting!" She dashed down the hallway, disappearing into her bedroom.

Nick laughed and shook his head. Jessie was one surprise after another. Maybe he was, too.

*

Lyle was at his desk at seven the following morning. After a sleepless night obsessing about the mysterious Hispanic lady, he intended to stay glued to his desk all day in the hope she'd call again.

Flipping through the Brady file, Barton knew it was time to talk to their last suspect: Michelle Davis, Tony Kendle's assistant cruise director. A sworn enemy of Jessie and Andrew. Lots of jealousy there. Fosselli had dumped Michelle for Jessie.

There was a reason Davis was last. Six months after Andrew had been killed, Michelle had vanished. Her last known address was West Eighty-First Street. Barton sent a team of detectives over to the Eighty-First Street brownstone to question neighbors. Every city dwelling had a resident busybody. Someone would come up with a lead.

Lyle's next order of business was to check on Santangelo's whereabouts. The last he'd heard, Eduardo was still in Genoa. It was afternoon in Italy at the moment. Barton would put Detective Mario Manganaro, a fellow paisano, on the phone to the Italian authorities.

Something had to break. The clock was ticking faster than a speeding bullet.

*

Gianni posed in front of the full-length bedroom mirror and straightened his tie. Charcoal silk suit. Pale tie and shirt. Appropriate attire for an early morning meeting with his accountant. And proper for his intended encounter with Jessica later. Gianni wanted to look his best, showing Jessica what she could have had. And tossed away for a barbarian.

He caught Abigail's reflection in the mirror as she slithered into her red halter dress. "What are you doing today?" he asked, turning around to admire her.

"I have an interview for a new lipstick campaign." Abigail stepped into her spiked sandals and grabbed her watch on the nightstand. "It's almost eight-thirty. I have to run home and change." She snatched her purse and headed into the living room.

"You should leave some things here. Makeup, change of clothes." Gianni followed her to the foyer door. "By the way, I'm having keys made for you today."

"Great ideas, both of them." She kissed him lightly on the lips. "You've given me a lot to think about, Gianni Fosselli."

If she only knew how much there was in his life to think about right now. "I almost forgot my briefcase," Gianni said easily. Returning to the bedroom, Gianni leafed through the dirty photos of Jessica and Nicholas in his briefcase. He removed one, pocketing it. Hurrying into the large cedar closet, he unlocked a teak cabinet. Quickly turning a small safe's combination, he secreted the rest of the photos inside and shut the door, checking twice to make sure it locked.

CHAPTER 21

Jessie padded down the back stairs wearing shorts and a tank top. She was set to work out in the new fifth-floor gym, filled with equipment she didn't know how to use. With the mercury already at ninety-two degrees at ten in the morning, it was too hot for a jog. "Where's Nick?" she asked Mary. "He's not in the suite."

Mary shrugged. "He got a phone call about an hour ago and hightailed it out of here. He was dressed for a run, if that helps."

Jessie heard the front door open and close. A moment later, Nick appeared in the kitchen wearing cut-offs and an Orioles T-shirt. Jessie couldn't believe it. "You went jogging in this heat?"

"I needed some exercise," Nick said smoothly. "I didn't go too far, took it slow. I'll do the gym later."

Jessie studied Nick. There were no perspiration stains on his shirt, and he wasn't winded. Why the charade? Was this something to do with Andrew's case? Nick had come back to New York early so he could help Barton. But so far he hadn't uttered a word about it. What was the man up to this time?

Nick poured a mug of coffee and pecked Jessie on the cheek before starting up the stairs. "I'll be working on the book for a while."

"In other words," Mary called after him, "you're not to be disturbed, right?"

"You're always right, Mary," Nick teased.

Jessie listened to Nick hustle up the stairs. He was hiding something. Was it for her own good? Or his? Jessie sighed. She wasn't naïve enough to think just because he'd opened up about Jeffrey he'd open up about everything. That's not how Nick was made. Jessie pushed away the thought of the other females in his life, desirable and eager women he could reach with one touch on his speed dial, playboy extraordinaire. She was the only woman who counted for Nick now. Jessie had to believe that.

*

Cobra shifted from one foot to the other. The heat was a fucking steam bath, and it wasn't even noon. The cement was cooking his feet as he waited for Aldo to answer the phone.

"Yes?"

"It's me. The Hispanic lady phoned."

"The brownstone?"

"No. Supercop phoned the brownstone."

"Who did the Hispanic lady phone?"

"Supercop."

"But you said Supercop phoned the brownstone."

"He did. After the Hispanic lady called him at his office."

"Shit, Cobra, you might as well be speaking pig Latin. Let's see if I got this straight. The Hispanic lady called Barton, and Barton called McDeare."

"Yeah."

"So who is this lady? What do we know about her?"

"Not much. No name. But she called from a pay phone booth at McClellan and Gerard."

"I'll put someone on it. How did McDeare react? Is he still on the case?"

"It didn't sound like it. I think Supercop's just keeping him in the loop. Being family and all."

"If anything changes, let me know. And do me a favor. Take some goddamn English classes."

*

Gianni Fosselli pushed through the brownstone's iron gate and rang the doorbell. Jessica opened the door. Where was Mary?

"Gianni! This is a nice surprise. I was going to call you in a little while. How did you know I was back?"

"Abigail told me you and Nicholas returned yesterday afternoon."

Jessica appeared flustered "Hey, come on in out of the heat." Gianni stepped into the foyer as Jessica closed the door. "Can I get you something to drink?"

"No. I can't stay long." Gianni looked her up and down, wondering how he'd ever found her desirable. "Just come from a run?" Jessica's shorts and tank top were stained with perspiration. A towel was slung around her neck, strands of hair dangling from her ponytail.

Jessica glanced down at herself. "God, I must look awful. I was working out upstairs."

"Where's Anthony?"

"Mary took him to a street fair up in Violet's neighborhood." Jessie led the way to the kitchen.

"Mary's sister Violet? Doesn't she live in the Bronx? That's not a safe area for a young white boy."

"You obviously haven't been up there in a while," Jessica said, perching on a stool at the island. "It's a mixed neighborhood. Very nice." She mopped her face with the towel and took a slurp of iced tea.

"And where's Nicholas?"

"Upstairs working. Why? You seem angry. Is something wrong?"

"Tell me something, Jessica. Were you really going to call me later?"

"Of course. Why would you ask? I was going to fill you in on my working again. A Bill Rudolph revival! I start rehearsals in a few weeks. Costume fittings begin--"

"When were you going to tell me you've been sleeping with Nicholas?" Gianni stared directly into Jessica's eyes.

"Sleeping with ..."

Gianni reached into his breast pocket and pulled out a photo of Nicholas and Jessica in the pool. Tossing it in front of her, he watched in delight as horror spread across her face. He'd purposely chosen the crudest of the photos.

"How did? ... where did? ..." Jessica fell silent, her face fire-engine-red.

"How long have you been lying to me? How long have you and that degenerate upstairs been carrying on?"

"Don't talk about Nick like that! You don't understand--"

"Oh, but I do," Gianni hissed. "I understand you are no longer the lovely woman I fell in love with all those years ago. I understand you've fallen under the spell of a womanizer, a man with a reputation of abusing women. You are my son's mother, and I'll be damned if I'll let Anthony be a witness to that, that kind of," he pointed at the photo, "perversion."

"You've got it all wrong!"

"Photographs don't lie. You and I both know that. We have the scars to prove it." Gianni pulled himself up to his full height. "History will not repeat itself. I won't allow it."

"History? What are you talking about?" Jessica's hands were shaking.

"I will not stand by and watch another man raise my son. Not again." Gianni stared at her with contempt. "Anthony will be eight on his next birthday. It's been two and a half years since Andrew died. I've lost eight years with my son, and I don't intend to lose another minute. It's time he knew the truth."

"Now wait a minute--"

"I'm through waiting. We're both going to sit down with Anthony tonight and tell him I am his father."

"You're out of your mind--"

"No more stalling. I'll be back tonight at seven. Make sure Anthony is here, or I'll take matters into my own hands. And you won't like it." He glanced at the picture again, hoping she got his meaning.

Jessica's jaw dropped. "Are you trying to blackmail me?"

Gianni smiled. "You can keep the picture. I had copies made. There are more where that came from."

"Where DID this come from?"

"Ask Nicholas. Maybe he knows. See you at seven."

*

Nick leaned against the suite's terrace door, his cell phone pressed to his ear. "This is getting out of control. I don't like this secrecy, sneaking around behind Jessie's back ... You've gone too far this time. Stop laughing, damn it. We have to regroup. Listen--"

"Nick!" Jessie's voice echoed up the staircase.

"Hold on." He covered the mouthpiece and yelled, "What?"

"NICK!"

"Got to go." Nick barreled down the stairs to find Jessie sitting at the island, in tears. "You're shaking. What's wrong?" Then he saw it. A photo on the counter. A picture of ... "My God ... What the hell?" Nick picked it up as if it were coated with a snake's venom. "Where ... where did this come from?"

"Gianni," Jessie choked out. "He was just here." She reached for a tissue. "And he's coming back tonight to tell Anthony he's his father. He didn't stop by to ask my permission either. He came to inform me this would happen tonight. Oh, my God." Jessie buried her face in her hands.

"Wait a minute. He's blackmailing you with this? The bastard." Nick paced in a circle. "And how the hell did he get his hands on that ..." Gianni had to have gotten the picture from Martinelli. It had be Martinelli's men who broke into the villa that night. Did Gianni give the order for the break-in? "Start at the beginning. Tell me word for word what Gianni said."

Nick listened with mounting anger as Jessie described Gianni's visit. "Why did he tell you to ask me about the photo? Why would I know anything about it?"

"He was so smug. So biting." She sniffed back her tears. "Of course, I guess he was hurt."

"I don't give a shit if he's hurt. The sonuvabitch is trying to blackmail you. Gianni hasn't given a thought of what this will do to Anthony."

"What will we do? Anthony can't ever know that Andrew wasn't his father. It will kill him!"

"How much more can the poor kid take?"

They both fell silent. Nick tried to will away a small voice in his head, whispering what he didn't want to hear.

"God," Jessie said, "if Gianni goes to one of the rags with those pictures, I'll never be able to show my face in public again. TO HAVE AND TO HOLD will be finished before it's even in rehearsal."

"Having my genitals on display isn't going to boost book sales either," Nick muttered. He could strangle Gianni with his bare hands. "Okay, let's calm down and think. We have to focus on Anthony. Our reputations have to take second place. Agreed?"

"Of course."

The small voice in Nick's head revved up. He knew what had to be done. He'd known all along, even while he'd let his anger have its say. He'd known months ago. And Jessie wouldn't like it any more than he did. He gazed at her compassionately.

"Nick, w-what is it? I don't like the way you're looking at me."

"I have to say something. You won't want to hear this. But," he said evenly, "I think Anthony should know who his biological father is. "

"Nick!"

"Hear me out." Nick put his hands on her shoulders. "Trust me, as an adopted child, I know what I'm saying. No child could love my parents more than I do. And part of that love's based on their having the honesty to tell me they were not my biological parents at an early age. Actually, about as old as Anthony. Anthony deserves the same honesty from you. He needs to know the truth about his father. He'll be grateful when he's older. But he'll forever hold it against you if you don't tell him."

"But Andrew's Anthony's only father. We agreed on that."

"And he always will be in every way that counts. But Gianni's his biological father, and he has his own relationship with him. We can't pretend he's not. Gianni has rights, like it or not. He can press it in court."

Jessie's eyes welled with tears. "I can't believe we're having this conversation."

"You know I'm right. I think we both knew this day would be coming. You had to know you couldn't hide this forever. You had to, honey. You know wishful thinking doesn't work in real life."

"How would Andrew feel? How can I do this to him?"

"I think," Nick said softly, "he knew this day was coming, just like we did. C'mere." Jessie fell into Nick's arms and he cuddled her. "We'll keep Anthony from Gianni until you're ready. We won't let him force your hand. I'll be damned if he chooses the time you tell Anthony this kind of news." Nick drew back and looked into Jessie's eyes. "I have an idea. Call Mary at her sister's and have her and Anthony stay with Violet tonight. Tell Mary to come home early in the morning."

"The villa! We should all go down to the villa. We'll be safe there."

"Jess, that picture was taken at the villa." His voice was gentle. "We knew someone broke in that night. Now it looks like they came back the next day. And this time they were successful. We're safer here in the brownstone."

"No place is safe, is it?" Jessie laid her head against his chest. "The villa was the one place Andrew and I felt secure. Andrew's whole world's crumbling. The villa. The plum tree."

"Andrew's whole world was you and Anthony. As long as you're both safe, his legacy's intact. Trust that. Besides, the villa's about to get a new security system. You'll feel safe there again."

"The only place I feel safe is with you."

Nick smiled and brushed Jessie's lips with his. "Let's take a break. Grab your sunglasses." Nick plopped twin Orioles caps on their heads from his hall closet collection and hustled Jessie out the door. The sun would do them good.

*

Lyle's mind was clicking on all cylinders. First, his detectives had found Michelle Davis, courtesy of a nosy neighbor in her old residence. The former ship lounge singer who'd worked her way up to cruise director had changed her name to Michaela David six months after Andrew was murdered. Soon thereafter, she started hanging out with a wealthy Long Island socialite who introduced her to Jack Greenwood, a wealthy real estate attorney with a suite of Park Avenue offices. Michaela and Jack had married and were expecting their first child in January. Unfortunately, Mrs. Michaela Greenwood wasn't returning Barton's calls. Maybe McDeare could handle this quietly. He was good with the ladies.

Second, Mario Manganaro had discovered Santangelo had left Italy. After which Lyle had called Fosselli. Gianni had verified that his nephew was in New York and living on the Upper West Side. What Eduardo did with his time was unknown to his uncle. Mario had circulated photographs of Santangelo to every street cop in the neighborhood and all patrol cars.

Now it was after two in the afternoon. One day almost down. Another day to go. Could McDeare wheedle out another extension? He called Nick and asked if Jessie was with him.

"We're heading to the Starbucks around the corner."

"Okay, I finally located Michelle Davis. She's now a society matron living on Park Avenue and not taking my calls. Think you could corner Michelle and get an interview?" At Nick's okay, Barton gave him Michelle's new name and address and hung up. Staring at the phone, he muttered, "Come on, Hispanic lady. Call!"

*

As seven o'clock neared, Nick spread cartons of Chinese food on trays across the bed in his suite. Jessie dug into the baby lamb with scallions. "Hey, stop right there. Ribs and spring rolls first. Thems the rules." Jessie laughed and reached for a spring roll. Nick was trying to keep the atmosphere light for this indoor picnic. Jessie deserved one last night of peace before all hell broke loose. They were cocooned behind drawn drapes, the rest of the brownstone dark, the phones set to voicemail. Nick's cell was turned off.

At seven on the dot, the doorbell and knocker began to sound. Nick and Jessie calmly finished the appetizers and moved on to the lamb, Singapore rice noodles, and sautéed Chinese vegetables. Fifteen minutes later, silence reigned again. Nick and Jessie eyed each other.

"Just remember," Nick cautioned. "We may've gained a night, but the clock's ticking. Gianni's a loose cannon, and he has those photos."

After dinner they stretched across the bed, Nick booting up his laptop while Jessie studied her script. Nick couldn't get that photograph out of his head. The villa had been searched thoroughly the night of the break-in. Someone had gained access afterward. How? It was making him crazy. He had only one more day before he had to beg the Commissioner for more time. Pulling up websites for the Virgin Islands newspapers, Nick scanned the articles, not sure what he was looking for. Until ... "Jess, what's the name of your exterminating company in St. John?"

"Mmm ... It's a funny name. Like a pun."

"Kritter Krunchers?"

"Yeah, that's it. Why?"

"Two employees and their truck have been missing for a couple of days. The day that picture was taken, you said the exterminators had been there that morning. I bet that's how our photographer gained access, with the exterminators. Someone probably came back for him the next day."

"Yeah, they did!" Jessie said, looking up at him, eyes wide. "Don't you remember? The exterminator's truck was pulling into the villa just as we were heading to the airport. I thought we had a new bug invasion. Hannah buzzed them right in."

"Damn, they were clever." He met Jessie's eyes. "It might be a good idea to start searching every vehicle at the gate. It'll mean hiring a guard full time, employee ID checks, the works."

"Whatever it takes. Every time I think of someone watching us like that--"

"I know. Me, too." Nick shut down the computer and double-checked the alarm clock. Jessie had to be back in her own bed before Anthony got home in the morning. He lassoed Jessie in his arms. "We'll weather this together. I won't let Gianni hurt us."

"I don't know what I'd do without you. I'll tell Anthony. You were right. I guess a part of me has always known I'd have to tell him. I just have to know what to say, rehearse it in my head. Just a little more time."

Nick watched as Jessie slipped into a deep sleep. He couldn't bear the thought of leaving her for London. Jess and Anthony would be walking targets. If anything happened to either one of them, he'd never forgive himself. He'd lived with guilt long enough.

Wait a minute ... Nick sucked in a breath, blinded by the solution. He could write the book here. He'd fly to London later for a few weeks to soak up the locations. Nick had lived in London off and on over the years. He knew it well enough. Relief swept through him. It would be a drastic change in his creative routine. His manuscript might not be as thick with atmosphere, a Nick McDeare hallmark. But life was a compromise. He'd learned that. And to ensure Jessie and Anthony's safety, he'd risk a chink in his reputation.

Nick glanced down at Jessie, all soft curves and pale hair and smelling of lilacs. She trusted him. He hated the lies to cover his secret. It hadn't been as hard before. He hadn't owed Jessie anything, just his promise to find Andrew's killer. He'd told himself there was no way around the secrecy. The ends justified the means.

Now everything had changed. That latent thing called a conscience was stirring. And Jessie had to have known he hadn't been out jogging this morning. He'd never come that close to being caught. If he wasn't careful, Jessie would guess he was seeing another woman. Nick turned on his cell and made a call from the bathroom, making sure Jessie didn't hear him leave his message.

*

Gianni padded out of the bathroom and slipped into bed beside Abigail. He was still fuming even though they'd just made passionate love. Even that hadn't helped.

Abigail snapped her cell phone shut and tossed it on the nightstand. "I just checked my voice mail. No word about the new lipstick campaign. I guess I'm yesterday's news. They want fresh young meat these days."

"Hmm?"

"Gianni, what's wrong? Tell me."

He might as well tell Abigail the truth. She'd find out eventually anyway. "You know me too well. I had a long talk with Jessica about Anthony earlier today. I told her I was tired of waiting to tell him the truth, and tonight was the night." He rubbed his eyes. "But when I went over there the house was dark. Either they weren't home or they weren't answering the door. Jessica can't keep me from my son!"

"Of course not. How ridiculous." Abigail stroked his chest. "What made you think she'd do the right thing this time?"

"Someone left some photographs for me yesterday. They were, well, they were explicit sex photos of Jessica and Nicholas on the beach at the villa. Vile pornography."

"What!? Who'd do that? That's crazy!"

"I think Nicholas took those pictures and left them for me to see. Who else? I, ah, showed one of them to Jessica and implied what I'd do with the picture if she didn't agree to tell Anthony who I am." Gianni wasn't sure how Abigail would take that.

Abigail burst out laughing. "That's too funny! That's great, Gianni. You used Nick's own spite against him." She continued to laugh.

Gianni looked at her in surprise. This was the last thing he expected. "Well, that's how I saw it, too. You're really not mad?"

"No, God, no."

"You are an amazing woman."

"And don't you forget it." Still smiling, Abigail turned onto her side. "I'll bet Jessie had a stroke when she saw that picture." She tittered and closed her eyes.

Gianni was too angry to sleep. Instead, he worked through his plan for tomorrow. It was time to do what had to be done.

Abigail's eyes fluttered open, and she looked up at him. "Is that why you asked me to marry you? Because Jessie's getting it on with Nick?"

"No, my darling. I've known I was falling in love with you all along. Seeing those pictures just confirmed that I was over Jessica. It's a relief. I feel free again." Gianni closed his eyes, content with his answer.

"Gianni?"

"Hmm?"

"Yes, I'll marry you."

*

The next morning, Nick found Mary making a batch of blueberry muffins that smelled good enough to bottle. Jessie sat across from Anthony in the breakfast nook. While he said good morning to everyone, she met Nick's eyes, a delicious smile passing between them. Nick couldn't wait to tell Jessie about London. "What's on your agenda today?"

"I'm meeting Bill and Kenny Harran, the composer, for a late breakfast," she glanced at her watch, "oh, God, in fifteen minutes. I'd better get going. Kenny's written some new songs, and he won't appreciate my being late. He's kind of high-strung, you know?"

She kissed Anthony, yelled goodbye to Mary, and jogged for the door, Nick at her heels. "Hey," he laughed, "let me kiss you goodbye at least."

Jessie kissed him full on the lips. After which, she whispered very low, "You're working with Barton again, aren't you? That's what that call was about yesterday when we were out."

- 230 -

Christ. "I … Be careful today, okay? And make sure Mary watches Anthony. I'll talk to her about it, too. But he can't catch on we're trying to keep him from Gianni. Hey, you'd better scram."

After a quick look into his eyes, Jessie dashed down the street to catch a cab on Fifth Avenue, Nick watching from the window. Jessie had come far since she was a recluse, locked up in her sanctuary. She was happy and full of life, able to put Anthony, the pictures and even the ever-present sense of danger out of her mind for a few hours.

But he couldn't brush his own troubles aside. Nick pushed his hands through his hair, staring out the window. Not only did he have to come clean to Jessie about the other woman in his life, but he had only one more day to solve his brother's murder, or at least prove reasonable doubt. Talk about mission fucking impossible.

*

Jessie's block had a charming little park on the corner of Madison and Seventy-Fifth, filled with fanciful statuary, a bench, and stone walkways. There was also a gazebo, a perfect hiding space for a man who wished to keep his eyes glued to the brownstone. Gianni had taken up his post at nine that morning. Jessica couldn't keep him from his son forever. What Gianni needed was a window of time and the right circumstances to right the wrong she was doing him. If it took months of waiting for the perfect moment to present itself, so be it. This was a personal mission—no lawyers or judge or hired minions could do this particular job for him. This was between a man and his son.

So far, so good. Jeremy Hoffman had arrived a little before ten, right on schedule. Gianni knew the agent would immediately take the elevator to the fourth-floor business offices, where he'd remain for the rest of the day.

Jessica emerged at ten-fifteen. Anthony's mother would present the biggest challenge, but now that she was working again his opportunity would come. Gianni's pulse quickened. Jessica was wearing a magenta suit, the kind of dress appropriate for a business meeting. He might be in luck. Unfolding the New York Times, he watched Jessica hurry towards Fifth Avenue and signal a cab.

Gianni blessed his patron saint when Nicholas emerged from the brownstone forty-five minutes later. It was harder to tell where he was going but he was hustling down the sidewalk, a set look on his face. Was it possible Gianni's meticulous plan would be operational on the very first day? He kept the newspaper over his face as McDeare swung by on the other side of the street.

Marveling at his good fortune, Gianni dug his cell phone from his pocket, waiting like a gambler in Vegas for a slot machine to hit the jackpot. Thirty minutes later, he got his payoff--sirens speeding up Madison Avenue. When they were a block away, Gianni punched out the brownstone's number, the adrenaline racing through his system. As he expected, Mary picked up.

"Yeah, hello?" Gianni asked frantically, raising his voice and trying to sound Spanish. "Are you Mary Bodine?"

"Yes. Can I help--"

"Yeah, listen, you don't know me, but your sister asked me to call you. She was just hit by a car and she kept yelling your name and asking me to call. She gave me this number. Can you hear me? The sirens are goddamned loud."

"Oh my God, is she all right?" Mary sounded panicked.

"I don't know, man. She's awake, but her leg's busted, bleeding all over. They're taking her to the hospital. She's hysterical."

"What hospital? Where?"

"Hold on." Gianni took the phone from his mouth and yelled, "Hey, man. Where you taking her?" He paused and came back on the phone. "North Central Bronx Hospital."

"On Kossuth Avenue? I know where it is. Tell Violet I'm on my way."

Gianni hung up, smirking at the thought of Mary's wild-goose chase. But the real point of this exercise centered on Anthony's terror of hospitals. Mary would never drag Anthony into a manic ER in the Bronx. She'd leave the boy in Jeremy's care—assuming Gianni's luck held and she couldn't contact McDeare in time to help her out. Busy men let their cell phone calls go to voicemail. Or Nicholas might well be on the other side of the city by now. As for Jessica, she'd never bothered to get a new cell phone after the murder. He'd nagged her about it often enough, in the days when he'd cared. Once Mary left the brownstone, Anthony was his.

CHAPTER 22

Mary tried to reach Nick on his cell for fifteen minutes. The phone kept going to voicemail, meaning he was talking to someone. She left frantic message after message and finally gave up. She had no idea where Jessie was meeting Bill for breakfast. God in heaven, this was a perfect example of why Jessie needed a new cell phone. Grabbing her purse, Mary gave Anthony strict instructions not to answer the door or the phone. If an emergency arose, he should ask Jeremy for help. Bringing him to the hospital with her was out. The child had been deathly afraid of hospitals ever since his father died. Buzzing the agent on the intercom, Mary explained what had happened and dashed out the door.

*

Eduardo met Aldo at a tiny restaurant in the Village. When Aldo had called last night, there'd been an edge to his voice Eduardo had only heard him use with one other person. Eduardo hadn't seen that person since.

Aldo remained silent as a waitress set a cup of espresso in front of Eduardo. After the woman left, Aldo quietly said, "You fucked up big time. You took five of those dirty pictures and gave them to your uncle. Don't insult my intelligence by denying it. I was the only one enjoying those pictures, and suddenly they turn up in Gianni Fosselli's hands."

Eduardo gulped. Did Martinelli have a million eyes watching everything that happened in this city? "How did you know--?"

"Shut up!" Aldo leaned forward. "It's only because of me you're still sucking air. Mr. Martinelli wanted you gone. You screwed up a plan we spent time and money putting together, you moron. And now it's fucked because those photos found their way from Fosselli to Nick McDeare."

Che cosa la scopata? They were just nudie pictures. How could this be so bad?

"You fuck up again, and it's out of my hands. You're getting something rare with Mr. Martinelli. A second chance. Now get the hell out of here and don't let me see your ugly face again until I want to see it."

Without a word, Eduardo slunk outside. He didn't want to screw up his future with the Martinelli family. And he definitely didn't want to disappear.

*

"Who is it?" Anthony yelled through the front door.

"It's Uncle Gianni." A moment later, he stepped into the foyer and smiled down at his son, such a beautiful child with dark curls and vivid blue eyes. "I have an imported carton of Italian spumoni in my freezer with your name on it, Anthony. How would you like to sit on my terrace and help me eat it?"

Anthony looked tempted. "I'm not supposed to go anywhere till Mom or Uncle Nick get back."

"Can't you ask Mary?"

"She's gone, too. Jeremy's upstairs, but Mary said not to call him unless it's important. Ice cream's not important. I know! I'll call Uncle Nick. I know his number by heart."

Smiling, Gianni made a simple suggestion. "Why don't we call him when we get to my place?"

Anthony hesitated. "If Mom comes home and finds me gone, she'll freak. I better leave a note." Anthony carefully printed a message on a piece of paper by the phone. He grabbed Gianni's hand. "Let's go."

*

Rosita had been holed up in her apartment like a mouse for forty-eight hours. After hanging up on the policeman the other day, she'd run, terrified the cops were watching her. Sure enough, from her hiding place behind two garbage cans she'd seen a police car squeal to the curb. Rosita had almost had a heart attack.

Now she needed groceries, and the rent was due next week. She needed a job, and for that she needed to be able to walk outside in daylight. Rosita knew she had to talk to that policeman, Lyle Barton. Maybe she should call him at home? It would be safer. Venturing outside, Rosita went to her friend Maria's and asked to see her phone book. She found an L. Barton in Flushing, Queens. None of any other names beginning with "L" looked like Lyle. None of the other initials in front of Barton were "L's" except a child's phone. Copying the number down, Rosita stuck it in her bra and hurried home, stopping long enough to buy an apple.

*

Nick clicked off his cell and glanced at his watch. Christ, it was after noon. That female could talk like she was paid by the word. But then again, she'd had a lot to say. So had Nick. They'd gone ten rounds to hell and back and settled nothing. He was on edge, the damn clock ticking down the day, and no closer to nailing Fosselli than he was this morning.

Switching gears, Nick composed himself and focused on the job at hand, another lady. He walked confidently into the luxury building on Park Avenue near Sixty-First Street and paused at the concierge's desk. He used his celebrity and two bills to get a pass from the man to the elevator to surprise his "old friend" Mrs. Greenwood in 23-H. Everyone in New York was out to make a buck. Nick rang 23-H's bell.

From inside the door he heard, "Cordelia! It's the bell." A pause. "It never fails." Footsteps to the door. "Who is it?"

"The super."

Nick kept his head down. This was probably Michelle looking through the peephole since Cordelia was in hiding.

"You don't look like the super."

"I'm new."

"Who are you really?"

- 234 -

Damn. "Mrs. Greenwood," Nick said, fixing his eyes on the peephole, "I'm Nick McDeare, the author. I'm also Andrew Brady's brother," he said evenly. "I'd like to talk to you about Andrew." Nick waited. Nothing. "Please, Mrs. Greenwood. I'm trying to find out who killed my brother." Nick angled a beguiling look at the peephole.

The locks turned and the door opened a crack. "You certainly look like Andrew." Michelle studied him a moment. "Are you really the famous author?"

Nick smiled the crooked smile that always worked. "In the flesh."

Michelle opened the door wider. "My husband's due home for lunch in half an hour, so please make it quick."

*

Digging into bowls of rich ice cream, Gianni and Anthony sat at the table on Gianni's terrace. It was a perfect summer day, the sun hot, the air cool on the skin. When Anthony said he should call Nicholas, Gianni reassured the boy he'd already called him when he was in the kitchen.

Gianni was in no hurry. This conversation had to be approached with delicacy. He'd given instructions to the building's doorman that he wasn't to be disturbed under any circumstances, sweetening the request with a tip the size of his Christmas bonus. Once Gianni said what he had to say and it was over with, it would no longer matter when Anthony's mother put in an appearance.

Gianni listened in amusement as the boy described his boredom with camp. His son should be spending his summers in Italy, taking in the museums and soaking up his heritage. Gianni feigned happiness as Anthony chronicled Jessica and Nicholas's surprise visit to bring him home. "Your mother and Nicholas came from the villa?" Gianni asked. Anthony had given him the perfect opening. "Did you wonder what they were doing there by themselves?"

"They were having fun. They used to fight a lot, but not anymore. I think Mommy really likes Uncle Nick now."

Gianni tried to mask his disgust. "I think it's gone beyond liking, Anthony. I think your mother loves Nicholas."

"Yeah?" Anthony broke into a grin. "I love him, too."

"I'm talking about a different kind of love." Gianni put his spoon down. "There's something I want to tell you. You're old enough now to hear the truth. If fact, you probably should have been told long ago."

"What's wrong, Uncle Gianni?"

"Nothing's wrong," Gianni said, smiling. "In fact, everything's about to get better." Gianni rested his elbows on the chair arms. It was important to stay calm. "A long time ago, before you were born, your mother and I, well … we were in love, too. Do you know what I mean by that?"

"You mean, like Mommy and Daddy?"

"Yes. Like that. We loved each other very much. But I had to go home to Italy for a little while. While I was there, your mother found out --" This was getting tricky. "She found out about you. You were going to be born."

"She married Daddy first."

"That's part of what I want to tell you. Your mother married Andrew after she found out she was going to have you. You see," Gianni continued, using his napkin to blot his brow, "Andrew loved your mother very much and wanted to marry her. I was in Italy, so Andrew told her I wasn't ever coming back, and ... well, then your mother decided to marry Andrew because she was lonely, and she didn't think she'd ever see me again." He set his hand on the boy's arm. "Do you understand what I'm trying to tell you?"

"Not really."

Gianni sighed. "Anthony, do you know where babies come from?"

The boy made a face. "Marc D'Agastino told me, but I didn't believe him."

Gianni chuckled. His son was a charming boy. "Well, when two people love each other, they have the power to make a baby with their physical love," Gianni waved a hand in the air, "just like that." There. That should suffice. "And that's what your mother and I did. We made a baby. We made you." Anthony's spoon paused and his mouth dropped open. Gianni smiled warmly at his son and ran his fingers through the boy's curls. "Andrew's not your father. I am."

*

"I don't know why you've come to me, Mr. McDeare," Michelle said. They were seated at the dining room table. Nick assumed Cordelia was busy making lunch somewhere in the bowels of the cavernous apartment. "I was hardly friends with Jessie and Andrew. In fact, we hated each other." Michelle fidgeted, a dragonfly poised to take flight.

Nick studied the woman. She was nothing like the harlot Jessie had described. Gone was the bright red hair, replaced by a smooth auburn bob. Her makeup was tasteful. She looked like every other wealthy Upper East Side matron, emaciated and coordinated. She was also agitated. There was a good chance she was hiding something.

"Look," Nick said easily, "I know you weren't in the terminal when Andrew was shot. But I'm talking to everyone who was on that cruise who knew Jessie and Andrew, just for their impressions." He was glad he hadn't called, the element of surprise on his side. "As I recall, you began as a lounge singer and worked your way up. You were Tony Kendle's assistant before taking over as cruise director when he died. Is that right?"

Michelle cleared her throat. "I don't mean to be rude, but what does this have to do with Andrew's murder? I'd rather not discuss my former career, if you don't mind."

"I'm just trying to keep everything straight in my head. As time has passed, has anything come back to you about that cruise that you think may be pertinent to Andrew's murder? Maybe you saw or overheard something?"

Michelle tried to look bored. "First of all, Andrew and Jessie stuck to their cabin for most of the cruise. And, secondly, I purposely put as much distance as possible between them and myself." She glanced at her watch.

"I know you didn't like Andrew or Jessie. That's your prerogative. But Andrew's son is going to grow up never knowing why his father was killed."

"Andrew's son?"

"What do you mean?"

"Look," Michelle said, rising. "I have nothing to tell you so--"

"Why did you say that?"

Michelle sat back down. "You're reading too much into my words."

"I don't think so." Nick leaned forward. "What is it you're not saying? I mean you no harm. I'm just trying to find out why my brother ended up in a coffin six feet under at the age of thirty-three when he had everything to live for."

"Look, I'm sorry you lost your brother, but I can't go back. My life's--"

Nick heard the front door open. "Michaela?" a male voice called. "Where are you?"

Nick watched the color drain from Michelle's face as Jack Greenwood walked into the dining room.

*

"It's true," Uncle Gianni said. Anthony listened to the words, but he didn't understand them. "I'm your real father. Andrew was your stepfather. You came from love."

Words-words-words. Maybe this was a dream. Another nightmare.

"I didn't know about you for a long time, not until shortly before we met on the Milano. Do you remember how we met in the little store with the ships? If I'd known about you, I would have come to New York immediately. Your mother and Andrew didn't want you or me to know the truth, but I finally found out."

Anthony felt like the time he'd fallen out of the tree in the back yard. When he'd gotten up, he could hardly breathe. Anthony started to breathe harder, feeling like that now.

"I'm sure you know your mother and Nicholas have ... become involved," Uncle Gianni continued. "They'll probably get married and want children of their own. You're no relation to Nicholas. But you'll always be my son. You're my only child. Why would I want any more children when I have you? Just you and me."

The bowl slid from Anthony's hands, crashing to the concrete. Shards of glass cut his legs, but it was like watching it cut someone else. It didn't even hurt. He leapt up. "No!"

Gianni rose. "Your leg is bleeding. Here, let me help you."

"No!" Gianni was like a stranger now. He didn't know this big man anymore. He wasn't even his uncle.

"Let me wash that for you." Gianni approached him, his hand extended.

"No! You're lying!" Anthony grabbed the sliding glass door and threw it open.

"Anthony, wait." Gianni grabbed him, but Anthony wiggled away and dashed for the front door.

"I'm telling you the truth," Gianni said, on his heels. "I'm the only one who's told you the truth. You can trust me."

Anthony started turning the locks frantically. He wanted to go home to his mom and his Uncle Nick, his real uncle!

"Stop that. Now, let's sit back down--"

Anthony finally found the magic combination and the door opened. When Gianni slammed it shut again, Anthony kicked him in the shin as hard as he could. Gianni grunted and staggered backwards, giving Anthony time to jerk the door open and run for the elevator. It opened right away. He punched the lobby sign just as Gianni barreled into the hallway. The elevator door slid shut in Gianni's face and whooshed downwards until he couldn't hear him yelling anymore.

*

Jessie clipped into the brownstone's cool hallway, relieved to be out of the summer heat. Humming one of the new songs from TO HAVE AND TO HOLD, she trotted down the hallway to the empty kitchen. "Mary?" She called up the stairs. "Mary? Anthony?" Smoothing a stray hair back into her French braid, Jessie decided Mary had probably gone to the store and taken Anthony with her. The bulletin board. There was probably a note.

Jessie crossed the kitchen and found two notes. One from Mary, the other from ... Dear God!

*

Nick offered his hand to Jack Greenwood, a small man, wearing a beautifully tailored slate gray suit and a sky-blue Hermes tie. His hair was thinning, every surviving strand perfectly barbered into place. "Hello, I'm—"

"Nick McDeare," Greenwood finished. "I recognize you. Ah, why are you sitting in my dining room?"

Nick flashed him a smile. "I knew Michaela years ago." Nick turned to look at Michelle. "We met through her friend--"

"Sally," Michelle finished for him, rising and moving to Jack's side.

"I'm trying to locate a mutual friend. Sally suggested I talk to Michaela, but it looks like we've all lost touch with Andrew."

"Andrew?" Jack asked. "What a coincidence. Wasn't your brother named Andrew? Andrew Brady? I read in the paper you were brothers."

"That's right." Nick chuckled. "Andrew Brady was my brother, but I'm talking about a different Andrew. Andrew Morse."

"I told Nick I'd lost touch with the old crowd," Michelle told her husband.

"In fact, I was just leaving," Nick said.

"I'll show you to the door." Fixing an adoring look on her husband, Michelle added, "Cordelia has lunch ready for us in the solarium. I'm so glad you could make time to discuss the benefit, dear. I'll be right there."

Nick shadowed Michelle through the living room into the marble foyer. "I'm sorry. I don't mean to cause you any trouble."

Michelle's smile changed her entire face. "I appreciate what you did back there."

Nick handed her his card. "If you want to talk, call me, okay? We can meet somewhere else, somewhere where your husband --"

"There's nothing to talk about. Really." Michelle palmed the card. "I do wish you luck. I hope you get your answers."

- 238 -

Nick cast Michelle the kind of smile he hoped she wouldn't forget when her conscience woke up. He headed for the elevator, the Greenwood's door closing behind him. His cell jangled. "McDeare."

"Gianni's got Anthony!" Jessie's voice was shrill. "I found a note from Anthony when I got home."

For a terrible second, Nick felt his world shatter into tiny pieces. He forced himself to regroup, fast. "Where's Mary?"

"She had an emergency. I'll explain later. What do we do?"

"Where's Gianni's apartment?"

"Seventy-Eighth and First Avenue, on the northwest corner. The penthouse."

"I'm at Sixty-Ninth and Park. You go to the restaurant. I'll head for his apartment."

*

Anthony galloped through the lobby. A second elevator opened and Gianni called his name. Anthony streaked past the startled doorman and out onto First Avenue. Glancing over his shoulder, he saw Gianni run after him. Anthony dashed down First Avenue. He knew how to go home from Gianni's. At Seventy-Fifth, the light was with him and he spun west, hurtling across the wide avenue, his legs pinwheeling. He wanted his mom and his Uncle Nick!

*

Gianni cut across Seventy-Eighth. The boy had to be heading for the brownstone. Gianni knew he was out of shape, and the reconstructive surgery after his attempted suicide made it worse. Still, he could outrun a small boy. At Park Avenue he turned south, intending to intersect his son at Park and Seventy-Fifth Street.

*

Nick dashed up the west side of Park Avenue. As he approached Seventy-Fifth Street, he tried to weave through traffic, but he might as well be stuck in a plate of metallic spaghetti. Nick finally worked his way to the median strip, but he couldn't find a damn path through the sea of cars to the east side of Park. A fog of exhaust and the drone of horns hung over the speed-and-stop traffic. He cursed. Then he saw them. Anthony was sprinting across Seventy-Fifth Street and nearing the northeast corner of Park, Gianni running down Park and approaching the same corner.

*

Anthony's marathon was wearing him down. His legs kept pumping, his breath coming in gasps, but his mind took on a dreamlike quality. The sounds, the running, the panic. His nightmare … He was in his nightmare. Fear choked Anthony as he hit the corner of Seventy-Fifth and Park and collided violently with someone. Gianni. He'd crashed into the man who was a stranger to him now. This was his dream, the stranger trying to catch him. Then Anthony remembered … His dad. If this was his dream, his dad would be across the street and save him. Gianni grabbed Anthony by the shoulders and shook him, yelling at him for running away.

Miraculously, out of the chaos, Anthony heard a voice call to him. It had to be Daddy's voice! He struggled to free himself.

*

Nick saw Gianni and Anthony collide. He fought to cross the jungle of cars. "Anthony!" he yelled. "ANTHONY!"

The boy raised his head and broke free. Nick watched, aghast. Anthony dashed towards him and directly into the street.

"Anthony, no!"

With a screech of tires, Nick saw Anthony's dark curls disappear. Nick tore into traffic, leaping over the hoods of cars as they swerved to avoid him. Nick zig-zagged, clawing his way to the spot he'd last seen Anthony. He halted, staring in horror. Anthony was sprawled on the pavement, his arms and legs splayed, blood trickling down his forehead.

Gianni was sobbing, muttering Anthony's name and kneeling over the boy. A cabbie pleaded with Gianni, "The kid just ran out in front of me, mister. He came out of nowhere."

In a rage, Nick lurched forward and jerked Gianni up by the lapels, tossing him onto the curb like a sack of garbage. Nick drilled in 911 on his cell and barked a call for help. He knelt beside the boy, taking his wrist and feeling a faint pulse. Thank God. "Hang in there," he pleaded with Anthony. "Help's on the way. I promise. I love you."

*

Gianni's haze lifted at the twin wails of an ambulance and a squad car, squealing to a halt. More sirens whined in the background. Nicholas was hovering over Anthony, EMTs rushing up. This was McDeare's fault. Swearing, Gianni grabbed the bastard by the arm, swinging him around and raising his fist. Gianni doubled over with a grunt as Nicholas landed a blow to his gut first. Two cops materialized, separating the men and pulling them to their feet. "What the hell's going on here?" one shouted. "Oh, you're Nick McDeare. Hey, sorry, sir."

"Let go of me!" Gianni shook himself free from the other cop. "Do you know who I am? I'm Gianni Fosselli. I own Oceano. I want you to arrest this man. If he hadn't interfered, the boy would be safe."

"If you hadn't kidnapped Anthony, he'd be home right now," McDeare shot back.

"Wait a minute," one of the cops said, coming between the two men. "Who's the little boy?"

"He's my son," Gianni said.

"Look," Nicholas squared off with the cop, "that boy's Anthony Brady, Andrew and Jessica Kendle Brady's son. I'm Andrew's brother, Anthony's uncle."

"Well then, who's he?" the cop asked, pointing at Gianni.

"He's nobody." McDeare spit.

*

Gianni wasn't at Oceano. Jessie took off for his apartment. When she reached Park Avenue, she spotted a cluster of police cars and an ambulance two blocks southward. Her eyes fixed on the swirling red, white and blue lights. Oh,

God, no. Fighting for speed in her high heels, hobbled by her tight skirt, Jessie ran towards them. Shoving her way through the crowd, she saw her son being transferred to a gurney. "ANTHONY!"

A policeman grabbed her. "Stay back, lady. Let the-- Oh, excuse me, You're Jessica Kendle. I-I'm sorry ..." The cop released her, backing away.

Nick appeared out of nowhere, blanketing her in his arms. "He's alive, Jess. He's alive. That's all that matters." Jessie couldn't take her eyes off Anthony. He looked so small. She burst into tears.

*

At Lenox Hill Hospital, Anthony was taken to the ER. Nick made a statement and made sure the cops kept Gianni away from Anthony, explaining he'd abducted the boy. A compassionate nurse led him and Jessie to a break-room, keeping them away from the curious stares and whispers.

"Gianni told Anthony, didn't he?" Jessie's eyes were dilated, her face white.

"I think so. I wish I didn't, but I do."

"This is his fault. If Anthony dies, it's Gianni's fault."

"Look at me," Nick waited until her eyes were locked with his. "Anthony is not going to die." Nick took Jessie's hand, willing himself to be strong for her. He recounted the events from when he saw Anthony running across Seventy-Fifth. He slowed, getting to the hard part. "Gianni grabbed Anthony and he was shaking him, yelling at him. It-it infuriated me. So I ... God help me, I yelled out to Anthony. When he saw me, he ran straight into the traffic. He was trying to reach me." Nick said the unthinkable. "If I hadn't called out to him--"

"Don't, don't blame yourself. This isn't your fault. Anthony had to be desperate to get away from Gianni. He knew you'd protect him. Why did this have to happen? He's just a little boy. He doesn't deserve this." Jessie dropped her head in her hands, the tears flowing.

Nick folded his arms around her and let her cry, kissing her forehead. He wasn't a praying man, but he was saying a prayer now. Please, God. Don't let Anthony die. Please let him be okay. I swear I'll spend the rest of my life making sure he's safe and happy. Please.

A nurse opened the door a crack and they followed her through the ER to a cubicle down a narrow hallway. Anthony lay motionless, his right arm in a splint, a large bandage over half of his forehead. One side of his face was bruised and swollen.

A young Asian man in a white lab coat introduced himself as Dr. Lars Ito. He told them Anthony's arm was broken in two spots. Ito pointed to Anthony's forearm and elbow, telling them he needed surgery to insert a pin, but he had to wake up first. He explained he'd cleaned and dressed the wound and Anthony had also cracked two ribs and had contusions down both sides of his body.

"But," Nick asked, trying to keep a grip on his emotions, "he'll be all right?"

Dr. Ito looked at them kindly. "I won't lie to you, Mr. McDeare. I'll be a lot happier when Anthony opens his eyes." Ito told them he'd arranged for a private room for Anthony next to the nurse's station on the seventh floor, where they wouldn't be bothered by fans.

*

Nick slumped in a chair in the seventh-floor waiting room, Jessie's hand gloved in his. They'd been waiting nearly two hours for Anthony to be brought up. Nick was close to losing his mind by the time Lyle and Mary materialized in the doorway. Mary hustled over to Jessie, encasing her in her arms. A single tear slid down her cheek. Mary was exactly what Jessie needed right now.

Barton caught Nick's eye and motioned him into the hall. "Listen," Lyle said, "Anthony's all over the news. The press is playing the poor Jessica Kendle Brady card. First her husband. Now her son. I could wring their fucking necks. Anyway, I called the Nineteenth, which covers the Upper East Side. Glenn Kersey's second in command, an old academy buddy. He's got the press corralled downstairs and out of your face. He's putting a guard here on seven to monitor access to the floor. The nurses are giving me a list of their patients. I need to know who can see Anthony."

"Mary, and maybe Abbie. Thanks."

Barton lifted an eyebrow. "Abbie? Is it safe to put the two of you in the same room?"

Nick shook his head. "How'd you hook up with Mary?"

"She called me hysterical a little while ago when your cell kept going to voicemail."

"I had to turn it off in the hospital."

"She said she couldn't reach you earlier this morning either. Anyway, I told Mary what happened to Anthony and swung by to pick her up. I thought Jessie might need her. How's Anthony?"

"Not good. In a coma."

"... I'm sorry. And Jessie?"

"Too quiet."

They walked in silence for a few seconds. "I've got the cops keeping Fosselli at bay," Lyle said. "He was making a scene, telling everyone he's Anthony's father, and he should be up here. Mary told me he's blackmailing Jessie with a photograph?"

Nick washed a hand over his mouth. "I could kill the asshole with my bare hands."

"You and me both. The sonuvabitch sent Mary on a wild goose chase up to the Bronx. Get this. The jerk had the balls to call Mary and say her sister was hit by a car and taken to the hospital."

"What? Gianni called ... I don't understand."

"I don't know for a fact it was Gianni, but it's pretty obvious. He wanted Anthony. The phone call was a scam to get Mary out of the house. Fosselli disguised his voice. He had to figure Mary wouldn't want to drag Anthony into an ER, not with the way the kid feels about hospitals. Mary was a basket-case when she realized Anthony was missing." Barton leaned against the wall, jingling his keys in his pocket.

"The bastard had Andrew killed," Nick said quietly. "I'm sure of it. Look, you know about the break-in down at the villa. And we know that Martinelli was behind it because of the lighter you traced to the Bronx strip joint. Now it looks like someone managed to get back into the villa. They came in on the exterminators' truck, hid in the brush and photographed Jess and me when we were ... well, in the pool and on the beach. A couple of exterminators turned up missing after those pictures were taken. Tell me how the hell Fosselli got his hands on that photograph he showed Jessie unless he's directly involved with Martinelli?"

"Maybe from his nephew. Santangelo." Barton stopped walking and faced Nick. "Santangelo's back in New York. I've had cops looking for him all over the Upper West Side. We hit pay dirt. A couple of detectives in the Twentieth spotted him and followed him this morning. Guess who he's working for? Martinelli."

Nick felt like punching a hole in the wall. "Goddamn it. Everywhere we turn, all roads lead to Santangelo! Who the hell's pulling his fucking strings?"

"There's more," Barton said tonelessly. "Time ran out for us. Commissioner Donahue wants Wexley behind bars tonight. Our two days are up. Bushman and a couple of street cops are picking him now at some seedy hotel on West Thirty-Sixth Street. I'm heading back to the precinct house to question him. We don't need to bother Jessie with this right now, correct?"

"Correct." Shit. The clock had struck midnight and all Nick had come up with was a pumpkin. Ian Wexley.

CHAPTER 23

Gianni slumped at his office desk, slowly draining a bottle of Amaretto. If only he could erase the horrific image of that cab slamming into Anthony, his poor son. He dropped his head into his hands. This was McDeare's fault. If he hadn't yelled out to Anthony ... He wished the interfering imbecile an ugly death.

"Gianni?" Abigail stood in the doorway. "I just heard." She closed the door. "What happened?"

"I never dreamed Anthony would react that way."

"You told Anthony ... Oh my God, you told Anthony you're his father?"

"I had to. Jessica never would have told him." Gianni took another swallow of Amaretto. He knew he was on his way to getting drunk, and he didn't care. "Anthony ran from me. I knew he'd be shocked, yes, but I never thought he'd reject me outright." Gianni motioned aimlessly. "We're so close. I'm his Uncle Gianni ..." He couldn't go on.

Abigail came around the desk and ran her fingers through Gianni's hair. "Why didn't you tell me you planned to tell Anthony today? I might've been able to help. To smooth the way." She leaned closer. "How is he? The news report just said he was struck by a car and taken to Lenox Hill."

"I don't know." Gianni lifted his head. "That gang of moronic idiots won't let me anywhere near him, my own son. Anthony ran away from me, and I finally caught up with him. I had him. Then McDeare shouted his name, and Anthony ran out into the street. It's--"

"C'mon," Abigail said. "Let's go home. You don't want anyone to see you like this. I'll go to the hospital later tonight to check on Anthony. First, I want to take care of you."

*

"Hi'ya, Ian," Barton said, striding into an interrogation room on Midtown North's second floor. "Long time no see."

Wexley slumped at the table. He looked like a bum on the streets. Bloodshot eyes. Stubble peppering his jaw. "You've got nothing on me. This is a joke."

Barton exchanged a glance with Bushman, leaning against the wall.

"No joke. We've got two eyewitnesses who put you under the West Side Highway early on the morning Andrew Brady was shot."

"Bullshit."

"Does this scenario sound like bullshit?" Barton straddled a chair backwards, staring across the table at the man. "You met some men down at a diner on West Street the night before Brady was shot. Around dawn you went to a warehouse on Tenth Avenue and came out carrying a gym bag. You took the subway up to Fiftieth Street and met a man beneath the West Side Highway. You gave this gentleman a leather jacket, leather gloves, and a gun." Barton smiled at the shock on Ian's face. "Ring a bell? Oh, yeah. One more thing. You were wearing the gloves Paula gave you for Christmas."

"Paula," he hissed. "My fucking wife's your witness."

"One of them. She followed you that night. She told us the whole story. It's over."

Wexley asked to make a phone call. An hour later, Jeremy showed up with an attorney. After conferring with both men for half an hour, Ian was ready to talk. He sat between the attorney and Jeremy as the two detectives reentered the room. "Okay," Ian said, "I want to tell you exactly what happened."

The two cops leaned against the wall, waiting.

"I fucking hated Andrew Brady. He screwed my career and then pushed it in my face, laughing at me. He told everyone I was washed up. He knew it would get back to me. Meanwhile he was cashing in on Jessie's dough, living in that palace on East Seventy-Fifth Street. So I bitched about him nonstop to my brother-in-law, okay?"

"Aldo Zappella?" Barton asked.

"Yeah, the man with the connections. Aldo finally got sick of my belly-aching and set it up for me. All I had to do was pick up the gun and jacket and give them to the kid. That was it. But Aldo never said anything about killing Brady, I swear. He was only supposed to do enough damage to screw the man's career like he screwed mine."

"And just exactly how was he supposed to do that?" Bushman asked.

"He said he'd take out his kneecaps or something. I don't know how these guys work. I'm an actor for crissake."

Barton chuckled. "You really expect me to believe that?"

"It's the fucking truth. Why would I lie about that when I'm telling you everything else?"

Lyle looked at Bush. He was laughing. Turning back to Wexley, he asked, "Who was the kid?"

Ian shrugged. "I never asked his name. I didn't exactly want to make his acquaintance, you know what I mean?"

Lyle slipped a picture of Santangelo from his jacket pocket. "Is this the man?"

Ian squinted at the picture. "Yeah. It looks like him. It was a long time ago."

Barton nodded, glancing at Bushman.

"Look," Ian said, "you should be going after Aldo. This was his idea. I admit my part, okay, but I didn't plan it. I didn't shoot Brady, and I didn't want Brady dead. I was just the deliveryman."

"A regular Santa Claus. Don't worry, Wex. We'll check it all out for you all nice and legal." Barton looked at Steve. "Mirandize him and get him out of here."

*

Time had stopped for Jessie. She sat stiffly in a chair beside Nick, staring at her motionless son in bed. This couldn't be happening. Not again. If only he'd open his eyes. Please wake up, she begged, the same mantra she'd been silently reciting for sixty hellish minutes. Jessie blindly reached for Nick's hand. "Now I understand how you felt when you lost Jeffrey."

"You won't lose Anthony. He'll be all right. C'mere," Nick said, pulling her onto his lap. Jessie nestled her head against Nick's shirt, inhaling his warm cotton scent that masked the hospital's antiseptic odor and the hideous memories it evoked. "Jess, there's something I've wanted to tell you all day. It never seemed to be the right time, but now's as good as any. I'm not going to London. I'm writing the book here in New York."

"Really?"

"I can't leave you. Or Anthony."

Thank God. "Nick, I-I love you. You don't have to say anything. It's okay if you don't feel the same way. I--"

Nick stopped her with a kiss. As their lips parted, he whispered, "I love you, too. Nothing's going to happen to Anthony. I promise."

*

Rosita slipped outside that evening and headed to a pay phone a few blocks away. A different phone. This time she'd only speak for a few seconds, even though she felt safer calling the policeman at home. Rosita had remembered from television crime shows how the police could trace a call if it lasted too long. That's how they found the phone booth last time. Everyone was a detective in America, even Rosita Hernandez. Rosita rehearsed her words in her head.

Dropping her coins in the slot, Rosita glanced around as the phone rang. "Barton residence," a female voice responded.

"Senor Barton, por favor."

"Uh, he just got home. May I ask who's calling?"

"I call about Andrew Brady."

A few seconds later, Rosita heard the familiar voice of Lieutenant Barton. "Yes?"

"It's me again," she said quickly in Spanish. "The lady you're looking for. Meet me tomorrow at five o'clock. Come alone, you must be alone. And don't tell anyone.

"Five o'clock," Barton repeated. "Where?"

"Where it happened. You know?"

"Yes. I understand."

*

Nick pushed through the hospital's front door, shaking off the press. He needed fresh air and a cigarette. After he crushed two and sniffed one, he pulled out his cell and turned it back on. Christ, there were messages from Abbie, Barton, his friend Michael at THE POST and a dozen other reporters Nick knew. He punched in Barton's cell. "It's Nick. You arrested Wexley?"

"The fucker confessed. He asked Zappella to set up the hit. And it looks like we were right. Martinelli used Santangelo. The kid made his bones."

"Did Ian identify Santangello?"

"Close. Looks like him but it was a long time ago. I just heard from our Hispanic lady. Things are moving. I'm meeting her tomorrow. I bet she ID's Eduardo. The Commissioner's giving a news conference in the morning. You want to be there?"

"No. But thanks. Thanks for everything. Great work." Nick clicked off, feeling numb. So he had gotten it wrong this time. He'd been so sure it was Uncle Fosselli asking Eduardo to do him a favor and connecting him to the organization. That would explain the Santangelo-Martinelli tie Barton had sprung on him. But, no, it was Wexley. In which case, Eduardo's involvement bypassed Fosselli. Gianni was in the clear.

Nick should be happy. They'd nailed Andrew's conspiracy of killers. Justice. Revenge. Did it really matter his record was no longer one-hundred percent and the NYPD got the credit instead? Did it really matter his instincts were screaming the NYPD had gotten it wrong?

*

Abbie cleaned up the spilled Amaretto and tucked an afghan around Gianni. He'd drunk enough liquor to knock out a seasoned lush. She'd listened all evening to his litany about how Jessica had turned Anthony against him and it was all Nick's fault. Gianni had finally collapsed on the couch, his glass sliding from his hand to the carpeting.

Writing him a note, Abbie explained that she was going to the hospital to check on Anthony. Then she was going home to sleep in her own bed. She said she had an early morning audition.

It was past midnight when Abbie arrived at Lenox Hill. Taking the elevator to the seventh floor, she hurried down the quiet hallway. Hospitals gave her the creeps in the middle of the night. They would forever remind her of Andrew, the two-day wait while her best friend was in a coma.

Abbie reached Anthony's room, pausing in the doorway. That sweet little boy, tubes branching out of his battered body. She glanced at Nick and Jessie, both asleep. Nick had slid down in his seat, his long legs stretched in front of him, his head resting against the wall.

Abbie tiptoed to Anthony, gently kissing his cheek. "You have to open your eyes, do you hear me?" she said softly. "You are so loved."

She reached into her purse for a tissue and mopped up her tears. Jessie and Anthony deserved better. Feeling watched, she found Nick staring at her. He put a finger to his lips and rose, heading towards the hall. Abbie dragged herself away from Anthony.

Nick leaned against the wall, hands in his pockets. "How's Jessie?" she asked.

"Not saying much."

"She has to be terrified. It's Andrew all over again."

Nick nodded. "How are you?"

"Not good." A sob caught in her throat and she leaned against Nick's chest, her forehead against his shirt. "I heard about Anthony on the news, of all places. Gianni didn't tell me what he was planning. Not a word. If only I'd known."

"Don't blame yourself." Nick put his arms around her. "I assume you've heard the other news, too?"

"There's more?"

"Wexley was arrested for Andrew's murder tonight," Nick said slowly. "He confessed."

Abbie backed away from Nick. "I don't believe it. There's no way Wexley did this. You and I--"

"It's over," he said wearily. "Ian arranged for Andrew's murder."

"It's not over. I don't accept that." She paced away from him. "How can you just give up like that? We were not wrong about Gianni!"

"I was wrong, and so were you. Our egos don't play into this."

"Listen to me, Nick McDeare. You've never been wrong before. What makes you think you were this time?"

"The man confessed. No one admits to murder if they didn't do it, unless they're protecting someone. Wexley doesn't care about anyone to protect." Nick looked tired to the bone, his eyes shadowed.

Abbie dropped her head in her hands. "Listen to me," she said as calmly as possible. "We've kept my cover under wraps all these months. Gianni trusts me. He's given me the keys to his apartment. I told you I caught him putting those pictures of you and Jessie in a locked safe in his closet. I'll bet that safe's full of enough evidence to win a murder conviction. The police are wrong. I won't stop."

"Don't do this, okay? It's dangerous. Your work's over. Let the NYPD handle it."

"I can't believe you're giving up."

"I'm not giving up. The evidence on the conspiracy to kill Andrew's solidifying, and Gianni's not part of it. I've been doing this a long time. I know when it's over. Now I'm going to try to get some sleep in that hospital chair and let the cops worry about wrapping this up."

"I'm going to prove you wrong. You'll see." Abbie turned on her heel and fled down the stairwell. They were not wrong. She was going to put that animal behind bars if it was the last thing she did.

*

Nick stirred, vaguely aware it was morning. Was that a noise? "Mommy?" Nick opened his eyes a crack. "Uncle Nick?"

"Anthony?" Nick gently shook Jessie, asleep in the chair beside him. "Jessie, Anthony's awake." Nick limped to the bed, his body cramped into one big pretzel. "Hi, kiddo."

"Am I in a hospital?" Anthony's face began to crumble.

Nick's heart went out to him. "Yeah, but you'll be fine. I promise. You were in a car accident. Your mom and I've been with you the whole time. We won't leave you for a minute. Not for anything." He turned to Jessie. She was struggling to her feet.

"Anthony," she said. "Thank God." She brushed the tears from her cheeks, quickly moving to her son's bedside.

Nick put his hand on her shoulder. "I'll get the doctor."

*

"The prognosis is good." Dr. Ito joined Jessie and Nick in the hallway after examining Anthony, the door wide open so Anthony could see them. Ito said he'd schedule the elbow surgery for the next morning. With a nod, the doctor left them alone.

A chill swept through Jessie. She wrapped her arms around herself. "Dr. Ito said Anthony remembers everything," she said dully. "That means he remembers his conversation with Gianni." She looked up at Nick, her stomach knotting. "He's going to want answers from me. I wish Andrew were here. He needs his father now." Jessie knew she was being irrational, but she was angry. Andrew should be here with her. "He'd know how to explain this to Anthony. He always said the right thing."

Nick rubbed Jessie's shoulder. "Just tell him the truth. Kids always know when you're lying."

"I'm scared. This comes out in the worst way possible and Andrew's not here. I'm alone in this." Jessie brushed a hand over her brow, her head throbbing like someone was taking golf swings inside her skull.

"You're not alone." Nick cupped her chin, holding her eyes with his. "Do you want me to go in there with you?"

"I'm still needy, aren't I? Yeah. I'd love for you to come with me. Thank you."

They walked into Anthony's room and Jessie explained the operation, assuring Anthony he could go home the next day. "And I'll let you eat whatever you want," she bubbled, "all your favorites. You can even have dessert for dinner. Wait till I tell Mary our new menu."

Anthony smiled weakly. "Honest, about going home?" Anthony looked to his uncle.

"Honest," Nick said. "You know I never lie to you. And you'll have a cool cast." Nick paused. "Dr. Ito said you remember what happened to you."

"Gianni was chasing me and--" His eyes darted from one face to the other before focusing on Jessie. "Is it true, Mommy? Is Gianni my real dad?"

Nick placed his hand in the small of Jessie's back and rubbed gently. "You're," she pushed the words out, "yes, you're related by blood to Gianni. But I wouldn't call him your real father."

"I know how you make babies. I told you Marc D'Agastino told me. Did you and Gianni make me like that?"

"Yes," Jessie said carefully. "Yes, Gianni and I were in love once and we created you, but ..." Jessie searched for the right words. She'd lived with the prospect of this moment forever, and it was still happening too soon. Jessie could feel the seconds tick away as she struggled for the magic words to explain.

Miraculously, she heard Nick's soft voice come to the rescue. "You know, Anthony, you and I have something in common. Gianni's your biological father, just like a man named Jason is mine. Gianni gave you life, just like Jason gave me life. But Charles McDeare raised me, just like Andrew raised you. That makes Charles my real father. He took me to soccer games. He taught me how to spiral a football. He was the first person to read anything I wrote. I loved him as much as a son can love his father. It was the same with Andrew and you. That's what your mother's trying to say. Gianni was the father who gave you life. Andrew was the father you loved because he was there for you every time you needed him."

"Andrew was the first person to hold you when you were born," Jessie said. "When I woke up that first night after you were born, Andrew was already rocking you and telling you all about your new family."

A tiny smile lit Anthony's face.

"I bet Andrew taught you your ABC's and how to tie your Reeboks," Nick added.

"And he taught me how to swim and dive, too," Anthony said. "And he used to sing with me. And he named a drink for me. The Bongo Bourbon."

Nick arched an eyebrow. "A Bongo Bourbon?"

"Ginger ale with lots of cherries." Jessie laughed. "Andrew put it in a special glass."

"We used to take bike rides at the villa, too," Anthony said. "I always sat in this basket behind Daddy. He was going to teach me how to ride my own bike when I got older."

"I'll teach you," Nick said gently. "You and Andrew did all the things that fathers and sons do together," Nick said. "That's what made Andrew your real dad."

"And your daddy understood blood isn't what makes a father and son relationship," Jessie said. "You know the only father Andrew had when he was growing up was my dad Tony. Andrew loved Tony so much that Andrew was the one who wanted to name you after him. You were his real son in every way that counts. He was so proud of you."

Anthony looked Jessie in the eye. "Gianni said you and Daddy weren't ever going to tell me the truth."

Calling on all her reserves, Jessie forced herself to stay calm. "Honey, I'm so sorry you found out the way you did. I'll be honest. Daddy and I didn't know when we were going to tell you. Even adults don't always know all the answers. When Gianni showed up on that cruise, we decided to discuss it when we got home, but then Daddy was ... When Daddy died, you were so sad I thought telling you right away would make things worse. But Gianni wanted you to know, so I talked it over with your Uncle Nick," Jessie glanced up at Nick, "and I decided now was the time. But, well ... Gianni beat me to it. You should have heard it from me, not Gianni."

Jessie was relieved to see Anthony absorbing every word in that measuring way of his. Nick was right. Anthony was wise beyond his years. He had always been an insightful little boy, but after Andrew died, he'd taken on a maturity and a gravity that had unsettled her more than once. Anthony turned his eyes on Nick. "How long have you known, Uncle Nick?"

Nick clasped Anthony's hand. "For awhile. It didn't make any difference to me, Bongo. I'm your uncle and I love you."

Jessie felt a weight lifted from her shoulders. The secret was out, and Anthony didn't hate her. She blessed Andrew for being such a loving father that Anthony was able to instinctively understand what being a father was all about. Jessie smiled. Andrew had been there for her after all. She'd underestimated him. "Is there anything else Gianni said that you want to ask me about?"

"He said ..." Anthony looked at Nick, "you're really not my uncle like you just said. That you and I aren't really related."

Jessie's voice tightened. "That's not true."

"Your mom's right. I'm your daddy Andrew's brother and I'm your uncle," Nick said firmly. A pulse clicked in his jaw. "We'll always be family. I promise you."

"He said ..." Anthony bit his lip.

"What?" Jessie asked. What other damage had Gianni tried to inflict?

"He said you and Uncle Nick would get married and have your own kids. He said you wouldn't want me anymore."

Nick started to say something, but Jessie cut him off. This she could handle herself. "That's not true. I don't know where Gianni got that. First of all, you're my son, and I'll always want you. I know you don't really believe what Gianni said." She hugged Anthony. "You'll be my little boy forever. And as for marriage," Jessie laughed, "Your Uncle Nick never wants to get married again, and I don't either. So that's something you don't need to worry about!" Jessie chuckled and glanced at Nick. He was looking down, his face expressionless.

"But you're not going anywhere, right, Uncle Nick? You'll keep living with us?" Anthony sounded anxious.

Nick remained still, his voice quiet. "That's right, Bongo. I'm not going anywhere. You can bet on it."

*

Abbie got up at ten and padded to the kitchen. It had been exhilarating to sleep in her own bed last night after so many nights at Gianni's. She glanced out the window. From the fifty-fifth floor of her West Seventy-Second Street apartment, Abbie had a spectacular view of lower Manhattan's new skyline. She still couldn't get used to the empty spot the World Trade Center once filled. Those twin towers had always defined New York for Abbie. It was a dangerous world these days.

Danger. That was the word Nick used for Abbie's undercover work with Gianni. Now Nick was willing to just let it go? Abbie chalked up Nick's capitulation to his worry over Anthony and Jessie. Nick McDeare didn't give up. But even before Wexley's arrest, Nick had been pressing Abbie to tell Jessie what she was doing or back off. Abbie wasn't blind. Nick had fallen hard for Jessie. From the first day of high school, Jessie Kendle had been a magnet for the male of the species. As cool as icicles, as warm as honey. The fusion drove men mad. And one man had ended up dead.

Abbie poured a cup of coffee and wandered to the picture window in the living room. Far below, the Hudson River stretched north to the George

Washington Bridge and south to New York Harbor. Pinpointing the West Side Cruise Ship Terminal on the waterfront, Abbie spotted the Milano, docked beside two other cruise ships. That's where Jessie and Andrew's saga had begun almost ten years ago, birthing ripples still felt today.

For over two years, Abbie had brooded about Andrew's murder. Even during the hospital vigil while Andrew was dying, Abbie had kept her eye on Gianni Fosselli. Jessie's former lover had shown up after six years, and Andrew had ended up dead? A coincidence? Abbie hadn't thought so then, and she didn't think so now.

Abbie's uncle in California owned a private investigation firm. After Abbie moved back to L.A., she apprenticed with Kevin, working around her magazine shoots. She vowed to find out who killed Andrew and she needed the tools to work with. With her training at Juilliard, Abbie was a natural for undercover work, delighting Kevin. She got the goods on three husbands cheating on their wives and an accountant embezzling from a major corporation. One of those husbands was the Italian photographer Abbie had used as her excuse for returning to New York. It was true enough; Abbie had fallen for the creep.

Abbie's lips tightened. But her real reason for coming back to New York had been Gianni. She and Nick teamed up that first night, Jessie almost catching them on the balcony of the suite. When Jessie had found them whispering in the study after the party, they'd gone underground, meeting outside the brownstone or by phone.

Abbie had known she'd have to sleep with Gianni to prove he could trust her. She was an actress; it was a role. But Abbie had never slept with Andrew. Andrew was gorgeous and talented, but he was a brother to her. Sex had never been an option. Abbie smirked. How convenient a lie to rope Gianni in.

Abbie rested her forehead against the cool windowpane. If Nick wanted to give up, fine. Abbie intended to keep investigating. Now she had to figure out the combination to that safe in the locked closet cabinet, the key to which was on Gianni's keychain. Abbie was sure Gianni's safe held the secrets to prove his complicity in Andrew's death. Letters. Photographs. Documents. Whatever it took to nail the bastard.

*

Gianni lifted his head. He'd fallen asleep on the couch in his clothes. He winced at his pounding head. Che cosa l'inferno? Anthony! Yesterday came hurtling back with all the intensity of a horror show. He hadn't been allowed to see his son, his injured, precious boy. He remembered. But last night ... last night was hazy. Groaning, he glanced at his watch. Eleven-fifteen? He hadn't slept this late since his days with Jessica aboard the Milano. The whore.

A shower. Gianni struggled to his feet, but collapsed back onto the couch. Maybe Abigail would take pity on him and bring him some broth from Oceano. Abigail. Where was she? He remembered her bringing him home last night, but after that ...? He spotted a note on the coffee table and breathed a sigh of relief. Gianni read the note. Abigail had seen Anthony last night. Reaching for the phone, Gianni punched in Abigail's cell, but it flipped to voicemail. Last night the hospital wouldn't release any information on Anthony. Maybe he'd have better luck today.

Gianni called Lenox Hill's information line. With fury, he heard the robotic operator repeat that Anthony Brady's status was private, for family only. "I am family, you idiotic, moronic, incompetent nobody!" he yelled into the receiver. Gianni hurled the phone across the room, jerking the cord out of the wall. He clutched his aching head. This was not over. This would never be over.

CHAPTER 24

Nick and Jessie caught a cab back to the brownstone after Mary relieved them at the hospital. They decided Nick would take over from Mary in the afternoon and Jessie would stay with Anthony overnight. Jessie leaned her head back, exhausted. As they sat in clogged traffic, Nick cleared his throat. "I, ah, have some news. Barton arrested Ian last night. Wexley confessed."

Nick had on his poker face, but this had to be hard for him. "I knew it had to be Ian all along," she said softly," Gianni may be a lot of things, but he's not a killer." Nick looked away. He was not a man used to being wrong. "I'm sorry. You were really convinced it was Gianni, weren't you?" She reached for Nick's hand.

"It doesn't matter now. What matters is cracking the case. It looks like you were right. Ian set it all in motion."

Jessie bit her lip. Her former lover had murdered her husband. She'd always known it. "Ian's a man you don't want to cross. He has to win. He plays dirty and enjoys it." Her voice caught. "I'm the one who blackballed him. He should've killed me."

"Don't say that. Andrew took joy in letting Ian think it was him. From what I gather, he taunted him every chance he got. I think Andrew's biggest crime to Wexley was being Andrew, the man who had it all." Nick squeezed her hand. "I can't picture you with Wexley."

"Back then Ian had this incredible ego, but it was attractive, you know? He was handsome in this lion kind of way, exuded so much confidence. He was a master at making me feel lucky that someone like him would even look at little me." She shook her head. "I was young and stupid. I wanted to find the kind of love affair my parents had. Ian knew how to romance a young naïve woman. So," Jessie laughed mirthlessly, "I created a great love affair."

"Let's hope your judgment in men's improved with age."

"You think I've regressed since Andrew?"

"Oh, I think you're in big trouble now, kiddo."

*

After running several errands, Nick arrived back at the hospital around two. Anthony's room was jammed with flowers, stuffed animals, and toys. Mary told him most of it came from strangers. "You should see the stuff I asked the nurses to take to the other kids." She patted Nick's arm. "See you at home tonight."

Nick nodded. Walking over to the bed, he set his shopping bag down and pulled out some of Andrew's journals. "I thought maybe you'd like to hear your dad's thoughts about you, Bongo."

"Hey, those are the books I found up in his old room on the third floor. Daddy told me where they were. Yeah. I want to hear them."

Nick reached in his bag, producing a chartreuse plastic glass, a bottle of ginger ale, and a jar of cherries. "A little refreshment while you listen?"

"Wow! That's my glass!"

Nick prepared Anthony's Bongo Bourbon. He dropped into a chair and read from the journals, mesmerizing Anthony with his father's tales about their adventures. Andrew had an eye for recounting the tiniest details.

"Uncle Nick, how did you find out you were adopted?" Anthony asked when Nick took a break.

"Well, I kind of figured it out myself. I didn't look like either of my parents. When I was about your age they told me the truth and made me realize how lucky I was.

"What do you mean?"

"They chose me," Nick said gently. "They went out of their way to adopt me. They wanted me more than anything else in the world, exactly the way Andrew wanted you. He chose to be your father. He couldn't wait to be your father."

Nick could see Anthony's mind computing his words. "You mean, most parents don't get to pick the kid they want, right? But your dad and my dad did. They got to choose."

"Exactly. You and I were lucky to be wanted like that."

"There's something I want to tell you, but I don't want you to tell Mommy because it will scare her, okay?"

"Absolutely."

"My nightmare came true," Anthony whispered. "Someone was chasing me. Then I ran into Gianni just like I ran into the man in my dream, and I heard you call me. In my dream, I thought it was Daddy. It sounded like Daddy."

"Everyone says my voice sounds like your dad's."

"But it felt like Daddy in my dream, even though I never saw him. The person across the street was trying to help me. Daddy always knew when I was scared. That's why I thought it was him. But it was you. You were trying to rescue me."

"I wish it had been your dad instead of me, Anthony. I wish he were sitting here right now."

"But he's not. You are." Anthony clasped Nick's hand. "There's more. I saw Jeffrey when I was sleeping."

Nick wasn't sure he heard right. "Jeffrey?"

"Your son. He looks just like you."

"When you were sleeping? You mean … after the accident?"

"He told me what a great dad you were. He said you'd take care of me now."

Nick tried to process the words. It was probably just a dream … except he and Anthony didn't just have dreams. He felt the hairs on his arms raise.

"He told me you'll be my dad now," Anthony continued, excited. "I don't want Gianni to be my dad. I want you to marry Mommy and be my dad. I choose you. You know how you felt lucky to have your parents? That's how I feel about you."

"That's how I feel about you, too, Bongo," Nick said hoarsely. "I choose you, too."

*

Lyle stepped cautiously into the deserted West Side Cruise Ship Terminal. With the exception of two security guards outside the front door, he was alone. Spotting the row of chairs where Brady had been shot, Lyle stared at the floor. His eyes drifted up to a bronze plaque set in the wall.

> 'Good night, sweet prince
> And flights of angels sing
> Thee to thy rest'
> Hamlet v, ii
> In memory of Andrew Brady
> The Broadway Guild

"Senor Barton?" Lyle swung around to face a Hispanic woman, her brown eyes huge. She looked to be in her late twenties, dark hair framing a heart-shaped face.

Barton took a hesitant step forward, glancing at the guards stationed by the door. Lyle had enlisted them to watch for the woman and signal whether she'd come alone. The guards nodded. Barton nodded back and the men disappeared.

"Thank you for coming forward," Lyle said in Spanish. "Let's sit down." He moved to the chairs below the plaque.

"No, not there, not where Cat Eyes ..." She moved to another set of chairs.

"Cat eyes?"

"That's what I call Senor Brady. Such beautiful eyes." She sat down hesitantly.

"Uh, I don't even know your name."

"No names."

"Look," Lyle said, sitting beside her, "I'll protect you. I have a friend in Immigration. There's no need to be afraid. Things like this are done all the time. I give you my word, Senora. I never break my word."

Unblinking, the woman stared into Barton's eyes. She must have found what she was looking for. "My name ... is Rosita Hernandez. My husband Miguel and I came here from Cuba a year before Andrew Brady was murdered."

"Where's your husband? Why isn't he here with you?"

"I ... don't know. He's been missing for a week."

Lyle jotted down the information in his notebook He promised to try to find out what happened to Miguel. So, why were you here in the terminal that day?"

"I was meeting a ship that was late. My cousin, she was ..."

"A stowaway?" Barton asked, keeping his voice gentle. "Is that how you got to America, too?"

"If I go back, they'll kill me."

"I gave you my word. You won't be sent back. Now," Lyle began, "on the phone you said you thought you saw what happened that morning. Why don't you tell me what you saw."

Rosita explained about a man who dropped a jacket. "I noticed him because the jacket made a noise when it hit the floor, like metal. When I started to reach for the jacket to give it back to him, he glared at me. His eyes were pure evil."

"The sound you heard was a gun hitting the floor beneath the jacket." Barton showed Santangelo's picture to Rosita. "Is this the man you saw drop the jacket?"

Rosita recoiled, as if he were holding a vial of poison. "That's him."

That old cotton candy smell filled Lyle's nostrils. Finally, a witness had fingered Eduardo Santangelo as the shooter. Barton smiled at Rosita. "I'm going to protect you. But first, I'm going to ask you some very important questions about what happened that morning. Then I'll find a safe place for you to stay."

*

When Jessie relieved Nick that evening at the hospital, they took a few minutes to themselves. Ambling down the hallway, Nick broached a subject that had been on his mind all afternoon. "I want you to think about getting a car and driver. You're about to begin rehearsals, and Anthony starts school soon. I think it would be safer for both of you."

"I've been thinking the same thing, ever since Gianni snatched Anthony. Andrew and I had a car and driver for years, Mary's nephew Willie; he used to be a cop. I think Mary said he's been working as a security guard."

"He sounds perfect. I'll ask Mary about him when I get home."

They reached the elevators. Glancing around, Nick hustled Jessie into a supply closet. "Listen, I called Mary a while ago. She offered to stay with Anthony his last night tomorrow so you and I can have a little time to ourselves."

"Mary offered?"

"Well, it might've been my idea. I don't remember."

"Uh-huh." Jessie's eyes teased him.

"Anyway, I thought maybe we'd do something special. Have a special dinner and ... see where it takes us."

"You know where it'll take us."

"So, it's a date." They kissed long and hard. Nick broke it off. "I better go, or we'll be in this closet for the next hour."

Nick decided to walk home. He needed some exercise. He strolled across Seventy-Seventh Street, pausing at the corner of Park to gaze in a jewelry shop's window, a party of gems on velvet. Nick patted his pocket, feeling a small box. Was he crazy?

As he crossed the broad avenue, Nick pulled out his cell, checking messages. Greta in Berlin. Delete. Two from Liz. Nick made a mental note to call his agent back later. Several from Abbie and two from Barton. He called Abbie first. She told him she was at the locksmith's having a duplicate key made to the closet cabinet, Gianni sick in bed from a collision with an Amaretto bottle. "I stopped by Oceano for some broth. The invalid lapped up every last drop and is out for the night."

"Get your ass back there pronto. He could wake up and find his key gone."

"The ten milligrams of valium I dissolved in the soup should keep him snoring until morning. Now I just have to figure out the combo to the safe."

"Be careful. If he catches you--"

"He won't. I'm not going near it while he's in the apartment, asleep or not."

They spent the next fifteen minutes arguing. Nick used every weapon in his arsenal of logic. It was too dangerous. The case was already solved. It wasn't right to lie to Jessie. Nothing worked. If it weren't for Anthony's ordeal he'd spill the whole deal to Jessie, beginning at the beginning. Nick eyed the cloudy sky. How did life get so complicated? He called Barton back after telling Abbie she was making a mistake.

Barton's voice was triumphant. "We got our witness. Rosita Hernandez, our mystery Hispanic lady."

"That's great." It was, Nick told himself. It was great.

"She positively identified Santangelo as the man who dropped the jacket and gun, exact time frame. But we may have an even better witness. When I questioned her further, Rosita mentioned a security guard standing a few feet away from her. I pressed and she remembered at the moment Santangelo scared her, she glanced at the guard. And the guard was staring at Santangelo. I'll bet my lucky Mets T-shirt Salerno saw the shooting."

"You sure it was Salerno and not some other guard?"

"She says it was the same man she asked earlier about a ship. Remember how Salerno said a Hispanic woman was questioning him about a ship?

"We knew Salerno was lying all along," Nick said, pausing at Seventy-Seventh and Madison. "Hell, Salerno wasn't on the far side of the terminal at all. He was just yards away from Andrew when he was shot. He was either involved or threatened."

"I'm not hauling Santangelo's ass in yet, not until we squeeze Salerno. He's what we need to make the case airtight, an eyewitness who saw Santangelo pull the trigger. Meanwhile, I'm putting Rosita in a safe-house. And in the Witness Protection Program after she testifies. Forget I told you anything about her."

Another secret. It was getting hard to keep them straight. Just as Nick clicked off, his cell rang. It was Ozzie with the information he'd requested.

"In three days? You're fast."

"I'm between cases. Besides, Eduardo Santangelo's an easy target. Everyone has something to say about him, and none of it is good."

"Shoot."

"A while back, Eduardo was working on one of the family ships, a bartender. He'd gotten into trouble in Genoa, so his mother sent him to his Uncle Gianni to keep an eye on him. All was quiet until he turned up again suddenly in Genoa two years ago, April. I looked up the date of Andrew Brady's death. It looks like the kid flew home the night your brother was murdered. He stayed in Genoa until last spring, when he returned to New York."

Nick knew what was coming. It was all falling into place.

"I nosed around some of Santangelo's former hangouts and got a bartender to talk."

"How much did it cost? I owe you."

"Forget it. You've done the same thing for me. Anyway, Santangelo got falling down drunk on grappa one night and started boasting he killed an American celebrity so big it made headlines for months. Said he made his bones with the Martinelli family in New York. He bragged somebody wanted the guy dead, and Martinelli gave Santangelo the honor because Eduardo had his own grudge with the celebrity. Eduardo said he was laying low in Italy until it blew over."

There it was. Wexley wanted Andrew dead, and his brother-in-law Zappella used his position in Martinelli's organization to contract Santangelo for the hit. Maybe he figured Wexley would treat his sister better for the favor. Eduardo was the perfect shooter. He worked on the ship and made no secret of his hate for Andrew. "Ozzie, thanks. You've been really helpful. I won't forget."

Nick hung up, reeling. My God. He'd been wrong from the get-go. Fosselli had nothing to do with Andrew's death. How could Nick's instincts have failed him so completely? Was he blinded by his love for Jessie? Had he been so intent on getting Gianni out of Jessie and Anthony's lives that he'd willed Fosselli to be guilty? But how did that explain his honing in on Gianni before Jessie was anything more to him than his sister-in-law? How could he have been so wrong?

*

Wexley lay on the filthy bunk in his cell, his arm tossed over his eyes. His life was over. He'd gotten his revenge on Brady, but in the end, Andrew had won. Andrew Brady always won, the fucking golden boy. Some people had all the luck. Others couldn't catch a break. If Ian didn't have bad luck, he'd have no luck at all.

Twelve years ago, Ian was the lead in an Off-Broadway play at a theater right down the street from Midtown North. Now he was housed in one of the precinct's cells. How had he gone from Rock Stone in SEARCH FOR LOVE to Edward G. Robinson in I AM A FUGITIVE FROM A CHAIN GANG?

If Ian had Paula in this cell right now he'd wring her neck. At least Ian could bring down Paula's brother Aldo with him. He'd still get one last curtain call.

*

Nick poured a bourbon and settled into the sofa in the study. After he'd spoken to Mary about a driver, she'd gone to bed early to watch television. That's what Nick should do. He wanted to be at the hospital early for Anthony's surgery.

Nick left a message for Liz, saying he was going to write the novel in New York and he had a new idea, something to blow his other sales out of the water. It had come to him on his long trek home this afternoon. Why write a book set in London? Why not write about New York? With excitement, he mulled the plot, working out the details.

Nick checked in with Jessie later and told her Mary's nephew Willie was eager to work for the family again. He stretched across the couch, missing Jessie like crazy. His eyes wandered to the majestic oil painting over the mantel, finished shortly before Andrew's death. His brother's murder was finally solved. So why did his gut say ... not yet? Nick went back to the investigation one more time: Ian Wexley ... Rosita Hernandez ... Joseph Salerno ... Eduardo Santangelo ... Roberto Martinelli ... Aldo Zappella. Dammit. Gianni Fosselli had to be in that cast of characters as sure as a shark was in JAWS. He knew it!

There had to be something he'd overlooked. And what about Andrew's secret? From the moment Nick had read that diary-- Nick bolted upright. The diaries. They stopped the day before Andrew boarded the ship for that final cruise. Andrew had diligently kept a diary from the moment he came to live with Jessie and her father, no gaps. He was religious about recording his impressions of the world around him.

Which meant Andrew kept a diary when he was aboard the ship. If he'd had it on him when he was shot, it would be in Midtown North's evidence room. Which Barton would've mentioned. So the diary had to be in the luggage. And Jessie said she'd never gone through the luggage, not wanting to see it again. Thankfully, Mary had ignored Jessie's words and stored the suitcases in the attic.

But where did everything go when it was removed from the attic? Nick dashed through the kitchen and up the back stairs. The old nursery at the back of the second floor was the new catch-all space. Nick hit pay dirt in the second room. That's where the attic items were stashed, everything organized and marked. Nick held his breath, hoping Jessie hadn't finally tossed the suitcases. Nope, there they were.

His pulse zooming into orbit, Nick searched both bags, combing through every inch of clothing, every one of Jessie's purses, leaving nothing unexplored. Frantically, he checked pockets, the insides of shoes, and Andrew's shaving kit. In his frenzy, Nick ripped out the suitcase's lining, remembering he'd used it as a hiding place for a plot in THE GREEN MONSTER. No journal. Stymied, Nick replaced the items in the suitcases one by one, lingering over Andrew's Broadway Cares T-shirt. "C'mon, Andrew," Nick muttered, "help me. I know you kept a diary on the ship. Where is it?" Where was his obnoxious ghost when he needed him?

Frustrated, Nick made his way to his suite, adding the journals he'd read Anthony that morning to the others stacked on a shelf. So many little books and notepads recording a man's life. They'd given up a secret Andrew had taken with him to the grave. Maybe it was time to put the journals away for good in that black dance bag and ... wait ... that black dance bag.

"My God!" Nick sprang up. Jessie said that dance bag went everywhere with them when they were working. And that cruise had been a working cruise. Nick flew to the closet and jerked out the bag Jessie had given him with the journals. He examined every inch of the soft black leather interior. Patting the stiff bottom, he felt a thicker section. Looking closely, he spotted an opening along the seam. Nick slid his fingers into the nearly invisible pocket and yanked out a thin leather notebook. His heart was running the race of its life.

For the next hour, Nick sat on the floor, intently absorbing every word of Andrew's final journal. His brother had even written several paragraphs that last morning, his closing words before he walked down the gangway ...

One of the ship's officers just brought me a message from the radio room, along with the early disembarkation pass I'd requested. Bill Rudolph's waiting for me in his car outside the terminal. He wants to do publicity for the Tony Awards, an interview and a photo shoot. I hope it's worth it. Jessie and I had better take home the gold this year.

I thought I'd escaped my worst nightmare by getting permission to disembark early. Jessie and Bongo would disembark with me and we'd all go home with Willie in the limo. Bill made it even easier—we'd get off the ship earlier yet. Jessie and Anthony would leave with Willie, and I'd go with Bill. Instead, Bongo wants to watch the luggage on the conveyer belt, and Jessie has packing to do. She wants to disembark later with the other passengers. Damn! All I can do is pray nothing happens in the next half hour without me at her side. If I make too much of it, Jessie will become suspicious. I have to let it go. Now I'm at the mercy of the fates. If things go wrong, when Bill drops me off at home I'll find my marriage over. Jessie will take Anthony and leave me.

Nick closed the little book, letting out a heavy breath. Jessie and Anthony never left Andrew. Instead, Andrew left them. Pulling himself off the floor, he drifted to the terrace door. Tiny pink bulbs illuminated the trees and path in the back yard. The plum tree was silhouetted, its barren limbs lifeless. "I know why you were killed, Andrew," he whispered. "I finally know who and why."

Nick wandered back to the black bag, secreting the diary in its hiding place. He stumbled into the bedroom, set the alarm, and fell asleep on top of the bed. A noise woke Nick shortly before sunrise. He opened his eyes, not surprised to see his brother. Andrew sat at the foot of the bed, a morose ghostly visitor.

"You're going to tell Jessie now, aren't you? She'll finally know what I hid from her all those years."

Nick sat up. "I don't have a choice. I'm sorry. It had everything to do with why you were killed. But I'll wait until I have more proof. She'll need it."

"Tell Jessie I ..." Andrew's voice caught. "She'll never understand."

"I'll make her understand when the time's right. She loves you. I know Jessie."

"Yeah, you do. You know her better than anyone. Better than I ever did."

"Stop it. You're her true love, not me."

"Jessie and I were kids playing at marriage. We grew up together. We were young and stupid and innocent. Jessie lost her innocence when I was killed. You're the man who was there for her when she came out on the other side."

Nick dropped his head, not knowing what to say.

"I knew you could do it. I knew you'd root out the truth even when all the odds were against you. I owe you."

"You don't owe me anything. We're even. You led me to Jessie and Anthony. I love them."

Andrew smiled. "Yeah, maybe we are even."

Impulsively, Nick stood up and threw his arms around his brother. The two men hugged tightly. He was hugging a ghost.

"We should've been able to do this our whole lives," Andrew said. "We should've been able to grow old together."

"I'll get him. I'll make sure Fosselli pays."

"The most important thing is Gianni won't get Jessie and Anthony. They belong to you now."

CHAPTER 25

Nick set off for the hospital early that morning, deciding to hoof it. The temperature had plummeted overnight into the mid-sixties, a shocking fall kiss hello. He punched in Abbie's number and got her voicemail. Which meant she was at Gianni's, her phone turned off. "Hey, it's me. I have great news. In fact, you're a genius. I'm on my way to the hospital, incommunicado until Anthony's out of surgery. We'll talk soon." A minute later, Nick reached Barton, on his way to the precinct. He rapidly filled him in on Andrew's final journal. "So Wexley didn't set up the hit. It's Fosselli."

"I see," Barton said slowly. "And Wexley's confession means ... what?"

"I'll figure it out."

"Let's get real. Andrew could've made it up."

"Why?"

"Beats me. He was an actor. He liked to tell stories. He was in a bad mood. He didn't like Gianni. It's a journal. I can write I arrested Bonnie and Clyde. Doesn't mean it's true."

Nick rolled his eyes. How could he tell Barton Andrew's ghost had confirmed Fosselli was their man? "Look, you know my reputation. I'll stake my entire career on the fact I'm right about this. It was Gianni."

A pause. "Wexley's supposed to be arraigned this afternoon." Another pause. "Just so you know, I'll need more evidence than a diary to arrest Fosselli. Or the DA will laugh himself sick."

"I'll get it. I won't let you down. Look, go ahead and arraign Wexley. He confessed. He's involved. But Fosselli's the reason my brother is dead." And when he had more proof, Jessie would realize it, too.

*

Roberto Martinelli strolled through the manicured gardens on his Long Island estate with Aldo Zappella. He was enjoying the vibrant roses in the late morning sunshine, the nip in the air refreshing. "So, it's finally finished," Roberto said. "Wexley's behind bars. Fosselli's in the clear."

"Ian confessed. It's over."

"It was a brilliant plan. Congratulations. Your brother-in-law thinking you were doing him a favor, inserting him as the middle-man with the jacket and the gun—it's rich. The poor schlub thinks he's guilty."

"So does Paula."

Roberto picked a rose, inhaling its scent. "I never did completely understand how you accomplished working your sister into this."

"It was easy." Aldo's smile revealed a row of piano-key teeth. "Before the cruise, I told Paula Ian was cheating again. Then I warned Ian Paula was sure he was cheating again. So the only night Ian had the balls to go out was the night before Brady was shot—to deliver the gun. Paula followed him like I knew she would, becoming our convenient witness should it ever come to that." Aldo chuckled. "I figured it was just a matter of time before Wexley had to dip his wick and Paula got wise. I urged her to go to Barton when she came crying to me a few days ago."

"Did Wexley implicate you?"

"The police paid me a visit this morning. I told them I didn't know what the hell they were talking about. I said my former brother-in-law was furious with my family because my sister was divorcing him. They thanked me and left."

"What about Santangelo? Did Ian finger him?"

"Not positively. I don't think they have enough to arrest him."

"I don't give a shit after what that little cocksucker pulled."

"Look, you weren't even sure you'd use those pictures. I'd just forget about it."

Martinelli looked his friend in the eye. "I don't forget about anything. That's why I'm still walking around a free man. Those pictures were insurance against McDeare's meddling. I could've stopped him cold if he decided to play investigator again. That Brady woman's got McDeare by the balls. He'd never let those pictures end up in the tabloids, which is exactly where I would've sent them."

"The kid won't step out of line again."

Roberto led his friend towards the vegetable garden, fingering the ripe tomatoes. "Look, you got to figure all the options. Wexley's arrested, but if McDeare doubts him and goes after Fosselli anyway, now we got nothing to hold over his head."

"We threaten him with the welfare of the Brady woman or the kid."

"Don't get stupid on me. McDeare would protect them with armed guards after the Othello. You think we want to attract the mayor's attention in an election year with that kind of business? And if we try to use the photos, now we run the risk of establishing a connection to Fosselli. Guess why?"

"Because Fosselli got his own hands dirty with those pictures, thanks to Eduardo. I get it."

"Listen to me, Aldo." Roberto picked a tomato, rolling its smooth skin between his palms. "Gianni Fosselli's an honorable man. He sold us the cruise line for a song. Customs suspect nothing about our little private import venture onboard those ships. It's a fucking gold mine. We're using his restaurant for money laundering. I have a great deal of respect for Mr. Fosselli. For years he never said a word about his parents' ... demise. When he approached Secchi with the cruise line, I jumped at it. Killing Brady was small potatoes for what we got. Now that little prick Eduardo might've fucked everything up in ways we can't imagine."

*

After Dr. Ito informed Jessie and Nick Anthony's surgery was successful and he'd make a full recovery, Jessie was elated. "He's fine, and he comes home tomorrow!" She mock collapsed against Nick's chest. "I'm so wrung out it's not funny. Why don't we go home and relax for awhile, until he's back in his room?"

"You go on home. I have some errands. Come on," he said, tugging Jessie into an elevator. "I'll put you in a cab."

"Errands? How domestic." As drained as she was, Jessie felt lighthearted enough to dance as they stepped into the fresh air and the whir of traffic. "What are you up to, McDeare?"

Nick hailed a taxi. "It's a surprise. For tonight. I'm planning to romance you."

"You're joking, right?"

"Why would I be joking?" Nick opened the cab door for Jessie.

"Well, you're not exactly the romantic type." Nick's face tightened, and Jessie cursed her big mouth. "Um, that's not what I meant. I'm just overtired."

"Get in. I'll see you later."

"Are you mad?"

"I'm not mad. Get in."

"You're mad."

"I'm fine. Get in. I have to get moving."

"You're really not mad?"

"I promise. Trust me."

*

Nick waited until Jessie's taxi was out of sight before making his call to Salerno.

"McDeare? That's weird. I been thinking about calling you the past couple of days. I just got back from California."

"A vacation?"

"My daughter, she ... died."

"I'm sorry," Nick said gently. "I lost my only child a few years ago. I know how it feels."

"Marlena was my only child, too. Uh, I was thinking that ... could we meet?"

This was a surprise. "Sure. Where? When?"

"The cemetery on Long Island where your brother's buried. His grave. Angela's buried there, too. And Mr. McDeare, bring that cop with you. Two o'clock tomorrow."

"We'll be there."

Nick hung up, puzzled. He'd called to put the screws to Joseph and insist on another meeting. Now Salerno was falling into his arms. And Nick didn't think it was his manly charm.

*

When Jessie got home, she filled Mary in on Anthony's surgery and warned her to be prepared for some odd menus. Jessie didn't care if Anthony wanted chocolate Easter bunnies for dinner every night. Her little boy was coming home!

Mary grinned, looking ten years younger. "I'll take his order tonight and go shopping in the morning." She put the laundry basket by the stairs. Jessie noted Nick's T-shirts folded neatly beneath Anthony's. "You're doing Nick's laundry?"

"He's a member of the family, isn't he? I've been doing his laundry for some time. Oh, by the way, the tree nursery was here. They took out the plum tree."

Jessie wandered to the window and looked at the empty spot in the back yard. "Maybe I'll have another one planted next summer for Anthony."

"Also," Mary added, smiling, "your birthday gift for Nick arrived early this morning. I had the men put it where you said you wanted it."

"Super!" Jessie dashed across the hall to the study.

"The old one's in Anthony's room, just like you wanted," Mary called after her. "And don't slip. I just waxed the floor."

*

Nick shivered as he headed down Lexington Avenue. Jeez, he should've grabbed his suede jacket. His cell jangled.

"Mr. McDeare? It's Michaela Greenwood."

"Could you speak up? You're competing with traffic."

"I don't want to be overheard."

"Wait a minute." Nick ducked into an Asian market where the noise level was a dull hum.

"I need your help." Michelle said quietly, "and you need mine. It's hard to explain. Can you meet me tomorrow morning?"

"Where?"

"Tug McGraw's Sports Bar at Broadway and Seventy-Eighth. Eleven o'clock."

"I'll be there." That's when Anthony was coming home. Jessie and Mary would have to handle it by themselves. He looked upwards. Why did everything happen at once?

"Mr. McDeare? Do you know if the Witness Protection Program still exists? You know. Where you can assume a new identity so no one can find you?"

"You've got information for me?"

"Yeah. In exchange you help me disappear."

"Do you mind if I bring the detective in charge of Andrew's case along? He'll be able to help you. You can trust him."

"Fine. But keep a low profile, okay? No sirens."

*

Barton looked his partner up and down. "You look like shit, Bush. What have you been doing to yourself?"

Bushman shrugged. "You know me. Burning the candle at both ends. A different lady every night, and last night's was a tiger. Life's good, man."

"It must be nice to be a single guy in New York City."

- 266 -

"Single and good-looking." Bush peered into the grimy office mirror and carefully arranged several strands of hair over his bald spot, which took up half his head.

"You ever going to settle down? You're thirty-five fucking years old. You saw the world when you were a Marine, sampled every type of female out there. Now it's time to pick one and procreate."

"Kids? Are you fucking nuts? Sometimes I think you don't know me at all."

At his phone's ring, Lyle picked up. It was Jeff Applebaum, up in the Bronx. Miguel Hernandez was John Doe number eighty-seven. Found off the Major Deegan Expressway with a bullet in his chest. Barton hung up, his face grim. America. Streets paved with gold. And danger.

"What's up?"

"Just something with Barb." Rosita had to remain a secret, even from Bush. Lyle changed the subject. "Get this, McDeare thinks we arrested the wrong guy. He's still convinced Fosselli did it."

"You got to be shitting me. Wexley confessed."

"Yeah, well--" Barton's cell rang. It was Nick, asking if he could talk. "Not really."

"Okay, just listen." Nick told him about two appointments tomorrow, Michelle and Salerno. "A suggestion," Nick added. "Clue in the Long-Island cops. Something doesn't feel right. Call me when you can talk."

Barton clicked off.

"Barb again?"

Barton got to his feet, rubbing the back of his neck. "I'm going down to the coffee shop. Want something?"

"I'll go with you. There's a hot little waitress I got my eye on. I have a feeling she's going to love me."

*

Abbie had been camped out in Gianni's stuffy closet for two hours. She was cramped and hot. Every combination of numbers she'd tried on the stupid safe had failed, and she'd chipped three nails in the process. Abbie punched the steel door. It was time for a break. Struggling up, she pulled her cell from her purse, checked messages, and immediately called Nick back, demanding to know his good news. Abbie listened in shock as Nick recapped Andrew's final diary. "I'm proud of you. You were right all along."

"We were both right," she said softly. "Poor Andrew."

"We need more evidence, but we'll get it. Any luck with the safe? And don't think I've forgotten about wanting to tell Jessie everything, as in today. The lies have to stop."

"She can't know yet. Please. Just give it a few more days. I know Jessie. We tell her and all hell breaks loose. We don't need that now. Know any good safecrackers?"

*

Nick shuffled into the hallway, his arms laden with packages. Mary hurried out of the study, closing the doors behind her. "What's this? Supplies for the winter?"

"Oh, this and that." Nick hustled to the kitchen, piling his bags on the island and emptying them.

Mary laughed. "You beat me to it. You bought Jessie a cell phone."

"I bought one for you and Anthony, too. He'll be safer with one. You all will be."

Mary raised a brow. "Do you think we're in danger? Ian was arrested." Nick could feel Mary's eyes boring into him as he emptied the bags. She put a hand on her hip. "What's going on?"

Those dark eyes could see through a lie like Superman saw through walls. Nick blew out a breath. "Okay. Wexley didn't kill Andrew. Gianni did. Jessie doesn't know yet. I need more evidence, but I'm positive. I can't say more than that. We can live our lives, but we have to be careful."

He watched Mary digest his words. "I can't say I'm surprised," she finally said. "I knew you suspected Gianni. I've had my own doubts about him. But this will hit Jessie hard. And I'm even more worried about Anthony. First he finds out Gianni's his real father. Now he's finds out that his real father killed Andrew. How will he handle that?"

"I'm worried about Anthony, too," Nick admitted. "We'll get him through it, all three of us." Four if you counted Andrew.

"He loves you," Mary said softly. "He looks at you the way he used to look at Andrew."

A large box on the island moved a few inches on its own. Mary jumped back. "Good Lord. What's in there?"

"Lobsters."

"Okay, come clean. What are you up to? Why am I really staying with Anthony at the hospital tonight?"

Nick took two potatoes to the sink to wash. "Do we have any wood for the grate in the study? It's freezing out there. And when the flowers arrive, would you please put them in Jessie's room?"

Mary's smile wouldn't quit. "Check the back yard for wood, stacked on the west side. Be sure to open the flue, or you'll have the fire department on the doorstep instead of Cupid."

*

After Lyle drove to the safe-house in Trenton to break the news to Rosita about her husband, he headed back to the city, mulling his next steps. Keeping Rosita in the States would require calling in a few favors. What a day it had been, Michelle and Salerno up next. Barton had alerted the Long Island cops, requesting a unit check out the cemetery before their meeting.

Would they ever get a real answer out of this case, or was it all smoke and mirrors into infinity?

*

Nick showered and shaved, changing into a pair of jeans and a black shirt. Before he left the suite, he grabbed a small box from the dresser.

Dinner was progressing nicely, water boiling, the potatoes stuffed and waiting to be popped back into the oven. Mary had laid out the black and violet Mikasa, with matching linen napkins and placemats. Nick set a corner of the massive oak table in the dining room, placing an ornate golden candelabra in the center.

Now for the wood. Nick stepped into the back yard, a brisk wind sending smoky clouds scudding across the sky. Nick drifted towards the barren spot where the plum tree had lived. Andrew had once raked autumn leaves here and played catch with his son. And he'd cared for a plum tree that had represented his place in the Kendle family. Now it was gone ... Wait. Nick squatted, looking closely at the ground. "I don't believe it," he whispered, brushing a hand over the earth. "Wait till Jessie sees this." Nick shivered and headed for the woodpile.

He swung into the study, tossing the wood next to the grate and grabbing the morning's TIMES. He'd wad up some papers, throw the wood on-- And then he saw it. Backing up, Nick stared up in shock. The oil painting of Andrew, Jessie, and Anthony wasn't holding court over the mantel anymore. In its place was an enormous oil of Andrew and Nick, standing side by side. They were both wearing tuxes, standing casually with their hands in their pockets, hair spiking their foreheads. Their heads were cocked in different directions, as if they were looking at each other.

"What the hell ...?" A red bow had a card attached: Happy belated birthday, Nick. All my love, Jess. His eyes fastened on the picture, Nick sank to the couch. "Dammit, Andrew, I wish ... God, how I wish."

*

Jessie closed the brownstone's front door behind her and clipped down the hallway. That smell ... a fire was burning in the grate. And the aromas coming from the kitchen. Yummy. "Nick?"

"In the study." He was sitting on the couch and staring up at the painting, a bourbon in hand.

"You built a fire," she said, dropping down beside him. "It feels good." Nick's eyes remained on the painting. "You like it?"

"I like it. I love you." Setting his glass on the coffee table, Nick roped Jessie into his arms. He kissed her with the kind of heat that started another fire, licking greedily at her insides until everything was melting together in a steamy drizzle. When their lips finally parted, he whispered, "How did you do it? It's wonderful. How was it possible?"

"The artist Leonard Blaine works from photographs," Jessie said, running her fingers through Nick's velvety hair. "I gave him some individual pictures, and Lenny melded them together. Anthony took some great ones of you on Tony night, remember?"

"The artist did this in a couple of months?"

Jessie nuzzled Nick's neck. "I made it worth his while. I'm so glad you like it." She straightened up. "Let me go shower and change. Give me a half hour to look gorgeous enough for you."

Jessie showered in record time, humming a memorable tune from the new show. She trotted back into the bedroom, spotting a wrapped floral arrangement. If Gianni thought flowers would make up for the pain he'd caused Anthony ... Jessie ripped off the wrapping paper and ... oh God. Dozens of white roses, lilies and lily of the valley in a black porcelain vase. They took her breath away. Jessie plucked the card from the attached spike. Nick? Was this the romantic surprise he'd talked about that morning? She inhaled deeply. Could life be so good, or was there a new catch lurking around the corner?

Jessie quickly slipped on a lilac gauze skirt and matching wraparound halter and silk shawl. Nick loved her in halters, and Jessie loved the slide of his fingers down her bare back. She ran a comb through her hair and hurried downstairs.

Nick was waiting for her. He looked her up and down, his eyes glittering. "You're gorgeous enough. And I hope you're hungry. Come with me, my pet." As he led her into the dining room, Jessie gasped. The room was a flickering mass of candlelight, the chandeliers on dim. Lobsters steamed on both dinner plates, joined by heated ramekins of melted butter. Twice-baked potatoes with bacon, chives and cheddar cheese, steamed summer squash, and sourdough rolls were on side plates. It was a dinner fit for royalty. Nick pulled out Jessie's chair and flipped a cloth napkin onto her lap with a flourish. He angled her a triumphant smile.

"Okay, okay, I take it back. You're the king of romance."

Nick sat down and reached for his own napkin. "You challenged me this morning. I couldn't ignore it."

"You and I are such competitive people." Jessie reached over and brought his fingers to her lips. "This is all beautiful, really. And I love the flowers. They're breathtaking. How did you know white roses are my favorite?"

"I thought pink roses were your favorite," Nick said, pouring Pinot Grigio into their flutes. "That's what Gianni always brings you."

"Pink roses are his favorite, not mine."

Nick lifted his glass. "To white roses and a happy little boy coming home tomorrow."

They both dug in, devouring every morsel of their first real meal in days. They talked about Willie's shopping for a car and Anthony's wanting fried chicken for dinner tomorrow night with strawberry cupcakes for dessert. Jessie stared at the hunk of man sitting beside her. She remembered that first April night, when Nick knocked on her door. They'd sat right here, strangers, until Nick's hellion ex-girlfriend had burst in, ripping up Andrew's books and knocking Nick out. It seemed like years ago.

"What?" Nick asked, sitting back. "You have a distant smile on your face."

"I was just thinking back." Jessie took a sip of wine. "You've been here less than five months. Not a very long time."

"Consider yourself lucky. My relationships are usually counted in days, not months. Hours in some cases." Nick stared at his plate.

"So," Jessie said, watching him, "what else have you got up your sleeve tonight? I mean, this fabulous dinner, flowers. What could top it? Making love in front of the fire in the study?"

"And have Andrew stare down at us? Maybe I've got something better in mind."

"What could be better?" Jessie reached over, looping her fingers through his.

Nick stared at their hands, running his finger over her wedding bands. "I want to ask you something, but maybe I should leave well enough alone."

"Just ask it," Jessie said, wondering at his sudden shyness.

He angled her a quick glance. "Well, I've been thinking a lot since we got back from the villa. The freedom we had down there. And then we came back to the brownstone, sleeping in separate beds ..."

"I know you hate it, but there's good reason for it."

"I do hate it. But that's not ..."

"What are you trying to say?"

Jessie could see a struggle going on inside his head. Releasing her hand, Nick dug into his pocket, withdrawing a jewelry box. His eyes cast downward, he slid it towards her.

Puzzled, Jessie opened the tiny box. Nestled on midnight velvet was a ring, a gold band set with three exquisite square-cut diamonds. The jewels snatched the candles' glow, multiplying the light into a million white-hot sparkles. Jessie stopped breathing. "My God. Are you ... Are you asking me to marry you?"

"Maybe." Nick had never looked more vulnerable, his walls down like Jericho. "I guess it depends on your answer."

Jessie looked back at the ring, spellbound. Nick McDeare wanted to marry her. Was she dreaming? "I ... I'm stunned."

"You haven't thought about it? I mean, as in doing it as opposed to not doing it? You really haven't considered getting married again?"

"I meant what I told Anthony. I thought I'd never get married again." Her eyes dropped to her wedding rings, her wedding rings that hadn't left her finger since Andrew had placed them there. She twirled them around her finger, something she'd been doing for years. It was hard to imagine not wearing them. How would it feel to ...? "I don't know what to say. I ..."

"You don't have to." Nick quickly retrieved the box and snapped it closed, the diamonds' light extinguished. "All I have to do is look at your face. Your expression says it all. You don't want to take those rings off. It would kill you. It means living a charade in front of Anthony, but so be it. He wants us to get married, you know. He told me."

"Nick, listen—"

"It's okay, I understand. You prefer to live in the past." He pushed his chair back. "I never should've brought this up. It won't happen again. I'm a quick learner."

Jessie dropped her head, wiping her eyes. "Nick, wait. I--" She looked up. It was too late. He was already out the front door, closing it softly.

CHAPTER 26

After Nick took a quick jog in the dark, working out his frustration on the pavement, he found his way back to his room. He dropped to the edge of his bed, clasping the jewelry box in his hand. Jessie had told him over and over she'd never take those rings off or marry again. It was his own damn fault.

"Nick?" Jessie was framed in the doorway.

"I don't feel like talking right now, okay?"

Jessie sat down beside him. "Can I see the ring again, please?"

Nick shrugged and handed her the box.

Jessie snapped the lid open, the light catching the diamonds and spraying the ceiling with tiny constellations of glitter. "It's gorgeous. I love it. Would you, um, mind if I hung onto it for awhile?"

"Do you have a jewelry fetish I don't know about?"

"Look, you surprised the hell out of me tonight. I never saw it coming. I thought you were a confirmed bachelor. And I-I never thought I'd ... You idiot. I'm not turning you down. I just need some time to get used to the idea, you know?" She looked down at the bands on her finger.

"Are you saying yes? Or maybe?"

"I'm saying probably. I think. Can you handle probably for now?"

Nick would never understand women if he lived to be two hundred. But he loved this particular woman. So instead of strangling her, he said, "I can handle probably. Maybe."

Jessie laid her head on Nick's shoulder and examined the ring. "Three flawless princess diamonds." She laughed. "God, this must have set you back. It's flattering to know you think I'm worth this much. How many carats?"

"None of your business. Not until you put that ring on your finger. But I will say this. I chose three diamonds for a reason. The three of us. You, me, and Anthony." Nick snapped the lid closed and slipped the box into his nightstand drawer. "I'll hang onto this for you. For a little while."

*

Nick was up early the next morning. He tiptoed around the suite, keeping his eyes on the sleeping woman in his bed, his future. Whistling his way down to the kitchen, he made a pot of coffee and began to check his cell messages. At the doorbell's buzz, Nick squinted through the peephole and quickly flipped the locks.

Abbie hustled inside. "Don't you check your messages? Where's Jessie?"

"Still asleep. What's wrong?" Nick spotted a gaudy diamond on Abbie's left hand. "What's that, a headlight?"

"Gianni gave it to me last night." Abbie waved the ring in front of him. "As you can see, he spared no expense. It'll be a nice souvenir, don't you think?"

"Christ--"

"Be quiet and listen to me. This is important." She leaned close to Nick, her voice hushed. "I came over to warn you. Gianni's lawyer's going to serve Jessie papers, maybe today. He wants a DNA test done on Anthony. He says he'll--"

"What's going on?" Draped in a blue silk robe, Jessie materialized in the middle of the staircase like a bad dream. "Is something wrong?"

The color drained from Abbie's face. Nick and Abbie sprang apart. Jessie descended the stairs, tying the robe's sash. "Is someone going to answer my question?"

Abbie shrugged. "I just needed to talk to Nick."

"You needed to talk to Nick?"

"We--"

"Is that an engagement ring on your finger?"

"Yes and no, I was telling Nick ..."

"You seem to be telling Nick a lot of things."

"It's complicated."

"I can see that." Jessie's eyes narrowed, gunning for Nick. "How many women do you intend to propose to at once? Isn't that a rather expensive hobby?" Jessie stopped a few feet away and crossed her arms.

Abbie's mouth dropped open. "Nick, you asked Jessie to marry you?"

"I'd like some answers, Nick. Now."

"When you calm down," Nick said slowly, "I'll give you answers. Not when you're like this."

"Oh, hell," Abbie snapped. "It's over. I know how much you hate lying to Jessie, so let's just put an end to it." Abbie turned to Jessie. "Let's sit down and I'll explain."

*

Jessie watched Abbie slide into the breakfast nook across from her. Nick leaned against the island, looking at a banana in the fruit basket.

"Before I forget," Abbie began, "Gianni wants a DNA test done on Anthony, so be on the lookout for someone trying to serve you papers."

"I expected as much. Get to the point." Jessie's stomach was in a million knots. What the hell was going on? Were Nick and Abbie having an affair right under her nose? She fought to keep her sanity and not explode.

"Okay." Abbie looked furtively at Nick before continuing, "I've been working undercover, trying to get the dirt on Gianni. You know. Looking for proof he killed Andrew."

Jessie's fear turned to horror. "You've been playing Gianni because you think he's the killer?" Jessie's eyes darted to Nick. "Where do you come into all this?"

"Nick's the only one who knew," Abbie explained. "Even Lyle doesn't know. Nick's been working with me from the beginning."

"You knew?" Jessie demanded. Nick nodded. "And you didn't tell me?" Jessie turned back to Abbie. "You've been sleeping with Gianni? For-for that?"

"I had to. It was the only way to get him to trust me."

Jessie turned her eyes on Nick again. "And you approved?"

"It was Abbie's choice," Nick said mildly, picking up the banana and examining it.

Jessie rose, glaring at Abbie. "That rock on your finger. It's from Gianni? He thinks you're going to marry him?"

Abbie nodded.

Jessie approached Nick. "And you knew about this sham of a marriage?"

"Yes."

Jessie snatched the banana out of Nick's hand, slapping it against his shoulder. "Who the hell are you, Nick McDeare? You stood by and allowed Abbie to use her body ... you APPROVED of her toying with a man's emotions, of going so far as to PRETEND to love him and want to marry him ... all to prove that my child's biological father's a KILLER?"

Nick looked down at her, his face grim. "Give me that." He yanked the banana from her hand.

"Wait a minute," Abbie pleaded. "Don't blame Nick. He had no idea I'd take it this far. He's been begging me to stop for months now." She got up, standing on Nick's other side.

"For crissake," Nick said, his eyes darkening. "I'm sorry for doing this behind your back, but you can't still be defending Gianni. Not after what he did to Anthony."

"Gianni wanted his son to know who he was. I can understand that. What I can't understand is your relentless desire to turn Gianni into Andrew's killer. The police arrested the right man. Ian Wexley!" What was wrong with Nick McDeare? Was his ego so huge he had to be right no matter what?

"Dammit, it wasn't Wexley. I have--"

Abbie touched Nick's arm. "Don't. Leave it alone for now."

Seeing the familiar gesture, Jessie had an epiphany. "My God," she shrieked, "you two have been pretending to hate each other for my benefit?"

"Partly," Abbie admitted, "but mostly for Gianni's."

Jessie stared at Nick as he calmly peeled the banana and ate it. Who was this man? "You couldn't trust me to know about this? You want to share your life with me, but you couldn't tell me about this? What other things should I be asking you about? Should we begin with Nick McDeare's list of handy bimbos?"

"Look," Nick said, tossing the peel into the trash. "There's no other female in my life. Abbie and I are friends. You have to trust me on that. And I've already apologized for keeping Abbie's work from you. It's been eating me up and I hated it, okay? I'm sorry. But Abbie insisted we couldn't tell you about Gianni, and she was right. Look at you. Even now, after everything Gianni's done, you're still defending him."

"Gianni's not a murderer."

"Says you. You're blind when it comes to men."

"Obviously. Look who I'm involved with now." Her fury boiling over like Vesuvius, Jessie marched towards the stairs. "Marry you? I don't even want to be in the same room with you!" Jessie flew up the steps to her bedroom and slammed the door. Hurling herself onto the bed, she burst into tears. Did Nick think she couldn't be trusted? Look who was talking about trust. How could she spend the rest of her life with a man who kept secrets from her on a daily basis? Why couldn't Nick be more like ... Andrew?"

*

Gianni relaxed at the desk in his office suite, a joyful man. His attorney was already taking the offensive with the DNA test. Abigail was now wearing Gianni's engagement ring, and a date had been set for a spring wedding.

Earlier that morning, Gianni had picked out a carved wooden ship for Anthony, arranging for it to be delivered that afternoon. It was Gianni's peace offering to his son, the beginning of a new relationship. Best of all, the hunt for Andrew Brady's killer had finally been resolved. Gianni was, as they said, off the hook. Wexley was an ass. The world would be a better place without him.

Gianni chuckled. The police were idiots, and so was McDeare. Getting away with murder, literally, was minor compared to having the last laugh on McDeare. Jessica and Nicholas deserved each other, both trash. But Anthony, ah, that was different. Gianni intended to rescue his son from the clutches of his vulgar mother and her disgusting lover. It wouldn't be long now.

*

Nick washed a hand over his face as he and Abbie left the brownstone. He was trying to remember why he wanted to marry Jessica Kendle Brady. He kept coming up blank. Abbie nudged him. "Calling Nick McDeare. Calling Nick McDeare."

"What?"

"I asked you twice already. You're in another world. What about Lyle? Will you tell him about my undercover work?"

"I don't know. I can't think about that right now. Look, I'm sorry. I'm in a crappy mood. I'll call you later. Good luck on the safe."

Waving goodbye, Nick veered in the other direction for his meeting with Michelle. He'd deal with Jessie later. As he approached Tug McGraw's on Upper Broadway, Lyle climbed out of a double-parked car. "I thought we'd go in together," the cop said. "I'm not sure I'd recognize Michelle, now that she's high-society."

The two men pushed through the door. Nick scanned the cavernous room, rapidly filling up with the early lunch crowd, televisions blaring. A woman at a table in the rear lifted her hand, signaling them over. "That doesn't look like Michelle," Nick said.

"How can you tell under the baseball cap?"

They joined Michelle, Nick examining her closely. The Park Avenue façade had vanished. Dressed in a baggy New York Giants T-shirt and jeans, her hair was tucked under a Yankees cap. Lyle reintroduced himself, and a waitress took their drink orders. Nick asked about the disguise. "Are you afraid your husband will see us talking? Is he following you?"

"Not Jack. His PI. Let me explain, Mr. McDeare."

"Call me Nick."

Michelle smiled. "Okay, Nick. This is the real me. This whole charade started as a lark. My friend Sally got in with a ritzy Southampton crowd, and we thought it would be fun to pull one over on them." She twirled her hand in the air. "Jack bought the whole package. His bitch of a mother didn't, and she's been a pain in my ass. She convinced Jack to hire a PI to look into my past. When you showed up at my apartment asking about our friend Andrew, the PI put it together. Andrew Brady's murder, the Milano, and moi. Now Jack knows I was a ship lounge singer, slash cruise director who lived my life like a refugee from the Sixties."

"I'm sorry. I didn't mean to--"

"Forget it. I'm actually relieved. It was exhausting, keeping up the pretense. I was in way over my head. Besides," she chuckled, patting her tummy, "I've got what I always wanted. A baby. When the PI told Jack about me yesterday morning, he threw me out. But the bad part is he wants custody of the kid. I told him to go fuck himself. Now he's got that damned PI following me again. I finally lost him, but it won't be long before he finds me."

Michelle sat forward, her face anxious. "If Jack's mother gets her hands on this baby, its life will be over before it begins. That's when I thought of you, Nick. I can help you nail your brother's killer. If you help me disappear."

"It depends on what you have to tell us," Lyle said evenly. "If you know who killed Andrew, I'll protect you every way I can."

"Oh, I know all right. What if I told you I overheard a confrontation between Gianni and Andrew on the back deck late one night during that cruise? I heard Gianni threaten Andrew's life. The man terrified me. When Andrew turned up dead, I never said a word. I didn't want the Italian stallion coming after me next."

Nick kept his surging emotions under lock and key. "How good is your memory of that conversation?" He glanced at Barton, his weathered face impassive, but his eyes intent on Michelle.

"It's permanently etched in my brain." Nick's pulse began to race as he listened to Michelle confirm every word Andrew had written in his final diary. "Finally," Michelle said, winding down, "Gianni bragged about what a powerful man he was, more powerful than anyone knew. He told Andrew to say good-bye to Jessie and Anthony because he'd never see them again after the cruise."

"That doesn't necessarily mean he killed him," Lyle interrupted, "just that Gianni intended to take Jessie and Anthony away from him."

"Well, how about this? As Gianni was making his dramatic exit, the last thing he said was, 'Isn't this ocean air invigorating? Breathe deeply. Air is what keeps us alive. Enjoy it while you have it.' Andrew looked like he was about to collapse. He asked Gianni if that was a threat. Gianni said, 'I always knew you were a smart man. The clock is ticking.' I was scared out of my mind."

Barton met Nick's eyes. "You were right." The cop turned his attention back to Michelle, thanking her for coming forward. After Lyle made some phone calls, they left the bar, driving in circles until Barton was satisfied no one was following them. Then he sped through the Holland Tunnel into New Jersey. Nick figured Lyle was taking Michelle to a safe-house, but he asked no questions. The less he knew, the better.

Lyle pulled up in front of a brick townhouse complex in Trenton. Before Michelle got out, she leaned forward and said, "Thanks for everything, Nick. I hope you get your justice. And for the record, you're nothing like your brother."

"That's what everyone keeps telling me."

*

Next up was Salerno. As Barton coasted along the Long Island cemetery's winding drive, Nick scanned the landscape. Even though the local cops had checked the place out, his nerves were thrumming. Nick spotted Joseph Salerno waiting at the top of a slight incline. So that's where Andrew was buried. Nick hadn't thought about Andrew's grave before now. His brother had become a living, breathing entity, a man who lurked around every corner in his dreams.

Nick and Lyle climbed out of the car. Salerno seemed older and faded, like a photograph that loses color with age. His pants looked too big for his legs. Nick tried not to stare at the Kendle burial plot. Now wasn't the time to visit the past. "Hello again, Mr. Salerno."

Joseph motioned to a stone bench. "Do you mind if I sit?"

Nick followed Salerno, the old man dropping heavily onto the bench. Barton pulled out a mini-tape recorder. Joseph glanced at it and nodded. Nick remained standing, his hands in his pockets. "Why did you want to see us, Mr. Salerno?"

"You already know my wife Angela died recently. Last week my only child dropped dead of an aneurism. I was in California for her funeral. I have no family left. No grandchildren. Angela and Marlena were the ones they threatened to kill, the ones I was protecting."

"Who are 'they'?" Nick asked, already knowing the answer.

"Roberto Martinelli's men. Let me start at the beginning." Joseph lit a cigarette, his gnarled hands shaking. "I saw Eduardo Santangelo shoot Andrew Brady. I actually saw it." He shook his head. "I never liked Santangelo. Whenever he was in the terminal, I kept an eye on him. That morning, he was one of the first of the crew to disembark. The terminal was still quiet."

"How soon did Brady come through?" Barton asked.

"A couple minutes later. Santangelo was hanging by the big windows, doing nothing. I thought it was weird, so I was watching him, you know? As soon as all the passengers started disembarking in a crowd, I see him sidle over to Brady, that leather jacket over his arm, and … he blows the man's brains out. I was in shock. I got to admit his timing was perfect."

"Why is that?" Nick asked.

"See, at the beginning of disembarkation, the terminal's chaos. Stevedores pushing those big dollies loaded with luggage out to the curb. People watching for their friends and family to come through from the inner terminal. Nobody pays attention to nobody."

"There's something I don't understand," Nick said. "Andrew thought a limo would be waiting for him. When he realized there was no car there, why didn't he just get back on the ship with Jessie and Anthony?"

"It ain't that easy," Joseph said. "Security's tight. Once he'd been through customs and immigration, it's near impossible to get back on."

"Even for a celebrity?"

"Even for them. On top of the security, Brady would be swimming upstream, hundreds of people are coming down the gangplank. It made sense for him to just sit there and wait for his family. Like a duck in the water. Santangelo planned it perfect, every detail."

Barton nodded. "So what happened next?"

"Anyway ... after he shoots Brady, I'm standing there scared stiff, not moving. And Santangelo's coming in my direction. All that quadrant stuff, me telling you I was on the other side of the terminal, it was a lie. Santangelo strips off his gloves and he drops them right there, the jacket and gun, too. This Hispanic lady, she starts to pick them up, but he freezes her with an evil eye. The kid sees me staring at him. I look away quick. But out of the corner of my eye, I see him go to a pay phone. When I turn around, those two guys, you know, uh—"

"Secchi and Zappella," Nick supplied.

"Yeah. Them two. They're right there, glaring at me. I get spooked and go to the inner terminal. Later that night, I got a phone call at home warning me Angela and Marlena would die if I talked about what I saw. I knew they meant it. They knew my wife and daughter's names. They done their homework."

Nick looked at Lyle. "So Secchi and Zappella were there to make sure Santangelo got the job done. I bet--"

"There's more you don't know," Joseph said. "I'm sick and I'm old. You got to know everything while I'm still alive." Joseph took a deep breath. "A few weeks before the murder, Fosselli, he suddenly showed up at the piers, after being away for years. My office was a little hole in the wall, on the terminal's lower level. Most people don't know it's there. The ships' crew disembarks down there. Otherwise, it's just for parking. Anyway, I saw Fosselli on that lower level on a day the Milano wasn't in port. A car pulls up, he gets in, and it takes off. A couple of hours later, back it comes and drops Fosselli off. Fosselli takes off on foot down the ramp to the Henry Hudson Parkway and Twelfth Avenue."

"Did you recognize the car?" Barton asked.

"I never seen it before. But the next week it's back, only it's Santangelo gets in this time. The car's gone maybe forty-five minutes before it drops the kid off again."

"Did you see who was inside?" Nick asked.

"Not until a few days later when the car turns up on a day the piers are deserted again. It just sits there, idling. Maybe they got there early. I don't know, but two guys get out and stretch their legs, the same two guys in the terminal that morning of the murder. A few minutes later, Fosselli appears. They shake hands, get into the car, and they're gone for maybe a half hour."

"Let me ask you something," Barton said, "why did you notice this car and its comings and goings in the first place?"

Salerno took a quick drag on his cigarette. "It aroused my suspicions 'cause when no ships are in port the piers are dead, Lieutenant. No one ever goes near the area. So I wondered about the secrecy. If you don't want nobody to see you, that's the place to meet."

Barton nodded, thanking Salerno for his help. He gripped the old man's shoulder. "I'm putting you in protective custody for your own safety through the trial, maybe longer. Now I'd like you to wait in my car while I discuss something with Mr. McDeare, okay? I'll send a cop over to pick up your car later."

Salerno rose, handing Lyle his car keys. He looked at Nick. "I always liked Andrew. He was a real nice kid when Mr. Kendle brought him around the ships."

"Thank you, Mr. Salerno." Nick shook his hand.

When their witness was in the car, Lyle started to pace. "Okay, let's put this together while it's fresh. I think the first meeting between Fosselli, Zappella, and Secchi was to arrange the hit. Then they met with Santangelo to give him his instructions. Either Fosselli suggested Eduardo, or the Martinelli family decided on their own to use him."

"I think they decided independently. Very clever. They used Fosselli's nephew to insulate themselves. If the cops nail Santangelo, it looks like a nephew righting a wrong for his uncle. That's what I thought, too. And Eduardo won't enlighten them, not if he's smart."

"Sonuvabitch. You're right. And then they met with Fosselli again to seal the deal."

"Okay, let's back up a minute. Why did Zappella and Secchi meet Fosselli at the piers? Why not the Martinelli mansion? It's more private."

"This kind of arrangement never takes place indoors. Too risky. Servants can be bribed. The cops are always around. The Feds can be watching, taking photos. But it's almost impossible to get a photo of occupants in the back of a moving vehicle. Which is why most hits are arranged in a moving car. What Salerno gave us is gold. It all fits ... We still have one problem though. How does Wexley come into this? The fucker confessed."

Nick's mind went into overdrive. Wexley, Wexley ... Wexley hated Andrew. Ian blamed him for his sorry life. He bitched at the top of his lungs to everyone about Andrew. He-- "Aldo set him up, Lyle. Aldo wanted it to look like Ian called the hit, deflecting any suspicion from Fosselli. Wexley hated Andrew so much, even Wexley believed he was responsible."

Barton's mouth dropped open. "In his confession, Ian said they weren't supposed to kill Andrew, just hurt him. I don't fucking believe this. Aldo made

Ian believe he was doing him a favor by setting up the hit. Only Wexley didn't know it was a hit."

"Or that it was all a cover for Fosselli." Nick shook his head. "Poor Paula stumbled into being an eyewitness because she thought her husband was cheating on her."

Lyle looked at Nick. "It's still an iffy case. Circumstantial, but a good D.A. might be able to make it work. Get an indictment at least. And with your connections, you'll get him convicted in the court of public opinion and poison any jury out there."

"I'd be happier if Fosselli admitted it."

"Forget it. Gianni's smug. He's got the fucking mob covering his back. He thinks he's home free and we can't touch him."

Nick felt a long-distance runner's rush of adrenaline. Barton was right. But Nick was determined to prove Fosselli was wrong. "What about the mob?"

"I'll talk to RICO. But you know racketeering and organized crime cases are never really over. They're always using one fish to hook a bigger fish."

"Are you arresting Fosselli and Santangelo tonight?" Nick asked casually.

"Tomorrow. I need search warrants for Fosselli's apartment and restaurant. I want everything in order before the two of them lawyer up on me. Or the D.A will have my ass."

Nick nodded, his face impassive. That gave him a small pocket of time to get Fosselli to admit he'd arranged Andrew's murder. Nick was determined to find a way to elicit an admission of guilt. A way that wouldn't land Nick in jail, too. Otherwise, he'd beat the hell out of him.

As Lyle headed down the hill to the car, Nick said he'd meet him at the gate. He watched Barton's car pull away before approaching the Kendle family plot. A cool breeze tousled his hair, but the sun was hot on his face. Pacing down the line of gravestones, Nick paused in front of Anthony and Katherine Kendle's marker, Jessie's parents. Tony Kendle. The man who'd become a beloved father to Andrew.

Moving on, Nick faced his brother's monument. Andrew Phillip Brady. Seeing the stone, the reality of his brother's murder hit Nick hard. He placed his hand on the cold marble and closed his eyes. He could see Andrew's face. He could hear his musical laughter, his baritone voice. What a waste.

Opening his eyes, Nick inched towards the last headstone. Crouching down, he ran his fingers over the marble etching. Chelsea Brady, beloved mother of Andrew. This was the woman who had given birth to Nick, given him away, and, Nick admitted, regretted it every day of her life. "Beloved mother of Andrew and Patrick," Nick whispered. "Your missing son is finally home."

CHAPTER 27

Jessie had spent most of the day with Anthony, watching television in his bedroom. Now her son was fast asleep, Hamlet melted against his spine. Jessie pressed her lips to Anthony's forehead. The excitement of coming home from the hospital coupled with the pain medication had worn the boy out. As Jessie left the room, she eyed Gianni's gift on the floor. Anthony had barely acknowledged the carved ship, discarding it after a quick glance.

Heading across the hall to her sitting room, Jessie poured a brandy and scrunched into a corner of the couch. It was past seven. Where was Nick? She hadn't heard from him all day. When he'd told her last night he wouldn't be able to help bring Anthony home, he hadn't volunteered any details. Jessie hadn't asked, assuming he had to be working with Barton.

Jessie swirled the brandy in the snifter, wishing she could take back the biting words she'd hurled at Nick that morning. She knew better than anyone how headstrong Abbie was. With calm had come the realization that the situation had gotten away from Nick. The secrets weren't right, no ... but his reasons were. Nick was Nick. He'd never be an open book. Jessie glanced down at her wedding rings. In her fury, she'd declared the marriage was off. That wasn't true ... was it? Her head began to throb. Could she remove Andrew's rings? She didn't know anymore.

"Jess?"

Startled, Jessie turned to see Nick just inside the door. "Where've you been? I was worried."

"I'll explain in a minute." He sat down beside her. "In fact, there's a lot I have to tell you." He placed a small leather notebook on the coffee table.

"If this is about Abbie, I'm--"

"It's not."

There was something about Nick's eyes that lodged Jessie's heart in her throat. "You're not leaving, are you? Because of this morning?"

"You can't get rid of me that easily." Nick mittened her hand. "But I have a lot to say, and you're not going to like most of it. It's about Gianni."

"I don't want to argue about Gia--"

"There's nothing to argue about. It's over."

"What do you mean?"

"Ian didn't kill Andrew. Gianni and Eduardo did."

This again. "You don't know that--"

"I do, and so does Barton. Wexley played a part in it, but it was Gianni who put the hit on Andrew. I finally have proof."

"N-no."

"Gianni," Nick said evenly, "made a deal with the devil. Roberto Martinelli. When Gianni sold the Martinelli family his cruise line, there was more to the deal than ships. A lot more."

Jessie stopped breathing. "A few months ago," Nick said gently, "I asked a PI friend in Italy to look into Gianni's family. He told me Gianni's grandfather had you investigated after Gianni returned to Italy. The old man discovered you'd married and were pregnant. After seeing pictures, he was convinced Anthony was Gianni's son. He intended to snatch Anthony at some point. Fortunately, Alzheimer's set in, and the file rotted away in a cabinet."

Pulling her hand away, Jessie stumbled to the window. She needed air. Nick shadowed her. "There's something Gianni never told you. When he got your letter about marrying Andrew, he got drunk and drove his Ferrari into a tree. Gianni spent years rehabilitating." Jessie opened the window and breathed deeply, feeling lightheaded. "He didn't tell you because it revealed how devastated he was to lose you to Andrew."

"That's why he has that scar on his hand. His accident in Italy. It was because of me."

Nick cupped her shoulder. "About four to six months before Andrew was murdered, Gianni's grandfather died. Apparently Gianni found your file when he cleaned out the old man's office. He sent some men to New York to take pictures of Anthony. In a matter of weeks, Gianni sold the cruise line and the family villa and relocated to New York. This was in February. Andrew was killed in April."

"None of this proves Gianni killed Andrew."

"I'm getting to that." Nick turned her around to face him. "Now comes the hard part. I have to tell you something about Andrew. It's something I discovered in his diaries, a terrible secret."

This couldn't be happening. Jessie placed her hands on Nick's chest. "No more. I don't want to hear anymore. Let it go, okay?"

"You have to hear this. It has a direct bearing on why Andrew was killed."

That weighted look in Nick's eyes, the burden of whatever he was carrying about Andrew ... It terrified her.

"Jessie," Nick said softly, "Ian didn't take those pictures of you and Gianni and send them to Italy. Andrew did."

"NO! Andrew would never do that. Never!"

Nick wrapped his arms around her, whispering in her ear, "It's true. It ate him alive. He didn't do it so he could have you for himself. He did it because he thought Gianni would hurt you." Nick cradled her face with his hands. "And he was right. Gianni's family never would've accepted you."

Numb, she searched Nick's eyes. This couldn't be true. But she could tell from Nick's face ... it was. All of it. All these years she'd believed a lie, an enormous lie. Her reality was a fake. Nick brushed a tendril of hair from her face. "When Andrew found out you were pregnant, he was devastated by the chaos he'd caused. But it was too late to fix things. The only thing he could do was marry you and raise the baby as his own. Andrew honestly thought he was doing the right thing."

Nick led Jessie back to the couch, sitting them both down. "He tried to tell you, so many times. But here's what's more important. It didn't take Gianni long to figure out Andrew took those pictures, not Wexley. I know this was a long time ago, but do you remember when Andrew's apartment was burglarized, the one he had before you got married and moved back here?"

In a daze, Jessie thought back. Andrew's old apartment ... "The burglary happened a couple of days before he asked me to marry him. Andrew said the burglars must have been scared off, because they didn't take anything."

"That wasn't true. They stole one thing. The negatives of the photos Andrew took of you and Gianni. The pictures were taken by a film camera, not a digital. The--"

"My father's old camera, he gave it to Andrew," Jessie said dully. "He treasured it."

"The package also contained the addresses of Gianni's grandfather and Bianca," Nick said gently. "Andrew figured Gianni was behind the burglary. Who else would want those negatives? Gianni needed them to prove Andrew took those pictures."

"If Gianni knew what Andrew did all those years ago why didn't he do anything about it? Why did he let it go?"

"I don't know. Maybe he thought it was over for good between you. He had his grandfather and Bianca to contend with. Then his accident and years of rehabilitation. That can take a lot out of a man. Sure, he hated Andrew, but not enough to do anything about it. Not until he found out about Anthony."

"God."

"Andrew was upset throughout that last cruise because Gianni was blackmailing him with the negatives. Gianni had a reason for coming between you and Andrew now: his son. He said if Andrew didn't tell you the truth before the end of the cruise, Gianni would tell you himself. But Andrew couldn't bear to spring it on you like that; he wanted to tell you in his own time, in the brownstone. With the two of you sticking to your cabin, he figured Gianni wouldn't be able to get to you."

"That's why he never wanted to leave the cabin. It had nothing to do with the fans."

"It was all about Gianni's blackmail. Andrew thought he was safe that last morning. You were all getting off early. He got the fake message Bill was picking him up, but he thought you'd all disembark earlier yet. He'd leave with Bill and you and Anthony would go home with Willie. But then you and Anthony decided to stay longer."

"Poor Andrew." Jessie buried her face against Nick's shirt.

"Once Gianni had you and Andrew separated and Andrew on a wild-goose chase, it was over. Andrew was a marked man. Nick stroked her hair. "You said Gianni was with you when you heard the lady scream in the terminal. How long was he with you?"

"Only a minute."

"He probably planned to tell you then, but Andrew's shooting happened too quickly. I think Gianni wanted to tell you the truth right before Andrew was killed. That way you'd hate Andrew and turn to Gianni. He didn't want you to mourn Andrew or revere his memory. That part," Nick laughed bitterly, "didn't go according to plan."

"Why didn't Gianni tell me about Andrew and the photos sometime over the past two years?"

"Because it would've thrown suspicion on him."

Jessie looked up at him. "How-how do you know all of this? The journals?"

"The journals, mixed with my ghost and the PI in Italy. And witnesses have come forward. That's where I was today. Barton and I met with witnesses who helped us put it all together, in detail." Nick reached for the notebook on the coffee table. "This is Andrew's journal from the last cruise. I found it concealed in the dance bag, hidden in the lining."

"The dance bag?"

"Makes sense, doesn't it? Andrew chronicled word for word a confrontation he had with Gianni on the back deck. Gianni accused Andrew of taking those pictures. He showed him those negatives he stole years ago and threatened his life. Andrew was frightened, but he never dreamed Gianni would move so fast—that his," Nick's voice caught, "… assassination was already planned to the minute. He took him seriously, but not seriously enough. Your old enemy Michelle overheard the argument. She confirmed Andrew's journal entry almost to the word. The threats, the blackmail, the negatives, everything."

Nick placed the notebook in Jessie's hands. "I want you to read this, honey. I know it won't be easy, but it explains a lot." He kissed her on the forehead, his eyes soft. "Read it now, okay? Find me afterwards and we'll talk." Rising, Nick left her alone.

Jessie looked down at the small notebook. Andrew, his secrets … And Gianni … A murderer … Jessie opened the book, her breath catching at the sight of her husband's flowing handwriting. She forced herself to read. A half hour later, she came across a section that produced fresh tears.

I'm afraid for my life. The Gianni who faced me tonight was a man I'd never seen before. A man with eyes as evil as Iago's. I don't think he'd have a problem snuffing out my life to get to Jessie and Bongo. Gianni will do anything to wrench my family from me. Anything.

When I tell Jessie I sent those photographs to Italy, she'll never understand I did it out of love. Jessie was always attracted to the men who hurt her most. When they shattered her, she always turned to me to put her back together. Boys in high school, then college, then Wexley. I saw it happening yet again with Gianni, and I dreaded seeing her fall under his spell. I dreaded being her second choice yet again. But I never intended to hurt her.

It isn't possible for a man to love a woman more than I love Jessie. And Bongo is my son, my greatest joy. If this is the end of my marriage, I don't care if I live or die. Life isn't worth living without my wife and my son. I'd rather be dead.

*

The hurricane lamps cast the back porch in shadow. Nick was on his cell, filling Lyle in on Abbie's undercover work with Fosselli. He held the phone away from his ear as Lyle blasted him. "I should haul your sorry asses in for obstructing justice and interfering with a police investigation. I should ..."

Nick rolled his eyes as Barton reamed him out. Lyle had never dealt with Abigail Forrester. The woman was a force of nature. It was better Lyle didn't know about their plan for Abbie to seduce a taped admission of guilt out of Gianni tonight, while he was in the throes of amour. They had to try. Once Gianni was arrested, the mob would have his back. The Mafia was skilled in the art of buying judges and intimidating jurors. A secretly taped admission of guilt may or may not make it into the courtroom, but it would give the D.A. leverage. And it would make him work harder for a conviction if he knew he had the right man.

Nick darted in a question while Barton took a breath. "When you turn this over to RICO, Jessie and Anthony are safe, right?"

"Safe from the mob, if not your own idiocy. You're all out of it then. It's RICO's baby."

*

After taking two aspirin, Jessie cried herself to sleep on the sitting-room couch, Andrew's journal clutched in her hands. A dream slowly crept into her slumber. She and Nick were on the beach at the villa, a half moon suspended in the sky. Jessie threw herself into Nick's arms and kissed him with abandon, as if she hadn't seen him in years ...

"Jess?"

"Hmm?" It felt so good to snuggle into Nick's arms. But why did he sound so far away? "Nick?"

"Open your eyes, Kendle, it's me."

Jessie cracked her eyes open. Andrew stood by the grate in the sitting room. Her breath caught. "Andrew?"

"It's me."

Jessie struggled to sit up, the journal dropping to the floor. Andrew glided towards the coffee table and sat on its edge, facing her. He looked exactly the same, breathtakingly handsome, sandy hair spiking his forehead, his amber eyes glistening. Andrew clasped Jessie's hands in his, and the clock spun backwards. There had been no shooting. No funeral. No two years of grief and loneliness. They were together again, the pain erased. If Jessie was dreaming, she didn't want to wake up.

She looked down at their intertwined fingers. "Your wedding band ...?"

"You took it off me in the hospital, remember?"

Tears filled her eyes. She wasn't talking to Andrew. She was talking to Andrew's ghost, a poor specter who lived in dreams.

"Don't cry, Jess. It's almost over."

"What is?"

"This miraculous little window that lets me communicate with all of you. We can't waste it on tears. You're even more beautiful, if that's possible. You've grown up. You're different." His eyes drifted to the floor, and he reached for the journal, flipping through the pages before setting it down. "So you finally read it. Now you know the truth … I'm so sorry about sending the pictures. If I'd only known you were pregnant … If I had it to do over again--"

"You'd do exactly the same thing," Jessie finished. She was talking to a ghost and it felt so … normal, as if Andrew had just returned from a walk. "I thought about it tonight," Jessie said, "over and over. You did it because you were sure Gianni would hurt me. And you were right. You were always right about the other men in my life. You were my protector, strong where I was weak. I think it's what our relationship was all about."

"Nick said you'd understand. But I was so sure you'd walk out on me if you learned the truth. I thought you'd never forgive me. Nick knows you better than I did."

"I never would've left you. You and Anthony were my life." She took his hand, stroking his fingers. "Why didn't you tell me you found your brother?"

"I found out only a few days before the cruise. I wanted to spring Nick on you, Kendle. You and Tony had been so sure I'd made him up. You have to admit it was rich. My favorite author Nick McDeare turns out to be my long lost brother. What a delicious joke!" Andrew dropped his head, his face sobering. "If I'd told you about Nick, he could've been with you at the hospital. The two of you could've shared your grief. Nick belonged with you."

"You really love your brother, don't you?"

Andrew's face softened. "Yeah. Nick's a sonuvabitch, but I can count on him. I brought him here to get to the truth. But," Andrew's melancholy eyes met Jessie's, "I also brought him here for you and Bongo. The three of you need each other. It's what I want, Jessie. Remember that. Nick will keep you safe."

"Safe? What do you mean? Gianni's about to be arrested."

A veil dropped over Andrew's eyes. "If Gianni goes free, none of you will be safe. He'll try to take Bongo away from you. You and Nick have to protect Anthony."

Fear streaked through Jessie. "Goes free? Andrew, you're scaring me."

"You hold the key. Only you can stop him. I want you to think long and hard about it. That's all l can say. Don't ask me any more questions."

"I'm sorry I ever got involved with Gianni. If I hadn't --"

"If you hadn't, Anthony wouldn't exist. Your son wouldn't be sleeping across the hall right now. Think of what your life would be like without Anthony."

Jessie shut out the image. She wouldn't want to live if something happened to Anthony. "There's something I don't understand. Why did you visit Anthony and Nick all this time and not me? Never me?"

"You were holding onto the past. Seeing me too soon would've kept you there. I had to wait until I was sure you wanted to make a new life for yourself. With Nick." Jessie had never seen her husband look so desolate. "Take care of Nick. You're good for each other." Andrew released Jessie's hands. "Time for me to go."

"Not yet," she begged. "Please, please don't go."

"I have no choice. You and I will see each other again one day. I promise you." Andrew stroked Jessie's cheek with his thumb. "Close your eyes. Go on. Close them and go back to sleep for a little while. Regain your strength. And when you wake up, protect your son with everything you have. Don't let Anthony down."

Jessie couldn't resist. So sleepy. She closed her eyes and felt Andrew's lips brush hers, sweet and gentle … When Jessie woke up, Andrew was gone.

*

Nick slumped on the wicker couch, his arms folded across his chest. Still no sign of Jessie. He had to let her deal with the shock her own way; he couldn't rush it. There was a lot for Jessie to process. He checked his watch again. Just as he was ready to leap up and storm Jessie's room, she floated onto the porch in a cloud of black silk. "I saw him," Jessie said softly. "Andrew. I fell asleep on the couch, and there he was."

Nick bolted upright. "You dreamed about Andrew?"

"He was real. As real as he is in your dreams. He called me Kendle, just like he used to. He kissed me. He was so sad. He seemed … resigned about what happened to him. About you and me."

Andrew kissed her? "You talked about us?"

"He loves you."

Nick eyed the floor. He'd never defined his feelings for Andrew. They were simply a part of him. "Are you okay?"

"I think I feel better now." Jessie tilted up her chin. "I told him I understood about the pictures, just like you promised I would. We talked about Gianni, too." Jessie bit her lip. "Andrew's afraid Gianni may get away with it. Is that true?"

Jessie did seem better, focused and rested. Nick explained the case was circumstantial and Gianni had the mob behind him. "The one thing that may help a conviction's an admission of guilt. Abbie tried to get the truth out of him tonight."

"Without Lyle knowing? That's crazy."

"It was a disaster. Gianni almost stumbled on the tape recorder, literally. Thank God he was called away by a crisis at the restaurant. Abbie was a basket case when she called me."

"It was too dangerous." Jessie suddenly grabbed Nick's hand and squeezed, her eyes widening. "Wait a minute. Maybe I could do it."

"Do what?"

"Get Gianni to admit the truth."

"Forget about it. You're not going to risk--"

"Listen to me. Andrew said something strange when we were talking about Gianni. He said I held the key. That only I could stop him. That I should think about it long and hard. I think he meant I was the one who could get the truth out of Gianni. I can do it!" Her eyes shot sapphire sparks. "Think about it. I know how to push Gianni's buttons, how to make him really angry. That's when he slips up, when he's mad. He once told me he hated getting angry because he always regretted what he said afterward. Self-control's everything to Gianni. You know I'm right."

Jessie had a point. If she could use Anthony to get past Gianni's iron self control...

"Let me do this. We have to keep Anthony safe."

Nick hated the idea. "If we do this, and I said if, we call in the cops for help. And even if you're successful, a taped admission of guilt may not be admissible in court."

"But it would color the whole case, you know it would. I have to do this. I have to hear Gianni admit he had Andrew killed. Then I can let it go. Then Andrew can rest, knowing we did everything we could to make Anthony safe."

Nick caught her urgency, even as he felt the room chill. For Anthony. Let her do this for Anthony. Were those his words ... or Andrew's? "All right," Nick said slowly, suppressing a shiver, "here's how it works. We go over what you're going say together. We rehearse it. Like opening night. Agreed?"

"Agreed." Jessie's eyes glittered.

Nick glanced at his watch. "I'll call Barton. It's late but this can't wait for morning. You're going to be wired by a professional. Bad enough Abbie put herself in danger tonight, but at least Gianni doesn't suspect her. You're another story."

*

Nick lay on his back, Jessie's breath light against his shoulder. They'd stolen time for lovemaking, counting on Anthony's medication to let him sleep through the night. At least the boy's nightmares were a thing of the past. Anthony had met his demons at Park and Seventy-Fifth Street.

Before leaving the porch, Nick had called Barton. After more curses, Lyle had finally agreed to Nick's plan, putting his own security requirements into play. In the end, success was too close for Lyle to pass up. The danger was minimal—everyone was out of the loop except for Nick, Jessie, Barton, and Abbie. There would be no leaks on this operation, no exterminators with cameras. After briefing Jessie, Nick had left Abbie a detailed voice mail about her role in the new operation.

It was way past midnight, but Nick was wired. He glanced at Jessie, her face pressed against his shoulder. "What are you thinking?"

"Mmm ... I was thinking how clear everything is for me for the first time in years. Andrew's visit lifted the fog. It was Andrew who made me see it." That dreamy look was for Andrew? Had Jessie pretended Andrew was making love to her tonight? Nick felt as if a gorilla had punched him in the gut.

"I loved Andrew," Jessie was saying in a far-off voice. "He was a good husband and father." Jessie pulled herself up, propping the pillows behind her. "There's something I have to say to you."

Fuck that. He'd rather not know he came in second to a ghost. "Jessie, I don't want to—"

"I've been thinking about your marriage proposal. I've thought about it all day. Seeing Andrew tonight brought back so many memories. He said he hadn't visited me earlier because the sight of him would've kept me locked in the past." Jessie spun her rings around her finger. "He was right."

"Look, just say it. You can't marry me because of Andrew. He reignited all the old feelings. You can't take the rings off. The past wins again."

"Wrong," Jessie said softly. "It's true I'd been wedded to the past because I couldn't stand the thought of a future without Andrew. But then you showed up. You challenged me and you outraged me, but you made me feel alive again. And in the process I," she waved a hand, "I guess I changed. Andrew saw it, too. He said I've grown up. He could tell I was different. Do you understand what I'm saying?" Looking down at her hand, Jessie spun the rings around slowly. Then she gently nudged them from her finger.

Nick sucked in his breath.

Jessie eyed Andrew's rings in her palm before carefully setting them on the nightstand. "I'll put them with Andrew's wedding band and save them for Anthony." She studied him. "Um, I think it's your move."

"Life with you is one manic roller coaster." Grinning, Nick reached into the nightstand drawer and snatched the diamond ring from its box, holding it up. "You're sure?"

"Yes, I'll marry you. As soon as possible!"

"You better believe it." Nick clasped her left hand and brought her fingers to his lips, kissing her knuckles. He slipped the ring on her finger. "We're official now. Too late to change your mind or you get locked in a dungeon." He nuzzled Jessie's ear, seeding little kisses from her jaw to her lips. "Remember the night of my birthday at the villa?"

"How could I forget?"

"Remember when I said you and Anthony gave me a second chance and I'd explain one day?" Nick held her eyes. "Jess, you both gave me a second chance to get it right this time. To be a good husband and father."

"Anthony and I love you, Nick."

"You'd better," Nick said lightly, not trusting his voice, "with what that ring cost me."

"Hey," Jessie said, looping her arms around his neck, "You promised to tell me--"

"Eight carats. A total of eight carats."

"Oh my God!" Jessie squealed, practically choking Nick. "You really do love me!"

*

It was Bush's day off, but Lyle had gotten to his desk just after sunrise. No day off for him. The devil was in the details and he had a ton of them. The first detail was taken care of. A judge had promised to have search warrants for Fosselli's apartment and restaurant on the lieutenant's desk by early afternoon.

Next, Barton clipped downstairs to the desk officer's station, commandeering a car from Harry Steinmetz. He wanted a tail on Santangelo immediately. The officers were to report in to Barton's cell at regular intervals.

"I'll be out from noon on, Harry. If you need me, call my cell." Jessie's confrontation with Fosselli was off the record. He was borrowing units from Kersey in the Nineteenth. Oceano was in his jurisdiction. It was a fail-safe operation, leak-proof. Jessie had been through too much to allow anything to go wrong. Not on his watch.

"Also, Harry," Barton lowered his voice, "I need a favor, for your eyes and one other only. I want a computer search of the phone logs for Midtown North the five months before Andrew Brady was shot. Put someone on this who can be discreet. Someone you trust with your life. Make sure you include the station's two pay phones. Barton handed Steinmetz a list of phone numbers for Martinelli and Zappella, their major soldiers, Fosselli, and the Milano. "Let me know if any calls were placed to these numbers."

Some crud in the department had fed Martinelli confidential police info on the Perv to obstruct the Brady investigation. Lyle might not be able to plug that leak, but he'd damn well try.

*

"Anthony?" Anthony rolled over and opened his eyes. Early morning sun was streaming through the shades. Spotting his uncle standing beside the bed, Anthony sat up, sleepy from his medicine. "Where were you yesterday, Uncle Nick? I didn't see you all day."

"I'm sorry about that. I was working. But we've got some news that might make up for it." His mom and Uncle Nick exchanged a secretive glance. "Well," Nick began, "normally I'd go to your grandpa with this. But seeing how you're the man of the house, I'll ask you. Your mom and I want to get married. Any objections?"

"Really?!" he shrieked. "You'll be my dad for real? Yay!"

His mom laughed and held up her ring. "I take it you approve?"

*

Abbie listened to Nick's detailed voice mail early that morning while Gianni showered. By the time he joined her in the kitchen for coffee, Abbie had her game plan down. "Honey, I want you to set a table in your office at Oceano and plan a special lunch for us," she cooed. "I'll be there around noon."

Gianni took a sip of coffee. "What's the occasion?"

"I think we deserve an engagement party. You're an established restaurateur in the city. Everyone in New York looks up to you. I want to sit down over an elegant lunch and plan the party."

"An engagement party is an excellent idea." Gianni set his mug on the counter and pulled Abbie into his arms. "We can have it at Oceano. I'll even shut down the restaurant for the occasion."

*

"Nick and I don't want a big fuss, Jeremy. We just want to get married quietly. No one but the people in this room plus Nick's agent and Abbie know we're engaged, and I want to keep it that way. No big announcement in the papers. No splashy pictures, okay?"

Jessie slumped in the corner of the breakfast nook, tired of arguing with Jeremy and Mary. She was exhausted from getting too little sleep. And ever since she'd told Nick she'd marry him, she couldn't get that new title song from TO HAVE AND TO HOLD out of her head. Round and round it went like a hamster on a wheel, the same melody, the same lyrics, about love and marriage. It was impossible to concentrate.

Nick was beside her, embroiled in his own heated argument with his agent on his cell. Mary sat across from them, reading glasses on her nose, a pencil and steno pad in hand. After bursting into tears of joy at the news, Mary had joined Jeremy in urging a large wedding.

"Dammit, Liz," Nick exploded, "you're not listening to me. We don't--" Nick looked at Jessie and rolled his eyes at whatever Liz was trying to sell.

"Jessie," Jeremy implored, "I know what I'm talking about. This will be the next big thing. Everyone will clamor to get an invitation."

"I keep telling you, Nick and I have--"

"Goodbye, Liz!" Nick tossed his cell on the table. "She's nuts. First she said I was throwing away my career by getting married, that my so-called allure is being a bachelor. Nice to know she thinks so much of my talent. When she finally realized this marriage will happen, she started talking about an extravaganza with lots of press. She called it cashing in on the publicity cow."

"She's right," Jeremy enthused. "Everyone will want a front row seat to see the woman who finally snared the infamous Nick McDeare."

Jessie dropped her head in her hands as her silent orchestra launched into its opening bars all over again. Shaking her head, she laughed softly.

Nick looped an arm around her. "What's so funny?"

Jessie groaned. "I can't get a new song Kenny wrote out of my head. Maybe I'll sing it to you at our gala of a wedding everyone seems to think we should have. It's all about marriage."

"Sing it," Jeremy urged. "I've got a great idea."

"Not now. I've heard enough of your ideas."

Mary smiled. "I haven't heard you sing in a long time, honey. I miss it."

"I've never heard you sing," Nick murmured, "not up close and personal."

Jessie relented. "I'll sing the beginning." She took a deep breath and launched into the opening stanza, getting into the captivating melody despite herself. Kenny had written a showstopper for the revival, the kind of song people left the theater humming.

"It's beautiful," Nick said. "Haunting. Unforgettable."

"Listen," Jeremy said. "You sing that at the wedding and we market the CD's! I'll call Kenny and--"

"Jeremy, no." Jessie sighed. "Could we talk about this later please? I have a lot on my mind this morning." An understatement. Only the most important performance of her life. And it wasn't a Broadway showstopper.

"We can talk about it anytime. And then we'll do it my way." Jeremy winked. "Great song. By the way, Nick, I want your agent's phone number by the end of the day."

"I don't think so."

Jessie heard Jeremy humming the song as he headed down the hallway for the elevator.

Nick lifted his jangling cell. "This is probably Liz telling me she booked Yankee Stadium for the ceremony ... McDeare." Jessie watched as Nick's scowl melted into a smile. He covered the mouthpiece and whispered, "It's Abbie. Everything's set for today."

"What's going on?" Mary asked, eyeing both of them suspiciously.

"By the way, give up on the safe, Abbie," Nick advised. "Barton's getting search warrants." Seeing Jessie's eye on him, he told her Abbie was still playing with the combination, no luck.

"Search warrants?" Mary asked.

"I'll tell you later," Jessie said. "I promise." She turned to Nick and asked to talk to Abbie. Nick shrugged and handed Jessie the phone.

"Abbie, maybe I know a combination you've overlooked." Jessie sucked in a breath, feeling goose bumps. "Try four-two-three-one-one."

"What does it mean?"

"Just try it, okay?"

Jessie could hear lock tumblers falling into place in the background. "Oh my God," Abbie screamed. "It opened! Jessie, you're a genius. Look at all this stuff. Give me Nick." Jessie handed the phone back to Nick. She felt as numb as Novocain.

Nick broke into a wide grin. "What about the negatives? ... Great. Don't touch anything. No fingerprints. Leave it for the police ..." Nick nodded, glancing at Jessie. "I'll ask her. Good luck with Gianni." He clicked off and turned to Jessie. "What's the significance of those numbers?"

"Four-two-three-one-one. April 23, 2011," she said tonelessly. "The day Andrew died."

CHAPTER 28

It was almost noon when Cobra stumbled home after a wild night of hot sex with a chick he picked up at a club in Soho. Melissa? Alyssa? Whatever. He was ready to hit the sack. Cobra's cell rang as he yanked his undershirt over his head.

Aldo wanted a report on the brownstone tapes. Aldo was a fucking fussy old lady. "McDeare's banging the Brady woman. Wexley's in jail. It's over."

"You're not the one calling the shots, asshole. Mr. Martinelli wants a detailed report, daily. McDeare's a loose cannon. You got that?"

"Got it." Cobra snapped his cell shut. He hadn't listened to the recordings since Wexley had been arrested. So much for sleep. Cobra jerked his bed away from the wall. Lifting the floorboards, he opened a small metal suitcase and pulled out a set of headphones, stretched across the bed, and began to listen ...

                        *

The wireless receiver taped in Jessie's bra was no larger than a dime, but it was starting to itch. She tried not to fidget as she sat in the back of Barton's car on East Seventy-Ninth Street, two blocks from Oceano. The small monitor on the dashboard would broadcast her conversation with Gianni to Nick and Lyle.

Glancing across the avenue, Jessie spotted two detectives idling in their unmarked car, search warrant in hand for Oceano. Another car waited outside Gianni's apartment building with another search warrant. His arrest was imminent, whether she was successful in prying the truth out of Gianni or not.

Nick sat in front of her. "It's two o'clock," he said. He glanced at Lyle behind the wheel before turning around and rubbing Jessie's knees. "You're on, kid."

"Remember," Lyle said, "if anything goes wrong, or you're afraid for your safety, say 'I don't feel well.' We'll be there in seconds."

"I don't feel well." Jessie mouthed the words, her voice booming from the receiver. Stepping out of the car, she took a deep breath and adjusted her black V-neck tunic over her jeans. The open neckline would prevent static interference.

Jessie glanced back at Nick, taking encouragement from his nod, as she began the short walk to the restaurant. Her step picked up confidence as Oceano materialized around the corner. She was Jessica Kendle, famed Broadway actress. And she was about to give the performance of a lifetime. This was for Andrew and Anthony. Wherever Andrew was lurking, he'd have the satisfaction of hearing his killer admit his guilt and know he'd moved heaven and earth to keep his son safe.

*

"It will be beautiful, Abigail," Gianni murmured, watching her close her notebook. They'd discussed every detail of their engagement party, from the flowers to the wine to the select guest list. Abigail was a class act.

The office door swung open. Gianni looked up, shocked to see Jessica. "What are you doing here?"

Jessica cruised into the office as if she owned it, ignoring him. "Hello, Abbie. Long time no see."

"I've been a little busy," Abigail said, her tone frigid. "Planning my wedding."

"You, too?" Smiling, Jessica held out her left hand, displaying a gauche ring.

Gianni snorted. "My condolences." He looked Jessica up and down. "Why the baggy clothes? Are you pregnant? At least you're marrying the baby's father this time."

Jessica folded her arms. "It must hurt to be rejected twice by the same woman. And for a pair of brothers no less."

Abigail rose. "Stop it!"

"What do you want?" Gianni asked.

"I came to discuss Anthony. In private." Jessica looked pointedly at Abigail.

"Abigail's not going anywhere."

"Then you'll never see your son again." Jessica rotated on her heel and headed for the door.

"It's okay," Abigail said. "The air in here has turned rancid. I have a manicure in an hour anyway." Abigail sauntered from the room.

Gianni lit a cigarette, staring at Jessica over the flame. Snapping his Zippo shut, he said, "We have nothing to discuss. I'll see you in court."

"Look," Jessica said, her voice softening. "For once, think of Anthony. He's been through so much. I don't want him hauled into court while we play tug-of-war."

"Fine. Give me full custody, and we can spare Anthony more agony."

"Not funny."

"I never joke about my son."

"Our son."

"My son!" Gianni shot back. "You've had him all these years. Now it's my turn."

*

"How's she doing?" Abbie asked Nick and Lyle as she climbed into the back of the car. "She made quite an entrance." Abbie's adrenaline was pumping. She and Jessie hadn't faced off as actresses in years.

"She's doing fine," Nick said, his eyes glued to the transistor. He pushed a hand through his hair.

Jessie's voice sang out. "You'll never get full custody. I promise you that. I won't allow it."

"You won't allow it?" Gianni's voice was hushed. "Do you know who I am?"

"A man who didn't have enough backbone to stand up to his grandfather, a sick old man."

"You don't know me at all."

"Oh, I think I do. You had to steal our son to get his attention. And what did Anthony do when he found out you were his father? He ran from you. He didn't want anything to do with you. He still doesn't. He'll sail that ship you sent him in the toilet."

*

"Holy shit!" Cobra threw off his headphones, leapt off the bed and speed-dialed Zappella on his own cell. No time to search for a disposable. How could this crap happen overnight? He blurted out Fosselli was being set up as soon as Zappella answered. "Jessica Brady's at Fosselli's restaurant right now. Barton's got her wired. They said something about two o'clock. They're trying to piss Fosselli off so he blows it. It's a trap."

"Why am I just hearing about this now, you imbecile?"

"Dammit, move. There's no time." Cobra clicked off and dropped onto the bed, his mouth dry. He forgot to tell Aldo about Gianni's girlfriend being a plant. There'd be plenty of time later, if he lived that long. This was a major fuckup. And he couldn't run, because there was no place to hide. Not from Roberto Martinelli.

He flopped onto his back. Out of nowhere an evocative song drifted through his mind. A song about marriage. That fucking song Ms. Broadway Star just sang at the brownstone to her admirers and fiance. Maybe they'd play it at his funeral as he was wedded to the freshly turned earth.

*

"You've poisoned my son against me," Gianni hissed.

"You did that yourself." Jessie felt invigorated. She was Jessica Kendle again, standing center stage, feeling the heat of the spot on her face. She could do this.

"It's time you faced cold reality. You need to see the complete picture." Gianni's entire body seemed to quiver from within, like a crouched cat when it corners a bird. "You see, it was Andrew who sent those pictures of us to Italy," he said softly, his eyes gleaming. "It was Andrew who sabotaged our relationship. I wasn't the villain. Andrew was." Gianni smiled. "I haven't told you to spare hurting you."

Jessie controlled her breathing. It was all she could do not to spring on him and slap him silly. "I know all about Andrew and those pictures."

"What? When did--"

"I've known for years. It wasn't hard to figure out. If Ian had done it, he would've bragged about it. I let it go. I never even told Andrew I knew. You see, I understood why Andrew did it. How could I blame him for protecting me from you?" Gianni's cell jangled. Jessie noticed a purple vein on his forehead begin to throb.

"That's a lie. Fool that I was, I loved you! I never would've hurt you." Gianni fumbled his phone out of his pocket and shut it off without a glance. "If I had known about Anthony, I would have taken the next plane back to New York."

"We both know you would've come back for Anthony, not me."

"You never gave me the chance to come back to you. You kept quiet and went along with Andrew's scheme, you whore."

*

Aldo swore. Gianni wasn't picking up. Beginning to sweat, he enlisted two separate parties to head for the restaurant to warn Fosselli. One would move north, from Chelsea, the other south, from Morningside Heights. Santangelo was closest, but he had the day off and wasn't answering his cell. Flipping rapidly through his rolodex, Aldo found Oceano's number. McDeare would pay for this. They all would. And Cobra's days were numbered. In the single digits. On one hand.

*

Lyle's radio crackled. "Lieutenant, Murphy reporting in. Santangelo picked up a sub at Blimpie's on Broadway, heading towards the park."

Barton had wanted to arrest Santangelo and Fossilli simultaneously, preventing the apprehension of one from tipping off the other. It was crunch time. Eduardo was out in the open, unaware of any trouble on the horizon. The peaceful pocket wouldn't last long. Lyle decided the element of surprise was too great to pass up.

Barton picked up the radio. "Take him. Arrest him for the murder of Andrew Brady. I'll be back at Midtown North soon. He could be armed and dangerous when confronted."

Pulling out his cell, Lyle punched in a number. Voicemail. "Bush, Santangelo and Fosselli are about to be arrested. I know it's your day off, but I thought you might want in on this."

*

"You know what?" Jessie backed up. "Forget I was here. Nick and I will take Anthony away where you can't touch him." She spun on her heel and headed for the door.

"Go ahead. Try to run." Gianni laughed, stopping her in her tracks. "I can get to Anthony anywhere. A-n-y-w-h-e-r-e. That's a harsh truth you'd be wise to remember."

Jessie whirled around. "You want harsh truth? Try this. Anthony will never recognize you as his father. You know why? He wants Nick to be his dad. They 'chose' each other in some sort of secret ceremony." Jessie stepped closer. "That's right. Anthony chose Nick. I'll bet that just kills you, doesn't it? First Andrew raised Anthony. Now Nick will finish the job."

Gianni's office phone shrilled.

*

Eduardo panicked when two police cars screeched to a stop beside him. This wasn't supposed to happen. Aldo had taken care of the cops. He tossed his sandwich and ran, taking a quick look over his shoulder.

"Don't do it, punk," one of the cops shouted after him, leaping out of his car and raising his gun.

No way was he going to rot in a fucking American jail! Eduardo sprinted like a demon down the sidewalk, the police in pursuit. He shoved an elderly woman walking her dachshund out of his path, knocking her to the ground. He immediately cursed his stupidity. Now the sidewalk was deserted. No pedestrians to hide behind.

"Stop, or I'll shoot!"

A bullet went wide. "That was a warning shot!"

Panting, Eduardo skidded to a halt, his hands in the air. "I want to make a call, man," he gasped. "I know my rights." Aldo would get him out of this. Eduardo Santangelo didn't get locked up for anyone.

"Eduardo Santangelo," the cop said, breathing hard, "you're under arrest for the murder of Andrew Brady. You have the right to remain silent. If you ..."

*

Gianni pointed a finger at Jessie as the desk phone rang its head off. "Nicholas McDeare will never raise Anthony. Never."

"Too late," Jessie said sweetly. "Anthony wants Nick to adopt him. In the state's eyes, his father's dead." Jessie was enjoying every minute of her performance. This is for you, Andrew.

"That's ludicrous." Gianni lifted the phone's receiver an inch and slammed it back down. "Anthony's father is alive and standing right here. A DNA test will prove--"

"DNA can be fixed." Jessie chuckled. "You seem surprised I know how to play dirty. You'd be amazed how different labs can come up with different results. Nick knows about these things. He has contacts you wouldn't believe."

The phone shrieked again. Gianni yanked the receiver to his mouth and shouted, "God damn it, no interruptions!" before slamming it down. "If you think I'm going to stand by and watch another man raise my son, I'll--"

"You'll what? You don't have Grandpa to run to anymore."

"Don't be an idiot. I'm a powerful man."

"You forget I'm Jessica Kendle, a famous actress and a very well known widow." Jessie laughed. "The public sympathizes with Anthony and me. Who are you? A local immigrant who owns the current hotspot in town. Big deal. Next year you'll be yesterday's news."

"This is McDeare's influence. He's done this to you."

"Life did this to me. I've learned the hard way how to fight. I'll do whatever it takes to protect my son. I want him raised in Andrew and Nick's image. I won't let you turn him into a miniature version of yourself."

"Nicholas McDeare will not raise my son. Do you hear me?"

Jessie turned away. "It's already done."

Gianni grabbed her arm and swung her around, jerking her within inches of his face. "You listen to me." His voice was barely a whisper. "If you try to keep my son from me, if Nicholas tries to adopt Anthony, you'll regret it. I mean it. You'll regret it for the rest of your life."

"Let go of me."

"Don't push me."

"Go to hell."

Gianni gripped Jessie tighter. "I am not a man to be taken lightly."

"I said let go of me!" Jessie cried, squirming to get away.

Gianni grasped her other arm, stretching Jessie up on her toes. "You have no idea how far I'll go to get Anthony. Don't underestimate me. Don't be as stupid as Andr--"

Fueled by adrenaline, Jessie drove on. "What were you going to say? What, Gianni?" Gianni released Jessie suddenly, making her stumble. "Don't be as stupid as Andrew was? What does that mean?" Horror transformed her face. "My God, what have you done?"

Breathing hard, Gianni remained silent, his eyes lasered to the floor.

"Tell me, what did you do?!"

"I took my revenge, you stupid puttana. I had Andrew killed. Do you understand what I'm saying? It was ME," he hissed. "Gianni Fosselli is responsible for your husband's murder. You'd be wise to remember that, especially when it comes to Anthony."

"You had Andrew killed?" Jessie whispered. "Why? To get back at him for those photos? What kind of coward has a man killed?" Jessie's voice began to steamroll, gaining strength as she released all her hatred and contempt and fury. "You sick bastard! I've been your biggest defender. How could you do it? Why did you do it?" Jessie moved closer, feeling his breath on her face. "Why? Why did you kill my husband? Tell me!"

"Because he took what was mine!" Gianni roared, backing up and punching his chest with each word. "WHAT-WAS-MINE!"

*

"Doesn't look like entrapment to me," Barton said, "but I'm no attorney. Time to get Jessie out of there." Abbie's heart was thumping. She and Nick exchanged glances as Barton called for backup. A cruiser two blocks away responded. Barton radioed the detectives across the street as he snapped the cherry on the hood of the car. Sixty seconds later three police vehicles squealed to a halt in front of Oceano. "Abbie, stay here," Lyle ordered as he leapt out of the car. "You too, Nick."

"The hell with that," Nick said, already swinging out the door after him.

Abbie watched the entourage sweep into the restaurant, Barton showing the startled hostess his badge before they scaled the stairs. She slumped in the back seat, drained. Out of the corner of her eye, she watched an SUV slow to an idle in front of the restaurant. The two men inside stared at the three police vehicles. A dark sedan pulled up on the other side of the vehicle, and the occupants conversed briefly before speeding away. A chill danced down Abbie's spine. Martinelli?

*

Gianni straightened up and smoothed back his hair, determined not to lose control again. "Andrew got exactly what he deserved. Now get out of here.

It sickens me to be in the same room with you. And if you try to use my words against me, I'll see to it that you bury another husband."

Someone chuckled behind him. Gianni spun around. Barton stood in the doorway, flanked by two uniformed officers and McDeare. "Keep talking," Barton said amiably. "The only one getting buried is you. With your own words." Barton and his entourage approached Gianni. Impossible, this was impossible.

Two more cops materialized, snapping on rubber gloves. They began to methodically search the bookcases and drawers. "What are you doing? You have no right--"

"Oh but they do," Barton said, the two uniforms preventing Gianni from moving. "This is called a search warrant," he added, holding up a paper. "Gianni Fosselli, you're under arrest for the murder of Andrew Brady." He turned to the uniforms. "Give him the spiel and take him to Midtown North."

How ...? Realization set in. As the officers cuffed him, Gianni turned his eyes on Jessica. "You were wired. Va fan culo!"

Jessica inched towards him, her expression as implacable as an ancient stone goddess in a Roman temple. She reared back and slapped him across the face. The crack of skin again skin brought everyone to a standstill.

"You killed an exceptional man," Jessica hissed, "and what did it earn you? Nothing but my contempt and your son's fear and loathing. I hope you rot in hell."

"I'll meet you there," Gianni spat. "No one treats me like this. No one."

*

Roberto paced along the boat dock on his estate. The sky threatened to burst at any moment.

Aldo hustled towards him, his face grim. He snapped his cell phone shut. "The cops were already at Oceano when our men got there. They kept on driving. Fosselli was arrested and taken to Midtown North. They heard it on their police scanner. Of course, now he joins Santangelo."

Martinelli watched his yacht bobbing in the choppy water. "Fosselli's a smart man. He won't contact us or involve us. Is Eduardo as smart?"

"I used to think so." Aldo looked away. "I was wrong. Cobra hears Eduardo panicked and ran when he was arrested. Now he's bragging about his connections to the cops. You were right. We should've cut our losses the first time he fucked up."

Martinelli shook his head. "The kid has no conscience. I liked that. But he's also stupid. Worse, he can't handle a fluid situation. If he involves us directly, you know what to do. Meanwhile, as a temporary measure, get Fosselli an attorney, someone not associated with us who owes us."

Roberto turned to his friend. "This is a high-profile case. If the Brady woman got Fosselli to implicate himself and that tape's ruled admissible, the DA will ask for the death penalty and it could get messy. It's not a risk I want to take right now, not with an election year and our friends feeling the heat."

"Any ideas?"

Roberto looked out over the bay. Whitecaps dotted the surface, smoky clouds churning overhead. "Cobra. Call him. If he pulls this off, he'll live to see another day."

*

The cruiser transported Fosselli to Midtown North. Barton dropped Nick and Jessie at the brownstone and Abbie at her West Side apartment. Bushman called as Lyle turned onto West Fifty-Fourth Street. "I'm on my way," Steve said. "The arrests are all over the news. They even know about the kid being Fosselli's. How the hell did the press find out about that?"

"Crap. Our leak at the precinct house." Barton slowed as he approached Midtown North. A crowd of news trucks jammed the street. "I got to go."

Barton pulled into the rear courtyard and slipped in the back way, avoiding the press. Steinmetz pulled him aside. "Lieutenant, I came up empty on that computer search you wanted. No calls to any of those numbers."

He wasn't surprised. Whoever had set up Brady's murder to look like the Perv was too smart to call from the precinct. He'd probably used pay phones out of the area or a disposable cell. Shit. "Thanks, Harry. Anything else?"

"The commissioner wants you downtown for a press conference about the arrests at seven."

An imposing man with a mane of salt and pepper hair interrupted them, "I'm Virgil Van Buren. I'm here to speak with my client, Mr. Fosselli."

"A new record." Barton looked at his watch. "You got here in forty minutes."

"May I see my client?"

"Your client's being booked for murder as we speak. Have fun."

*

Mary met Nick and Jessie at the front door. "It's all over the news," she said, agitated. "They even know Anthony's Gianni's son. How did they figure that out? Anthony saw it on TV before I could--"

"Is it true?" Anthony stood at the top of the stairs. "What they're saying on TV," Anthony said in a high-pitched voice. "Tell me, Mommy. Is it true?"

Nick glanced at Jessie. She looked exhausted, too close to the edge herself. They all were. "What are they saying, Anthony?" Nick asked evenly.

"That Gianni killed Daddy."

"Anthony," he said softly. "We need to talk."

"It's true! Gianni killed my daddy!" Anthony took off. Nick raced up the stairs after him, Jessie on his heels. A series of crashes echoed down the hallway. They both stopped short in Anthony's doorway.

With his good arm, Anthony was hurling the carved wooden ships onto the floor, reducing them to kindling. "I hate Gianni. I don't ever want to see him again. I hate him!" Anthony jumped up and down on the shredded boats. He slipped and tumbled to the floor.

Nick quickly picked Anthony up. "It's okay, Anthony. We all feel the same way." Nick met Jessie's dry eyes. Without a word, she crossed the hall to her bedroom, closing the door behind her.

*

"It's arranged. All of it." Aldo approached Roberto on the estate's back terrace. Zappella had spent the last hour on the phone.

Glancing up at the menacing sky, Roberto shoved his hands in his pockets. It was too damned cold for this time of year. "Did Cobra give you trouble?"

"Are you kidding? He knew the alternative. Now for Santangelo. He called me, babbling like a parrot, wanting a lawyer. I hung up on him. Then I was told he tried to make a deal."

Roberto looked at him, his eyes as emotionless as a pair of grapes. "Don't worry about it. I fixed that, too."

"What a fucking moron. Ah, well. He performed a service for us, and he served his purpose, hmm? You live and you learn, my friend. At least, some of us do." Martinelli parked his cigar stub between his teeth. "You contacted our news sources?"

"I told them Gianni had been kept from his son for years. They're sympathetic, telling the world his side of the story."

*

Fuming, Gianni paced his cell. He'd been forced to spend an hour with a pompous attorney sent by Martinelli. The man kept telling him not to worry. Scopata. He was behind bars, accused of murder. Gianni had used his one phone call on Abigail, only to get her voice mail. To make the situation more surreal, he'd seen Eduardo during the booking process, arrested as well. Gianni had put it together instantly. Eduardo had been recruited by Martinelli to shoot Andrew. Clever. By using Eduardo, Martinelli could walk away with clean hands, making it look as if the uncle and nephew were doing business. It made perfect sense, and Roberto Martinelli was a very sensible man.

Gianni looked to his right. Eduardo was somewhere on this cellblock. He'd passed by Gianni when the cops took him to his hole.

A heavy door clanged. Gianni looked up and Abigail walked into view. The sight of her sent Gianni's spirits soaring. He pressed against the bars. "Abigail, thank God. Did they tell you why I'm here? They actually think I killed Andrew--"

"Don't. I don't want to hear it."

"Don't tell me you believe this garbage--"

"I heard you admit it. I was listening with Nick and Lyle."

Gianni's breath caught. "Nick and Lyle?"

"That's right." Abigail flashed her winning smile. "I'm an actress, remember? All that Juilliard training came in handy. You bought the whole package."

As her betrayal sank in, Gianni almost vomited, exerting all his effort to hold back his gag reflex. He'd never trust another woman for the rest of his life. Whores, all of them. He grabbed the bars, his knuckles turning white. "You've been lying to me all this time, sneaking around behind my back? You--"

"Get over it. You were lying to me, too. You think I didn't know you wanted to marry me to better your chances of getting Anthony? You killed Andrew, my closest friend--"

"Get out. Get out of my sight!"

"Enjoy what's left of your sorry life. I'm going to get a real ..." she smiled, "jolt out of watching your execution." She turned to leave. "Oh. One more thing." Abigail waved her engagement ring, "Thanks for this. I'll sell it and use the money to buy Christmas gifts for Anthony. That little boy hasn't had a real Christmas since you killed his father."

"I'm his father!"

As Abigail strolled away, Gianni heard Eduardo's quiet laughter echo down the cellblock. "You lose, Uncle," he taunted. "I win."

*

It was close to midnight when a man strolled down Midtown North's deserted corridors. Cobra approached the sleepy guard at his desk outside the cellblock and flashed his ID. The young cop nodded towards the sign-in sheet, and Cobra scribbled his name and the time. "I won't be long. Just want to check on the day's prized catch."

Junior flashed him a grin before going back to his Nascar magazine. The dumb shit was too young and stupid to realize the hotel's new guests were not your everyday felons. Before punching in the locked door's code, Cobra glanced at the monitor mounted over the kid's desk. The black and white picture showing the cell corridor was grainy at best.

He hustled into the small cellblock, empty but for two prisoners. Clipping past Fosselli, Cobra hurried by the next space to the third cell and leaned against the bars, keeping his back to the surveillance camera. Santangelo was stretched out on his bunk, his arms propped behind his head. "What do you want?"

"Do you know who I am?"

"Should I?"

Cobra was dying to wipe the smart-ass glare from the kid's face. "Think back. Two years ago. In the terminal, right after the shooting ..."

"Yeah, I remember you now." Eduardo spit on the floor and turned to face the wall. "Get the fuck out."

"Ever heard of Cobra?"

Santangelo rolled back over, eyeing the man. "You're Cobra?"

"That's right. Martinelli sent me."

Santangelo sat up, giggling "You're Cobra. Shit. Martinelli's got everyone in his pocket." Still laughing, he rose and approached the bars. "I knew he'd send someone for me. He doesn't want me talking to the cops. He has a plan."

"You thought right." Cobra slid a gun with a silencer from his pocket and shot the punk through the heart. Eduardo's shock was etched on his face, his mouth cracked open like an egg, as he fell backwards onto the cement with a grunt.

Cobra stared down at the bastard. When you were that stupid you deserved to die. His mind wandered back to his days in the Central Intelligence Department of the Naval Investigative Service. Undercover work, drug busts. He'd been decorated twice for bravery, shot three times, and had lost track of the number of lives he'd ended. All in a day's work.

Pulling latex gloves from his pocket, Cobra snapped them on, reminding himself to wipe down the outer door and guard's desk on his way out. He walked back to Gianni's cell. The prisoner was perched on the end of his bunk, his eyes fearful. Cobra smiled. Hearing the whoosh of a bullet and a body crash to the floor might have that effect on an unarmed man in a cage.

Cobra turned as he heard the locked door's code punched in. The night janitor pushed through with his mobile mop and bucket. The man looked about seventy-five years old, but for a full head of dyed black hair. Ah, vanity, vanity. "Evening, Sam," Cobra said.

"Evening, Detective Bushman."

CHAPTER 29

Gianni eyed the detective, a squat mass of muscle, and he suddenly knew the meaning of cold sweat. Detective Bushman was Barton's partner. And he'd just killed Eduardo? "Sam," the detective said to the janitor. "Push the buzzer for the guard. I'm worried about this prisoner."

Gianni leapt up. "No, he--"

"Shut up. Move it, Sam." As the old man set off, Gianni backed up against the wall, his eyes fixed on the detective. "Martinelli sent me," Bushman whispered. "I'm here to help you." Gianni's mouth dropped open. Before he could say a word, the guard materialized, the janitor at his heels.

"What's up, detective?" the guard asked, yawning. "I'm not supposed to leave my desk."

Bushman whipped out his gun, jamming the muzzle against the kid's chin. "Your hands over your head and face the bars." The janitor froze in place. Bushman snatched the guard's gun, tossing it down the cellblock. After patting him down, the detective slid a plastic card from the man's pocket. He jerked the guard out of sight, towards the cells. Gianni heard a jail door clang open and shut. Bushman jogged back, opened Gianni's door with the card, and motioned the janitor inside. "Exchange clothes," he ordered, "including the specs, Sam."

"Y-you won't hurt me, will you?" the old man asked. "I won't tell no one. I swear."

"You can trust me, Sam," Bushman said. "I like you."

With shaking hands, Gianni removed his prisoner jumpsuit and shrugged on the janitor's worn gray slacks, shirt, and eyeglasses. Bushman asked the janitor to lie on the bunk and face the wall. His eyes pleading like a beagle's, Sam did what he was told. As soon as his head was turned, the cop shot him through the back of the skull. Bushman looked down at the still body. "Thanks for dyeing your hair, Sam. It was the perfect touch."

The detective quickly moved to the other cell. Gianni heard a yelp, choked off by the whoosh of another bullet. Bushman hustled back. "We have to move quickly," he said, pulling a slip of paper from his pocket. "Mess up your hair to look like Sam's." His heart banging against his ribs, Gianni swirled his hair with his fingers. "That's good. Here's the code for that door. The code beneath it's for the back door. This is a map on how to get out of here. Keep your head down. Focus on your bucket. You'll exit into an inner courtyard. Follow the alley to the street. I'm parked on Tenth Avenue and Fifty-Second. A dark blue Honda. I'll be waiting for you. And I want this paper back." He started towards the door.

"Wait a minute. My nephew. He's--"

"Dead. He dropped Martinelli's name to the wrong people."

"What's going to happen to me?"

"Martinelli has a plan."

For the first time in hours, Gianni smiled.

*

Nick sat in Anthony's bedroom for most of the evening. A slashing rain rattled against the windows, the clouds finally bursting. The poor kid was exhausted after his fit of fury. So was Jessie, sleeping in her own bed. That song Jessie sang this morning, the lyrics kept coming back to him. "To have and to hold." He'd say those words to Jessie soon. And mean them.

"Uncle Nick?"

"I'm here, Bongo. I thought maybe you'd fallen asleep."

"Not really. What do I tell the other kids? Everybody's going to know my real dad's Gianni and he killed Daddy. It's on TV. I'm a freak. They already think I'm different because Daddy was famous, and he was shot."

Nick blew out a breath. Children could be cruel. "I don't know. I'll think of something, okay? I promise." Nick ran his hand across the boy's curls, a clap of thunder shaking the window. "Ignore that storm. Try to get some sleep."

*

"Any problems?" Bushman asked, eyeing his sodden passenger.

"None." Fosselli climbed into the detective's car, handing him the paper with the codes. "Is it always that quiet at night?"

"If there's a poker game going it is." Bush pulled into traffic, windshield wipers snapping back and forth. He congratulated himself on the poker game, a stroke of genius. He'd set it up from home that afternoon. Bush had joined the game after the press conference, cashing in his chips around midnight and heading for the cellblock.

The two men rode in silence through the driving rain to Tenth Avenue and Fourteenth Street, where Gianni was transferred to another car. Whistling that damn tune he couldn't get out of his head, Bush sped away, a happy man. To reward himself for a job well done, Steve pointed the Honda towards Bottoms Up, Martinelli's strip club in the Bronx.

Why not celebrate in the spot where it had all begun? For years, Bush had been a regular customer, favoring the private rooms reserved for select patrons with select girls. Nothing changed until early one Sunday morning over two years ago, when Bush awakened in a drunken haze in one of those rooms, a dead hooker with a garrote around her neck in bed with him. Bushman had no idea how it had happened. They'd been having fun ... He couldn't remember a thing.

The manager of the club with a rep for being connected had rescued Bush that morning, disposing of the girl's body. Aldo Zappella had told Steve it was the least he could do for one of New York's finest. Two weeks later, Aldo had pleasantly asked Bushman for confidential police information on the Perv. When Bush had balked, he'd just as pleasantly produced a photo of Steve in bed with the dead hooker. Cobra knew he was fucked. Shortly afterwards, he'd been instructed to call the docked Milano's radio room at seven A.M. one morning and leave a detailed message for passenger Andrew Brady to meet Bill Rudolph in a private car outside the terminal.

It hadn't fallen into place for Bush until he and Barton were called to the piers to investigate Brady's shooting that same day. The murder had the Perv's stink all over it--the jacket, the gloves, the gun left behind. He'd been set up—and now the mob owned Steve Bushman.

That's the day Cobra sprang to life, Bush's code name in the Marines. If he was going to be forced to lead a double life, he'd create two personalities, one for each. It made it easier. Cobra had no principles. Detective Steve Bushman did. That's what he told himself anyway.

Cobra's next assignment had been to bug the brownstone, monitor the tapes, and watch Lyle spin his wheels for two years. And then that asshole McDeare fucked things up. Steve crossed the bridge into the Bronx under sheets of battering rain. He glanced down at the sign-in sheet and guard surveillance tape on the seat beside him. He'd burn them before discarding them in the first dumpster he passed.

*

Barton was jolted awake in the middle of the night with a call every cop dreaded. Fosselli had escaped. Santangelo and two other men were dead. Lyle snapped into action. "Put out an all-points bulletin. Cover the airports, tunnels, bridges, buses, and trains. All cars leaving Manhattan are searched."

Jamming the SUV's pedal to the floor in a torrential downpour, Lyle dashed into Midtown North forty-five minutes later. Barton listened to the coroner's summary as the bodies were removed. White with anger, he called his men together and gave them hell, unsparing in his contempt and disgust. And then he yelled that he was going to talk to each and every one of them personally. " I'll start with you, Grogin. My office. Five minutes. Now get out of my sight, all of you. You make me sick." Barton strode down the hallway, taking the stairs two at a time. Reaching his office, he slammed the door, making the night detectives jump.

Lyle paced his office, trying to shake off his anger. Fosselli had walked right past those Keystone Kops downstairs, dressed as the janitor and pushing a mop and bucket. And the sonuvabitch had a couple hours lead time. He could be fucking anywhere. Barton alerted the airlines worldwide with photos of Gianni and an order of extradition. A hotline was set up with a toll-free number for tips or sightings. The media outlets and wire services ran with the story, flashing Gianni's picture and the hotline number.

Finally, Barton had to face a hard truth he'd pushed away for too long. Fosselli's blood-soaked escape had been an inside job. An outsider couldn't have breached the cellblock. Martinelli had a man somewhere in Midtown North who was a force to be reckoned with.

*

Early that morning, the Milano steamed up the Hudson River following a routine run to Bermuda. Rain pounded the decks, and the wind rocked the liner as she was nudged into her berth by the tugs. After the ship was cleared by customs and the passengers had disembarked, Aldo and five men emerged from a dark limo and ducked into the nearly deserted terminal. They were the guests of the master of the ship. Captain Vincenzo Verde had left the men's names at the security guard's checkpoint. The guard issued them guest tags in exchange for their driver's licenses. All six men handed over fake ID matching the aliases on the list.

An hour later, the guests departed, exchanging their tags for their licenses. One of the original six had been replaced by Captain Verde's thirty-six year old son. Orlando Verde had arrived from Italy a week ago to visit his father. With his thick dark hair and sensual good looks, Orlando was a ringer for the man left behind. He wore the man's hat and jacket over his own slicker, slipping them off once they left the terminal and were out of sight. Aldo snapped his fingers and a minion grabbed the clothing.

Aldo and his four men returned to the limo. Orlando hustled to an adjacent terminal, took the escalator to the lower level, and loped back to the Milano's terminal, re-boarding on the lower gangway. He flashed his crew pass to the guard, which gave him access to restricted crew areas. Back aboard, Orlando scaled the stairs to his father's quarters, as successful as a rat in a maze. "It worked."

Captain Verde nodded and turned to his special guest. "You're sure you can handle a power boat?"

The man smiled faintly. "Of course."

*

Nick was awakened at six by his cell's jangle. He'd fallen into bed less than three hours earlier. It was Barton, with bad news. Fosselli had escaped, and Santangelo was dead.

"What!" Nick bolted up. "How?"

"We've got a dirty cop, Nick. I could use your brain." Lightning ripped the muddy sky outside the window.

"I'm on my way."

As Nick dashed for the door, Mary padded down the front staircase. He filled her in on Gianni's escape and told her to leave the alarm system on and keep Jessie and Anthony inside. Barton had a unit parked outside, but God knew what Gianni was capable of.

*

Barton's instincts told him a poker game had been in full swing during the escape. Scanning the squad room, he spotted Danny Dombrowski, a top-notch detective who'd recently been switched to nights. Lyle called Dombrowski into his office, asking if he'd seen anything unusual. Nothing. Barton asked about a poker game.

"Yeah, there was a game. I figured you knew about it. Bush called me to see if I wanted to play. I turned him down. Too much paperwork."

"Bush organized the game? Has he done this before?"

"I don't know. I'm new to the shift, remember?"

"Did you see him last night?"

"Yeah, but not playing poker. I was coming down Fifty-Fourth Street after getting a sandwich around twelve-thirty. Bush was hustling out the door and took off towards Tenth Avenue. I yelled to him, but he didn't hear me."

"Okay, thanks." Barton slouched back in his chair. If Bush had left at twelve-thirty that was within the timeframe of the murders, according to the coroner. Lyle brushed his hand over his cropped hair, dismissing the notion of Bush being his termite. Steve was Mr. Clean Marine. Glancing out the office window, he saw Nick squish his way across the squad room, his hair dripping in his face.

*

After a night of steamy sex in the bowels of Bottoms Up, Bushman dragged into the detectives' squad room around nine. Sliding off his rain slicker, he headed for Barton's office. Ah, there was McDeare, joining the pity party. Bush smiled. "Hey, Nick, did the boss-man call you in to fix our royal fuckup?" He turned to Lyle. "It's all over the news. How the hell did this happen?"

"Why don't you tell me? I heard you organized a little poker game here last night."

Bush dropped his head. "Guilty as charged. C'mon. The graveyard's been playing poker since you and I were rookies."

"How late did the game go?"

"I don't know. I left around midnight. Hot date. Why?"

"I thought maybe you saw something. Heard something. The escape could've happened anywhere from eleven to two." Lyle's brown eyes were as flat as a paper bag.

"It was quiet. Like a morgue." He glanced at his watch. "I'm testifying in the Parker kidnapping trial. I just wanted to check in and see if there was word on Fosselli. Good to see you, McDeare. Congrats on your nuptials. Mrs. Brady's one helluva lady." Bush left the office whistling.

*

"You're getting married?" Barton asked. He wasn't surprised. He just wished he was in a better mood for congratulations.

Nick knifed a hand through his hair. "You saw the ring Jessie was wearing yesterday. You even heard her tell Abbie and Gianni she was engaged." Nick's brow furrowed as he watched Bushman's retreating back, the cop still whistling that tune.

"I thought that was for show, for Fosselli's benefit. So I guess congratulations are in order ... Why the weird look?"

"Hmm? ... Uh, Jessie and I made a point of not telling many people ... Abbie and Anthony ... Jeremy and my agent. Mary." He continued to stare after Bushman. "I figured you knew because of the ring. But ... how did Bushman know? He wasn't with us yesterday."

"Maybe he overheard the news." Barton felt his stomach lurch as the smell of cotton candy filled his nostrils. "Where've you and Jessie discussed it?"

"Just the brownstone, yesterday morning." Nick rose slowly and walked towards the door, staring at Bushman taking the stairs down. "How ...? That tune Bush is whistling ... It's a brand new song from Jessie's show. No one knows that melody. Just the composer. She sang it for us that morning, right before we left to--" Nick swallowed. "Christ." He leaned across Barton's desk, shock etching his face. "Bushman," he said softly. "Bushman's your Judas.

They bugged the brownstone. That's how Bush knew. The engagement. The song. He HEARD it."

The five cups of coffee Barton had consumed that morning threatened to spew all over his desk. Shaking off his nausea, Lyle reached for his phone. "Mike? It's Barton. I need a handful of your best men for a residence sweep. You tell those men their jobs are in jeopardy if they breathe a word of this to anyone."

Barton clicked off, lifting his eyes to Nick. "Bush's out of commission, testifying at that trial. One small blessing." He punched in another number. "Fisk? Barton. I need a big favor. I want a record of calls made from a cell phone. I'm authorizing you to do whatever needs to be done A-SAP. I'll take responsibility. I'm looking for specific numbers called ..."

*

Nick called Jessie, warning her some of Lyle's men were on their way over to search the brownstone. "They," Nick exchanged a glance with Barton, "ah, they'll be looking for hidden microphones."

There was a moment of silence. "Someone's ... been listening to us?"

"That's what we want to find out. There's a dirty cop in the department. Lyle's on it. How's Anthony?"

"Terrified Gianni's coming after him. When will you be home?"

"I don't know." He glanced at the windows, coated with a glistening gel of rain. "If this storm keeps up, I may have to swim."

"I heard some of the subways are flooded."

"Maybe I'll build a raft," Nick said, trying to lighten the conversation. "Don't worry. I'll get home. Talk to--"

"Jesus, the Milano!" Barton shouted, smothering Nick's goodbye as he hung up. "Martinelli owns the fucking ship." He punched up a screen on his computer. "The Port Authority schedule ..." He scanned his monitor. "Bingo. The Milano docked this morning and sails back to Bermuda at five." Barton flung the office door open. "Okay, listen up, everybody. The clock's ticking. This precinct is the joke of the department. Time to make up for it."

Nick watched Barton spin into action, scrambling detectives and uniforms to search every inch of the Milano until its departure. Lyle notified the Bermudian authorities to watch the airport and waterways once the Milano docked. He called a contact at the Port Authority who e-mailed a manifest of the Milano's passengers and crew for that afternoon's sailing. Barton quickly focused on late bookings and any new crew or guests boarding.

*

Detectives Mario Manganaro and Bernie Loman were the lead team sent to the Milano. Barton arranged for the two detectives to stay aboard and sail to Bermuda if Fosselli was still MIA. That afternoon, they questioned the passengers who booked within the last forty-eight hours: An elderly couple who spent most of their time at sea. A redhead named Heidi Campbell whose husband had just walked out on her. And Brian Boca, a middle-aged executive ordered to take a vacation by his doctor. All three cabins were searched. No sign of Gianni.

Manganaro and Loman moved on to question the senior officers and search their cabins. Entering the captain's quarters, they found Captain Verde in his living room, deep in conversation with a handful of officers. Fluent in Italian, Manganaro listened as the men discussed potential hazards of the inclement weather. The detectives searched both the captain's cabin rooms. They scoured closets, under the bed and desk, in cupboards, and the shower. Nothing.

*

Barton's afternoon from hell raced by, each passing moment multiplying his anxiety and fury. The brownstone search had revealed more than a dozen bugs strategically planted in all the first-floor rooms, plus a phone tap. The upper floors were clean. Barton gritted his teeth. Early in the investigation, Bushman had been in the brownstone often, the dutiful detective.

Manganaro and Loman reported back the Milano search yielded nada. The captain had entertained six guests early in the afternoon. Mario reeled off the names, and Barton checked them against his roster of known Martinelli employees. No matches.

*

Captain Verde dismissed his officers, sending them back to the bridge. Locking the cabin door, he said, "They're gone. It's safe."

In the far corner was a built-in wooden divan topped with black leather cushions. Vincenzo watched as the divan cushion seat lifted. A man crawled out of the storage space like a locust out of the earth.

*

Barton glanced at his watch. Five-fifteen. The day squad had headed home. The Milano had set sail. Barton was beginning to believe Gianni Fosselli had slipped out of the city before anyone had known he was missing. He looked across his desk at McDeare, sitting with his arms crossed, his eyes cast to the floor. They might as well be at a wake.

Don Fisk rapped on the door and dropped a computer printout on Lyle's desk. "There it is, Lieutenant, the calls from the cell phone."

Barton devoured the sheet as Fisk shuffled from the room. It only took a minute. A minute that lasted a lifetime. Slumping in his chair, Lyle scrubbed a hand across his eyes.

"Proof?"

Barton nodded. There it was in black and white. Bush's cell phone records. Lyle's eyes widened. "Bush called the Miilano's land-line the morning of the murder."

Nick's lips thinned to a razor's edge. "Jesus Christ. The bastard set up Andrew to meet with Bill Rudolph."

"If I didn't have the records in front of me, I wouldn't fucking believe it." Lyle's eyes zapped to Bushman's vacant desk outside the glassed-in office. His own partner had betrayed the department. For how many pieces of silver? Lyle Barton was a clown, the joke of Midtown North. Wordlessly, he passed the sheet to Nick.

- 311 -

"Look at this," Nick grated, studying the sheet. "Bushman called Zappella yesterday, when Jessie was with Gianni. Jessie and I discussed the plan on the back porch the night before. The shit heard us and tried to warn them."

Barton felt himself go dead inside. He picked up the phone and placed two calls. One to Internal Affairs. The other to Bushman.

*

The Milano was twenty nautical miles beyond Sandy Point, the last marker for New York City. Captain Verde picked up the microphone in his office and clicked on, asking for attention. He announced they'd be shutting down the engines briefly to fix a minor glitch. "It's best if you remain indoors. The rain is heavy, the wind is gusting, and the decks are slippery. In the meantime, enjoy your dinner. Thank you very much."

Vincenzo turned off the microphone and looked at the man dressed in rain gear and goggles, his dark hair slicked back. "You'll use the starboard power boat closest to the bow. It's being swung out now. Once you're aboard, two mates will lower you. Don't hurt them. They'll say nothing."

*

Jessie heard the foreboding in Nick's voice as soon as she picked up the phone. "You better sit down, honey." Nick took a deep breath. "Steve Bushman's been working for Martinelli. He's the mole. It's Bush."

"Steve ...?" Jessie froze as she was transported back to the Othello Hotel. The bathroom. That horrible cologne. The garlic breath. And the voice ... that voice ... "It was him!"

"That's what I said."

"I mean at the Othello ... in the bathroom. It was Steve Bushman who tried to .... It was his voice."

"Are you sure?"

"I'm positive." She placed her hand over her heart, as if she could still its pace. My God. She knew this man. She'd offered him coffee in her home. He'd eaten Mary's cookies. And he ...

"Okay, stay calm. Barton's on top of it. I'll be home soon."

Jessie remained on the line after Nick clicked off, staring into space. Steve Bushman was the brutal animal who had tried to rape her. He'd used her like a piece of meat. Lyle's partner. Another traitor she'd welcomed into her home. How many more shocks could her mind absorb in such a short time? How many nightmares could one life hold?

*

Nick stuffed his cell in his pocket, rage sweeping through him. "Bush is the animal who attacked Jessie at the Othello."

Barton's face aged ten years in ten seconds. "After all my years on the force, I'd thought I'd seen it all. Bush proved me wrong. I'm sorry. I'm sorry I let this happen. It's my fault."

"You can't—"

Barton looked up. "Here he comes. Don't do anything stupid. Remember, you gave me your word. We do this my way."

Nick nodded, watching Bushman hang his dripping raincoat over his desk chair and head towards them. On his way, he nodded to cops on the graveyard shift. "You still here?" he asked Nick, entering the office. "What's up? What's so important I had to come all the way into town again? Fosselli?"

"Close the door, Nick," Lyle directed.

Nick fought for self-control. All he could see was Jessie's broken body after her attack. His head hummed with such rage it felt like a swarm of bees living inside his brain. He pictured himself leaping at Bushman and ...

"Nick," Barton repeated sharply.

With a glare, Nick sprang up and closed the door, leaning against it.

"What the hell's wrong with you, man?" Bush asked, eying Nick.

"Bush," Lyle said. "I'm going to give you one chance to come clean."

"What the fuck's going on?" Steve's eyes darted from one man to the other. Nick saw the first flicker of doubt.

"Look at me." Lyle's voice was even, his eyes ice. "I know you've been working for Martinelli."

"What ...? What the hell are you talking about?"

"It's over. I have proof. Records from your cell phone."

"Oh, that. Listen," Bush said, looking embarrassed, "I had no choice. Let me explain." Nick cocked his head in amazement. The squat man standing in front of him was talking as if Lyle had caught him fixing a parking ticket.

Nick saw Jessie half naked on that bathroom floor, swollen and bruised. This pig had left his handprint on her breast. With a reflex action, Nick reared back and slugged Bushman hard in the face, sending the man sprawling.

Bush stumbled to his feet, blood trickling from his nose.

Ignoring Barton's bark to step back, Nick hissed, "You piece of shit. You tried to rape Jessie. She recognized your voice." Nick flexed his hand, his fury bubbling over. "And you set my brother up to be murdered. I could kill you with my bare hands!"

*

Bushman pulled out his handkerchief and swiped his bloody nose. With a powerful thrust, Barton shoved Nick back against the wall, separating them. "Look, Lyle, let me explain. They set me up. I had no--"

"You killed two good men last night. You freed Fosselli. You--"

"I can help you, man." Bush thought fast. The Witness Protection Program. He could still get out of this. "I know how Martinelli's organization works. I'll flip. I've been on the inside. I--"

"It's over, Bush." Lyle was looking at him like he was a freak who molested little girls. Steve dropped his eyes, unable to meet that look. "You'll either die at the hands of the state or you'll die in prison," Lyle said, a tremor in that gruff voice. "I promise you. You're going down."

Lyle glanced beyond Steve into the squad room. Bush looked over his shoulder. Two suits from Internal Affairs stood on the other side of the door. It was over. Or was it? Maybe Cobra had something to say about that. It was his life, too.

"Your shield and your gun," Barton snapped.

Cobra leered at McDeare. "Jessie was sweet, man. Sweet pink flesh. Yum." He jerked his gold shield from his pocket and tossed it on Lyle's desk. "I slept like a baby after almost getting a piece of that tasty ass." McDeare was breathing hard, like he was being strangled. Cobra clenched his hands. He wanted to tear Nick's heart out and roast it. If McDeare hadn't messed things up, he'd be sitting in the fucking catbird seat right now.

Without taking his eyes from Bush, Barton said, "Not a word, Nick. Not another move, or I swear I'll have you arrested for obstruction. The gun, Bush," Barton prodded.

Bushman reached into his shoulder holster, gripping the revolver's smooth handle. Think. He didn't want to kill Lyle. Barton was a good cop, a loyal partner. He was the most decent man Bush had ever known. But Cobra, Cobra would love to drop that prick McDeare where he stood.

Bushman gauged how far the IAD goons and Barton stood from him. He saw the sequence of events in a flash. Take out McDeare with a bullet through the throat. Bang. Fast-forward to Barton drawing his gun and taking Bush down, freeing him from this nightmare. No media circus. No prison. But Detective Lyle Barton would never recover from shooting his partner dead. He'd relive every minute every night in his sleep for the rest of his life. That's how Lyle Barton was made. Bush had a fragment of a second to decide what to do. THINK.

He saw only one way out that eliminated prison and what happened to cops in prison. One way that spared Barton more pain.

His way.

"The gun," Lyle barked.

Bushman swiftly jerked his service revolver out of its holster, lifted the muzzle to his temple, and pulled the trigger. The last thing he heard was Barton's shriek, "Bush, no!"

*

At Captain Verde's announcement, Mario Manganaro and Bernie Loman left the dining room. Mario's instincts were screaming this didn't feel right. They found the captain's quarters empty. The steward said he was in the engine room. As they trotted down the staircase, Mario paused. "What's that?" A grinding, as if metal were straining against metal. Had the ship hit something?

Clattering down the stairs, they found themselves on the main deck of shops and public rooms. Two young seamen stumbled in from the outer deck, soaked to the skin and winded. Mario showed them his badge and asked in Italian about the strange noise. The two boys exchanged a glance and dashed down the stairs, turning a deaf ear to Mario's shouts.

Mario sprinted across the lobby, leaving Bernie lumbering behind. He burst onto the outer promenade. The wind and rain whipped his hair and clothes, blinding him. Covering his eyes, he struggled forward, slipping on the slick teak deck. Moving to the rail, Mario noticed a tanker. He'd been a Navy man. Ships were required to keep a reasonable distance between each other. This tanker was too close, stopped dead in the water.

As he scanned the horizon, he noticed an empty davit hanging over his head, its lifeboat missing. Leaning over the railing, Mario spotted the lifeboat bobbing up against the Milano in the choppy sea. As the small boat's engines revved, he tried to focus on the lone man at the helm. His dark hair was slicked back by goggles, his profile hazy in the cabin lights' dim blue glow. The swirling rain didn't help, but Mario saw enough to be sure it was Gianni Fosselli. Fosselli guided the powerboat away from the Milano. The bastard was transferring to the other ship!

Manganaro reached for his gun and aimed over the side, firing two shots but hitting nothing. The third bullet hit the gasoline tank. He watched in horror as the small craft exploded into a giant fireball.

CHAPTER 30

Mario requisitioned another lifeboat to take the two detectives and a small crew out to the smoldering wreckage. All they fished out of the sea were singed pieces of boat and a charred shoe. Mario wasn't surprised. No one could've survived that blast.

They questioned a badly shaken Captain Verde who swore he'd been forced to go along with the escape plan. Vincenzo stammered that Fosselli had warned him people would be watching to make sure the escape was successful. If anything went wrong, they'd come after the Verde family. The captain didn't know who those people were by name. No one asked the Mafia those kinds of questions. Not if they wanted to live.

Mario couldn't argue that.

*

After Bush's body was removed from Lyle's office, Internal Affairs took over. Barton responded to the never-ending questions in a monotone, trying to ignore the bloodstains on his clothes. Bush's blood. His partner.

Despite the interrogation, Barton demanded periodic updates on the unfolding case. This was still his precinct, his watch. Dombrowski reported a search of Bush's Brooklyn apartment unearthed over two-years' worth of brownstone recordings.

RICO checked in after paying a visit to Martinelli. The big man had never heard of Steve Bushman. They also talked to Zappella at the Martinelli estate. Aldo admitted he knew Bushman as a regular at a Bronx club Zappella managed. When RICO produced Bushman's cell records showing a call to Aldo during the Fosselli sting, Zappella shrugged. Sure, Steve had called to say he'd be coming by Bottoms Up that night. Regular customers often phoned ahead of time, asking for special favors with special girls. And Bushman was a very regular customer.

As IAD was finishing with Barton, Mario phoned with news of Fosselli's death. Lyle shook his head. So many people dead, so many lives scarred, and for what? What did any of it mean in the end? When he returned to the squad room, Barton found Nick slumped at an empty desk, arms folded, clothes and hair splattered with blood. Barton repeated what Manganara had told him, his voice as flat as a weatherman's.

By the time Lyle and Nick left Midtown North, it was almost ten. The rain had finally stopped, a haze settling over the lights of Manhattan, dressing the city in a misty beauty. As Barton pointed his SUV in the direction of the brownstone, the numbness began to wear off.

He remembered.

Quickly turning onto Central Park South, Lyle wrenched the car to the side of the road. He threw the door open and crouched on the ground, his stomach heaving. When nothing was left in his belly, he looked up to find Nick standing a few feet away. "I'll drive," Nick said, pulling a handkerchief out of his pocket and handing it to Lyle. "I'll cab it home from your place."

Barton nodded, wiping off his mouth. He climbed into the passenger seat, and the two men rode in silence to Flushing. Nick pulled to a stop in front of Barton's home. As Lyle reached for the door handle, he hesitated. "I thought you were a dead man, Nick. Steve wanted to take you out. I saw it in his eyes when he grabbed his revolver."

"He knew if he killed me, you'd have to shoot him. He didn't want to do that to you."

Barton shook his head. Steve had betrayed the department and assassinated God knows how many men in his lifetime, but he'd remained loyal to his partner that last minute. Go figure.

*

It was all over the news, Gianni killed during an aborted escape attempt. Abbie felt nothing. She flipped off the TV and stood in the darkness. She watched out the window as the Milano glided up the Hudson River back to her berth. No trip to Bermuda today. Elegant and sleek, her deck lights ablaze, the Milano was the last of the Victorian dowagers. Maybe if that floating palace had never existed, Andrew would be alive today.

*

Roberto paced his terrace. The RICO agents had come and gone two hours ago. Cobra's loss was a blow, but there were other cops to be had, other friendly eyes in the department. Aldo had been impeccable in covering his tracks. So where was he? There were more important events than Cobra's demise on Martinelli's mind. He'd been waiting in the damp muck for twenty minutes.

As if summoned, Aldo rounded the corner. "Sorry you've been waiting. The passengers were questioned after the Milano docked. It took Heidi a while to call."

Roberto allowed himself a smile. "I saw the news reports. Heidi Campbell has a future."

"Heidi wasn't the one who took the boat out. The fucking cops did it."

"What?"

"The cops caught onto Fosselli's escape route. We both know Barton's no idiot. Heidi was questioned by the police as soon as she boarded because she was a late booking. They searched her cabin."

"Get to the boat blowing up."

"It went according to plan. The captain stopped the engines and slipped Heidi the gun always locked on board. He had no idea why. She got into position as the lifeboat was lowered. When she had the boat in her sights, she heard gunfire and the fucking boat exploded. It was the cops! They must've heard the lifeboat being lowered or something. Do you believe our luck?" Aldo threw back his head in laughter. "One more thing. Afterwards, the captain told the cops Fosselli threatened the lives of his family if the escape didn't go off without a hitch." Aldo continued to laugh.

Martinelli grinned. "Vincenzo Verde's been a good friend to Fosselli for years. I knew he'd cooperate. He must've gone crazy when that boat blew up. He didn't count on an explosion being part of the favor."

"Heidi said he was stunned, but he kept his cool."

"It's time for a celebratory drink." Roberto clapped his friend on the back. "Andrew Brady is finally out of our lives." They started towards the house. "What about the Wexley situation?"

"Being taken care of right now."

*

At the sound of the front lock turning, Jessie hurried down the hallway. It was after eleven. She took one look at Nick as he stumbled through the door and panicked. "You're bleeding!"

"I'm fine," he said, relocking the door and setting the alarm. "It's a long story. You've heard about Gianni?" He fondled her cheek, dropping his hand.

"Abbie called. She said it's all over the TV and Steve Bushman's dead, too. I-I didn't want to watch. I didn't want Anthony to find out about Gianni on TV either. Mary and I kept him busy, and he played those computer games you bought him. We'll tell him tomorrow. Please. Whose blood is that?"

"I'm starving. All I've eaten today's a stale package of cheese crackers. Anything to eat?"

Jessie paused. She reminded herself Nick McDeare was not a package that opened easily. "I, um, kept your dinner warm."

"I've been sitting around in wet clothes all day. I need a hot shower first. Then food. Don't worry about me, okay?"

*

Nick threw his bloodied clothes in the trashcan. They smelled of crushed cigarettes and police stations and tragedy. He slipped on jeans and grabbed a turtleneck from the dresser drawer. Spotting Jeffrey's ring box in the corner, Nick stared at it long and hard. Tonight he'd come within seconds of seeing his son again.

Jessie was lighting a fire in the grate when Nick joined her in the study. He warmed his hands over the flames, trying to chase away the chill in his bones. He wasn't sure he'd ever be warm again.

"Your dinner's on the coffee table. I'll get a bottle of wine."

Nick dropped onto the couch, digging into the food. A thick slab of prime rib, mashed potatoes with gravy, buttered peas, and crusty French bread. Jessie returned with a bottle of Cabernet. "The meal was Mary's idea. She said we needed comfort food." She uncorked the bottle, filled two flutes, and curled beside him.

Nick emptied his plate methodically, forcing the evening's events from his mind.

"What happened tonight?" Jessie asked quietly.

"I don't want to talk about it." Nick dredged the last piece of beef through gravy.

"Whose blood was that?"

"Enough, okay?" Nick took a slurp of wine and collapsed against the back of the couch, closing his eyes. When a case wrapped in the past, Nick went home to a quiet apartment and a bottle of bourbon. Tonight he came home to a hot meal, a good bottle of wine, a fire, and Jessie. Full of questions.

When he opened his eyes, Nick found Jessie staring at him, those turquoise eyes glistening. Nick pulled her into his arms. She radiated warmth, her rosy flesh … Bushman. Bushman said something about Jessie's flesh. Nick pushed the thought away. "How's Anthony doing? He liked the computer games?"

"I'm worried about him. He stayed in his room most of the day. Yeah, he liked the games. He has enough junk in that room to hibernate for the next five years. I unplugged his TV so he wouldn't find out about Gianni. I told him it was broken. Eric called and invited him over, but Anthony wouldn't budge. He wouldn't come down for dinner. I think he's upset about what his friends are saying, among other things. Maybe we should look into a therapist?"

"He mentioned his friends the other night," Nick said slowly. "I've been thinking. Maybe there's something I can do, something computer games and a therapist can't." Nick skimmed his fingers across Jessie's arm. Sweet pink flesh. He pushed Bushman out of his head. "Jess, I have an idea…"

*

Huddled under a Mets blanket in his den, Barton stared glumly at the television screen. The news of Bushman's death and double life screamed back at him on every news channel, the details of his suicide mercifully covered up. Bushman wasn't the lead story, however. That honor belonged to Gianni Fosselli.

Forget Fosselli. Barton dropped his head back and closed his eyes, seeing that frozen moment in time, Bush's hand on his gun, his eyes fixed on McDeare. The stone-cold eyes of a killer. And then, for a brief second, Steve had flicked his glance to Lyle. In that moment, his partner had come back to him, as surely as night turns into dawn. It was Bush, the man he'd trusted with his life, the man he'd been as close to as a brother. Steve. That look would haunt Barton to the end of his days. That look, and the bloodstain on his office floor.

*

As the fire in the grate burned down to embers, Jessie and Nick nodded off on the couch, tucked beneath an afghan. Later that night, Nick roused Jessie from sleep. Feverishly pressing his body to hers, he clutched her tightly, his staccato kisses frantic. Nick's every move built in pitch, as if some unseen force were driving him. Jessie held him close, returning his desperate kisses as their bodies came together in frenzied motion.

Afterward, Nick collapsed in Jessie's arms, his face buried in her neck, his breath coming in gasps. "It was Bush," he said, his voice barely a whisper. "The blood. He shot himself in the head, Jessie, in front of Lyle and me." Nick swallowed. "But first he wanted to kill me. I saw it in his eyes. His hand was on his gun. You and Anthony flew through my mind."

In the darkness, Jessie cradled the man she loved as he continued to whisper, painting a picture of a few seconds in time when Nick's life had flashed before his eyes. A few seconds in time when Jessie had come close to losing Nick the same way she'd lost Andrew.

*

Nick awoke the next morning to find Jessie gone and sunlight streaking through the study's windows. He stared at the ceiling, an arm crooked over his forehead. Nick wandered across the hall. Jessie sat at the island, reading the Sunday TIMES. He poured a cup of coffee and sat across from her.

Jessie looked up at him. "Mary's out buying the fixings for a good old fashioned Sunday dinner, something that used to be a tradition around here. Abbie's joining us, Lyle, too. Barb and his daughter have tickets to the ballet."

Nick washed a hand over his stubbled jaw. "Where's Anthony?"

"In his room."

"Want to talk to him about my idea?"

"I think you should talk to him alone. This is about the two of you. He already knows how much I love him." Jessie glanced up, smiling. "Now it's your turn. Talk to him."

"What about Gianni?"

"Play it by ear. He may take it better coming from you. Man to man. You decide. If you want me there, let me know." She cupped his hand and squeezed. "You're great with him. He loves you."

After a quick shower, Nick found Anthony staring out the window. He plopped down in the easy chair and asked the boy if he remembered what they'd talked about the other night, about the other kids teasing him.

Anthony rolled his eyes. "Sally Pritchard told Eric she's afraid I'll kill her. She said killing's in my blood."

"That's nonsense. Blood has stuff like white cells and red cells and antibodies. Forget Sally Pritchard." Nick cleared his throat. "Your mom and I talked last night. I've come up with an idea, but if you don't like it, we'll forget about it. I'll never bring it up again. Deal?" Anthony nodded. "Okay. How would you feel about my legally adopting you? It would make us father and son."

"You can do that even if everyone knows Gianni's my real dad?"

Here it was. "Anthony, I have something to tell you about Gianni--"

"I know. Gianni died. Eric called me this morning and told me. He tried to escape and he died." Anthony dropped his eyes. "I'm glad. Gianni killed Daddy, and I'm glad he's dead, too." He peeked up at Nick. "I know I'm bad for feeling that way. It makes me bad like Gianni."

Damn Fosselli to hell. If he wasn't there already. "You know something? I feel the same way. We can't help our feelings. Gianni hurt us both. It's normal to have not-so-nice feelings about him. It doesn't mean we're bad, just human." Nick saw relief flood the boy's blue eyes. "Anyway," Nick said carefully, "I could adopt you, yes, even if Gianni's your father by blood. But I

- 320 -

want to be clear. Andrew was your real daddy. I'm not trying to take his place. I just want to make it easier--"

Anthony sprang up and looped his good arm around Nick's neck. "I want you to be my dad for real, not just because you marry Mommy!"

"Wait, there's more. The other kids? If I adopt you, you could take my name—if you want to. You'd be Anthony Brady McDeare. If your mom and I enroll you in a new private school, you can have a fresh start. Everyone will get to know you as Anthony McDeare. Then later you can decide what to tell your new friends, if you want to tell them anything." Nick sat back. "So? What do you think?"

Anthony broke into laughter. "C'mon," he said, tugging Nick to his feet. "Let's tell Mom and Mary." He skipped out of the room, yelling, "Hey, everybody! I'm Anthony McDeare. Daddy's still my daddy, but I have a new name just like Mommy's!"

Nick trailed after the boy. He found mother and son in the back garden. Anthony was babbling a mile a minute before running back into the house to find Mary.

"Look at him," Jessie said, gathering dead twigs littering the yard after the storm. "I haven't seen him that happy since Andrew was alive ..."

"I know something that might make you just as happy." Nick took Jessie's hand, leading her to another spot in the back yard. "Look."

"Oh ... my ... God." Jessie dropped the branches and crouched down, studying the ground. Out of the barren dirt where Andrew's plum tree had once stood, two new leafy sprouts had popped above ground. Two new plum trees would rise from the original. Fingering the sturdy leaves, Jessie looked up at Nick, a stunned expression on her face.

Nick shrugged. "Andrew works in mysterious ways."

*

Barton arrived at the brownstone for dinner later that evening. He still felt raw, but better. "C'mon," Nick said to Barton, while Jessie and Abbie chatted. "I could use a drink."

"A scotch sounds good." Lyle followed Nick to the bar in the study.

Nick poured the drinks and slid a glass towards Lyle. "So tie up the threads for me. What happened to Rosita?"

Barton took a swig of scotch and winced as the burning liquid slid to his gut. "Rosita Hernandez disappeared off the face of the earth. Rosa Hererra is a legal immigrant with a green card to prove it. The WPP promised me they'll find her a good place. This miserable saga deserves at least one happy ending."

"Gianni's dead. Another happy ending."

"Look at the carnage he left behind."

Nick paced to the window. "You know something? All this could've been avoided. Gianni made one fatal mistake."

"Falling in love with Jessie?"

Nick spun around to face Barton. "Not phoning Jessie when he went back to Italy. If he'd called her instead of writing weeks later, I bet Jessie would've told him about the baby. Gianni would've come back in a heartbeat if he'd known Jessie was carrying his child. All our lives would have turned out differently. Jessie would've married Gianni. Aldo never would've had any use for Bush. And Andrew and I would've spent the rest of our lives getting to know each other. Think about it." Nick glanced up at the oil painting of the two brothers. "A simple phone call."

*

Jessie looked around the table and smiled. Over Mary's rack of lamb, rice pilaf and steamed broccoli, Sunday dinner was an event, the way it used to be in the old days. Anthony was animated, talking with his mouth full of food. Mary and Abbie were full of ideas for the upcoming wedding, turning deaf ears to Jessie's protests about keeping it simple. Lyle and Nick were deep in conversation about Nick's new novel. After peach cobbler and coffee, Mary began clearing the dishes, Abbie rinsing. Anthony bounded from the room, eager to call Eric and tell him about his new name.

Lyle's cell buzzed. He spoke in muffled tones and hung up, his face grim. "Ian Wexley was shivved last night in prison. He's dead."

"Shivved?" Jessie asked.

"It's a makeshift knife."

Nick shook his head. "Martinelli tied up everything in a nice neat little package, didn't he? There's no one left to point the finger at him."

Jessie dropped into her chair. Andrew was dead. And Gianni. Now Ian. The final domino had fallen. Dominos which had begun to tumble when Andrew sent those photographs to Italy. A lifetime ago.

"No guilt, Jess," Nick said, taking her hand. "Ian played a part in Andrew being killed. He controlled his own destiny."

Nick was right. No guilt.

It was over.

*

Jessie awoke with a start. She flicked on the bedside lamp and glanced around the room. Nothing. She felt silly sleeping alone when she could be snuggled up in Nick's arms. But until she and Nick were married she didn't want Anthony to see them share a bedroom. She smiled. She'd never realized how old-fashioned she was. Poor Nick. Poor her. Leaving the light on, Jessie closed her eyes again. Just as she began to drift off, someone's lips brushed her forehead.

"I love you, Kendle."

Jessie bolted upright, her eyes darting around the room.

The rocker was moving by itself, as if someone had just risen from it. Jessie touched her forehead. Andrew.

*

Abbie was having the funniest dream. She and Andrew were back at Juilliard, hurling water balloons off the school's roof onto Lincoln Center Plaza. "For God's sake, Andrew, that's a condom! You can't throw that."

"Remind me to buy some more. That's my last one."

"Abbie?"

"What?"

"Abbie. It's me. Can you hear me?

"Andrew?"

"No man ever had a better friend than you."

Abbie opened her eyes. Goose bumps chased up and down her arms.

*

Nick had fallen asleep on the couch in the study, watching TV. He cracked his eyes open and yawned. What he needed was his own bed and twelve hours of steady sleep. Hell, what he needed was a bedroom he shared with Jessie. Then maybe he could keep warm in this drafty house. He flicked off the television. Stumbling up, Nick grabbed his glass and took it to the kitchen sink.

"Nick?"

Nick swung around. Andrew sat in the breakfast bar. "You scared the hell out of me."

Andrew laughed. "I seem to do that a lot. I came to say goodbye. Time to go."

"You're leaving for good?" Nick had assumed Andrew would always be around, happily pointing out his shortcomings.

"Unless I get special dispensation from someone on high." He grinned, but his smile faded. "I got what I wanted. Jessie and Anthony know Gianni for who he is and what he's done. It looks like Fosselli lost, and you won." Andrew's amber eyes bored into Nick's. "Thanks, Nick. For everything." He smiled a melancholy smile. "Anthony Brady McDeare. I began the job. You'll finish it, no matter what shadows come your way."

His ghost was depressed. So was he. "I ..." Nick couldn't find his voice. The writer who made his living from words didn't know what to say.

"I know. Me, too."

Andrew rose, and Nick threw his arms around his brother. "If only ..."

"Yeah. If only."

Nick awoke abruptly, but he wasn't on the couch. He was standing in the kitchen, hugging the air.

*

"Bongo? I love you. You will always be loved. Look for the love."

Anthony cracked his eyes open, feeling his daddy hug him. "Daddy?" He sat up, switching on the lamp. Anthony looked all around. How was he supposed to look for the love? That's when he saw a small box on the bedside table. His name was printed on a card beside it. Opening the box, Anthony found a ring inside. A gold band with a shiny stone in the middle. Did Daddy bring this? He opened the card. It was from his uncle. Wow. Uncle Nick gave him a ring with a stone like Mommy's. No, he was his dad now. Dad N. Daddy wanted him to know Dad N would always love him. Anthony tumbled out of bed, running towards the hallway.

*

Nick leaned against the island in the kitchen. He felt as if he'd lost Andrew all over again. At pounding footsteps, Nick looked up to find Anthony running down the stairs. "What are you doing up in middle of the night?

"Daddy was here. You weren't in your room." Anthony wiggled his fingers. The ring sparkled in the stove's light. "Did you leave this for me? I think Daddy woke me up to tell me it was there."

Nick looked skyward. Thank you, Andrew. "A little while ago, while you were asleep. You like it?"

"I love it! It's a little big."

"We can fix that."

"But how come you gave it to me? It's not my birthday or Christmas. It looks old. Was it yours?"

Nick brushed the boy's curls from his forehead. "It was Jeffrey's. I want you to have it, Bongo." Jeffrey had gone to great lengths to make sure his ring was returned to Nick. There had to be a reason, and that reason was Anthony. Nick could hear Jeffrey's words: "Promise me if you find your family you'll do a bunch of stuff with them. Picnics and Christmases and birthdays and baseball games. Promise me you won't be sad."

"C'mon. Let's hit the sack. Have you ever been to a Mets or a Yankees game? Or the Giants? Have you ever been to a football game? I bet if your dad ever took you, it was so long ago, you don't remember. See, it's cold out, and you eat hot dogs and …"

***

EPILOGUE

Two Weeks Later

"Mrs. Panfiglio, I haven't seen your husband in months," Aldo said. "Now, please, I have to go, and your car's blocking my driveway."

"Mr. Zappella," she begged, tears wetting her cheeks, "Frank said you were sending him on some secret mission, and he'd be back in a week. That was two weeks ago, and I haven't heard a word."

"I don't know anything about any secret mission, and Frank's not working for me. I don't know where you got that idea. Now, please, move your car."

*

Jessie and Nick jogged out of the park and up Fifth Avenue. She glanced at her watch. Eight-thirty. Still plenty of time.

"Excited about starting rehearsals today?"

"Yeah. And scared." They jogged a few minutes in silence as they turned the corner onto East Eighty-First Street. "Anthony looked so cute, getting into the car and having Willie drive him to school."

"Willie's better than a guard dog. I felt sorry for that poor guy who asked for our autographs. Willie practically threw him to the ground."

Jessie laughed. "Willie's a driver and a bodyguard all in one."

Nick and Jessie reached Madison Avenue and turned south, slowing to a walk as they stared across the street at what had been Oceano. The restaurant had shut down the day Gianni died, but the building was buzzing with activity. Workmen came and went through the etched glass doors, and the front window sported a large sign. Coming Soon: Aladdin's Falafel.

*

Max Callaban paid for his groceries with a credit card, smiling at the pretty blonde checkout girl.

The young girl dimpled. "Um, are you new around here?"

"So new I'm new to the country."

"I thought I heard a slight accent. Where are you from?"

"Brazil."

"What brings you to our sleepy Ohio town?"

"I sold my business and retired."

"You don't look old enough to be retired," she said flirtatiously. "No wedding ring?"

"I'm older than you think," Max said, flirting back, "and I'm divorced."

"Well, you have a nice day, uh," she looked at the credit card receipt, "Mr. Callaban."

"You, too, honey." Max left the store and tucked the groceries in the passenger seat of his black Fiat. He drove out into the country, pausing in front of an iron gate. With the push of a button, the wrought-iron gates swung inward, closing behind him. Max sped up the winding driveway, continuing on past the old Victorian house, and pulled into the three-car garage.

Dropping his purchases on the kitchen counter a few minutes later, Max opened windows wide, breathing in the fresh country air. He'd been here only a week, but already he was in love with the old house. He intended to renovate it himself, something he'd always wanted to do. He'd pour all his love into fixing it up, taking his time and getting it exactly right. He always liked things exactly right, the way they should be.

After putting away the groceries, Max eyed several crates that had been delivered early that morning. Grabbing a crowbar on the sideboard, he pried one open and lifted out a bone china plate. Pale blue, with a shadow of a gull in the center. Opening the second crate, he lifted out delicate crystal stemware.

Max carefully hand washed and dried the crate's contents, stowing them away in an antique mahogany china cabinet in the dining room. There was one more small box to open, but it could wait. Everything in due time.

He climbed the curved staircase, tossed his clothes in the hamper, and stepped under a steaming shower. Running his fingers across his bald pate, he grabbed the shaving cream and lathered his head. It had become a daily ritual.

Dressed again, he stared at his reflection in the bedroom mirror. Bald head. Slender and fit. Of course, the green contact lenses would take some getting used to, but he liked the look. Heading back downstairs, he tackled the last box in the kitchen as his cell phone shrilled. "Yes?"

"Just checking in," a familiar voice said. "The money was transferred to three banks. One in Grand Cayman, one in Zurich, and a large amount to the local bank in town."

"I appreciate it." With one hand Max eagerly lifted the lid from the last box, revealing hundreds of matchbooks. Matches with a cruise ship on the front. Souvenirs from another life. "You've been a good friend, Aldo." Gianni Fosselli clicked off.

Of course, Gianni Fosselli no longer existed. Gianni Fosselli had died on a rainy night at sea in a fiery explosion. Gianni had never asked the name of the man who took his place aboard the Milano that evening. Aldo had said he owed Roberto a vast amount of money, a man who thought his debt would be wiped out by impersonating Gianni. The world didn't work that way, not Martinelli's world.

Gianni Fosselli was now Max Callaban, formerly of Rio, entrepreneur and independently wealthy. Max was fluent in Italian and Portuguese, as well as English, Spanish, and German. He was a new resident of Canton, Ohio, an average Midwest American town nestled in the northeastern corner of the state.

It was a new day. A fresh start.

Time to look to the future. To his-- Gianni shivered as a blast of cold air swirled around him, and he quickly shut the windows he'd opened. He hadn't realized how cold it was. He laughed at himself, so caught up in his daydreams that ... Wait. Was that an echo of his own laughter vibrating in the still air? No. It was a deep baritone laugh, not his. So rich in timbre it reminded him ... Impossible. He was not a superstitious man. Gianni wrapped his arms around himself, a bone-chilling draft seeping into the house through the old windows.

He quickly poured himself a Sambucca.

And he tried to wipe away the figment of his imagination that lingered on that laugh.

The laugh of a dead man. Watching him.

*****

The Authors:

Deborah Fezelle trained as an actress at Juilliard in NYC. For 25 years she worked on Broadway, Off-Broadway, and in regional theaters around the country. She began writing at the age of 10, when she penned her first play. EVIL marks her publishing debut, a story inspired by her sister's untimely death.

Sherry Yanow is the author of COOPER'S LAST STAND, an award-nominated Harlequin romance. She's also been a film and theater critic and an avid soap-opera buff, hosting a soap-opera message board. And then she met Deborah on that same board …

When Deborah decided to check out her favorite soap actor, serendipity took over and she and Sherry began a writing collaboration that has spanned 10 years, including six staged plays, two web series, and THE EVIL THAT MEN DO, the novel that began it all. Deborah and Sherry love writing all kinds of popular fiction, from complex tales of love and loss to political thrillers to supernatural karma. In Sherry's "other life," she enjoys her family, her cat, her eclectic classes, and her new home in the beautiful Hudson River Valley. Deborah returned to Ohio in recent years, formed a theatrical company, and turned to directing. After serving as acting coach on the feature film UNDERDOGS, Deborah is now filming a web series based on THE EVIL THAT MEN DO.

Made in the USA
Charleston, SC
28 April 2013